"A bite?"

Sophie blinked when a forkful of the chocolate dessert appeared before her eyes. She stared at it with surprise, and then shifted her gaze to the man holding it out to her.

Alasdair smiled. "It is really good. Decadent. My taste buds are humming with pleasure with every bite. It would be a shame if you did not at least try it. I am willing to share."

Sophie stared at him. A voice that sexy should be outlawed, she thought a little weakly, and then realizing she was just gawking at him like a lovesick cow, she leaned forward and opened her mouth as Alasdair urged the forkful of deliciousness forward.

He didn't shove it in her mouth, he eased it in, slow and almost gently, as if being careful not to rub it on her teeth or lips. When she closed her mouth around it, he then drew the fork back out just as slowly so that she could catch all of the dessert with her lips and keep it from leaving with the fork. All the while, he was watching with eyes that were beginning to glow, and Sophie really wanted to examine that effect. She wanted to understand what happened with his eyes, but her own were closing as the taste of the dessert exploded on her tongue. Chocolate, cherry, almond, whipped cream, and a hint of rum, the flavors struck her one after the other, and it was amazing. She'd never tasted anything so good. It was heavenly. Finally she opened her eyes and whispered, "Thank you."

"You are welcome," he whispered back, his eyes glued on her lips.

By Lynsay Sands

LYNSAY SANDS

Bad Luck
VAMPIRE

AN ARGENEAU NOVEL

AVON

An Imprint of HarperCollinsPublishers

BAD LUCK VAMPIRE. Copyright © 2023 by Lynsay Sands. All rights reserved. Printed in the United States of America. No part of this book may be used or reproduced in any manner whatsoever without written permission except in the case of brief quotations embodied in critical articles and reviews. For information, address HarperCollins Publishers, 195 Broadway, New York, NY 10007.

First Avon Books mass market printing: September 2023
First Avon Books hardcover printing: September 2023

Print Edition ISBN: 978-0-06-329210-9
Digital Edition ISBN: 978-0-06-329211-6

Cover design by Nadine Badalaty
Cover art by Tony Mauro
Cover images © Ekhphoto | Dreamstime.com; Shutterstock

Avon, Avon & logo, and Avon Books & logo are registered trademarks of HarperCollins Publishers in the United States of America and other countries.

HarperCollins is a registered trademark of HarperCollins Publishers in the United States of America and other countries.

FIRST EDITION

23 24 25 26 27 BVGM 10 9 8 7 6 5 4 3 2 1

Bad Luck Vampire

Prologue

"Aren't you getting a drink with your dinner?"

Sophie turned from the waitress she'd been giving her order to, and peered with confusion at her blind date. "I asked for iced tea."

"A Long Island iced tea?" Carl suggested.

"No. Just iced tea."

She started to turn back to the waitress, only to pause when he cajoled, "Oh, come now. You have to have a proper drink. How about a margarita? That's a girly drink, isn't it?"

Sophie stiffened at his words. *A girly drink? Seriously?* Irritation sparked in her, but she pushed it down. "No, I'm good with the iced tea," she assured him, and turned away to smile at the waitress as she reaffirmed, "A straight iced tea, no alcohol please."

Carl wasn't done pushing, though. "Well, if you don't like margaritas, what about a mai tai, then?"

Sophie frowned at the man. "No."

"A mojito?"

"No."

"Oh! Sex on the beach," he suggested with a grin, and told the waitress, "She'll have a sex on the beach."

"*She* won't have sex on anything," Sophie said grimly, losing her patience. Arching one eyebrow, she asked, "Are you a date rapist or something?"

Carl jerked back in his seat, shock on his face. "Why would you ask a thing like that?"

"Because you appear to have trouble accepting no for an answer, and I gather that's an issue with date rapists too," she explained sweetly. And then her expression went cold as she said, "I don't want an alcoholic beverage. I don't like the taste of alcohol. I want an iced tea."

Carl relaxed at once, a slimy smile oozing over his face. "Oh, well, no one *likes* the taste of alcohol, Sophie. That's not why anyone drinks."

"Really," she said dryly. "So, you only drink to get buzzed?"

"Exactly," he said at once.

"Riiight," Sophie drew out the word, her eyes narrowing. "So aside from giving off a date rapist vibe, you acknowledge you have a drinking problem. Good to know, and thanks for revealing all of that right away so I don't have to waste any more time than necessary on this blind date."

Picking up her purse, Sophie pulled out a twenty as she stood up. She handed the money to the waitress then and offered her a smile. "For your trouble. Please scratch the iced tea and Caesar salad you just wrote down. I won't be staying. Have a good night."

Grabbing her coat off the back of her chair, Sophie

headed for the exit, more than eager to be done with this nasty-ass blind date.

"Hey!" Carl shouted.

Sophie heard the scrape of a chair pushing back from the table and just knew it was his. Of course Carl couldn't just let her leave quietly and calmly. No, jerks like him always had to make a scene.

"Hey!" His hand on her arm stopped Sophie as she reached the door.

She turned slowly and peered at the man with dead eyes. "Let go of me."

"You can't just walk out like that. We're on a date."

"The date is done," she said firmly, and tugged her arm free to push the door open and slip outside.

"It's not done. You didn't even give me a chance," Carl protested, following her out into the cool night air. "Come back in and finish the date."

"No, thank you." Sophie picked up speed, nearly jogging in her high heels to get away from him. She'd had a long day, and this blind date she'd let her co-worker Lise rope her into was the crappy cherry on top of a crap day. She just wanted to go home, kick off her heels, veg on the couch in front of a movie, and forget this day—and specifically this date—had ever happened.

"Come on, stop playing hard to get. I make good money and I'm a good-looking guy. I'm a real catch. I know you want me."

"Yeah, right," Sophie muttered with disgust as she cut through the rows of vehicles to get to where her own car was parked in the outer lane of the lot. Her shortcut ended when he grabbed her arm and jerked her around, the action so abrupt she was brought up against his chest. He immediately grabbed her other arm to keep her there when she tried to pull away.

"Come on, sweetheart, you're not fooling anyone with this ice maiden act," he assured her, his hands dropping from her arms to her behind to force her groin tight against his. "Let's—"

Whatever he would have said next ended on a curse as she kneed him in the balls. The moment he released her to grab for his injured testicles, Sophie turned to rush away. She was pissed, but she was also eager to get to the safety of her car before Carl recovered.

She'd made it past the first double row of vehicles when Carl again grabbed her arm and jerked her around. Sophie took in a lungful of air as she spun, fully intending on blasting the asshole for both his persistence and his laying hands on her, but the words died abruptly when she found herself staring at . . . nothing?

Carl was gone.

Sophie peered around the parking lot with bewilderment, rubbing her arm where he'd grabbed her. *He had done that, hadn't he?* she suddenly wondered with confusion. Where the hell had he gone? He couldn't have got back inside the restaurant in the few seconds it had taken her to turn.

Scowling with both irritation and suspicion, she gave the parking lot a much slower perusal, wondering if he'd ducked around the nearest car intending to leap out at her or something. However, a more thorough search, which included dropping to her haunches to look under the cars on either side of her, didn't reveal any sign of him crouching nearby.

Straightening slowly, Sophie glanced around again,

now unsure what to do. The man's sudden absence was almost supernatural in nature and was giving her the heebie-jeebies.

A short whistle caught her ear and Sophie peered into the darkness. She couldn't see anything . . . until a flashlight suddenly popped on in the grassy area next to the parking lot.

Not a flashlight, Sophie realized as she took in the two men under a tree. It was a phone flashlight, she noted as her gaze slid over a handsome dark-haired man in all black clothes, and an equally handsome blond who was also dressed all in black. The dark-haired guy was smiling at her cheerfully; the blond, however, had an exasperated look on his face.

"This fellow seemed to be annoying you so I thought I'd better step in," the cheerful man announced, shifting his phone so that the light splashed over the person at the end of his extended arm.

Sophie's eyes widened incredulously as she saw that Carl was dangling in the air, kicking and struggling to pull the hand away from his throat and free himself.

The phone's light shifted back to the other two men now, and the dark-haired man asked, "Was I wrong? Should I let him go?"

"Oh, hell no," Sophie said at once, and then caught herself and added more calmly, "You were right. He was being a pain."

"Well, then I shall happily hold on to him until you're safely away," her Sir Galahad in black told her with a charming smile.

"Sounds good. Thanks," Sophie offered with a nod.

"My pleasure," Sir Galahad said easily, raising his arm again and then scowling and turning to stare at

Carl briefly when the dangling man managed to kick him in the side. After a moment of his staring, Carl went still and the stranger turned back to smile at her again.

Sophie found herself grinning in response, then shook her head and turned to start toward her car, saying, "Thanks again."

"Tybo," he said.

Sophie stopped and peered toward the three men with confusion. It sounded like some kind of martial art. Was he asking her if she knew any? Or suggesting she should learn it?

"That's my name," the man explained with what sounded like amusement. "Tyberius Verde, but everyone calls me Tybo for short."

"Oh." Sophie relaxed and nodded. "Hi, Tybo. I'm Sophie Ferguson. Thanks again for your help."

"My pleasure. Always happy to help a damsel in distress," he said easily.

Sophie gave him a wave as she quickly walked to her own car. She was at the driver's door when it occurred to her that while she might be escaping this situation, it probably wouldn't be the last she'd hear from Carl. He had her phone number. Lise, a coworker at the insurance company where she was employed, had texted it to him when Sophie had finally given in to her harassment and agreed to go on this date. He'd then called to firm up the time and place. Sophie had no doubt she'd hear from the jerk again, if only for him to blast her for leaving him hanging, literally, and not calling help for him or something. He'd probably try to sue the guy for coming to her aid like this too, and maybe even her, she thought with irritation. He seemed the type.

"If you want, I could erase your phone number from this guy's phone before I let him go."

Sophie swung around to see that Tybo and his blond friend had moved parallel to her. She could just make out the faint shadow of Carl outside the light from the phone. He didn't seem to be struggling anymore. She hoped that didn't mean he was dead or something. Not that she really cared, except she wouldn't want this man to get in trouble for trying to help her. He was too pretty to go to jail.

"He's fine," Tybo assured her as if she'd spoken the concern aloud. "I won't hurt him. Just keep him here until you're safely away." He paused a beat, and then asked, "So? Should I remove your number from his phone so he doesn't trouble you again?"

Sophie nodded. "Yeah, that would be good," she said, and decided she'd call Lise the minute she was out of the parking lot and threaten her with something horrible if she gave him her number again.

"Would you mind . . ."

Sophie had been reaching for the handle of her car door, but stopped and glanced around at that to see Tybo hesitating and looking uncertain. Then he shrugged as if to say *what the hell*, and offered her another charming smile. "Could *I* have your number?"

Sophie's eyebrows shot up at the question. It was the last thing she'd expected.

When she just stood staring at him in surprise, he added, "I'd love to take you for coffee or something to prove that not all guys are jerks like this one." He gave Carl a shake and her gaze skated to the man he was holding when the light splashed over him again. Carl's eyes were open and he was grimacing. He was no longer struggling, though, she noted before the light shifted again and Carl disappeared into the darkness.

Sophie returned her gaze to Tybo and his friend. This was the craziest situation she'd ever encountered. The guy was dangling her blind date in the air and asking for her number. They were complete strangers. For all she knew he was a serial killer or something. On the other hand, he *had* saved her from an awkward and even potentially dangerous situation by dragging Carl away from her. Still, Sophie wasn't sure it would be smart to accept a date from this guy.

She was about to say no when she noted that the blond was looking at Tybo as if he'd lost his mind. Sophie was self-aware enough to know that was what changed hers. As one of the workers at a group home she'd lived in had put it, she'd always been a "contrary bitch." Tell her she couldn't do something, and it was as good as done. The fact that his buddy obviously didn't think she was good enough for Tybo was enough to convince her to go out with him.

"Sure. We could do coffee," she said now. "If my number's not in his contacts, it'll be in a message from Lise Cunningham. Give me a call sometime," she added, and then turned away, opened her car door, and slid in.

"Tell the truth . . . you've lost your mind."

"Huh?" Tybo glanced at his partner, Valerian, with confusion at those words, but then just shook his head and looked back to the white Nissan exiting the parking lot. Sophie Ferguson was a pretty little thing. He couldn't wait to call her. That thought had him lowering Carl so that he could search his pockets for his cell phone as he said, "She thinks you don't think she's good enough for me."

"What?" Valerian said with surprise.

"You were looking at me like I was crazy when I asked for her number," Tybo explained as he went through Carl's pockets.

"That had nothing to do with her," Valerian said at once. "She seems fine."

"Yeah. I know, but it's probably the only reason she said yes to going out with me," Tybo told him as he found and pulled out Carl's phone. Lowering the other man, he cast Valerian a smile. "Thanks for that."

Valerian snorted at his words. "I was looking at you like you were crazy, because what you're doing is crazy. You do remember what happened the last time we went vigilante, don't you?" Shaking his head, he predicted, "Lucian's going to be pissed if he finds out about this."

"No, he won't," Tybo said with certainty, and then held out Carl to him. "Hold this asshole while I remove Sophie's number from his phone."

Valerian's mouth twisted with irritation, but he caught Carl by the collar and took over holding him while Tybo quickly went through the phone in search of Sophie's number. It hadn't been entered into contacts yet, so all he had to do was erase it from messages and recent calls. After a hesitation, he then snapped the phone in half. The bastard deserved it. Carl's intentions had not been good. Despite Sophie's obvious disinterest, he'd decided she was just playing hard to get and if he hadn't been able to coerce her back into the restaurant to continue their date, he'd intended to follow her to her car, force her into it, and take what he felt he deserved and was sure she was just withholding to tease him. Carl had been positive she'd be glad in the end.

Reading those thoughts from the man's mind was what had moved Tybo to intervene. The guy was an arrogant asshole who figured if a girl agreed to a date, she was agreeing to sex and he was going to get it one way or another.

Bastard, Tybo thought, dropping the phone on the ground and stomping on it for good measure. It was guys like Carl who made women leery of the rest of the men in the world.

"Can we let this douchebag go and get back to work now?" Valerian asked when Tybo turned back to him.

Tybo considered Carl with dissatisfaction. A broken phone was hardly much of a punishment for what this guy had intended. Finally, he said, "Let him go."

Looking relieved, Valerian released the man and then eyed him warily, no doubt expecting Carl to freak on them. Instead, the man turned and began to skip away from them across the parking lot.

"What did you—?" Valerian began, but his question died as Carl kicked off his shoes and began to remove his suit jacket. Once that was off, he tossed it away. Even as it landed on a little Hyundai, Carl was skipping along again, working on the buttons of his shirt. A moment later the dress shirt was flying into the back of a pickup.

"Oh man. We are dead," Valerian almost moaned as they watched Carl push his pants and underwear down next and then pull his feet out and kick the clothing under a nearby van.

"No, we're not," Tybo assured him, grinning evilly as he made Carl pirouette in the middle of the space between the first double row of cars and the door to the restaurant, his junk swinging out from the movement.

A squeal drew his attention to the restaurant to see two women frozen in the open door, gaping at the man dancing naked outside. After a shocked moment, both women backed into the building and the door closed. But they didn't move away from it. Instead, their gawking faces were visible through the glass of the upper part of the door. When other faces began to join them, as well as several phones suddenly popping up to film, it was obvious they'd reported what was happening outside to the other patrons. Which meant the police would be called.

Smiling with satisfaction, Tybo began to lead Valerian to the SUV where they'd been waiting and watching for the arrival of a suspected rogue.

"He's still dancing," Valerian said tightly as he got behind the wheel. Turning on the engine, he asked, "Are you going to release him?"

"Eventually," Tybo said mildly, his gaze still trained on the man as he controlled him and had him start hopping around like a bunny, his bare butt jutting out and junk flopping with each hop.

"Jesus," Valerian muttered, and then stiffened and glanced sharply at Tybo as his phone began to ring. Mouth tightening, he growled, "We're so dead."

"No, we're not," Tybo assured him, and answered, putting the call on speakerphone.

"The cops are on the way. Wait till you hear the sirens and then get out of there," Lucian barked.

Tybo grinned when Valerian's eyes widened incredulously at their boss's words. *Told you*, he mouthed to him silently.

Valerian scowled in response, but then leaned toward the phone and asked, "What about watching for Adamso—"

"He won't show up with the police here," Lucian cut in. "The minute he sees the police cars, he'll turn around and return to his hole. We'll have to stake out the restaurant again another night. It's inconvenient and irritating, but you could hardly stand by and let a woman be raped while you watched for Adamson."

"What?" Valerian asked with disbelief.

"What, what?" Lucian asked mildly.

"Is this the same man who gave us royal hell for rescuing a woman from being kidnapped a couple years ago?" Valerian asked dryly. "I thought for sure you'd be pissed about this."

"You didn't get hell for rescuing that woman, you got hell for showing your superhuman strength and speed while doing it and getting caught on camera," Lucian growled. "This time you played it smart. The bastard will get arrested and charged with public indecency and probably get added to the sexual offender database since the restaurant is across the street from a school. You saved the woman and played it smart while doing it. Good job. Now get out of there. I can hear the sirens. The mortal police are close."

Lucian ended the call without a goodbye, and Tybo grinned at a flummoxed Valerian as he bragged, "I played it smart."

A short laugh slid from Valerian at his preening, and he shook his head as he shifted the SUV into gear. "Yeah, yeah. You were right and I was wrong."

"It happens," Tybo said with mild amusement, returning his attention to Carl and encouraging him to start doing cartwheels. He then winced as he watched him. There was just something really undignified about a naked man doing cartwheels, his junk swinging around in circles as he did.

"I was sure Lucian would skewer us for this one," Valerian muttered as he steered the SUV toward the exit.

"And yet you didn't try to stop me when I intervened, and didn't protest much even after Sophie was gone," Tybo pointed out, twisting his head to continue to control Carl as their vehicle carried them out of the parking lot even as two police cars pulled in.

"The guy planned to force her," Valerian said tightly. "Of course I didn't try to stop you." Grimacing, he admitted, "I was willing to take the shit for intervening. I just wasn't happy anticipating how much shit we'd be in."

Tybo chuckled at his words and finally released Carl as the police cars squealed to a halt in front of the naked man, their headlights spotlighting him as he came out of his last cartwheel and did another pirouette before stopping and shaking his head like a wet dog. Tybo didn't watch to see what would happen next. He was already getting a crick in his neck from twisting his head around. Besides, his job was done. The guy was in deep doo-doo no matter what he did now.

"So, are you really going to call Sophie?" Valerian asked a moment later.

Tybo smiled and glanced down at the phone in his lap. He'd texted himself Sophie's number before erasing every sign of her from Carl's phone. A quick check now showed that the text had gone through and he did have her number.

"Well? Are you?" Valerian asked when Tybo was slow to respond.

"Sure," he said finally, slipping his phone into his pocket. "She's a cute little thing. I'm thinking she'd make a great date for your wedding."

"Yeah?" Valerian glanced over to give him a quick smile before turning his attention back to the road and asking, "But you were able to read her, right?"

"Yeah," Tybo said sadly. Like the mythical vampires that most mortals would think of them as, immortals—which was what his kind preferred to be called—could read and control the minds of mortals, as well as other immortals younger than themselves. Except for possible life mates. In fact, not being able to read someone was a sure sign of a possible life mate, which is why most immortals read, or attempted to read, every new person they encountered. Life mates were precious. They made living such long lives bearable.

"Sorry. She seems nice," Valerian murmured.

"Yeah." Tybo sighed. He supposed it was foolish to be so disappointed that he had been able to read her. After all, he'd only been born in 1920. That made him young for an immortal, and his kind didn't usually find their life mates until much later in life. That didn't mean he couldn't hope, though, or suffer disappointment when he encountered someone he liked but could read.

Pushing his disappointment down, he said, "Oh well, it's fine. I'm young. Dating is a thing and she's a nice gal. She'll be a fun date for your wedding."

One

"Packing up already?"

Sophie glanced up from the bag she was tucking her computer into and noted the confusion and concern on Megan's face as she entered her office.

"Yes. I'm leaving early today," Sophie said as she zipped up her computer bag.

"*You?* Leaving *early on a Thursday afternoon?*" Megan asked with amazement, and then a worried frown took over her expression and she asked, "Why? You're not sick, are you?"

"No, I'm not sick," Sophie assured her, understanding her concern. Sophie never left work early unless she was deathly ill. Well, actually, she'd only ever left early once and then it had been on a stretcher, headed for an ambulance and the hospital. Appendicitis. She'd been suffering pain in her lower stomach most of the day, but then she'd started vomiting and had managed to stumble and hit her head against the bathroom's tiled wall. Megan had found her lying on the floor, still heaving and her head bleeding, and had immediately called 911. It turned out hitting her head had been a lucky break. If Megan hadn't called 911, Sophie very well might have gone home thinking she just had the flu or something, and her appendix could have ruptured, which was extremely dangerous. At least that's what the doctor had told her after the emergency surgery.

"So, why leave early?" Lise asked, poking her head into the office. "A hot date?"

Sophie scowled at the woman who had set her up with the horrid Carl of the rapey/alcoholic vibe. Something she still hadn't forgiven her for. Seriously. The guy had apparently gone streaking around the parking lot after she'd left, flashing his bits for everyone to see. Sophie had read about it in the paper the next day and then seen the video online. Several videos actually. He'd gone viral. Sophie had figured out pretty quick that he was a dirtbag, but this was just beyond, which had made her even angrier at Lise. How the hell had her coworker ever thought Carl would be a good match for her?

"It's not a *hot* date," she told her with irritation, and then deciding to ignore the other woman, turned her focus back to Megan and reluctantly admitted, "More like a favor date."

Megan's eyebrows shot up. "Seriously? You *are* leaving early, on *Thursday*, for a *date*?"

"I had no say in the day or time, Megs," Sophie said with amusement. "It's a wedding."

"Who gets married on a Thursday?" Megan asked at once, looking outraged at the very idea.

Before Sophie could answer, Bobby—Megan's brother and also a coworker—slipped past Lise to enter the office and asked, "Is it a family member?"

"Family?" Sophie echoed with amusement. "Why? You getting married?"

"Oh, hell no," Bobby said at once, his eyes widening with horror. "Elizabeth and I just started dating. Besides, I'm like you, planning to stay single forever."

"Well, then, since you, Megan, and Mama and Papa are the only family I have, I guess it can't be family who's getting married, can it?" Sophie asked with an affectionate smile for the man who had been like a brother to her since his parents had taken her in as a foster child in her early teens.

"Ahhh. That's so sweet, and we love you too," Megan said, smiling with affection, and then abruptly asked, "So, whose wedding is it?"

Sophie sighed with resignation. She'd known this would happen if they found out. It was why she'd hoped to sneak out unnoticed. She should have known better. Everyone in what had become her family worked in this branch of the insurance company, except for her foster mother, Deb. Her foster father, George, owned and ran it and she had started working here after finishing university, just like her foster siblings, Megan and Bobby, had. And just like most siblings, she'd known they'd be all up in her business if she didn't slip out unnoticed.

Knowing she wouldn't get out of the building without telling all, she cast a glare at Lise, one of the few nonfamily workers here, and said, "Well, you all remember that awful date I had last weekend?"

"I said I was sorry," Lise said with exasperation. "Carl seemed like a nice guy. How was I to know he'd turn out to be a perv?"

Before Sophie could respond, Megan exclaimed with horror, "Ohmygawd! You are *not* going to a wedding with that pervy Carl that Lise set you up with, are you?" She then straightened her shoulders and said firmly, "As your older sister I forbid it."

"You're only a month older, Megs," Sophie pointed out with amusement. She didn't, however, add that technically they weren't really sisters either, mostly because as far as she was concerned, they were. The Tomlinsons were the only family she had. She'd considered them family almost from the moment they'd taken her in to foster when she was fourteen and she knew they felt the same. Instead, she said, "It's okay. I'm not going out with Carl. My date is Tybo. The guy who helped me out."

"You mean the hero who picked up Pervy Carl by the throat with one hand?" Bobby asked with interest.

"Yeah. Him." Sophie nodded.

Rather than soothe Megan, that made her sister's eyes go wide and incredulous. "The hero actually called you and your first date with him is going to be accompanying him to a wedding?"

"It's not our first date," she admitted. "He called Monday night and we met up for a coffee." Pausing, she pursed her lips and then asked, "That counts as a date, doesn't it?"

"No," Bobby said with amusement.

It was Megan who said, "A proper date is dinner and a movie, or dinner and dancing, or a concert or something of that nature. Not twenty minutes in a noisy, overbright cafe with coffee in cardboard cups and donuts on cardboard plates."

"Oh. Then yeah, I guess our first date is going to be a wedding," Sophie said with a shrug. The coffee date had actually lasted an hour rather than just twenty minutes, but she didn't think mentioning that would help matters.

"Ohmygod, Sophie!" Megan said with exasperation. "Seriously? When did you become a risk-taking masochist?"

"It's not a risk," Sophie assured her. "Tybo's a cop. I should be safe enough with him."

"A policeman?" Bobby asked with amazement. "Really?"

"Yeah." Sophie smiled faintly at his surprise. It was rather how she'd felt. Tybo just did not seem the type. Or maybe she just had no idea what policemen were like.

"Okay," Megan said now. "Right, he's a policeman. So, you're less risk-taker and more just pure masochist."

"I am not," Sophie protested on a laugh, although she was starting to wonder about that. After all, weddings weren't exactly first date–type outings. She'd be meeting his friends, coworkers, and maybe even family depending on who all had been invited to this shindig. That wouldn't make for a relaxing first date where she could get to know him.

Sighing inwardly, she admitted, "I kind of felt like I owed him for his help with Carl and couldn't say no."

"You don't owe him squat," Megan said firmly.

Sophie shrugged. "It's all good, Megs. Tybo's polite and funny. He's good-looking too, and seems nice. And, I mean come on, how much more respectable can you get than a wedding for a first date? I definitely won't have to worry about getting attacked or anything on the arm of a cop with a wedding hall full of people dancing the funky chicken around us."

"Hmm. I suppose," Megan acknowledged, still not looking impressed.

"So, Black Widow, have you told him about your curse?" Bobby asked suddenly.

Sophie cast a scowl at him. "I'm not cursed and stop calling me Black Widow."

"Right." Bobby nodded and then asked innocently, "How many boyfriends have died on you now? Is it three or four?"

"Two," Sophie said shortly. "Only two died and they were accidents."

"Is it really only two, though?" Bobby asked dubiously. "I mean, I know you were only engaged to be engaged to Andrew, and he is technically still alive in body, but he's basically brain dead and on life support."

Sophie let her breath out on a sigh, picked up her purse, and said quietly, "I'm not cursed. The fact that the three men I was engaged, or almost engaged, to were all in terrible accidents is just a coincidence."

"Sweetheart, two is coincidence. Three is a curse," Bobby said dryly.

Sophie just shook her head, slung her computer bag over her shoulder, grabbed her sweater off the back of her chair, and headed out of her office. "I'll see you guys tomorrow."

"Wait!" Bobby shouted. Leaving Megan and Lise behind, he followed her out to reception. "Where is this wedding?"

When Sophie paused and turned back with irritation, he smiled apologetically and said, "You know I was just teasing you about the curse."

"Yeah," she said unhappily, relaxing a little. And it was true, she did know he was just teasing her. The problem was after losing her parents when she was young, and then one good friend, two fiancés, and one almost fiancé to accidents, well, she was starting to believe she *was* cursed, so his teasing was striking on a raw nerve.

"You should really let us know where you're going to be, Sophie," Bobby said solemnly. "Just in case. We'd at least know where to start looking if you disappear or something."

Sophie smiled crookedly and said with light sarcasm, "That's why I love you, Bobby, you always see the bright side of everything."

"And you can always count on me to worry about you when no one else does," Bobby pointed out.

"Yeah," she breathed. Her sarcasm giving way to affection, Sophie walked back to give him a hug and a kiss on the cheek. Straightening away from him, she admitted, "I'm not sure where the wedding is. I didn't think to ask. But I'm sure it'll be fine. I'll call if there's any trouble," she promised.

"You be sure to do that," Bobby said sternly. "Fully charge your phone beforehand, and don't forget it. Then text me the minute you know where you're going," he insisted. "If you have *any* issues at all you call me and I'll come get you."

"Thanks, Bobby," Sophie said quietly, and gave his arm a squeeze before turning to head out of the building.

TWO

"How are you doing? All right?" Tybo asked as he led her toward the tents set up at the back of the Shady Pines Golf Course. At least, that's what Sophie thought Tybo had said the name of the place was where the wedding was to be held. She wasn't completely sure that's what he'd said, however. She'd been a little distracted at the time by the helicopter he'd been leading her to.

A helicopter, for heaven's sake! When he'd said they were catching a ride with the groom, Valerian, she'd thought he'd meant in a limo or something. Not a helicopter. Sophie had never ridden in one before. She wasn't certain she really wanted to do it again either. They were noisy and . . . not planes.

Realizing that she hadn't answered his question and that Tybo had slowed to eye her with concern, she managed a smile and said, "I'm good." She then blurted, "That was my first ride in a helicopter."

"I never would have guessed," he assured her, expression solemn, but eyes twinkling.

Sophie just snorted at the obvious lie as he picked up his pace again and escorted her into the crowd of guests around the tents behind what she guessed was the golf course's clubhouse. There were two tents, one filled with rows of seats separated by an aisle leading up to a large dais where she suspected the wedding ceremony was to take place, and another, larger tent filled with tables and chairs around what appeared to be a large dance floor. Sophie didn't notice much more than that about the tents, though, she was too distracted looking at all the people milling around.

Dear God, it was like she'd stepped into a magazine shoot or something. Damned near every person present was gorgeous, young, and dressed to the nines.

Sophie glanced down at her own dress now. She hadn't been sure what to wear to an early evening fall wedding. In the end she'd decided on a navy A-line dress with a fitted top, short sleeves, and round neck, that had midsized pale pink flowers along the bottom of the skirt that then darkened as they went up until the fitted top was a pure dark navy blue. Much to her relief, she hadn't either underdressed or overdressed for the occasion and should fit in just fine with the other women in attendance. She hoped.

"You look perfect."

Sophie glanced to Tybo with surprise at the quiet compliment, and then smiled faintly and relaxed.

"As the best man I have a couple things to do before the wedding," he told her apologetically. "But I've arranged for some friends, Marguerite and Julius Notte, to look out for you before and during the ceremony."

"Of course," Sophie murmured as if that were to be expected, which she supposed it should have been. She'd known Tybo was the best man. She should have realized that would mean she'd be on her own not just during, but before the ceremony. But honestly, that hadn't occurred to her at all. She'd thought he'd at least spend some time with her before the ceremony started.

Great, she thought on an inner sigh, alone in a sea of strangers who were all family or friends of the bride and groom that she didn't know. What on earth had she been thinking when she'd agreed to be his date tonight?

"It'll be fine," Tybo said soothingly as if he could tell she was now regretting agreeing to come. "They're Valerian's aunt and uncle. You'll like them."

"I'm sure I will," she said, not sure at all. But positive the poor older couple had probably felt obligated to agree to look out for her and resented being burdened with her.

"They'll love you," Tybo said encouragingly, apparently having read her worries on her face.

Sophie stifled the scowl that wanted to claim her lips and instead smoothed out her expression. But she was irritated that he had read her so easily. People usually couldn't. She had learned young how to suppress her emotions and give nothing away by word or expression. It was safer that way. Keep things light, stifle all emotion, and give nothing away to anyone. That was her motto and how she usually rolled, but for some reason, Tybo seemed to have no problem figuring out what she was thinking and feeling. It was kind of annoying.

"Trust me," Tybo added. "You and Marguerite will get along like a house on fire, and the minute the ceremony is over I'll collect you for the meal."

"'Kay," she said mildly, keeping her expression bland as she reassured herself that it wouldn't be for that long anyway. Wedding ceremonies were short, weren't they? It was just the "Do you take this woman?" and "Do you take this man?" Then the "Kiss the bride" and done, right? That's how it was on TV anyway.

"Oh, there's Marguerite."

Sophie blinked her thoughts aside and glanced around to see that they were approaching the tent where the ceremony was obviously to take place. The news that the groom had arrived must have spread, because everyone was now gravitating to this tent to claim their seats. Including the aunt and uncle Tybo had mentioned. The nice older aunt and uncle, she'd thought. Now she stumbled in surprise as she took in the couple he was pointing out.

"Whoa," Tybo said, catching her arm to help her keep her feet. "All right?" he asked once she'd steadied.

"Yeah. Thanks," she said. "But that can't be Valerian's real aunt and uncle, right? It's just a joke nickname or something, isn't it?"

"No. They're his real aunt and uncle," he assured her, then tilted his head. "Why?"

"They don't look old enough," she said simply.

Tybo chuckled at the comment and just said, "Come meet them. You'll love them."

When he urged her forward again, Sophie didn't fight him, but shifted her gaze back to the couple to examine them more closely.

Valerian's aunt didn't look more than twenty-five

or so. She was also gorgeous with a killer figure, auburn hair, large eyes, and full lips. The man next to her, presumably the uncle, was nothing to sneeze at either. Also in his mid to late twenties, the man had dark hair, swarthy good looks, and was sexy as hell. He looked nothing like the fair-haired Valerian other than seeming to be around the same age, which was unusual for an uncle, Sophie thought as Tybo drew her to a halt in front of the aunt and uncle he planned to palm her off on for the ceremony.

"Marguerite, you look lovely as always," he greeted, releasing Sophie to give the woman a quick hug and shake the hand of the man with her. Stepping back then, he took Sophie's arm again to draw her forward as he added, "This is my beautiful date, Sophie Ferguson. Sophie, this is Marguerite Argeneau-Notte, and her husband, Julius Notte."

"Hi." Sophie offered her hand in greeting, holding it out to the aunt first. Much to her amazement, rather than take, shake, and release it as she'd expected, Marguerite Argeneau-Notte grasped her hand in both of her own and held on.

Sophie wanted to arch an eyebrow and look down at their hands meaningfully to get her to release her, but found her attention caught by the woman's eyes before she could. They were a beautiful silver blue. The color was eye-catching on its own, but the fact that the silver appeared to be shifting and growing to overwhelm the blue as the woman tried to drill a hole in Sophie's forehead with her stare was what really got her attention. It was bizarre and discomfiting, both of which just made her want to snap at the woman to "take a picture or something already, lady." But the words died along with the feeling when Marguerite suddenly broke contact and turned to Tybo.

"She's lovely, Tybo . . . and special," the woman announced solemnly.

While Sophie blinked in surprise at the comment, Tybo merely grinned and said, "I couldn't agree with you more," to the woman, before turning to Sophie to add, "I told you Marguerite would love you."

She merely smiled dubiously in response. They'd just met, for heaven's sake. Calling her special at this point seemed ridiculous to her. But before she could comment, Marguerite announced, "I know a certain male who will love her even more."

Sophie felt her eyebrows rise at the cryptic words, but she wasn't the only one surprised by the comment.

"What?" Tybo asked with dismay.

"I believe she will suit someone here perfectly," Marguerite added.

Sophie was just bewildered by this. She had no idea who or what the woman was talking about. She would suit someone here perfectly? What did that even mean? She was Tybo's date, and much to her relief he pointed that out to Marguerite, although his voice was more complaining than outraged when he said, "But she's *my* date."

"She may be your date, Tybo, but I believe Alasdair needs to meet her," Marguerite responded, her tone solemn.

Sophie was now staring at the woman with complete and utter disbelief. Tybo, however, just looked resigned as he asked, "Really?"

Marguerite nodded.

"But I like her," Tybo said unhappily, and Sophie

stared at him with disbelief. It sounded to her like he was on the edge of caving in to Marguerite's suggestion that she belonged with someone else. What the hell was going on here?

Elbowing Tybo sharply in the side to get his attention, she gave him what Bobby called her "death stare" and asked, "Care to explain this little conversation here? I'm *your* date. Not some chick to be passed around at parties."

"Of course not," Tybo said quickly. He then ran a frustrated hand through his hair and muttered to himself before glancing at his wristwatch and scowling. "I don't have time to explain right now. I really have to go put the wedding rings in Sinbad's basket."

Before Sophie could respond, he turned to Marguerite and said, "You're going to have to handle Sophie. But she's *my* date tonight. She came with me and she's leaving with me."

"Tybo," Marguerite began in warning, and he scowled harder.

"I'll be a complete gentleman the whole night and then see her home safely, but I'm not dancing with myself at this wedding. She's *my* date tonight, Marguerite. Alasdair can have her tomorrow." He didn't wait to hear what Marguerite had to say about that, but simply turned and strode quickly away.

Sophie watched him go, hard-pressed not to chase after him and demand an explanation. She didn't understand what the two had been talking about, and didn't like not understanding. But she definitely didn't like the bit about Alasdair could have her tomorrow?

"Sophie dear."

She tore her gaze away from Tybo's retreating back

and turned to the other woman, fully expecting her to explain what Tybo hadn't been able to.

But instead of explaining anything, Marguerite's gaze became intense again as it had when she'd taken her hands earlier and she said, "Everything is fine. The discussion I just had with Tybo is of no consequence whatsoever. You should forget about it."

Oddly enough, Sophie felt herself nodding in agreement, suddenly quite sure that this was true and that the conversation she was so concerned about was of no consequence whatsoever. Hardly worth remembering. She should just forget all about it really, Sophie thought, as Marguerite took her arm to usher her into the tent.

Three

"Is Valerian finally here, then?"

Half-asleep in his chair, Alasdair stirred at that question from Lucian Argeneau and turned to glance at the man who had apparently settled in the seat next to him with his wife, Leigh, and their son and daughter on his other side. The head of the North American Council of Immortals, Lucian was both powerful and ancient, but you wouldn't know it to look at him. At least not the ancient part. With platinum blond hair, silver-blue eyes, and youthful good looks, the man didn't appear more than twenty-eight or twenty-nine years old. Nowhere near the thousands of years old he actually was. As for the powerful part, the way Lucian carried himself and the ice chips in his eyes definitely gave that away, Alasdair thought, and then realized the man wasn't speaking to him but someone past him.

Alasdair turned his head to see his twin brother, Colle, easing sideways along the row of empty seats toward them. While Colle had collected people from the helicopters as they arrived and driven them in a golf cart to the tents, Alasdair had helped out by setting out chairs for the ceremony. He'd finished his job ages ago and had been mostly standing around and then sitting, waiting for everything to begin since. Hence why he'd been nodding off in his seat.

Damn, weddings were boring as hell so far, he thought with mild irritation. He hadn't been to any before this. Valerian was the first of their generation to marry.

"Yes, Valerian's here," Colle answered as he took the seat next to Alasdair. "He flew in with Tybo and his date, so now everyone's here. The wedding should start on time."

"Good. Then we'll be eating soon," Lucian growled with satisfaction. "I hope Natalie made those peanut butter chicken wrap things I like so much."

"Thai chicken wraps," Alasdair corrected.

"Yes. Those," Lucian agreed, although Alasdair had no doubt the man would just keep calling them "peanut butter chicken wraps."

"Really?" Lucian's wife, Leigh, gasped with disbelief. The petite brunette scowled at her husband. "You can't be hungry already, Lucian. I made you a meal before we left to tide you over until the dinner."

"Salad is not a meal, Mother," their son, Luka, said from the other side of Leigh, drawing a grunt of agreement from his father.

"It was Caesar salad," Leigh said with exasperation. "And Caesar salad *is* a meal."

"Lettuce with *imitation* bacon bits and vegan parmesan made from garlic and cashews," Lucian growled with disgust.

"And vegan Caesar salad dressing," Luka added.

"Caesar salad and garlic bread," Leigh said firmly, ignoring the commentary. "That *is* a meal."

"Rabbit food," Lucian and Luka muttered under their breaths in stereo, making Leigh glare from one to the other with irritation.

While Colle didn't hold back his laughter at this exchange, Alasdair didn't want to offend Leigh, so turned his head away to cough into his hand to cover his laugh. It was then that he noticed the woman making her way along the row of seats toward them. Alasdair paused and stared. The lass was lovely with tan skin, large eyes that were a brown so dark they almost appeared black, a small high-bridged nose, and full almost heart-shaped lips. Her hair was a long, wavy chestnut. She was beautiful, and slightly exotic. His guess was that she had a mixed ancestry . . . and he didn't know her from Adam. That was somewhat unexpected. He'd met all of Natalie's friends prior to the wedding, and the rest of the guests were Argeneaus, Nottes, MacKenzies, or hunters, most of whom he knew.

Curious, he glanced toward the couple following the lass and his eyebrows rose when he recognized his uncle Julius and aunt Marguerite. His gaze barely skated over Julius, but caught on Marguerite when he noted the gleam in her eyes and the satisfied, almost knowing smile on her lips.

Wariness creeping over him, Alasdair stood even as Colle did. It was habit, manners drummed into them from youth. A man always stood when a lady approached.

"Alasdair darling, and Colle," Marguerite said, her smile blossoming into a full one. "Let me introduce Sophie Ferguson. She's Tybo's date and is kind enough to have agreed to sit with us while Tybo is busy with his best man duties."

Alasdair's gaze slid back to the lass and he gave a polite nod of greeting, then simply stared at her as Colle did his usual charming routine, starting with proclaiming that he was fortunate enough to have already met the lass when he collected her and the boys from the helicopter, and going on to say how pleased he was to meet a lovely lassie like her again and so on.

Normally, Alasdair found his brother's ability to charm members of the opposite sex amusing. Especially since he knew Colle would never do anything more than compliment and flirt with them. Colle, like he himself, had lost interest in sex centuries ago as was wont for immortals past a certain age, but Colle did still like to flirt for some reason, and Alasdair was usually fine with that. This time, however, his brother's effusive compliments and charming smiles kind of annoyed him. Alasdair wanted to cuff him in the back of the head and tell him to shut up. He did neither. Instead, it was Marguerite who interrupted Colle's charm-fest.

"Goodness, Colle, you'll turn the girl's head," Marguerite said with a laugh. "Save your charm for the other unattached females here. Sophie isn't for *you*."

The way she gently emphasized the word *you* and then turned a solemn, meaningful look on Alasdair had him stiffening where he stood. She met his gaze, gave a small nod, and then smiled and added, "Besides, she's Tybo's date . . . for tonight."

That pause was another message, Alasdair was sure, but he wasn't certain what it meant. Had he misunderstood the first look and she was telling him that Sophie was Tybo's life mate? Or was she a possible life mate for someone else, maybe even himself, so was only Tybo's date for tonight? He had no idea, and since Marguerite was older than him, he couldn't read her mind to find out, so he simply turned his attention back to the beautiful lass.

She had a petite figure that showed nicely in the lovely dress she was wearing. She was no more than five foot three or five foot four, slender, but with definite curves and shapely legs.

"Come, come, we should sit down," Marguerite said suddenly, making him realize he'd been gawking at the lass. Fortunately, a quick glance back up to her face reassured him that Sophie didn't seem to have noticed. In fact, she was doing a little gawking of her own, her gaze traveling over his body like a caress he could almost feel now that he was aware of it. He was so distracted by the sensations suddenly rolling through him—sensations he hadn't experienced in centuries—that Alasdair wasn't paying much attention when everyone began to take their seats. Not until he realized he and Sophie were the only ones still standing.

Sophie appeared to notice that at the same time, and a pretty flush covered her cheeks as she hurried to claim the chair Marguerite directed her to . . . which was right beside the only empty seat still remaining, between Sophie and Colle. His twin had taken the seat next to Lucian that Alasdair had been occupying prior to this. Refraining from comment, he simply settled into his brother's now empty chair, but he did wonder why Colle had moved. Apparently, he wasn't the only one to wonder.

"Why are you sitting there, Colle? Alasdair was sitting next to me, not you," Lucian said suddenly, sounding suspicious.

"Marguerite waved me over when I started to sit in my own seat," Colle explained quietly enough Alasdair was sure Sophie couldn't have heard it. He did, however, and glanced at Marguerite in question.

The woman merely smiled and gave a slight nod toward Sophie and then raised her eyebrows and nodded toward her again. Alasdair knew his aunt was trying to tell him something. He just wasn't sure what it was. Letting that fact show in his expression, he raised his own eyebrows in question. This brought an exasperated roll of the eyes from Marguerite, but then she heaved a sigh and glanced at Sophie, who was peering at the flower-covered arch on the temporary dais at the front of the tent and wasn't paying them any attention. Marguerite quickly pointed at her forehead and then to him, and finally to Sophie.

Alasdair narrowed his eyes, trying to translate.

"She's telling you to try to read the girl," Lucian growled with impatience and then leaned forward to peer at Marguerite and said, "Stop it."

"Stop what?" she asked innocently.

"Stop stealing my men. Alasdair and Colle are supposed to be here to help out until Valerian gets back from his honeymoon. The last thing I need is for you to hook up one of them with their life mate. You'll make him useless."

"Oh, do not be silly, Lucian," Marguerite said on a chuckle. "You cannot stop destiny."

"The hell I can't," Lucian snapped, and then narrowed his eyes and added, "You've gone through my men this last decade like women go through toilet tissue. It has caused me nothing but headaches trying to keep the Enforcers numbers high enough to do their work. I *will* ban you from being anywhere near my Enforcers if you keep up with this nonsense."

"You would not," Marguerite said with fond amusement. "You want your men happy. Besides, you'd have a mutiny on your hands if you did. Every immortal wants their life mate, Lucian. You know that better than anyone," she added, her gaze sliding to Leigh, Lucian's life mate.

Lucian growled under his breath, but didn't argue the point, and simply sat back in his seat and bent to the side to press a gentle kiss to Leigh's lips as she slipped her hand into his.

Alasdair smiled faintly at the loving look the couple shared, and then turned his gaze to Sophie. She didn't appear to have heard the exchange, her attention was still on the flowers on the dais. It was possible that she was pretending not to hear, but he didn't think she was. Aside from the fact that Marguerite and Lucian had kept their voices low enough that a mortal would have had trouble catching the conversation, he suspected one or the other was also controlling her. Otherwise, they wouldn't have spoken so freely.

"Well?" Lucian said after a moment had passed.

Alasdair leaned forward slightly to peer past his

brother and see that Lucian was looking at him. "What?"

"What are you waiting for? Read her," Lucian said dryly. "Or try to. We all know you will not be able to, else Marguerite would not have brought the girl to you."

Alasdair raised his eyebrows at the command. First the man was griping about it, and now he was demanding he prove Sophie was his life mate.

"Just get it over with already," Lucian muttered with a combination of irritation and resignation. "As Marguerite said, you can't fight destiny. Besides, whether you can read her or not does not mean you will end up together. That's up to her."

Alasdair frowned at that comment and shifted his gaze back to Sophie. He didn't try to read her right away, though. Instead, he allowed himself a moment to look her over again. She really was a beautiful lass . . . to him anyway. A bit small, though, he noted, suddenly worried that if she was his life mate . . . Well, he could crush the girl with his mass if he—

"Do it," Lucian growled impatiently.

Alasdair turned a hard stare on the man for a count of three just to let him know he found him annoying, and then shifted his gaze back to Sophie and this time tried to read her. Despite the fact that Marguerite had become renowned for pairing life mates, Alasdair was still a little surprised when he came up against a blank wall of nothing and could not read the lass. It was just so . . . well, unexpected. The last thing he'd imagined while preparing to attend this wedding was that this would be the night that he found his life mate.

But there were other considerations running through his mind now that he knew he *had* met his mate. Not least of which was his brother, Colle. They were twins and while it wasn't always the case that twins were close, or that their lives were intertwined, both were true for he and Colle. They worked together, lived together, and did pretty much everything together short of showering and shitting. They were the best of friends and as close as could be, which was interesting considering the two of them were somewhat opposites. Colle was the lighthearted, charming, chatty, and impulsive one, while Alasdair was quieter, more introspective, and as far from impulsive as it was possible to be. Alasdair always thought before acting, and that was what he was doing now, thinking about how this would affect various aspects of his life. First, and most importantly, his relationship with his brother.

As twins, Alasdair and Colle couldn't read or control each other, so had been able to live together with few issues. In truth, Alasdair supposed their brotherly bond had taken the place of a life mate for the last more than three hundred years. While many immortals grew lonely and bored with life after centuries alone, he and Colle had always had each other to prevent that. This was definitely going to change their dynamic. On top of that, he almost felt guilty that he was finding his life mate before Colle.

"You think too much, bro," Colle said quietly. "I'll be fine. I'm happy for you. Besides, if I know Marguerite, she'll now be actively looking for a life mate for me. Trust me, soon enough, we'll both be settled with life mates."

Alasdair turned to peer at him with surprise. "You can read my mind now?"

Colle smiled crookedly and shrugged. "New life

mate brain, brother. Every immortal here can now no doubt read you like an open book. Even me."

Alasdair sank back in his seat at this news. New life mate brain. It was a thing. Even Lucian, one of the oldest and most powerful immortals, who no one had been able to read previously, had temporarily been easily read by everyone after finding his life mate, Leigh.

Alasdair shook his head. Damn. Sophie was definitely his life mate, or a possible life mate at any rate. As Lucian had so kindly pointed out, whether she became his official life mate was up to her. It wasn't something he could force. He'd have to woo her, charm her, and convince her to—

Dear God, he thought suddenly. Charm was something he was sadly lacking in and knew it. Colle was the twin who had inherited that ability. He himself didn't have the patience for it, and found the tendency to chatter, flirt, and compliment others somewhat disingenuous. He usually left that up to Colle while he remained silent and alert for trouble and knew that tended to intimidate people. How the hell was he going to woo Sophie?

"Colle, take your brother for a walk," Lucian said suddenly.

Blinking away his thoughts, Alasdair glanced at the head of the North American Council in question as Colle stood up.

"You're panicking," Lucian Argeneau said dryly. "It's painful to hear. Go for a walk and clear your head."

Alasdair scowled at the man, but didn't argue, mostly because he *was* feeling panicky at the chore ahead of him to gain his life mate. He stood to follow Colle as his brother scooted past Lucian, Leigh, and their teenaged twin son and daughter, Luka and Gemma, to get out of the row.

Sophie sensed motion beside her and turned to see that the men Marguerite had introduced as Colle and Alasdair were making their way to the aisle. Her gaze traveled over the pair and then settled on the one named Alasdair. Other than the fact that Alasdair was wearing a charcoal gray suit, and Colle had on a lighter gray one, they were identical. They were also both gorgeous. At about six feet tall with short dark hair and muscular bodies, they fully fit the tall, dark, and handsome description, but it was their eyes that made them something special. Like herself, both had eyes so dark a brown they appeared black, but their eyes had gold flecks that she found beautiful.

Sophie watched until they disappeared into the crowd, and then turned to peer at the dais at the front again. It was what she'd been doing since sitting down, mostly to keep from gawking at the man who had been seated beside her, which had been really hard not to do. Big as he was, he'd taken up more space than most men would in the chairs that had been set out. Enough that his outer leg had pressed lightly against hers the moment he'd sat down, and his arm had brushed her own whenever he'd shifted in his seat to talk to his brother or the other man next to his brother.

Sophie had been aware of the conversation taking place next to her, but she couldn't say what had been said. Their voices had been so low they'd been hard for her to hear. Besides, while she'd been staring at the dais and its trappings, her attention had been on her body's reaction to the leg pressing and arm brushing going on . . . and what a reaction it had been. Never in her life had she had such a visceral response to such a harmless and unintentional action. Alasdair most likely hadn't even noticed what was happening, but she had. Goose bumps had broken out all over her body, her nipples had pebbled, and a liquid heat had swelled low in her stomach and rushed down between her legs leaving her wet and a hair's breadth away from panting and squirming on her seat. How pathetic was that?

The worst part was that she was reacting like that to a complete stranger, all while here on a date with Tybo, who was perfectly nice, and a good-looking guy to boot. Not as good-looking as Alasdair, of course, but—

"Idiot," she muttered under her breath with self-derision.

"What was that, dear?" Marguerite asked.

Sophie felt herself flush at being overheard, but she shook her head and muttered, "Nothing. Just talking to myself. A bad habit I have."

"One I have myself," Marguerite said sympathetically.

Nodding, Sophie focused on the dais again, ready to let the conversation die, but Marguerite apparently wasn't done with her.

"Colle and Alasdair work with Tybo."

Sophie turned to her with interest. "They're cops too?"

Marguerite blinked, and hesitated a beat, then smiled. "They are in law enforcement, yes."

"Hmm." Sophie twisted in her seat to look in the direction the men had taken, but they'd got lost in what was essentially a sea of tall men. Seriously, they seemed to grow them big out here, she thought, and then frowned as she noted that there appeared to be several men who looked very like the twins. Most of the men had the same dark hair and eyes, and were equally tall, but few were quite as wide and muscly. However, they were all either sitting on the opposite side of the aisle or heading that way.

"That's the MacKenzie side," Marguerite told her, taking note of where she was looking, and then added, "The groom's side."

"And this is the bride's side?" Sophie asked.

"Technically, yes." Marguerite smiled. "However, Natalie doesn't have any close family other than her daughter, and has only a handful of close friends and employees in the area, so it was decided that some of us would sit on her side to support her. So, even though Alasdair and Colle are MacKenzies, they took seats on this side for Natalie."

Sophie thought that was kind. She didn't really have any family other than the Tomlinsons and would have found herself in a similar predicament.

"So, Alasdair's last name is MacKenzie?" Sophie asked with interest.

"Actually, I think it's Notte this decade," Marguerite murmured absently as she glanced around.

"This decade?" Sophie asked with confusion.

Marguerite's gaze shot back to her with realization, and then she gave a small laugh. "Sorry. That's a family joke, dear. Alasdair and Colle's mother is a Notte and their father is a MacKenzie, so actually they're Notte-MacKenzies."

Sophie nodded, but didn't really understand the joke. Still, of the two names, she thought MacKenzie fit better since she'd noted a slight Scottish burr when the two men had spoken. Sophie loved Scottish accents. She loved everything Scottish and hoped to visit there someday. Her favorite movies were all set in Scotland too, from the animated *Brave* to the dramatic *Braveheart* and thrilling *Highlander* and so on. Put someone with a Scottish accent in the movie and she was down for it.

Perhaps that was why she was so oddly attracted to Alasdair, Sophie thought. He was Scottish and she loved his accent. Of course, he hadn't said a word to her, but his brother Colle had. She supposed that it would make more sense to be attracted to Colle, who had been laying the compliments on thick. But she wasn't. She'd recognized Colle's chatter as practiced charm and empty words and hadn't been impressed. It was probably the same deal with Tybo and why she wasn't attracted to him either. While he'd helped her out of a sticky situation and was charming and funny, she suspected he was a player, just out for fun. Alasdair, on the other hand . . .

Sophie continued to peer at the flower-covered arch on the dais and wondered if she'd ever marry. She'd come close three times now. Her first love had given her a promise ring, not an engagement ring, but then they'd both been teenagers in high school at the time. However, she had been properly engaged twice now as an adult. Unfortunately, her high school sweetheart and both of her fiancés had been in terrible accidents that had brought an end to her dreams of having a husband and family of her own. While Bobby had joked that she was cursed, she was half-afraid that the universe was trying to tell her something. Or she *was* cursed. Which meant it was probably better for her to date guys like Tybo and Colle rather than the Alasdairs of the world who she might actually get interested in. She'd had enough heartbreak in her life and really didn't think she could bear any more.

Four

"I need to woo Sophie," Alasdair growled as he and his brother finally made their way out of the tent and into the darkening night. The sun was setting. It would be full dark soon.

"Aye." Colle nodded in agreement.

"But I'm no' guid at wooing," Alasdair said fretfully.

"Yer Scottish is comin' out. It only comes out nowadays when yer upset or anxious," Colle said, his own accent thickening.

"Well, yer Scottish is comin' out too," Alasdair pointed out with irritation.

"Because yer upset, so I'm upset fer ye," Colle said with exasperation, and then paused, took a deep, calming breath, and said soothingly, "It's perfectly understandable. Ye've just met yer life mate, and now are frettin' o'er how to convince her to be yours. But 'twill be fine. I'll help ye woo her."

"The whelp's found his life mate?"

Alasdair stiffened at those words, and then turned slowly to find four men standing behind him. His uncle Connor, and his great-uncles Ludan, Inan, and Odart. All four men were at least two hundred years older than them and still considered him and Colle wet behind the ears. They were also all rogue hunters in Scotland and tended to hang around together when not on the job, which meant they hadn't really changed with the times. They remained the uncivilized barbarians of their eras. He wasn't surprised to see that each of them wore a short dress jacket, kilt, and sporran, or that each had a large plastic drinking glass full of ale in hand. He was only surprised they hadn't brought their own steins for their drinks.

"Well?" Connor asked impatiently. "Did I hear right? Allie's found his life mate?"

Alasdair winced at the childish nickname that only his uncles insisted on still using.

"Aye, *Alasdair* has met his life mate," Colle said, emphasizing the full name.

"Damn," Odart breathed, turning his attention to Alasdair. "Ye're a lucky bastard, ye are."

"Aye," Inan agreed on a sigh, and then shook his head. "'Tis no' fair, though. We're older. We should be meetin' ours first."

"Hell, if life were fair we'd ha'e met ours ere both their grandda' Caillen or at least their da' Gillie found their women," Ludan pointed out.

"Aye, but ye should ken by now that life is no' fair," Connor said with a shrug, the *now* sounding more like *new*.

All four men nodded and grunted in glum agreement to that, and then Connor shook off his malaise and asked abruptly, "So, if the lad's found his life mate, why are the two o' ye out here looking glum as guppies?"

"Because he's concerned about wooing her," Colle explained.

"Why the devil would he worry about that?" Ludan asked with obvious surprise.

"Because if he messes up, he could lose her. Forever," Colle pointed out, his tone turning a tad dry. "Just because they're life mates doesn't mean she'll agree to be one."

"Oh, aye," Odart muttered, scowling now as well.

"Nay, no' 'oh aye,'" Connor said with exasperation to the other man, and then turned to Alasdair and added, "Stop being a numptie. Ye're no' alone in this. Ye've got family. We'll help ye claim yer lass, lad."

"Aye, we'll help ye woo her," Inan said, looking pleased at the idea.

Alasdair managed to control his expression to hide his alarm at this announcement. But inside he was cursing up a blue streak. He couldn't think of anything worse than his uncles "helping" him woo Sophie, and was quite sure their idea of helping would scare Sophie off. Alasdair groaned inwardly at his bad luck in meeting a possible life mate when his uncles were here, which, as it happened, was the first time the bastards had ever set foot in North America.

"Buck up, lad," Connor said, with a comradely blow to his arm that would have knocked Alasdair over if he hadn't known his uncle so well and been prepared for the move. "We'll ha'e yer lass in yer arms in no time."

"Aye, we will," Inan agreed, giving him a slug as well. "With us helpin', the two o' ye will be standing before the priest ere ye can say 'Foos yer doos.'"

Alasdair blinked at the greeting he hadn't heard in a long time, which was common in Aberdeen and actually translated to "How are your pigeons?" He then winced as Odart too slugged him in the arm, hard.

"We'll help," he growled, the two words sounding like a threat.

"Aye" was all Ludan said, and Alasdair half suspected he only bothered so that he too could give him an arm punch.

"So, where's yer lass?" Connor asked, turning to peer into the tent of people.

"She's the pretty brunette seated beside—ouch!" Colle stopped when Alasdair elbowed him in the side and gave him a meaningful look. The last thing he wanted was help from their uncles. In fact, it seemed like a bit of bad luck that they were even here when he found her. Not only were his uncles old and stuck in their ways, they were also nosy as hell and a good part of the reason that he and Colle had left Scotland. They'd wanted to live without their constant interference.

"Well? Where is she?" Connor asked, pulling his gaze from the people in the tent to arch his eyes at Alasdair.

"It does no' matter," Alasdair said firmly. "She's someone else's date tonight. I'll have to wait to start wooing her."

"She's on a *date*?" Inan asked, horrified at the very thought.

"With *another maun*?" Connor asked with equal horror.

"Well, that's no' on," Ludan said with disgust. "What kind o' ass would date yer life mate?"

"It can no' be an immortal," Inan decided. "No immortal would be foolish enough to date another maun's life mate."

"He didn't know she was anyone's life mate when he asked her out," Colle said soothingly.

"Hmm," Inan said, looking disgruntled. "That's a bit o' bad luck then, is it no'? Findin' yer life mate when she's datin' another?"

Odart and Connor grunted in agreement, but Ludan scowled and asked, "Does he ken now that she's yours?"

Alasdair frowned, unsure of the answer to that. Marguerite hadn't mentioned whether Tybo knew or not.

"Tybo?" Connor jumped on the name in his thoughts. "She's his date?"

Alasdair merely scowled in response. It was so annoying when others could read your thoughts. He'd briefly forgotten that his uncles could, and it wasn't like this was something new. Centuries older as they were, his uncles had always been able to read his mind, as had anyone else older than him. Normally that was at the forefront of his mind and he either controlled his thoughts, or took steps to try to mask them. However, finding his life mate had made him forget to do either.

"We should probably get back in there now," Colle said, glancing past him with a small frown. "Val and Tybo are on their way out. The wedding must be about to start."

Alasdair glanced over his shoulder to see that what Colle said was true. His cousin Valerian and Val's best man, Tybo, were just coming around the side of the clubhouse, heading for the tent. That meant the bride and the rest of the party wouldn't be far behind.

"Aye, we'd best go in," Ludan decided, tossing his now empty glass into a garbage can set up outside the tent. Once the other uncles had dumped their own empty glasses, Ludan began urging the group toward the tent entrance, before adding, "But don'y worry about claiming yer lass, boyo. We'll help ye with that. We'll get together after the ceremony and have a think on how to do it. Right?"

Alasdair merely grunted, and tried not to think that that was possibly the worst idea he'd ever heard. He wouldn't put it past them to think clubbing her over the head and dragging her to the nearest cave was the best approach. Truly, his uncles were old barbarians and he cursed his luck that they were here.

Five

Sophie heard a disturbance to her right and glanced over to see that Colle and Alasdair had returned. Or were trying to, she realized as she watched them interact with four other men, two of whom definitely looked like relatives. They weren't quite as tall as Colle and Alasdair, but they did have the dark good looks, and the two in question were also twins. At least, they looked identical to each other and very similar to Alasdair and Colle. The other two men had similar facial features to the rest of them, but both had dark auburn hair rather than black. All four of them, however, had the builds of linebackers or something. She'd thought Colle and Alasdair big and brawny, but these men surpassed even them. They also wore kilts, she noted, and had a brief vision of them in a scene from *Braveheart*, wielding broadswords as they charged across a glen at their enemies.

"Those are Alasdair and Colle's uncles," Marguerite announced.

Sophie glanced around with surprise. "Really?"

Marguerite nodded, her gaze narrowing on the group of men in the aisle.

"But they don't look old enough," Sophie protested, and then smiled wryly. "But then neither do you and Julius look old enough to be his aunt and uncle. Were his parents a lot older than you all, or a half-sibling from the father's first marriage or something? Because those men cannot possibly have the same mother as whichever of Valerian's parent they're related to. She would have been ancient when she had Valerian."

"Oh dear. It looks like there is a bit of a disagreement as to where the uncles should sit," Marguerite murmured, rather than answer her question.

Sophie peered back to the group to see that Colle and Alasdair appeared to be trying to direct the four newcomers to the chairs on the other side of the center aisle, while the uncles seemed determined to follow Colle and Alasdair down the row of seats to sit with them. Which wasn't really possible. The tent had continued to fill up since the two men had left. Every seat in their row was now taken except for the two Colle and Alasdair had briefly abandoned.

Sophie was just beginning to worry that they would march on down the row and order others to abandon their seats for them, when the man with platinum blond hair stood up with an exasperated huff to join the men.

"Lucian will handle it," Marguerite said with satisfaction.

"Lucian?" Sophie queried with curiosity. "Is he one of the friends of the bride that you mentioned, or—"

"Not a friend exactly, no. More a . . . Lucian Argeneau is the boss of Valerian and Tybo's boss," she finished finally.

"Oh," Sophie murmured as she watched Lucian "handle" the uncles. She had no idea what he said, but whatever it was seemed effective. Within minutes, the uncles were moving off to claim seats on the other side of the aisle, but not before every one of them turned to look her over.

Not welcoming the sudden scrutiny, Sophie scowled slightly and then simply turned her head away and gave them her back as she asked Marguerite, "So, Lucian is Valerian and Tybo's boss's boss."

"Yes. And that lovely lady is his wife, Leigh," Marguerite told her.

Sophie eyed the woman in question briefly, but then shifted her gaze to the men again to see that while the uncles had moved off to find seats, Lucian, Colle, and Alasdair were still in the aisle talking.

"And the handsome young man and pretty girl beside Leigh are her children, Gemma and Luka," Marguerite continued. "They are fraternal twins."

Sophie's gaze moved back to Leigh and the young teenagers next to her. The boy had Leigh's dark hair, while the girl had her father's fair hair, and their features were a mixture of both parents; both had Lucian's silver-blue eyes, but otherwise Gemma looked more like a younger version of her mother, while Luka had his mother's lips but his father's nose. Both were as ridiculously attractive as the rest of this crowd. Well, except for the people in the first row in front of them, Sophie thought, glancing toward the guests now occupying the seats in the last row before the dais. Some of those guests were young, some were even attractive, but none were as attractive as the rest of this congregation, and there were even older people filling those seats. No twins, though. But then how many could there be in a group? Three had to be above the odds.

Turning to Marguerite, she said, "Twins seem to be a thing in this crowd. Gemma and Luka, Colle and Alasdair, and I'm pretty sure two of the uncles were twins too. At least they look like identical twins."

"Inan and Odart," Marguerite said with a nod. "Yes, they are twins."

"Inan and Odart?" Sophie echoed.

Marguerite glanced at her with surprise and then seemed to realize the names weren't exactly standard. In fact, Sophie had never even heard them before.

"Yes. Well, I'm not surprised you have never heard them before. They are old-fashioned Scottish names. Very old and rarely used now," Marguerite said.

Sophie didn't doubt that for a minute but then frowned as Marguerite's words played through her head. *I'm not surprised you have never heard them before?* She hadn't said that out loud, had she? She'd just thought it. Hadn't she? No, she must have muttered what she was thinking. It wasn't like Marguerite could read her mind.

"Here come the boys. Oh, and Tybo and Valerian just entered the tent. The ceremony must be about to begin."

Shaking away the ridiculous idea that Marguerite could read her thoughts, Sophie looked to the end of the row to see that the men were now easing past Leigh and the twins to regain their seats. She then turned to look toward the back of the tent to see Tybo leading

Valerian up the aisle toward the dais. When he spotted her and grinned, she smiled back and then raised her eyebrows quizzically when Tybo's grin morphed into a frown as it shifted to Alasdair just as he reached and reclaimed the seat beside her. Then her view of Tybo was blocked by Alasdair's chest. By the time she leaned to the side to be able to see Tybo again, he was walking past their row and had turned his head to face forward.

Wondering what that was about, Sophie shifted to sit properly in her chair to watch Tybo and Valerian mount the dais. The two men had barely taken up position on the dais, side by side, facing the people here to witness the wedding, when a murmur had her glancing back toward the entrance of the tent to see a minister starting up the aisle, his white robes fluttering out around him as he hurried to join Valerian and Tybo.

Once the minister was in position on the dais, music started. Sophie, along with everyone else, immediately turned to look toward the back of the tent. She wasn't sure what she'd expected to see, but it wasn't the adorable little cherub in a pretty pink dress with a crown of pink- and mulberry-colored flowers on her head and the huge white dog she was holding on to by the fur with one hand as she teetered up the aisle. A soft *ah* went through the crowd, and as if it were a cue, both the dog and child stopped and the little girl released her hold on the animal to reach into the basket she was carrying and pull out and toss a handful of petals on the floor. She then grasped the big dog again by the hair and took a couple more steps before stopping to repeat the exercise. Sophie had to bite her lip to hold back the laugh that tried to escape her. It was such an adorable scene, and the dog was wonderful, moving when the little girl did, stopping at once when she stopped.

"That is Natalie's little girl, Mia," Marguerite whispered. "And her dog, Sinbad. He's so good with Mia."

Sophie nodded silently, never taking her eyes off the pair as they made their way up the aisle. The sweet little cherub was just a couple feet from the dais when she reached into her basket again, only to frown, peer into it, and then tip it up. The basket was empty. For one moment she looked distressed, but then Valerian gave a soft whistle to get her attention. Spying him on the dais, she beamed a smile, squealed, and dashed forward with Sinbad hard on her heels.

Sophie held her breath as the little girl negotiated the stairs, and everyone gasped when she lost her footing on the top step and began to teeter backward, but Sinbad was there. The dog caught her by the collar of her dress and lifted her off her feet even as Valerian rushed forward to scoop up the little girl.

"Good boy," Valerian said, patting the dog before straightening with Mia now clutched safely to his chest. Mia immediately showed both men her empty basket, which from her chatter, appeared to be quite disappointing to her.

"I think I'm in love," Sophie whispered with amusement as she watched the little girl chatter away, hands and basket waving around. She didn't think she'd spoken loud enough for anyone to hear, but the words had Alasdair swiveling around to look at her wide-eyed.

Flushing with embarrassment, Sophie shrugged and said almost apologetically, "She's just so darned cute."

Alasdair relaxed a little and nodded. "She is."

Sophie peered up at him with curiosity. That was the first time he'd spoken to her, and she was fascinated by the husky, almost rusty sound of his voice. As if he didn't use it much.

A murmur that started at the back of the tent and moved forward like a wave had her looking around again then to watch a pretty strawberry blonde start up the aisle. She was wearing a lovely mulberry-colored gown with the front reaching just below the knees and then swooping down in the back where it reached the floor. It had a fitted bodice and a pleated sash around the waist and looked beautiful on the woman.

"That's Jan," Marguerite murmured helpfully. "Natalie's dear friend and assistant chef here at the golf club. She's the maid of honor to Tybo's best man."

Sophie nodded and watched the woman make her way up the aisle, admiring the dress and the way the chiffon skirt flowed out as she moved.

The bride was next. Walking alone and carrying a mixed bouquet of white, pink, and mulberry toned flowers in hand, she was absolutely beautiful. Her hair was down, falling in soft waves around her lovely face, with a crown of flowers on her head just like her daughter wore. Natalie had bypassed the usual long white gown that was traditional for weddings, and instead had gone with a gorgeous white satin and black lace gown. The skirt was white satin with a black lace trim along the inside bottom hem, easily seen since the skirt, like the bridesmaid's, was asymmetrical with the front reaching just below the knees and then curving down on the sides so that the back drifted across the floor. The bodice of the gown was short sleeved, with a princess scoop neck of black lace over white satin. It was absolutely stunning.

When Natalie reached the steps to the dais, Valerian was there, offering his hand to see her safely up, and the smile the pair exchanged was so full of love it made Sophie's heart hurt. Valerian didn't put Mia down for the ceremony as she'd expected, but simply held her and gazed lovingly from the child to the mother even as Natalie did the same.

"They're so in love," Sophie whispered as the minister began to speak.

Alasdair grunted what sounded like agreement, and Colle leaned in front of him to tell her, "'Twas the luckiest day o' his life when Val met Natalie. They were meant for each other."

Sophie nodded because that seemed obvious from the happiness and love the couple were exuding. Curious, she leaned toward Alasdair and asked, "How long have they known each other?"

He hesitated briefly before saying, "I think it's been three and a half—"

"Closer to four," Colle corrected.

"Four," Alasdair conceded with a nod. "Four weeks tomorrow."

"*Four weeks!*" Sophie gasped with disbelief . . . much more loudly than intended, or at least more loudly than she would have meant to had she not been so shocked. When he'd started with the three and a half business, she'd expected *years* to follow, not *weeks*. Surely that would have shocked anyone?

Unfortunately, this was a wedding, where everyone was silent, straining to hear the minister. That silence became deafening after her bellowed words, and absolutely everyone in the tent turned to look at her, including the bride, groom, and minister. Sophie didn't dare look at Tybo to see how angry he must be at having his date interrupt the ceremony like that.

Face going hot as a poker, and no doubt red as a tomato, Sophie froze for a moment, her brain slow to figure out what the correct course of action was to fix this situation. Then she finally offered an embarrassed and very apologetic smile to the happy couple on the dais and gave a kind of scooting gesture with her fingers, silently begging them to continue the ceremony . . . and hopefully get the attention off her.

Much to her relief, the bride didn't appear upset about the rude interruption, in fact she grinned at Sophie and then turned to her almost husband and the couple chuckled then turned back to the priest. The ceremony continued and most of the eyes that had been trained on her shifted to the happy couple again.

Letting her breath out on a sigh, Sophie closed her own eyes and tried to calm herself. God, that was embarrassing. But who the hell married someone four weeks after meeting them?

"Dear, if you slouch any lower in your seat, I fear you will fall on the floor."

Those gentle words from Marguerite had Sophie's eyes popping open. She glanced to the woman's kind face, offered her a crooked smile, and forced herself to sit up in her chair. She hadn't really realized she'd slunk down in it in an effort to be less visible. Frankly, she'd been hoping the ground would open up and swallow her, but sliding off her chair to the floor was not a good alternative.

Sighing, she glanced around to see if anyone else

had noticed her childish actions, but no one seemed to be looking her way anymore. Except for Alasdair. Sitting stiffly upright, his big arms crossed over his even bigger chest, he was eyeing her with twinkling eyes and twitching lips she suspected were fighting a smile. Before she even knew what she was doing, Sophie had stuck her tongue out at him.

Much to her surprise it brought a bark of laughter from the big stoic man . . . and once again brought a halt to the ceremony as everyone turned to look their way once more. This time, though, they were looking at Alasdair, and while they'd all had surprised expressions when they'd turned at her shouted *Four weeks!*, they were all now looking absolutely shocked at one little bark of laughter from Alasdair. Honestly, the reaction seemed a little over-the-top to her. They were all acting like the man was a deaf-mute who had never spoken or laughed in his life. She actually felt sorry for him as she watched his face turn red and he made the same finger scooting gesture as she had to urge the ceremony along.

Natalie and Valerian glanced at each other with raised eyebrows, but then turned back to the minister and the ceremony continued, but the man named Lucian suddenly leaned in front of Colle to growl at them, "If you two cannot behave and be quiet, perhaps you should go for a walk so this ceremony can be done. I am hungry and you are delaying my eating."

Sophie blinked at the words and had to bite back a laugh of disbelief to whisper, "We'll be quiet. At least I will," she added, since she had no right to speak for the man beside her.

Alasdair then grunted what she assumed was agreement. Lucian spared a moment to scowl from one to the other of them like they were naughty children, and then sat back in his seat to watch the rest of the ceremony.

Shaking her head, Sophie sat back in her seat and tried to pay attention to what the minister was saying, but honestly, it was kind of boring. He seemed to go on and on for quite a bit about love and God and family, and as he droned on, Sophie found her mind beginning to wander to the fact that both Marguerite and Lucian acted like old folks. She was quite sure that at thirty-one years and ten months–she wasn't thirty-two yet and would hold on to that fact until it wasn't true anymore—she was older than both of them. Yet every time Marguerite called her "dear," she felt like she was being spoken to by her grandma. As for Lucian . . . well, he acted like the lord of the manor . . . or God. It was obvious he was used to his word being law.

Weird, she thought, and then the minister's boring drone was replaced with Natalie's sweet voice, and Sophie tuned back in to hear what she was saying. It turned out Natalie and Valerian had written their own vows, which were really quite lovely and sweet, and much to her embarrassment actually made her eyes glaze over with tears, especially when Valerian included little Mia in his vows and promised to love and cherish her too. At which point Mia piped up and asked, "And Sinbad?" which made everyone chuckle, including the groom before he promised solemnly, "Yes, and Sinbad."

The rings were then retrieved from a basket that sat on a harness on the big white dog's back, and exchanged, including a little one for Mia, which moved Sophie to murmur, "That's sweet."

"What is?" Alasdair leaned closer to her to ask in a whisper.

"Mia getting a ring too so she wouldn't feel left out," Sophie whispered back, trying to ignore the sensations his nearness stirred in her. Dear God, she was here with Tybo. She had no business getting all squirmy inside because Alasdair's arm was touching hers, and she could feel his breath on her cheek when he spoke.

"It's not so she won't feel left out," Alasdair informed her quietly. "Mia's ring has the MacKenzie family crest on it. It's a formal welcome to the clan."

"Oh," Sophie said with surprise, and thought that was even sweeter. Then the bride and groom were pronounced husband and wife, kissed each other, and then each pressed a quick kiss to either side of Mia's head to finish the ceremony. The guests immediately broke out in smiles and clapping and all stood to watch as the bride, groom, daughter, and dog all started off the dais, followed by Tybo and Jan.

Once the happy couple had cleared the first row, the people seated there began to file out behind them. Their row followed next with Lucian ushering his family along, saying, "Come on, girls, let's go. Time for food."

"Dad," Luka complained. "You always call us 'girls.' I'm not a girl."

"And your mother is a woman not a girl," Lucian pointed out and then shrugged. "It is easier to say girls than daughter, son, and wife." When Luka looked less than impressed with this explanation, he snapped, "Just move. I am hungry."

Sophie bit back a chuckle at the teenaged boy's look of disgust and followed when Alasdair and Colle moved toward the aisle.

Six

"Well," Marguerite said as they stepped out of the tent into the cool night air a few moments later. "That was lovely."

"Yes," Sophie agreed, looking around for Tybo. He'd said he'd collect her for the meal, but she didn't see him anywhere. She didn't see the bride and groom either, though. The group must have moved on quickly to the other tent. Sophie was just thinking she should probably find him when a tap on her shoulder had her turning to see him next to her.

"Oh, hi," she said with relief. "I was just looking for you."

"I had to slip around the outside of the crowd to get back to you," Tybo explained.

Sophie nodded in understanding, but narrowed her eyes on him. He was looking a little nervous, like he had bad news he wasn't looking forward to giving.

She understood why when he said, "I'm sorry, Sophie. I have to go back into the tent for pictures. We're just waiting for the last of the guests to leave for the reception tent and then they apparently want pictures of the wedding party, and family and such."

"Oh. Of course." She nodded with understanding.

"And then," he added with a wince, "again, I'm sorry. I thought we'd be able to sit together for the meal, but it turns out I'm expected at the head table with the others. It's a very small head table," he said apologetically. "There's just room for the six of us."

"Six?" Marguerite asked, joining the conversation. "Natalie, Valerian, Mia, Jan, you, and . . ." She raised her eyebrows. "Not Jan's husband?"

"No. The minister," Tybo explained. "Jan's husband is sitting at the table with Natalie's friends and employees. He knew ahead of time, and was fine with it, but I didn't think to ask about seating arrangements for the meal," he explained apologetically. "Sophie, I'm sorry. But—"

"She can sit with us," Marguerite interrupted soothingly, and then asked her, "You don't mind keeping us company a little longer, do you, Sophie?"

"No, of course not," she said politely. What else could she do? She didn't want to kick up a fuss, and it wasn't like she had other options. If she'd known more about weddings, she supposed she would have seen this coming.

"Thank you," Tybo said with obvious relief. Taking her hands, he gave them a squeeze and bent to press a kiss to her forehead. "I'll see you after the dinner. The first dance is for you," he promised. "We'll dance the night away."

Sophie nodded.

When he stepped back, she saw Alasdair and Colle had been standing behind him, watching and listening. Colle's eyebrows were slightly raised, as if surprised that Tybo had kissed her, but Alasdair looked like stone, as if he took offense at the tame show of affection. Sophie found that a bit surprising considering Tybo had kissed her on the forehead, which was more a fatherly or even grandfatherly gesture than anything that could be considered racy. It wasn't like he'd French kissed her mouth or anything.

Speaking of which, she thought now, what was with that peck on the forehead business anyway? Certainly, it was their first date, and no they hadn't kissed yet other than that peck, but he *was* her date. He could have placed the peck closer to her mouth, or even on it and she wouldn't have taken offense.

"Well, I suppose we had best head over to the other tent and see where we are sitting," Marguerite suggested. "Alasdair, will you escort Sophie? The ground is a little uneven and she—like the rest of us ladies—is wearing high heels."

Alasdair was at her side and taking her arm before Marguerite even finished speaking, and Sophie—who had just opened her mouth to politely refuse his aid—stilled at the tingles his touch sent up her arm and through her body, stirring some intense reactions from her. She then closed her mouth and withheld her protest. Purely because she'd already crossed the grass once that night and knew Marguerite was right, Sophie told herself. Negotiating grass in high heels was tricky. The heels were likely to sink into the grass and dirt. The last thing she needed was for a heel to get stuck and her to fall flat on her face and embarrass herself more than she already had with her squawking during the ceremony. That was the only reason she allowed it, she told herself. It had absolutely nothing to do with the warm tingling sensation that was making her nipples pebble under her gown, or the liquid heat sliding down to the apex of her thighs like warm caramel.

"Liar," she breathed under her breath.

"What was that?" Alasdair asked, and Sophie glanced up at him quickly and then kind of froze like a deer in headlights because while his question suggested he hadn't heard what she'd said, something about his eyes and expression told her he'd heard her perfectly and perhaps just didn't understand the reference. Deciding it was better off if he didn't know, she simply shook her head and then turned quickly forward as the cool night air was replaced with light and warmth. They were entering the second, larger tent, and now that they had she was getting her first real look at the setup.

Sophie had seen part of the tables with place settings and accompanying chairs through the opening on first arriving; what she hadn't seen was that they were set up with a rectangular table in the center of the far wall across from where they were entering. The head table, where the wedding party would sit once the pictures were done, she knew, her gaze moving on to the rest of the tables. Large round tables that sat eight or nine people filled up the rest of the space, except for a large square in the middle left for dancing. At least that was what she assumed it was for when she saw the shiny white tiles on that area where the rest of the floor of the tent was some kind of woven rug of rattan.

The tables were lovely with white chairs, white tablecloths, white dishes, what looked like real crystal wineglasses and champagne flutes, and beautiful pink, white, and mulberry floral arrangements in the center of each round table. The warm air was coming from outdoor heaters at each corner of the tent and spaced out along the sides. It was the latter half of October and while the last couple of days had been unseasonably warm, the nights were growing cooler, so the heaters were handy, but they were also somewhat concerning to her. What if the material of the tent got too hot and caught flame?

"The tent is made of fire-retardant cloth," Colle said, stepping up on her right side, the opposite of where Alasdair was holding her arm.

"Oh, right," Sophie said with a nod, but her attention had already moved on to the ceiling of the tent where chandeliers hung. Good Lord, there must have been twelve of them spaced out across the ceiling. Six running down either side. There were also four ceiling fans running down the center peak between them. The fans were one thing, but chandeliers? In a tent? Crazy, she thought, and then frowned, pointed up at them, and asked, "How are they powering those?"

Both brothers peered up at the chandeliers, and then Alasdair shrugged and said, "Electricity."

Sophie rolled her eyes with exasperation. "Well, I know it's—"

"Sophie dear! Boys! Come along now, I found our seats."

Giving up her curiosity about electrical issues, Sophie headed toward Marguerite, who stood by one of the round tables closer to the right side of the head table. Presumably the bride's side again, she thought as she led Alasdair and Colle to Marguerite.

"Here we are, dear," Marguerite said cheerily, sitting in one chair and tapping the one next to her.

A glance at the table showed name cards on top of each plate, and it appeared Marguerite hadn't had to offer to have her sit with them, Sophie's name was on the one Marguerite was directing her to. They'd been stuck with her anyway, she thought, and then as Alasdair pulled her chair out for her, she noted that his name was on the plate next to hers.

"Thanks," she said as she sat down. Sophie watched him take his own seat next to her and then glanced around at the other empty chairs at the table and wondered if Lucian and Leigh and their children would sit with them. Their table was one of the ones that sat nine, so there were obviously four more guests joining them.

"Oh, look! There are Decker and Dani," Marguerite said suddenly. "I wonder if they have heard any news about Martine."

Marguerite was talking to Julius, and Sophie had no idea who Martine was, but still looked in the direction Marguerite was, trying to guess which of the people settling into chairs farther down their side of this section of round tables she was talking about. She couldn't tell; there were several couples at the table she seemed to be looking at.

"We should go say hello," Marguerite decided after a moment, and stood up. Pausing then, she glanced worriedly down at Sophie. "You will be all right for a few minutes, will you not, dear?"

"Of course," Sophie assured her, thinking to herself

that Marguerite talked like she imagined her grandmother might have if she had lived long enough to be a grandmother. Unfortunately, she'd died giving birth to Sophie's mother and had never met her daughter let alone Sophie, her granddaughter.

"Alasdair, look after Tybo's date, please," Marguerite instructed as she headed away.

"Of course."

Sophie's head swung around at the sound of his voice. It was just as husky and almost rusty sounding as the first time he'd spoken. God it was sexy, she thought. So deep, and with the perfect timber to send shivers down her back. He should be a radio DJ or one of those readers for audiobooks or something. She'd listen to everything he narrated.

"I will not be long."

Sophie turned toward Marguerite in time to see Julius escorting her toward the table she'd been looking at. She watched them go until the pair stopped by a couple and bent to hug first the dark-haired man, and then the blonde woman beside him before either could stand.

"Decker is Marguerite's nephew by her first marriage. The pretty blonde is his wife, Dani. She's a doctor," Alasdair told her quietly.

"So, you *can* speak whole sentences," Sophie teased, continuing to watch the table where everyone was now standing to greet and receive hugs from Marguerite and Julius. When Alasdair didn't respond, she turned to look at him, and had to fight to keep from frowning when she noted the discomfort on his face. He didn't know how to take her words, she realized. Had he thought them serious, or a put-down? Letting a light grin play on her lips, she said, "I was teasing you, Alasdair. But you do have a very nice voice. You should use it more."

His eyes widened and they stared at each other briefly. Sophie was staring at his mouth. It looked so firm and soft at the same time and she wondered what it would feel like if she reached out a finger to touch the pillowy pad of his lower lip. Or what it would feel like on hers. She felt her heartbeat pick up and her eyelids begin to droop as she imagined him kissing her. Would he be a good kisser? Would he take her hand, drag her onto his lap, and then just envelop her in his arms and—

Bad Sophie, she chastised herself, forcing her eyes back to fully open. *You're here on a date with Tybo. Remember him?* Cute, laughing, good-humored Tybo, who had rescued her from rapey Carl? He— Damn was Alasdair's face lowering toward hers? Oh God, was he going to kiss her?

You should stop him, Sophie told herself. She was not the type to kiss one man while on a date with another, and yet she found herself unable to move or say anything to stop him. Her heart was beating a rapid tattoo in her chest, and she had goose bumps rising on her arms just at the thought of him kissing her. More than that, the skin on her face was tingling the closer his got to hers, as if the skin were trying to pull itself off her and wrap around him. That or she was getting little electrical shocks off the man. Dear God, this was odd, and why were her nipples hard again? They'd just begun to calm down after he'd released her arm.

Distracted as she was with her imaginings and her body's response to his nearness, Sophie hadn't stopped him and his mouth was perilously close to hers when Colle suddenly cursed.

Both of them froze for half a second, and then pulled away from each other and shifted to look at the other man.

"What is it?" Alasdair asked, his voice all gravel.

For a minute, Sophie had thought Colle's cuss was in reaction to Alasdair's obvious intention to kiss her, but he wasn't even looking at them. He was leaning sideways in his seat, his attention shifting between the card on the plate next to his own and the card he'd apparently plucked off the plate next to that.

"Odart's next to me and Inan next to him. I cannot read the other two cards but I'm betting—"

"Connor and Ludan," Alasdair finished for him on a growl, not sounding pleased at the prospect. It was an impression that was only reinforced when he muttered, "Another bit of bad luck."

Sophie was surprised at the words, but was a little distracted with issues of her own. Her response to Alasdair was paramount among them. Obviously, he was her kryptonite for this event and she would have to watch herself. She did not want to become the gal who cheated on her date. It made her extremely grateful that Colle had intervened, if only accidentally. But she couldn't count on that again. She would have to control herself, Sophie decided, and forced herself to sit up, then crossed her legs to make something of a barrier between her and the tempting Alasdair as she asked lightly, "Is there a problem with your uncles sitting with us?"

When both men turned surprised expressions her way in response to her knowing who they were, Sophie explained, "Marguerite told me who the four men were in the aisle with you before the ceremony, and I'm pretty sure there can't be more than one man at this wedding named Odart. Or Inan for that matter," she added, her smile turning wry. "So . . . your uncles? Would their sitting with us be a problem?"

Alasdair and Colle exchanged a glance, and then Alasdair turned back to her and started with, "They are . . ."

"Ale-swigging, foulmouthed barbarians," Colle finished for him with something between amusement and exasperation.

When Alasdair grimaced, but nodded agreement with his brother's description, Sophie chuckled and shrugged. "Well, that should make this evening more entertaining than I expected. I mean, from what I've heard, weddings are pretty boring, but ale-swigging, foulmouthed barbarians don't sound boring."

While Alasdair took on a surprised smile at her words, Colle burst out laughing.

Sophie shared a smile between the pair of them and then turned to glance toward Marguerite again. Her gaze was on the people milling around the auburn-haired beauty and her husband, all laughing and chatting happily, but her mind was on her breathing and trying to make it slow down. Dear God, Alasdair's smile was heartbreakingly beautiful. She wished Colle hadn't interrupted their kiss.

Ho! her mind bellowed.

What was wrong with her? She'd never acted like this before. She was a one-woman man. No, wait, she was a one-man woman. Whatever, Sophie thought with exasperation, she knew what she meant. But that little mix-up just showed how much Alasdair messed with her thinking, and she had no idea why. Sure, he was good-looking, and he had that whole silent, stoic sexiness about him, but Tybo was good-looking too.

Maybe it had something to do with his scent, she thought suddenly. Sophie hadn't really noticed it until she'd pulled away and could no longer inhale it so readily, but Alasdair had this sexy, woodsy, spicy aroma about him that just made her want to bury her nose in his neck.

That was it, she assured herself. It wasn't him, it was whatever amazing cologne he was wearing. Spray a bit of that on Tybo and she'd want to climb all over him too, sniffing like a drug dog.

Swiveling her head around to look at him, she asked, "What cologne are you wearing?"

Alasdair's eyebrows went up in surprise. "I'm not. Wearing cologne, I mean."

"Oh," Sophie said weakly, and spun away to pretend to look at Marguerite once more. Dear God, he wasn't wearing cologne. That was just . . . him. Someone needed to bottle that shit. They'd make a killing on the market selling his natural scent as cologne. Women all over the world would be attacking any man who wore it.

A laugh from Colle had her glancing over her shoulder with curiosity, but he quickly shook his head and muttered, "Sorry. Just thought of something . . . so adorably funny."

"Oh," Sophie said with uncertainty, and then her gaze slid to Alasdair to find him staring at her, his eyes smoldering with that golden glow growing in them again. Damn those were some beautiful eyes. The way the light played with them was almost mesmerizing and she found herself leaning toward him again to get a closer look at his burning irises. A big mistake, she realized almost at once. His scent immediately enveloped her again and she found her eyes dropping to his lips once more and her body swaying closer to his, straining toward him like a flower toward the sun. Even worse, Alasdair was doing the same, his body leaning and mouth lowering toward hers.

Dear God, it was going to happen, Sophie thought with a combination of dismay and eagerness. They were going to kiss. A man who wasn't her date was about to kiss her and she wasn't stopping him. It was bad and awful, and she'd definitely owe Tybo an apology, but Sophie couldn't seem to help herself. He was close enough now that she could feel his breath on her lips and she let her eyelids droop closed.

"Oh hell, here they come."

Sophie straightened abruptly, her eyes blinking open at Colle's words. She then turned away from Alasdair out of a desperate need to reclaim her equilibrium. She immediately found her gaze landing on the four burly men making their way toward the table where she and the twins sat. She was so overset at her second almost-kiss with Alasdair and the shame that she was actually disappointed it hadn't been accomplished, that it took until the men had nearly reached the table for her to recognize the uncles. Inan, Odart, Connor, and Ludan. She knew their names, just not who was who.

Sophie tried to watch the approaching men with interest rather than the resentment she was feeling at their arrival interrupting their almost-kiss. But then she realized what she was thinking, and forced herself to push those feelings away. She should be grateful. She had no business letting Alasdair kiss her, and she doubted he'd think much of her if she did.

That thought troubled her enough that she made herself push him from her mind and concentrate properly on the four men approaching, which turned out to be easier than she would have thought. It was the way they were dressed. She'd seen men in Scottish dress in magazines or perhaps online before. The kilts, short jackets with silver buttons, matching vests, white winged collar shirts, bow ties, sporrans, high socks, and odd shoes with long laces she thought were called brogues. But she'd never seen anyone dressed like that in real life, and real life was fascinating. It was a really hot outfit, she decided, and suspected Alasdair would look amazing in it.

All four men had longish hair as well as beards and mustaches, and while Sophie usually wasn't a fan of facial hair, on these men it looked good. Between their outfits and general handsomeness, Sophie decided she might like to take a trip to Scotland one day. Maybe she could convince Alasdair to—

Sophie stopped her thoughts right there. Dear God, she was here with Tybo! What was the matter with her?

"Here we are, at the best table in the place and with the bonniest lass."

Sophie blinked her thoughts away and stiffened in surprise when her hand was taken by the first of the men and pressed to his lips as he bowed before her. She stared at him wide-eyed, and then a startled burble of laughter slipped from her lips when the devil lifted his head just enough for him to wink at her before he straightened and moved aside as the next man stepped up to perform the same action.

"A pleasure, lass," the second man said as he too bowed to press his lips to the back of the hand he'd claimed.

"So bonnie," the third complimented as he too performed the ritual.

"We are truly lucky men to be able to enjoy yer company at this celebration," the fourth said before kissing her hand.

Sophie simply watched as they moved around the table to claim their seats. She then turned to Alasdair and whispered, "They don't seem foulmouthed or like barbarians."

"Och now, who's been tellin' tales?" the first one who had kissed her hand demanded as he settled in his seat. Although the word *now* had sounded more like *new*.

Sophie blinked at him with alarm. She'd been sure she'd whispered quietly enough they couldn't have heard.

"No tales, Uncle Connor," Colle said, not looking the least bit upset that her words had been overheard. "We were just describing the four of you to Sophie."

"And ye did a muckle fine job o' it, lad," the third man who had kissed her hand said with good humor. Sophie knew this speaker was Inan only because he was sitting one seat over from Colle and she knew Odart was beside Colle, and Inan beside him. That meant the other two men were Connor and Ludan.

"Oh, good, you gentlemen found our table."

Sophie glanced around at that gay comment to see that Marguerite and Julius had returned.

"O' course we did," Connor said with a smile. "The

best table in the house, with the loveliest lassies? E'en blind we'd ha'e sniffed it out."

Marguerite chuckled at the claim as she settled into the chair Julius pulled out for her. "Have you been here long?"

"Nay. We jest arrived. Only had time to get seated and hear the fine description our nephews had given Sophie o' us. Did we no', lass?"

"Aye, I mean yes," Sophie corrected herself with a shake of the head, but the men just laughed at her slipping into their speech.

"There ye go, Alasdair. She's already talkin' like a Scottish lassie, she'll make a fine *bean ghradhach*."

Sophie blinked in confusion at the words, and then turned to Alasdair, intending to ask what a *bean ghradhach* was, but Marguerite tapped her arm to get her attention.

"I should introduce you, dear," Marguerite said with a smile. "Sophie this is Connor, Ludan, Inan, and Odart MacKenzie," she announced, pointing to one man after the other in order from left to right. She then added, "Gentlemen, this is Sophie Ferguson, *Tybo's* date."

She said the last with an emphasis that made Sophie consider that perhaps Marguerite believed the men had mistaken her for Alasdair's date since they were seated beside each other. It made her think that perhaps *bean ghradhach* was Gaelic for "girlfriend" or something, and let that question go because she didn't want to embarrass Alasdair. It wasn't his fault that her date was part of the wedding party and he and the others had been tasked with looking after her until Tybo was free.

"Ferguson?" Ludan growled, eyes narrowing. When Marguerite nodded, he said with satisfaction, "A Scot."

"A lowland Scot, though," Inan pointed out.

"But still a Scot," Connor countered.

"Aye. Ye've a point," Inan said with a nod. "Better a lowlander than no' a Scot at all."

"Er . . . well, I'm not exactly a Scot," Sophie said, almost apologetically. "My father's grandfather—my great-grandfather—came over from Scotland, but my grandfather and father were born here in Canada. And my mother's side is Filipino and English."

She was sorry to disappoint them, but she didn't feel right claiming to be a Scot when she was basically a mongrel. She just considered herself Canadian.

"Lass, we're all mongrels," Connor said with a faint smile. "Our own ancestors traveled to Scotland from Rome and various other places before that. But having Scotland in yer heritage makes ye a fine match fer Al—"

"Wine?"

Sophie turned with relief to the tall, blond waiter who had appeared at her elbow. She suspected the man had been about to say "Alasdair," and it would have been embarrassing when he wasn't her date. Now she noted the two bottles the waiter held, one white and one red, but she shook her head, just managing to hold back a grimace. Sophie was not a wine drinker. "No. Thank you."

"A soft drink, or water, then?" the man asked.

"Water is good," she said gratefully.

The waiter set the bottles on the table to free his

hands and leaned past her to pick up a crystal pitcher of water she hadn't noticed on the table.

"Oh, I can do that," Sophie said at once, feeling bad for putting him to extra work when there were so many others at the table to look after.

"It's no trouble," the young man said, smiling at her.

Sophie smiled back, and then thanked him once he'd finished. Nodding, he moved on to Alasdair next, but he didn't even get the opportunity to ask what he wanted. Alasdair simply waved the waiter on, and picked up the pitcher of water to pour into his own glass.

Colle also got water, but the uncles all asked for ale, which had the waiter scurrying away to find some. In the end it was only Marguerite and Julius who had wine.

"So, Sophie, how did you and Tybo meet?" Marguerite asked once the waiter had finished at the table and moved on to the next.

"Oh." She smiled faintly. "He and Valerian rescued me from a blind date gone bad."

"Ye had a date with a blind man that went bad?" the man Marguerite had introduced as Connor asked with a frown.

"Oh, no," she laughed. "I was on a blind date. He could see."

When all four men just stared at her rather blankly, Alasdair got an evil smile on his face and told them to "google it."

Much to Sophie's amazement all four uncles pulled cell phones from their sporrans and began to tap away on them. Turning to Alasdair, she asked, "They really don't know what blind dates are?"

"They're from Scotland," Alasdair said as if that should explain everything.

"A social engagement or date with a person one has no' previously met," Inan read out, apparently the first to get the answer since the other three were still tapping. They stopped now, though, and glanced at him, then grunted with understanding and put their phones away.

"Right o'," Connor said as they all finished tucking away their phones and turned to her. "So, this blind date went bad how?"

Sophie grimaced, and hesitated, but finally said, "I realized early on that we weren't compatible and ended the date before we even finished ordering. But when I then tried to leave, he followed me out of the restaurant and was making a nuisance of himself. Tybo intervened."

"The bawbag tried to force hisself on ye," Inan growled, apparently seeing through her polite wording.

"We'll be needin' his name, lass," Ludan said grimly.

"Aye," Alasdair agreed.

Sophie peered at him with surprise, amazed to see the fury on his face and . . . in his eyes. The gold in them seemed brighter even than it had got before, almost as if it were a banked fire, and it actually seemed to be swelling to fill the black. That wasn't possible, was it?

"Goodness! I think I need the ladies' room before dinner," Marguerite announced suddenly. "Sophie? Will you join me?"

Sophie turned as the other woman stood up, and then found herself standing up as well. "Yes, of course."

She then spent the walk to the clubhouse wondering why she'd agreed and followed as she had. Sophie didn't have to go to the bathroom, and she didn't really decide to accompany Marguerite, she simply had, and didn't know why. Weird, she thought.

Seven

"The tadger who attacked our wee Sophie was named Carl Breckham."

Alasdair turned from watching Marguerite and Sophie leave the tent and raised an eyebrow at his uncle Connor. "You read her mind."

It wasn't a question but his uncle nodded anyway.

Alasdair's mouth tightened with irritation. Sophie was his life mate, and aside from dreading the very idea of his uncles "helping" him, he didn't like the idea of any of them poking through her thoughts.

Connor clucked his tongue. "Now don'y fash yerself o'er it. I ken ye feel possessive o' the lass since she's yer life mate, but our being able to read her can help ye in yer wooin'."

"Aye," Inan agreed. "For instance, we can tell ye that the lass is gaggin' fer ye, lad."

Alasdair straightened abruptly, his irritation forgotten. "She is?"

"Aye, I was reading her mind as we came up and she wants to bottle yer spunk and inhale it," Inan told him with a grin.

Alasdair was just blinking in horrified disbelief at this, when Ludan cuffed Inan in the back of the head and growled with disgust, "No' his spunk ye daft eejit. His scent."

"She thinks you smell good," Colle explained quickly. "She wants to bottle your scent so she can breathe it in as she likes. She thinks all women would love it."

Alasdair let his breath out on a sigh. The spunk business would have been just weird, at least as he suspected his uncle had intended it, which had nothing to do with the proper definition of spunk being his mettle or spirit, but more along the lines of the slang use where it was a term for ejaculate. But liking his scent was good.

"She likes yer eyes too," Connor told him. "Thinks they're bonnie."

"And she was fightin' the want to kiss ye, because she's supposed to be here with Tybo," Colle informed him solemnly. "Speakin' on that, you might want to hold off on anything until this night is over. I suspect she'd suffer terrible guilt for mucking about with ye when on a date with another, and that could slow ye down. Better to just keep a bit o' distance tonight, and start the real wooin' tomorrow when this business with Tybo is done."

"Tybo," Alasdair sighed the name, and then frowned and asked, "What about this blind date that Tybo and Valerian handled for her? Carl?"

"Tybo did the handling," Valerian announced, and

Alasdair turned with surprise to find the groom standing behind him. Smiling, Valerian added, "He took control of Carl and made him strip naked, then dance around and do cartwheels in the restaurant parking lot."

"How long have you been here?" Colle asked even as Alasdair wondered that very thing.

"Long enough to catch the gist of the conversation," Valerian answered Colle, and then glanced to Alasdair and said, "There's no need to punish Carl. The police were called, and he was arrested. We checked later and Carl was charged with a lot of things including public indecency. He will also be put on the sex offender registry."

"For streaking?" Alasdair asked with surprise.

"For streaking across the street from a public school," Valerian explained. "Even though it was night and the school was closed, it can still land you on the registry. Or at least they're trying to put him there. Whether they succeed or not depends on the mortal courts." He shrugged. "Tybo thought it was what he deserved. And I agree. We read his thoughts that night and he did intend to force himself on Sophie. She was lucky we were there."

"Aye," Alasdair agreed. "Thank you for helping her."

"You should ha'e cut his dobber off," Inan opined with disgust. "I can'y stand men like that. Tryin' to take what isna on offer."

Alasdair grunted his agreement, his gaze moving to the mouth of the tent where he'd last seen Sophie. He couldn't imagine how an attack like that might have affected her had Carl succeeded, and was grateful Tybo and Valerian had been there to intervene.

"And if we hadn't, she wouldn't be here now for

you to meet," Valerian pointed out with a faint smile, obviously having read his thoughts. Resting one hand on Alasdair's shoulder, he squeezed slightly and said, "Tybo told me Marguerite says she's your life mate. Congratulations, cousin."

Alasdair let his breath out on a slight huff. "Do not congratulate me yet, I still have to win her."

"You will. I have faith in you," Valerian said with a grin.

"And so ye should, lad," Connor said. "Especially with us here to help him."

The other uncles all nodded and grunted agreement, then clanked their glasses of ale together before gulping down their beverages.

Alasdair groaned under his breath. The very last thing he needed was these old barbarians to help him woo Sophie.

"I suppose you'll want more of that, Uncles," Valerian said with amusement as they each set their empty glasses back on the table with solid thuds. "Although I don't know why you drink ale when the alcohol doesn't affect you."

"Because we like the taste, boyo," Inan said dryly.

"'Sides we can'y drink blood with mortals about," Connor added grimly, his gaze sliding around the guests in the room.

Alasdair glanced around as well. There were really only a dozen mortals as guests at the wedding. Natalie's employees and their dates, as well as a few locals who were friends or friends of the family. But it still meant they had to be careful.

"That reminds me," Valerian said now. "There's blood in the refrigerator in Natalie's office if anyone needs a top-up. Just make sure you close the door so none of the mortal guests walk in and see something they shouldn't."

He waited for everyone to nod acknowledgment and then started to turn away, but paused, hesitated, and then swung back to suggest, "And if you want to avoid questions, you should probably take plates of food when they're offered and try to eat at least some of it to avoid arousing suspicion too." Grimacing, he admitted, "That's actually why I stopped here on the way to the head table. Natalie wanted me to remind anyone sitting close to mortals to at least pretend to eat."

He raised his head then to glance around the tent, and smiled when he spotted his bride at another table with mixed mortal and immortal guests. "She thought of it while the photographer was taking pictures and spoke to Tybo and me, so we decided to stop and have a word where we could on the way back to the table."

"A word with the immortals while mortals are sitting right there?" Colle asked dubiously.

"Well, she won't say anything out loud that might sound off to mortals. But the immortals can read it from her mind while she's at the table," he pointed out. "I told her to say, 'If you could read my mind, you'd know how good the food is' and then think that they should at least pretend to eat in front of the mortal guests." Valerian shrugged. "Fortunately, I didn't have to bother with that since Sophie isn't here. Where is she, by the way?"

"Ladies' room with Marguerite," Alasdair muttered.

"Ah." Valerian nodded. "Well, that made telling you all to pretend to eat easier. Just push the food around on your plates and try to distract her so she doesn't notice you aren't gulping down food like the big men you are should do."

"Don'y fash yerself, lad," Connor said. "We'll eat."

"We eat at least once a week still and this week put it off for the weddin' feast," Inan explained, and when Valerian looked startled at this news, he asked, "Did ye really think a diet o' blood would be enough to keep up these braw bodies?"

Alasdair rolled his eyes when his uncle stood up and flexed to show off his muscular arms and chest. His other three uncles just grinned at the display. They were all beefy hulks, the cloth of their shirts straining under the stress of their muscles at chest, forearms, and biceps.

"Yeah, yeah," Colle said with exasperation. "Sit yourself down, Uncle. The mortal lasses are suitably impressed and gawking now."

Grinning, Inan retook his seat, and Connor said, "The point is, we always eat at least once a week to help keep up our muscles."

"Aye," Inan agreed. "We may no' enjoy feastin' anymore, but we do it anyway so we don'y lose strength. Hunters need to be strong."

The uncles all nodded, their gazes sliding scathingly over Alasdair, Colle, and Valerian as if to suggest they were not up to snuff despite the fact that Alasdair and Colle were at least as big as them if not bigger.

"Right," Valerian said with a laugh, obviously unconcerned by the attempted insult. "Well, I'm just glad I can reassure Natalie that you won't be sitting here not eating or doing anything else unusual, so . . ."

Turning on his heel he headed away, calling out, "Enjoy dinner."

"Lud," Connor said idly as they watched the groom walk to the head table.

"Hmm?" Ludan asked, glancing his way.

"I don'y think our nephews were impressed with our point about strength helping in the hunt."

Ludan grunted what might have been agreement.

"Aye," Inan said with a slight scowl for his nephews, and then his expression faded and he said judiciously, "But then they don'y ken any better. They don'y have the huge old bastard rogues we've been getting in Europe. Most o' the rogues in North America are younger, born when pistols and muskets were the weapon o' choice and muscle was no' in fashion. Not the longsword-wielding rogue bastards that ha'e been growin' in number in Europe lately."

Alasdair's gaze sharpened with interest on his uncles. "You've had older, larger rogues across the pond lately?"

Ludan nodded. It was Connor who said, "Aye. A fair number o' late. Children and grandchildren o' pairings from the last conciliare are reachin' the age when some who are still unmated are losin' their will to live and goin' rogue."

"The last conciliare?" Alasdair questioned with confusion, not recognizing the word.

Inan goggled at him. "Ha'e ye been taught naught about yer own people?"

Before Alasdair could respond, Connor suggested, "Google it."

Recognizing the words he'd tossed out to them about blind dates, Alasdair knew they wouldn't explain and pulled out his phone even as Colle did. His brother was faster at typing, however.

"It's Latin for *to reconcile*," Colle said with a frown.

"And that means?" Ludan asked patiently.

"I ken what *to reconcile* means," Colle snapped, his accent thickening with his irritation. "That doesn'y explain—"

"Does it no'?" Connor interrupted, and then arched an eyebrow and suggested, "Google *to reconcile*."

With a little huff of irritation, Colle bowed his head to his phone and started tapping again. After a moment, he began to speak in a tone suggesting the meaning was exactly what he'd thought. "According to Oxford Languages to reconcile means to restore friendly relations between, cause to coexist in harmony; make or"—he paused briefly and then finished more slowly—"or show to be compatible."

He read that last part with a growing understanding even as Alasdair himself understood. He glanced sharply at his uncles. "A conciliare is what you used to call a life mate matchmaker like Marguerite?"

The men nodded solemnly. It was Connor who said, "The last time we had a conciliare as proficient at matching life mates as Marguerite was more than a thousand years ago."

"At a time when men wielded clubs and longswords," Inan added, and pointed out, "They had to be big and muscular for those weapons."

"As did the children o' those matches, at least the ones born over the next three or four centuries or so."

"And the last conciliare made hundreds o' pairings ere passin', and those pairings resulted in twice that many first and second born bairns. Now those children are old, many unmatched, and some no' doin' well," Inan said quietly. "A guid number o' them are now goin' rogue."

"They're big bastards," Connor told them. "Strong and cruel. Tearing their victims apart with their bare hands some o' them." He shook his head.

"Time to change the subject, boys. The ladies are on the way back," Julius said suddenly, and Alasdair turned to peer at the man with surprise. He'd been so quiet that Alasdair had forgotten he was even there.

Shifting his gaze past the man, he spotted Marguerite and Sophie walking back toward the table. The two women were laughing over something, and damned if Sophie wasn't the loveliest flower Alasdair had ever seen.

Movement from Julius had him looking to see that the other man was standing to pull out his wife's chair. Alasdair immediately stood as well to do the same for Sophie as she reached them.

"Thanks," she said with a wide smile as she settled in her seat.

"My pleasure," Alasdair murmured as he reclaimed his own. He then reached for the pitcher of water and topped up her glass, earning another thanks. Silence fell on the table as she drank. Alasdair watched her, but didn't realize everyone else was too until she peered over the glass, and then lowered it and raised her eyebrows at his uncles. He glanced their way to see the concentrated expressions on all four faces and knew they were reading her.

"Is there something on my face?" Sophie asked with sudden amusement. "Or maybe my hair is a mess from the breeze outside?"

"Nay, lass," the uncles all said as one.

Connor added, "Ye're perfect as a picture."

"Aye, bonnie," Odart growled.

"Ha'e ye any sisters fer poor wee lads like us to meet?" Inan asked.

A surprised laugh burst from Sophie, but she shook her head and set her glass back on the table. "I'm an only child."

"Ah," Inan said sympathetically, but there was no surprise. He had been reading her. Even so, he still asked, "And yer parents?"

Alasdair cast his uncle a grateful glance, appreciating that Inan was only asking these things so Alasdair could learn what they already knew from reading her mind.

"My parents died when I was eleven," Sophie said softly.

"So, no family left?" Connor queried gently.

Sophie hesitated and then just shook her head before asking, "Do you all live in Scotland?"

"We do," Connor said, gesturing to himself and the other uncles. He then pointed at Alasdair and his brother and said, "But these laddies jumped ship to the Americas ages ago."

"After we spent eons trainin' 'em on how to be good and proper Enforcers too," his uncle Inan said almost resentfully. Turning, he scowled at Alasdair and his brother. "They've been here ever since. Broke their ma's heart, they did."

Alasdair scowled at him for the guilt trip, and then turned swiftly to Sophie when she asked him, "Enforcers? What is that? I thought you worked with Tybo."

"We do," Alasdair assured her.

"But he said 'enforcers,'" Sophie pointed out with confusion.

Alasdair had one moment of panic as he tried to come up with an explanation, and then the answer came to him. "We're in law enforcement. *Enforcers* for short among those on the job in Scotland and we just call it that by habit."

"Oh." Sophie nodded and relaxed at this explanation from the men. She supposed it made sense. Law enforcement. Enforcers. Simple, she thought and then glanced around swiftly when the waiter suddenly appeared at her side and leaned past her to set a large platter of appetizers on the table. Sitting back to give him more room, she offered a "sorry" for being in his way, because . . . well, she was Canadian.

"That's fine, miss," the waiter said, offering her a smoky smile.

"Och, away and boil yer head, boyo," Connor growled at the man.

Sophie had no idea why until Inan said, "Aye, the lass is taken, so ye can jest keep those cow eyes to yerself."

When the waiter flushed and turned quickly away to collect another platter, Sophie scowled at the men for embarrassing him like that. She then looked to Alasdair for an explanation for such behavior, and saw that he too was scowling at the young man.

When the waiter finished setting down the second platter, he moved to the other side of the table to place a third one down. It wasn't until the man had moved away that Alasdair glanced her way and saw her looking at him questioningly. He immediately smothered his scowl and shrugged mildly. "My uncles are a tad protective."

"Huh," she muttered, eyeing him narrowly. Turning to peer at the uncles, she said, "But I don't need protecting."

"Lass," Inan said, his tone condescending, "if ye kenned what that tadger was thinkin', ye'd be thankin' us fer interfering."

Sophie arched one eyebrow. "And how would you 'ken' what he was thinking?"

"I read—" Inan stopped on a grunt of pain, and then scowled toward Alasdair as if he were the source of pain.

"I'm a maun," Inan said now in answer to her question, and then added, "And he was peekin' down yer décolletage while layin' out the platters. Did ye no' notice how slow he was with the task while on yer side? 'Twas so he'd get a longer gander at yer chebs."

Sophie had never heard the word *chebs* before, but suspected she knew what it meant and immediately glanced down to see that the way she was sitting had allowed her neckline to gape a bit, giving a lovely view from above of her black lace bra. Sophie calmly straightened in her seat, making the gap close. She then said mildly, "It isn't like there's much to see other than my fancy ass bra, and it covers as much as a swimsuit, so . . ." She shrugged with studied unconcern and hoped she wasn't blushing and giving away that she was embarrassed and uncomfortable.

Silence reigned for a moment after her comment,

but Sophie ignored it, as well as the stares she could feel trained on her, and leaned forward to inspect the food on the platters.

A moment later the uncles apparently gave up their staring at her, and turned their attention to the food as well, because Inan asked with dismay, "These little bite-sized bits are no' the meal, are they?"

"They are just the hors d'oeuvres," Marguerite said soothingly.

"Hmm." Connor grunted. "What are they?"

"This platter has little mushroom quiches, vegetable spring rolls, and Brie crostini with onion jam and cranberry compote," Alasdair said, and Sophie glanced at him with surprise to see that he was reading from a small card.

"Where did you get that?" she asked with interest.

Alasdair smiled faintly, set down the card, and reached across in front of her to tug a small card out of a holder she hadn't noticed on the bottom of the raised edge of the large platter. When he offered it to her to read, she quickly shook her head. She had never been much for public speaking, but simply said, "I like listening to your voice. You read it."

His smile widened at her words and he read out, "Mini shrimp cocktails with cocktail sauce, fish tacos with tequila lime corn salsa, and tuna sashimi wontons."

"This one looks like meat," Connor announced, turning the last platter that sat closest to him until he found the card for that one. He then read out, "Garlic and lemon chicken skewers smothered in garlic sauce, pulled pork tostadas with mango salsa, and mini Montreal smoked meat sandwiches with Dijon and pickles."

"So," Sophie said, "a vegetarian plate, a seafood plate, and a meat plate of hors d'oeuvres."

"Something for everyone," Marguerite said with a nod. "But I'm sure it's all delicious. Natalie is a brilliant chef."

"The bride cooked these herself?" Sophie asked, wondering where she would have found the time. If Natalie had only known Valerian not quite four weeks, she couldn't imagine she'd had more than a day or two or perhaps a week to arrange everything.

Alasdair shook his head. "Valerian said La Bonne Vie was catering."

Sophie's eyebrows rose at this news. She recognized the name. It was a fancy restaurant in Toronto, some place she couldn't afford. Sophie didn't say that, though, and simply commented, "I didn't know they catered."

"They do not," Marguerite agreed, picking up her small plate and surveying the various appetizers on offer. "However, the owner, Alex, is a relative and she was kind enough to close down one of her restaurants for the day and brought her people down here to prepare and serve the meals so no one from the clubhouse restaurant had to miss the wedding," she explained, and reached out to select several appetizers and place them on her small plate. "But all the recipes used are Natalie's."

Sophie nodded, and considered the offerings briefly, then reached for a chicken skewer even as Alasdair did. Both froze when their hands collided, their gazes shooting to each other as electricity sparked between them.

Sophie was the first to retrieve her hand and shift her gaze away from his. She was sorry she had to, but until this date with Tybo was over . . . The thought made her wonder if she'd ever encounter Alasdair again and get the chance to pursue this crazy attraction between them.

Maybe she should ask for his number, Sophie thought. Would that be a bad thing to do while on a date with another? She was fretting over that when Inan suddenly spoke.

"Tell us a little bit about yourself, Sophie, lass," he suggested. "It'll let us get to know ye better while we wait fer the food to come."

Sophie froze like a deer in the headlights of an oncoming car as all eyes turned to her. She so hated being the center of attention.

Eight

Alasdair had actually been glad when his uncle Inan had suggested Sophie tell them more about herself. He'd just been wondering what she did for a living, and worrying that it could be a career that might be made difficult by being an immortal. It would be hard enough to convince her to become his life mate without the threat of losing her career being part of the decision.

But his feelings on the question changed when he saw Sophie's reaction to it. She had a hunted, almost horrified look on her face, and he realized she'd kind of been put on the spot and wasn't comfortable with it. He was just trying to think of a way to ease the situation for her, when she cleared her throat and finally spoke.

"Well, there isn't much to tell," she said slowly. "I live in Toronto in a small apartment I own, have a bachelor in computer science, and work for my family's insurance office."

"You sell insurance?" Alasdair asked with a small frown. She didn't seem like a salesperson. In his experience, people in sales usually enjoyed attention and Sophie definitely didn't if he were to judge by her reaction just now, as well as during the wedding when her startled outburst had temporarily drawn all eyes her way.

"No," she said quickly, and then frowned and said, "Well, not so far anyway. Officially, my title is information technology manager."

Alasdair nodded, relieved to know that her job would not affect her decision about whether to become immortal or not.

"But?" Connor asked. "I hear a *but* in your tone."

Alasdair's gaze shot to his uncle at those words, and then bounced back to Sophie as she smiled faintly at his uncle and nodded.

"Good catch. Yes, there's a *but*," she admitted. "Our branch is too small to need a full-time IT manager, so while I'd say fifty percent of my time is spent on that, the other half of my time is spent wherever I'm needed. Sometimes on office stuff, sometimes helping out the adjuster, sometimes the claims examiner, but usually I play assistant to my boss, the owner, when not needed for IT work."

"So ye were hired fer a job, but only get to do it half the time and otherwise play general dogsbody?" Inan asked with a slight frown.

Sophie gave a small shrug. "Obviously, they don't really need a full-time IT manager. In fact, they wouldn't even need a half-time IT manager if it weren't for certain employees who—despite repeated warnings—insist on opening sketchy websites and downloading from the internet, inviting viruses and whatnot."

"Do you mind?" Alasdair asked, and when she glanced at him in question, he explained, "That you only do what you trained for half your workday?"

"Oh . . . no," Sophie said after a hesitation that made him think she wasn't being completely truthful. As if sensing his thoughts, she added, "It makes the workday more interesting. Sometimes I'm working IT all day, and sometimes it's ten minutes and then I'm off making calls, checking through insurance policies, or running to pick up lunch for my boss, so . . ." She shrugged. "It's all good."

Alasdair wasn't sure she was being completely honest, but her smile was infectious, and he found himself smiling in return. However, his smile dropped into a scowl when the cheeky waiter who'd been trying to look down her top wheeled another cart to their table. This time it was to collect their empty platters and appetizer dishes, and to show them the dinner options and have them select what they wanted.

There were four options: a pasta dish that could be vegetarian or not; a vegetarian-only meal that Sophie didn't show the least interest in; a chicken dish featuring creamy herb chicken and a choice of sides; and a steak dish that Marguerite told them was the best thing she'd ever tasted and was well loved by the locals. It too had a choice of sides. Sophie went for the steak, as did Alasdair and everyone else at the table except for Julius, who chose the pasta, but the nonvegetarian version.

This time, the waiter was both professional and

swift about his job without any loitering or leering. Sophie and Marguerite said thank you to the young man as they gave their orders, and Julius and Colle nodded politely, but Alasdair and his uncles all glared at him until he'd left.

"You know he's going to spit in our food before he brings it, right?" Sophie said, her gaze sliding over Alasdair and his uncles' sour expressions with amusement.

"What?" Alasdair asked with surprise.

"It's never smart to be rude to your server, Alasdair. The things they can do . . ." She shook her head. "I've heard of people licking steaks, spitting into mashed potatoes, and jerking off into cream corn. So . . . yeah, I'm always nice to waitstaff," she assured them and then smiled and admitted, "But if they're complete jerks, I always get the waitperson's name and leave a bad review once I'm out of there. I think the business should know what their people are doing if they're creeps or rude."

Alasdair stared at Sophie with horror as what she'd said went through his head. Licking steaks? Spitting into mashed potatoes? He didn't even want to recall the creamed corn business. Thank God there hadn't been any of that on offer as a side dish. But he *had* ordered steak. Dear God, he thought, and decided that when the bastard returned with their meals, he was definitely reading his mind to be sure he hadn't tampered with anything. One glance at the determined expressions on his uncles' faces told him they would probably all do the same. Mortals! he thought with disgust.

"I am sure Alex would not employ someone who

would do anything like that," Marguerite said sooth-ingly. "And I really do not see his flirting a little with Sophie as that much of an issue. She's not wearing a ring. He probably thought her single. And he barely glanced down her top. I do not think it was on pur-pose."

Alasdair snorted at the suggestion. He had read the little creep's mind and . . . Well, all right, it hadn't been on purpose, but he certainly had en-joyed the view he'd accidentally got, and he hadn't looked away from it quickly. In fact, he'd done a double take and slowed his movements as he gaped at what was apparently a really sexy bra if he was to go by the guy's thoughts. It had pissed Alasdair off. She was his. No one should be seeing her intimate apparel but him, and he was jealous as hell that the waiter had.

Whatever, he thought with irritation. Margue-rite might not think Alex would hire someone who would tamper with their food, and being immortal, Alex would be able to read the minds of her em-ployees so probably wouldn't. But he was still going to double-check and read the waiter's mind when he returned, just to be sure everything was as it should be and nothing had been tampered with. He and Colle, like his uncles, ate every week or two to help keep up the muscle they'd built up when young and still growing. But aside from the occasional bite of this or that at celebrations for politeness's sake, most of what they'd eaten before this was just raw steak, nice and bloody. Nothing cooked fancy, be-cause it hadn't been worth the trouble when they didn't really have an appetite for food anymore. His appetite was back, however. Finding a life mate did that to an immortal, and he was looking forward to the meal . . . sans spit.

"That was mighty quick."

Alasdair glanced up at his uncle Connor's comment and then followed his gaze to see that several carts were being wheeled in with dinner plates of food on them. The first two carts went directly to the head table. The next three went to the table nearest the head table opposite theirs where Valerian's parents, Uncle Gill, and Aunt Effie sat with other relatives. The three carts after that were led by the waiter who had been serving their table and came their way.

Alasdair immediately focused on the waiter and slid into his thoughts. He was relieved to find that Marguerite was right. He hadn't messed with their meals. In fact, he felt bad about what had happened earlier, and kind of felt like a creep for it. Relaxing, Alasdair sat back in his seat and simply waited for dinner to be served. This time, he didn't scowl at the man. He didn't smile either, but he didn't scowl.

"Oh look, the boys are setting up."

Sophie tore her gaze away from the yummy-looking chocolatey dessert Alasdair was eating, to glance toward Marguerite at that excited comment. She then followed her gaze to where two men were pulling back two sides of the tent to make an opening that revealed what could have been the raised dais from the wedding tent, or just another one holding a drum set, an electric piano, speakers, and other miscellaneous things she didn't recognize but suspected had to do with sound. Amps or subwoofers or whatever they would be called. She didn't know much about music herself and what was needed by a band.

"I wonder where Giacinta is?" Alasdair murmured as they watched four men get on the stage and move to their positions.

"Who's Giacinta?" Sophie asked him.

"She's a member of the band too," Alasdair explained. "She— Oh, there she is."

Sophie looked to see a petite woman with bleached blond hair stepping onto the dais to join the men. She watched them get set up, and then asked Alasdair, "You know the band?"

"Yes, they're the NCs and family from the Notte branch," he told her. "NC stands for 'Notte *cugini*.'"

"*Cugini?*" Sophie echoed with confusion.

"Italian for 'cousins,'" he explained with a faint smile. "They are all cousins." His gaze slid back to the dais. "Natalie was having trouble finding a band or even a DJ for the reception on such short notice, so Colle suggested Valerian ask the NCs. Fortunately, they agreed."

"Ah, a family band," Sophie said, trying not to sound too dubious, but she was thinking the music might be the only part of the wedding not as spectacular as everything else.

Apparently, despite her efforts, Alasdair heard her misgivings in her voice, because he said, "They're a professional band. Very popular in Italy. They're really very good."

"I'm sure they are," Sophie said apologetically, and

then glanced down at his dessert again. It was almost half-gone and she sighed with regret that she hadn't ordered dessert herself. But she simply hadn't had room in her stomach after the meal. Marguerite hadn't been kidding about the steak. It was marinated in something that was . . . well, just amazing. The sides had all been yummy too and she'd eaten every last bite of everything on her plate. It hadn't left even a bit of room in her stomach for dessert. Although, staring at Alasdair's chocolate cake with cherries and she didn't even know what else in it, she was sure she could have made a little room for it.

"A bite?"

Sophie blinked when a forkful of the chocolate dessert appeared before her eyes. She stared at it with surprise, and then shifted her gaze to the man holding it out to her.

Alasdair smiled. "It is really good. Decadent. My taste buds are humming with pleasure with every bite. It would be a shame if you did not at least try it. I am willing to share."

Sophie stared at him. It was the most he'd spoken since she'd met him and his raspy voice had a peculiar effect on her. Very peculiar. It kind of made her feel all warm and mushy inside, like she might very well melt into a puddle in her chair.

A voice that sexy should be outlawed, she thought a little weakly, and then realizing she was just gawking at him like a lovesick cow, she leaned closer and opened her mouth as Alasdair urged the forkful of deliciousness forward.

He didn't shove it in her mouth, he eased it in, slow and almost gently, as if being careful not to rub it on her teeth or lips. When she closed her mouth around it, he then drew the fork back out just as slowly so that she could catch all of the dessert with her lips and keep it from leaving with the fork. All the while, he was watching with eyes that were beginning to glow, and Sophie really wanted to examine that effect. She wanted to understand what happened with his eyes, but her own were closing as the taste of the dessert exploded on her tongue. Chocolate, cherry, almond, whipped cream, and a hint of rum, the flavors struck her one after the other, and it was amazing. She'd never tasted anything so good, and didn't want to swallow and end the experience. It was heavenly. But finally, she did with a sigh, and then immediately opened her eyes and whispered, "Thank you."

"You are welcome," he whispered back, his eyes glued on her lips.

Thinking she must have got some chocolate or whipped cream on her lips, she licked them and then glanced around for their waiter. Maybe she could fit some dessert in, after all. She didn't spot their waiter right away, but her gaze did land on Tybo. He was looking their way, and had obviously witnessed Alasdair sharing his dessert with her, at least that was the only reason she could imagine for the sad expression she caught on his face before he quickly changed it to what to her seemed a forced smile.

Sophie smiled back, but guilt was seeping through her now. Was trying one man's dessert bad when you were on a date with another? She didn't really think so, except that it had been more than trying the cake. She'd taken the cake from his fork, and he'd served it to her. That was kind of intimate, wasn't it? Maybe? Couples did that kind of thing. It probably would have been better had she taken the fork from him and served herself, or even asked if he would just cut off a bite and let her take it with her own fork.

But worse than that was the way she'd been staring at Alasdair with cow eyes before taking the bite. She'd been doing that a lot, looking at Alasdair. Her eyes seemed to be drawn to the man and she'd kept finding herself looking his way during the meal. Much to her excitement, every time she'd looked, he'd been looking back, so she suspected the attraction was mutual.

Had Tybo witnessed that? She hoped not. She didn't want to hurt his feelings, but she was attracted to Alasdair. Strongly. Sexually. In a way she wasn't attracted to Tybo. But she was Tybo's date. It was probably disrespectful to be lusting after another while on a date with him. She needed to show some respect for her date and rein in her mounting attraction to Alasdair. She wouldn't like it if their roles were reversed and she'd invited someone on a date and they had then obviously been attracted to another woman.

A person couldn't control who they were attracted to, but they could control their actions. The respectful thing to do would be to concentrate on Tybo tonight, and keep her distance from Alasdair. It sucked because she had no idea if she and Alasdair would ever encounter each other again, but she didn't want to be the girl who went to a wedding with one man and left with another.

It was probably for the best anyway, she told herself to reinforce the decision. If she was cursed as she and her friends joked, then it would definitely be safer for Alasdair not to get involved with her.

Sighing, she picked up her glass and took a sip, then offered Tybo another smile. Now that the wedding was done and dinner was nearly over, he would be able to spend time with her. She was his date. Time to start acting like it.

"**A**re you all right?"

Alasdair tore his gaze away from where Sophie and Tybo were dancing to glance at Marguerite. "O' course," he assured her, and then suddenly concerned that he might look as miserable as he felt, asked, "Why? Do I no' look all right?"

"Do ye look a'right?" his uncle Connor echoed with disbelief. "Ye've got a face like a melted welly, lad. And yer natural accent's makin' a show. Ye're obviously hurtin' to watch the lass with Tybo."

"No' that we blame ye," Inan put in. "I'd be ragin' if another man was pawin' all o'er me life mate."

Alasdair scowled and glanced toward the dance floor again. Tybo wasn't pawing all over Sophie right now. The song playing was a fast one and they were a foot apart, dancing to the beat. But during the slow songs, he did hold her as anyone would while dancing to a slow song. Those were harder to watch. Still, he wouldn't call it pawing. Tybo held her hand with one of his, and kept the other firmly at her center back, not lower back, or anywhere near her behind. Much to his relief, Tybo didn't even hold her as close as he could have during those songs. He still kept an inch or two of space between them and Alasdair appreciated it . . . even if it was still hard to watch.

"I'm thinkin' we lure Tybo away from the party, give the bastard a good thrashin', and tie him up to keep him oot o' yer way," Inan suggested. "Then ye can take Sophie behind the tent and—"

"Oh dear God! You will do no such thing," Marguerite interrupted with dismay. Shaking her head, she said more calmly, "She is Tybo's date tonight. You should be grateful he brought her here allowing Alasdair to meet her." Turning to peer toward the dance floor at the couple, she added, "He understands she is a possible life mate to Alasdair and is behaving like a gentleman. But she is *his* date tonight. Do you expect him to just dump her in Alasdair's lap? How do you think that would make her feel? She has no inkling about life mates and that she is Alasdair's. She would not understand. She would either be hurt at Tybo's rejection despite her attraction to Alasdair, or feel like he saw her as a piece of meat to be passed around."

Turning back, she scowled at the uncles. "If you have read her mind, then you know she is, of course, attracted to Alasdair, but she is also suffering some guilt about that because she is on a date with Tybo. Just let them be tonight. Tomorrow is soon enough for Alasdair to start wooing her. In fact, it gives him time to come up with a plan."

"Aye. A plan," Connor said with a nod. "We can help with that."

Lord, help me, Alasdair thought and cursed his bad luck in their being present for this momentous time in his life.

Nine

"So? How was the date?"

Sophie glanced up from her computer and smiled at Megan as she led Bobby and Lise into her office. Their arrival was not a surprise. She'd arrived at the office a little early this morning and already been hard at work when the others had shown up. Despite the fact that they were all employed by the family business, she'd known they'd wait for break time to grill her about her date the night before and they had. It was now ten thirty. Break time.

"The date was fine," she said with a faint smile as she stood up and moved around her desk to head for the door.

"That's it?" Megan asked, following her out of her office. "Fine? We need deets, Soph. 'Fine' is not an answer."

"Okay, okay," Sophie said on a laugh. "The wedding was held in big tents at a golf course. The bride wore a white-and-black dress and—"

"Who cares about the wedding?" Megan interrupted with disgust as they entered the break room where George Tomlinson was seated with a coffee, reading the newspaper. He always took the first break with them, while the other office workers were split between the second and third break. They split lunches the same way, taking them in shifts.

"Hi," Sophie said in greeting, just stopping herself from adding Papa at the last moment as she affectionately squeezed his shoulder in passing.

"Hi," Megan said too, and then simply continued on with their discussion. "We want details about your date and if he— Wait, did you say the bride wore white and *black*?"

"Yeah." Sophie grabbed four cups and moved to the coffee machine to start pouring coffees as she explained, "It was mostly white, but with black lace along the hem and over the bodice. It was actually beautiful."

"Hmm," Megan muttered as she retrieved cream from the refrigerator. Her expression suggested she was trying to visualize it, but after a moment, she shook her head and said, "Anyway, more importantly, how was the date part with . . ."

"Tybo," Mr. Tomlinson supplied from behind his newspaper when Megan hesitated, apparently unable to recall Sophie's date's name.

"Right. Thanks, Dad. Tybo," she agreed, and then muttered, "Sounds like a martial art."

"It's a nickname," Sophie explained. "Short for Tyberius. He was named after his great-grandfather." That was something she'd learned last night. They'd done a lot of talking and actually got along really well once he'd been free of his best man duties. In fact, if she hadn't found herself so attracted to Alasdair, Sophie might have been happy to date Tybo. However, she had been seriously attracted to Alasdair, which had placed Tybo firmly in the friend zone for her. Fortunately, he'd seemed to feel the same way and hadn't even tried to kiss her good night at her door. At least not a proper kiss.

"Okay, so . . . How was the date side of things with Tybo?" Bobby said now, pulling the sugar and sweetener out of the cupboard while Lise grabbed spoons. "And don't deflect with more descriptions of the wedding itself. We don't care about what people were wearing or how the food was, or—and hey," he said suddenly, interrupting himself. "You texted me that the wedding was three and a half hours outside of Toronto?"

Sophie nodded. "It was at a golf course called the Shady Pines or something. Tybo said it was about three and a half hours southwest of Toronto . . . Or was it southeast?" she pondered now, not sure anymore.

"That's a heck of a drive," Lise commented.

"It is," Bobby agreed. "What time did you get home this morning?"

"About one o'clock. Maybe one thirty," Sophie answered.

"Wow," Megan said with surprise. "You didn't stay long at the wedding, then. You must have left shortly after the meal."

Sophie shook her head. "We stayed until well after midnight," she told them and explained, "We didn't drive. We took a helicopter down and a plane back."

"What?" the three of them said as one. Even Mr.

Tomlinson glanced over his paper with eyebrows raised.

Sophie grinned at their reaction and nodded. "I know, right? It was definitely interesting. Although, I have to say I preferred the plane."

Sophie had turned to finish pouring the four cups full of coffee when Bobby asked, "So, how was Tybo? Another Carl or a gentleman?"

"Definitely a gentleman," Sophie assured them. "Actually, he was sweet and kind and we got along great. He's a nice guy."

"So, will there be another date?" Megan asked at once.

Sophie shook her head as she added sugar and cream to her coffee. "No. I mean he's good-looking and nice and makes a great date, but there was no chemistry."

"On your end or his?" Bobby asked at once, glancing past her to the open door of the break room.

"On either end," she said, stirring her coffee. "We talked about it and agreed to just be friends." Actually, much to her relief, it had been Tybo who had brought it up, saying that while he thought she was beautiful and he'd enjoyed their date, he suspected the groom's cousin, Alasdair, was attracted to her and he was pretty sure she was attracted to him too. Sophie had immediately felt guilty that her attraction to Alasdair had been obvious enough that the man she was on a date with had noticed, but he'd assured her it was fine. These things happened, he'd said, and then asked if it would be okay if he gave Alasdair her number if he asked. She'd said yes, and he'd kissed her on the cheek and left her at her door.

Sophie had spent most of her waking time since then wondering if Alasdair would call.

"If you agreed to just be friends, then who's sending you flowers?" Bobby asked.

"What?" she asked with confusion.

Bobby gestured to the doorway. "Janice just carried flowers into your office. A big arrangement with tons of red roses and a heart balloon. I'm pretty sure friends don't send friends those kinds of arrangements, so if you and Tybo are just friends, who sent the flowers?"

Eyes widening, Sophie looked toward the door to see Janice passing, obviously returning from one of the offices. Not really sure if Bobby was telling the truth or just teasing her, she headed out of the break room, unsurprised when the others followed. She was surprised, however, at the floral arrangement sitting on her desk when she got to her office.

"Dear God," Sophie breathed with amazement as she slowed to approach her desk. The floral arrangement was a thing of beauty. And huge. At least two dozen red roses had been arranged with baby's breath and various pink and white flowers in a bloodred vase.

"Yeah. I'm thinking Tybo didn't get the message that you're just friends," Megan said dryly, moving up beside her.

"Maybe he's just thanking you for being his date," Lise suggested. "I mean, agreeing to be a date for a wedding is a big deal if you aren't already dating someone. Especially if the other person is a member of the wedding party."

"Then wouldn't it be a *thank you* balloon rather than a *thinking of you* balloon?" Bobby asked.

Sophie's gaze finally shifted from the arrangement

to the balloon that stuck out above the flowers. It was a medium-sized, heart-shaped red one and did read *Thinking of You*.

"There's a card," Lise pointed out. "See what it says."

"Ooooo, a card," Megan said, reaching for it.

Sophie snatched it up before her friend could grab it and quickly opened the envelope to pull out the little card inside. Her eyes widened and her heart stopped briefly.

"Who's Alasdair?" Megan asked, reading over her shoulder.

"No one." Sophie quickly slid the card back into the envelope, her heart pounding like a drum. Alasdair had sent her flowers.

"Oh yeah, right. You went out last night with Tybo, and today get flowers from someone named Alasdair . . . who is no one?" Megan snorted. "Come on, fess up. Who is he? Someone you've been having secret trysts with?"

"Trysts? What are you, eighty?" Bobby teased his sister. When she punched him in the arm in response, he just laughed and turned to Sophie to raise his eyebrows. "So, who is Alasdair? You know Megan won't leave it alone until you explain this."

"What I know is that none of you will leave it alone until I explain," Sophie countered a bit irritably as she headed back to the break room. She needed a minute to absorb the situation. Alasdair had sent her flowers. Alasdair. Whom she had lusted after last night like a bitch in heat, but had hardly exchanged more than a handful of words with. What did it mean?

"So?" Megan prompted as they entered the break room. "Who is Alasdair?"

Sophie rolled her eyes, but picked up her coffee cup and gave an uncaring shrug before saying, "He's the groom's cousin and one of the people who kept me company while Tybo was busy with his duties as best man."

"Right." Megan nodded, and then asked, "So, just how did he keep you company? A little footsie under the table? Sneaking away for a little make out session?"

"Yeah, and then we went behind the tent and had a quicky," Sophie said dryly.

"Really?" Lise squealed with excitement.

Sophie scowled at her with irritation. "No, not really. Jeez. I would never have a quicky behind a wedding tent with a virtual stranger, especially while on a date with someone else."

"You didn't have sex and still got flowers like that?" Lise's expression was dubious.

Sophie scowled at her coworker. "It's the truth. Alasdair and I didn't even dance, and hardly said more than a handful of words to each other. He literally just sat beside me during the ceremony and then during the dinner."

"Really? That's it?" Megan asked, not bothering to hide her own doubt.

"If you only exchanged a handful of words, how did he know where you work to send the flowers here?" Bobby asked before she could respond.

Sophie stared at him blankly. She had no idea. She did recall mentioning that she was an IT manager for the family business, but she hadn't said the name of the insurance company or anything. He must have learned where she worked from Tybo, she decided, though she didn't recall telling him where she worked either. Shrugging that aside, she said, "Tybo must have told him."

All three said "Humph," one after the other, and Sophie shook her head at the trio. "You guys are too much. A man sent me flowers. It's not a big deal."

"Right, you just keep telling yourself that," Bobby said with amusement.

Shaking her head again, Sophie grabbed her coffee and headed for the door. "I should get back to work. I came in early this morning and planned to skip my breaks and lunch to make up for leaving early yesterday."

"You don't have to do that," Mr. Tomlinson said from behind his paper.

"I know," Sophie said, smiling at the man despite the fact that his paper was up and he wouldn't see it. "But I don't want to take advantage."

Mr. Tomlinson grunted. "Good girl."

Sophie grinned, and without waiting for further comment, left the room to return to her office.

The sight of the flowers on her desk made her smile as she entered. They were beautiful, and such a cheery addition. But on top of that, *they were from Alasdair.* She hadn't really believed Tybo when he'd said Alasdair was obviously attracted to her. Well, she kind of had. She'd noticed that every time she'd looked his way he was looking back. And there had been those two brief moments when she'd been sure he was about to kiss her, which would have been a terrible awful thing since she was on a date with Tybo, she reminded herself. But she hadn't been sure that would mean Alasdair might call her, let alone imagined that he would send such a beautiful floral arrangement.

Thinking of You the balloon and card both said. She didn't know if that was true and he was thinking of her, but the flowers and card were certainly making her think of him. In fact, she suddenly wondered if he'd already tried to call her.

Sitting at her desk, she bent to the side to open the large bottom right-hand drawer to reveal her purse. She then dug through that for her phone and checked to see if there were any missed calls. There weren't. Alasdair hadn't called.

Sophie set the phone on her desk rather than return it to her purse, and then found herself staring at it, hoping it would ring. But after a couple of moments, she realized what she was doing and gave herself a mental slap.

"Back to work," she muttered firmly, and managed, with some difficulty, to force her attention back to work.

"**A**rghh!" That shocked roar exploded from Alasdair's mouth as he shot upright in bed. He then blinked in confusion and anger at his four uncles who stood around his bed, watching him blink water from his eyes.

"There ye are, lad. Are ye awake now?" his uncle Connor asked with amusement.

"Am I awake?" he bellowed with disbelief. "I'm soakin' wet! What the devil did ye throw on me?"

"Just water, boy," Connor said. "We were tryin' to wake ye up."

"I'm soakin' wet!" Alasdair repeated, glancing down at his chest and the wet blankets that were now sliding down his stomach to pool in his lap.

"Aye, well, that's o' no matter," Inan said now. "Ye'll get wet in the shower anyway."

"But my bed would not," Alasdair pointed out grimly, his accent fading as he tamped down his temper and tried for reason. His gaze slid to the bedside clock and a combination of disbelief and outrage immediately brought his accent back. "Why the devil wid ye be wakin' me up at this ungodly hour?"

"Because ye need to shower and shave do ye want to go collect yer lass and take her to lunch," Connor said calmly.

"What?" he asked with disbelief. "What are ye talkin' about?"

"This is Friday, the start o' the weekend," Inan told him. "Ye need to take her to lunch today, and then take her to dinner after work do ye want to get any houghmagandie tonight."

"What?" Alasdair asked again, beginning to wonder if he'd hit his head at some point while sleeping and was suffering brain damage. He had no idea what they were talking about.

"The three-date rule," Odart growled.

"Aye." Inan nodded and explained, "See, we were researchin' courtin' lasses fer ye while ye were workin' last night. To help ye along," he added, and then held up a magazine open to an article with the large headline "When to Have Sex: The Three Date Rule." "See now, there's apparently rules to these things nowadays, and the third date is considered the right time fer sex without her havin' to feel like a hurdie."

"She shouldn'y be made to feel like a hurdie," Odart said firmly.

Inan nodded. "But as life mates, ye ken ye'll ha'e the lass in bed in no' time. I'm thinkin' ye'll no' be lasting past this night without introducin' her to yer wee tadger."

"It's no' wee," Alasdair snapped.

Inan waved his words away, and continued, "The point is, ye'll need to squeeze in lunch and dinner to get ye to three dates so ye can bed her tonight and no' leave her feelin' bad."

Sighing, Alasdair sagged in the bed and pointed out, "Lunch and dinner are only two dates."

"But the weddin' last night makes three," Connor pointed out, and before Alasdair could protest the wedding being a date for them, added firmly, "Ye spent as much if no' more time with her than Tybo did last night. We're thinkin' it can be counted as a date."

"She may no' agree," Ludan pointed out grimly.

There was a moment of silence as the men looked at each other and then Inan brightened and said, "After dinner, ye take her to another restaurant fer dessert. Three dates."

"That wouldn'y be counted as a separate date since they were already out," Connor pointed out with a frown, and then suggested, "Mayhap take her home after the sup, and then leave, go and buy dessert, and take it back to her . . . well, then ye'd be on a whole new date. The third one."

Alasdair stared at them all, wondering when his uncles had lost their minds. Although, truthfully, he wasn't sure they'd ever had minds to lose. The foursome had always seemed like men out of time to him. They were ale swigging, foulmouthed barbarians as his brother had said and just had not managed to move with the times. Although, to be fair, it appeared they were trying to, he thought, his gaze dropping to the women's magazine Inan was holding. It must belong to Sam, he thought. She was his direct boss Mortimer's wife and the only female living at the Enforcer house at the moment. That, or his uncles had gone out to a store to buy it. The very idea of his uncles leafing through women's magazines to find articles on dating and when it was appropriate to have sex had him shaking his head.

Taking a breath to try to regain his patience, he said, "I appreciate that you want to help me. However, I cannot just show up at Sophie's job and expect her to go to lunch with me."

"Well, ye'd best else she'll be wonderin' where ye are and why ye didn'y show," Connor warned.

"What?" he asked again. "Why would she expect me to—?"

"'Twas on the card," Inan told him. "Ye invited her to lunch."

"What card?" he asked with mounting alarm.

"The one with the flowers," Connor explained.

"Flowers?" Alasdair squawked.

"Aye, ye sent her flowers with a card invitin' her to lunch," Connor said, talking slowly now, as if he thought Alasdair might not understand.

"Well, we did it fer ye, really," Inan pointed out judiciously.

"Why the devil would ye do that?" Alasdair barked with alarm.

"To help ye," Inan said with exasperation. "The way

ye were just sittin' there like a lump on a log last night at the wedding, it was obvious that ye'd need help claimin' the lass." His mouth pursed and he added, "I ken ye had to be careful since she was Tybo's date, but ye didn'y e'en make an attempt at talkin' to the lass after the meal was o'er."

"She spent most of the time on the dance floor," Alasdair reminded them. "Because she was *on a date with Tybo*."

"Aye, well, and today she'll be on a date with you."

"Two dates," Connor added, and then glanced at his wristwatch. "Speakin' o' that, it's a quarter past the hour. Ye'd best get up and get showered. Ye'd no' want to be late fer yer date."

Cursing, Alasdair tossed his damp sheets and blankets aside and leapt out of bed.

Ten

A soft tap at her door drew Sophie from the paperwork she was going over. Today was a slow day for IT, so she was helping out their claims adjuster. Setting the papers down, she called out, "Yes?"

Janice, the company receptionist, entered and offered her an uncertain smile, and then said tentatively, "Sophie, there's a . . . man out front who insists on seeing you. But he won't explain why and—" She hesitated and flushed, before admitting, "I'm afraid I got a little flustered and forgot to ask his name."

"Alasdair!" Sophie stood up with amazement as she spotted him towering behind the receptionist.

Janice immediately spun around, hand going to her chest. Her voice was breathy when she said, "Oh. You followed me."

"I thought you were taking me to Sophie and I was meant to follow," he explained, his voice deep and smooth.

For a moment, Janice seemed to sway on her feet and Sophie was afraid the older lady was going to swoon. She couldn't blame her. Damn, the man was big and beautiful and had a killer voice. It made her glad he hadn't spoken much the night before. She might not have been as well-behaved as she had managed to be if he'd used that against her.

"Oh!" Janice was suddenly blinking with recognition. "Sophie called you Alasdair."

"Yes," Alasdair agreed mildly.

"Then you're the man who sent those beautiful flowers to her."

The words made Sophie's eyebrows rise slightly. The receptionist hadn't been anywhere near her office when she'd opened the card. Either Janice had snooped and read the card before bringing it back to her office, or Megan, Bobby, and/or Lise had blabbed and told her who the flowers had come from. She suspected the latter. Not that Janice was above snooping, but Sophie knew her coworkers had probably been gossiping about it since she'd left them in the break room nearly two hours ago. In fact, she was only surprised that they hadn't all invaded her office to grill her further on the subject.

Rather than speak this time, Alasdair merely nodded, his gaze moving to the flowers on her desk. She thought she saw surprise and relief flicker across his face as he took them in.

"Well, they're beautiful," Janice told him, and then stood smiling, her eyes eating him alive for a moment that drew out into two before she suddenly gave herself a little shake, and offered Sophie an apologetic smile before saying reluctantly, "I suppose I should get back to the front."

"Yes," Sophie agreed gently. "Thank you for showing him back, Janice."

Nodding, the woman turned her gaze back to Alasdair and slowly eased past him as he stepped into the room. She then, just as slowly, drew the door closed, her gaze taking in as much of Alasdair as she could before the door was shut and she could no longer see him.

At least I'm not the only one affected by the man, Sophie thought as she switched her gaze to Alasdair and offered a smile she hoped was light and unconcerned. "Thanks for the flowers. They're beautiful."

"Welcome," Alasdair responded, his gaze moving over her where she stood behind her desk.

Back to the one-word answers now that we're alone, Sophie thought with amusement. *At least he wasn't just grunting.* Considering him briefly, she tried to think what to say next. Flat-out asking why he was there seemed kind of rude and she was trying to come up with a way to say it more diplomatically when he asked, "Am I late?"

One eyebrow rising, she asked, "Late for what?"

"Our lunch date," he explained. "Or maybe I'm early. I should have asked Janice what time you normally take lunch. If I'm early, I can just wait."

He was talking in actual sentences again, but nothing he was saying was making any sense. Sophie tilted her head and considered him, then said, "I'm sorry. Did we have a lunch date?"

She didn't recall anything like that. Had he asked her to lunch at some point last night? If so, she didn't remember it, which made her wonder how much she'd had to drink. She'd thought she'd only had a glass of champagne to toast the bride and groom, and then another with dinner, but there were a few holes in her memory of last night that suggested otherwise. Just fuzzy spots in her memory where small things like bits of conversation were missing. She'd remember the start and end of a conversation, but there were obvious holes in the middle sometimes, as if someone had just plucked out a chunk of her memory. So, she supposed Alasdair could have asked her out last night and she didn't recall the conversation. Although, she was quite sure she wouldn't have agreed to a lunch date with Alasdair while on a date with Tybo. She would have simply given him her number and told him to call her in the morning.

"The card," Alasdair said, drawing her attention back to him. "Did it not say—?" He paused and frowned. "I should have called to be sure you wanted to go to lunch, rather than just assume you would be willing to accept an invitation on a card."

Sucking in a breath, Sophie snatched the envelope from where it was tucked into the flowers and tugged out the card. His name had been the only thing on the front of the card, but she hadn't checked the back. Maybe— No, she saw as she turned the small card over. It was blank.

Returning her gaze to him, she asked, "I presume you called in the order and what to put on the card?"

When Alasdair merely raised his eyebrows in question, she held up the card for him to see and said, "It looks like someone messed up and didn't add your message, just your name."

"Oh." He frowned.

Sophie hesitated. Lunch with Alasdair would mess

up her plans to make up for leaving early the day before, but with him standing there looking incredibly handsome and smelling so damned amazing, her good intentions were slipping a bit. She could always go out for an hour lunch and work later to make up the time.

Decision made, she gave a small nod and slid the card back into the envelope as she asked, "So there was supposed to be an invitation to lunch on the card?"

Alasdair smiled faintly. "Who me? Invite you to lunch through a card and then not even think to call and verify that you were all right with it?" he asked with wry good humor, and then shook his head. "Never. But since I am here, I would be delighted to take you to lunch. If you are free?"

A short laugh slid from her lips, and then she affected a blasé voice and said, "Well . . . *since you're here* . . . I guess we could do that."

They smiled at each other briefly, and then Sophie retrieved her purse, snatched her phone off the papers it was lying on, and walked around her desk to join him. "I only have an hour for lunch. Where were you thinking of going?"

"Actually, I do not know this area well," he admitted solemnly as he opened her door. "Mayhap you could suggest somewhere?"

"This is nice."

Sophie glanced around from shrugging out of her jacket and raised her eyebrows at that comment. They were at a Swiss Chalet, about a five-minute walk from her office. She'd chosen it because it was convenient . . . and because Megan hated Swiss Chalet so she'd been relatively certain she wouldn't run into her coworkers there and be forced into explanations and introductions.

Smiling with amusement at Alasdair now, she commented, "You make it sound like you've never been to a Swiss Chalet."

"I haven't," he admitted.

Sophie was blinking over that announcement, finding it hard to believe anyone could have just never been in one of the franchises at some point in their life. It was known for its rotisserie chicken and chalet sauce, something many people found addictive. There had to be at least nine of them in the Greater Toronto Area. Worried now that he hadn't ever been to one because—like Megan—he didn't care for their food offerings, she opened her mouth to ask and then paused as their waitress arrived at their table.

Letting the question go for now, she requested an iced tea, and then turned her attention to her menu as Alasdair asked for the same.

It wasn't until their waitress returned with their drinks and they'd given their food order that she then got back to the subject.

"Why have you never been to a Swiss Chalet?"

After a hesitation, he simply said, "I haven't been in Toronto long."

"How long?"

"A week or so."

Sophie's eyes widened slightly. She knew he worked with Tybo, but hadn't realized he hadn't worked in the city long. He must have transferred to Toronto from somewhere else, she supposed. And obviously somewhere small enough not to have a Swiss Chalet.

"Where were you before Toronto?" she asked with interest.

"I was at Shady Pines for a few weeks before coming to Toronto."

Sophie recognized the name of the golf course where the wedding had been held, but couldn't imagine it had its own police station. Perhaps he'd been vacationing there or something, she thought, and asked, "And before that?"

"I've lived and worked in New York for dec—" He paused momentarily with his mouth open on that last unfinished word, and then closed it and cleared his throat before substituting, "years."

That made her sit back and eye him suspiciously. "I thought you were a policeman like Tybo?"

"I work with Tybo, yes," he agreed.

"So, were you a police officer in New York too?" she asked, trying to understand how a policeman in New York could end up working in Toronto. She was pretty sure they couldn't just be transferred from the US to Canada. That wasn't how things worked. At least, she didn't think so.

"Colle and I worked in Enforcement in New York as well," Alasdair admitted, and then changed the subject and asked, "What made you get into IT?"

Sophie scowled slightly, dissatisfied with not being able to find out how he'd managed to work as a police officer in Toronto so quickly. She would have thought that they'd be expected to take some sort of course or something to ensure they knew the different Canadian laws as opposed to the American ones, but maybe that wasn't the case. Maybe being a police officer in New York was considered good enough and they just handed them a gun and a badge and sent them on their way.

Shaking her head, she let the matter go for now and said, "I don't know. I just like computers. Always have. I find them challenging, and I love new technology, learning the next language, the next program." She smiled faintly. "My training is in coding and networks. The job I presently have is kind of . . ." She paused and frowned, not wanting to be insulting to her boss, who was basically like a father to her. Finally, she said, "Really, I'm not utilizing all my skills at my present job. I was hired because Mr. Tomlinson, my boss, wanted to switch to new computers and a more efficient system. He wanted me to set it up. I was fresh out of university and happy to help for a month or two before looking for a job more suitable to my training. But once the new system was up and running, he wanted me to stay. He doesn't really need me. At least not full-time. There are the occasional issues, but mostly I just do minor things like help people reset passwords, or clear out viruses and stuff, and when I run out of things like that, I help out coworkers with paperwork and stuff like that."

"You do not seem happy when you talk about it," he commented with concern.

Sophie shrugged. "I'm not really unhappy, it's just not what I trained for. I thought I'd be writing code and developing programs and such."

"Then why stay at the insurance company?" Alasdair asked reasonably.

Sophie grimaced at him for the logical question. It

was one she'd asked herself several times in the past. Sighing, she said, "It's complicated."

She'd meant to leave it at that, but found herself admitting, "Mr. and Mrs. Tomlinson are the closest thing I have to parents, and their children, Megan and Bobby, are my best friends and like siblings to me. It's a family business and I'm fortunate enough that they consider me part of that family."

"You feel like you would be throwing that relationship in their face if you left and do not want to hurt, and possibly lose, them by leaving," Alasdair said solemnly, understanding more than she'd expected.

Sophie let out the breath she hadn't realized she'd been holding and nodded. "Yeah."

"And your real family?" Alasdair asked.

Sophie shrugged and picked up her drink. "I think I mentioned last night that my parents died in a house fire when I was eleven."

"No brothers or sisters?"

"I was an only child," she said, and took a drink of her iced tea.

"I'm sorry."

Sophie's eyes shifted quickly to him. She wanted to say it had happened a long time ago and it was fine, but suddenly had a lump in her throat, so she merely nodded.

"What happened after your parents died?" Alasdair asked. "Did the Tomlinsons raise you? Is that why they are like family to you?"

Sophie shook her head. "We were neighbors. Megan was my best friend growing up, and we were having a sleepover at their house the night of the fire. That's the only reason I wasn't home when our house burned down."

.She fell silent for a minute, remembering waking in Megan's room that night. She could see her best friend standing by the open window, silhouetted by the light coming through the window from the fire next door. She'd heard the scream of sirens in the distance and had stumbled out of bed to join her at the window. Just in time to see Mr. and Mrs. Tomlinson running to the house next door in their pajamas, shouting for her parents.

"So, if not them, who raised you after your parents died?" Alasdair asked.

Blinking away her memories, Sophie set her glass back on the table. "I went to a group home for the next three years."

"You didn't have family that could have taken you in?" Alasdair asked with a frown.

Sophie shrugged. "My father had a big family, but they apparently turned their back on him when he married my mother. She was half Filipino and they were racist, didn't consider her good enough for him," she said dryly. "When social services contacted them after the fire, their stance was that they had no son and weren't interested in his 'foreign brat.'"

"Ouch," Alasdair said with a wince.

Sophie smiled faintly at his expression. "They were strangers, so I wasn't bothered," she told him, and it was the same thing she'd told herself at the time, and in the years since, but—

"And your mother? Did she have family?" Alasdair asked, interrupting her thoughts.

Sophie shook her head. "Her parents both died before she married my father. And there was only a sister on her side, my aunt, who was a single mother of three kids already and said she couldn't afford to take me in. So, it was the group home for me," Sophie said with a shrug, and then added, "But I wasn't there long. Three years and a bit."

"What happened then?" Alasdair asked.

"High school," she said with a grin. "I ended up going to the same high school as Megan." She chuckled as happier memories began flooding her mind. She distinctly recalled Megan's excitement and happiness as well as her own. "We picked up where we'd left off before the fire, and were BFFs again."

"BFFs?" Alasdair asked uncertainly.

"Best friends forever," she explained with a smile. "You know, hanging out, giggling over boys, sleepovers. Best friend stuff."

"And her parents adopted you?" Alasdair guessed. "That's why you were no longer at the group home."

"They *fostered* me," she corrected. "And it didn't happen right away. There were some hoops for them to jump through. Mr. and Mrs. Tomlinson had to do some training, and home study, and had to be screened by the police and whatnot, but they did it."

Absently turning her glass on the tabletop, she added, "My caseworker said that both George and Deb, the Tomlinsons, took weeks off work to get through the preservice training and home study more quickly. They wanted me out of the group home as quickly as possible."

Alasdair's eyebrows rose. "Then why did they leave you there for three years?"

"I guess they thought I'd gone to live with a family member. They were very upset to learn I'd been in a group home since my parents' death."

"Ah." Alasdair nodded. "So, you got to move out of the group home and live with your best friend, Megan, and her parents."

"And her brother, Bobby," Sophie put in. "And now they're family and I work with them all. Well, not Deb, Mrs. Tomlinson," she explained. "She's a grade school teacher."

Alasdair opened his mouth to say something, but then paused and sat back from the table. It made Sophie glance around. She wasn't surprised to see their waitress approaching from behind her with their meals. She sat back at once to stay out of the way, and murmured, "Thank you," as the woman set down their food.

"Mmmm." Alasdair closed his eyes and inhaled once the woman moved away. "It smells delicious."

"Which part?" Sophie asked with amusement. She'd ordered the spring rolls and pierogies as appetizers for them to share, and then had ordered a quarter chicken dinner for herself. Alasdair had ordered the quarter chicken dinner as well, at first, but she'd recommended he get the half chicken dinner instead. While the quarter chicken was more than sufficient for her—in fact she knew from past experience that she'd be taking away half her meal in a doggy bag, especially with the appetizers there—she just hadn't thought the quarter chicken would fill him up. The man was huge.

"Everything," he decided, opening his eyes to survey the food, before reaching for a spring roll as she did. They paused to look at each other when their hands collided over the appetizers and Sophie swallowed thickly as a rush of tension and excitement slid through her.

If they weren't in a restaurant, she'd . . . But they were in a restaurant, she reminded herself, and gingerly retrieved her hand then lowered her head to concentrate on her meal as she waited for her body to stop buzzing.

Eleven

"So, unlike me, you have a big family."

Alasdair stopped chewing and glanced up quickly to Sophie at that comment from out of the blue. They'd been eating in silence for several minutes now. This was the first thing either of them had said since the food had arrived, and her words caught him somewhat by surprise.

Smiling at his expression, Sophie said, "I mean, there's your brother, Colle, your cousin Valerian, and then your four uncles. Plus, I'm pretty sure Tybo mentioned that Julius was an uncle or something too, and there were obviously others. The groom's side was full," she pointed out.

Alasdair finished chewing the food in his mouth which was a bite of delectable chicken, and then swallowed and nodded. "Yes."

He took another bite of chicken.

"Seriously?" Sophie asked with obvious amusement. "That's all you're going to give me? Yes?"

"Yes, I have a big family?" he tried.

Sophie snorted at the pathetic offering. "Sure, I spilled my guts all over the table, answering your questions about my family, or lack thereof, and now that it's your turn to talk, you revert to the caveman again."

"Caveman?" he asked, sitting up straighter in his seat with alarm. That didn't sound like a description of a man a woman would be attracted to.

"Yes, caveman," she said firmly. "And now that I know you can actually talk in whole sentences, the caveman act simply won't pass muster, so you better start talking, mister."

Her tone was teasing, but Alasdair suspected the message was not. It was also probably fair. She had answered every one of his questions. Turnabout was only right. He set down the chicken leg he'd been devouring, used the lemon water to clean his fingers, dried them on his napkin, and then reached for his drink for a quick sip before admitting, "I apologize. I have never been much of a talker. Colle is the chatty one of the two of us."

"Why?" Sophie asked at once.

Alasdair considered the question. It was something he'd never really wondered about. It had always just been that way. Colle chattered away, charming everyone, and he watched and listened, silent and alert. But now that he was thinking about it, he supposed the truth was—"I really do not like people much."

He wasn't sure what reaction he'd expected from

Sophie, but it wasn't for her to nod with understanding and say, "I feel you there."

"You do?" he asked with surprise.

"Of course," she said as if that should be expected. "I mean, really, people kind of suck."

Alasdair stared at her, hardly able to believe she agreed with him. He was pretty sure she was the first person who had. At least openly. Usually, on the rare occasions when he'd said something of the like to others, they'd immediately started in with the *"people aren't so bad"* nonsense, when really, they were. And he should know, he'd been alive a hell of a long time, more than three hundred years, and a lot of those years as an Enforcer, seeing the worst of the worst. People could be pretty awful.

"Mind you," Sophie said now, "I suppose I should say people kind of suck *in general*. I mean, I've met a lot of assholes so far in life, but I've met a few pretty nice people too. Like the Tomlinsons. Not only did George and Deb take me in and raise me like I was one of their own, they actually put me through university too, and then they gave me a job. They've really tried to be there for me and they didn't have to. I was just the neighbors' kid and a friend of their daughter's. They really went above and beyond."

Alasdair nodded, but was wondering about the assholes she'd encountered.

"And I've known other wonderful people like my parents and friends and . . . others." Sophie paused and pursed her lips briefly, before saying, "Mind you, they're all dead now. So, I guess that saying about the good dying young is true."

"Except for the Tomlinsons," he said solemnly.

"Yes, except for them," she agreed, and then tilted her head and smiled at him faintly. "And you, of course. So far you seem nice enough. As did Marguerite and Julius, and Tybo, of course."

"Not my uncles?" Alasdair teased.

Sophie grinned. "Your uncles are definitely interesting. I haven't decided yet if they're nice or not, though they seemed nice enough last night."

"They were on their best behavior," Alasdair assured her in dry tones.

Sophie smiled faintly at the comment and responded lightly, "Probably afraid you or Colle would take them to task if they weren't."

"Not us. Julius."

"Seriously?" she asked with open disbelief. "Marguerite's husband?"

Alasdair nodded.

"But he was so quiet and . . . well, sweet," she protested. "Especially compared to your other uncles at the table last night."

Alasdair chuckled at the description. Julius seemed quiet and gentle, but he was more lion than pussy cat when the need arose. But all he said was, "Julius is older than Ludan and the others. He probably would have cuffed every one of them if they'd got out of line. It's undoubtedly why they were put at our table with Julius. Valerian knew he'd keep them in check."

"Huh," Sophie muttered, and shook her head. "Never would have guessed it. I didn't find him the least scary or intimidating."

Alasdair grinned at her comment. Few would find Julius scary or intimidating . . . until they pissed him off.

"So, did you get today off because of the wedding?" Sophie asked, changing the subject.

Alasdair shook his head and picked up his chicken again before answering, "I worked last night after the wedding."

"Seriously?" she asked, looking shocked.

Alasdair nodded. "Myself, Colle, and several other Enforcers were on the first plane back to Toronto at midnight to take up our shifts."

"So that's where you disappeared to," she murmured.

Alasdair nodded and tried not to grin at the knowledge that she'd noticed his absence.

"Hmm," Sophie said now. "So, you work . . . What? One A.M. till nine A.M.?" she guessed.

"Midnight to eight," he corrected. "The guys on the earlier shift knew we might be a little late because of the wedding and offered to work our shift until we could take over."

"Oh, that was nice of them," she said with a smile.

Alasdair merely nodded. It had been nice, he acknowledged, and then noted that Sophie was frowning at him now and asked, "What?"

"So, you haven't been to bed yet?" she asked. "I mean it was noon when you got to my office and if you got off at eight A.M. . . . . You also took the time to order those flowers. You must sleep in the evenings before work," she guessed, and then frowned with dissatisfaction at her own deduction and added, "Although you were at the wedding in the evening yesterday."

"I normally sleep through the day," he said, telling her what she was trying to figure out.

"But not today obviously," she said with apparent concern. "You must be exhausted."

"I caught a nap after work," he assured her. "And I'll probably lie down again after our lunch for a couple hours. Probably," he added grimly because he had a bone to pick with his uncles first. They'd gone to bed as he'd left. Maybe he should wake them up by tossing a pail of cold water over each of them as they'd done to him. Then he could point out that there hadn't been anything about a lunch on the card with the flowers. Once he had them wide-awake and soaking wet, he could lie down in his own probably still damp bed for a bit. With the door locked this time.

Not for long, though, Alasdair recalled. He was supposed to invite Sophie out for dinner to get their second date done and get to the third where they could have sex. Which seemed kind of cold now that he was thinking about it. After all, they were having a lovely meal without any crazy life mate passion cropping up to get in the way. Well, other than the brief spark of electricity between them when their hands had collided over the spring rolls. Still, he could last another day before the next date so long as he made sure there was no more contact and—

Alasdair's thoughts died as he glanced at Sophie to see that she was cleaning chicken grease from her fingers by popping them into her mouth one after the other and then pulling each digit out with a soft sucking sound, before turning her attention to the next. He watched the activity with fascination, noting the way her eyelids drooped in concentration and her lips puckered around each finger in a soft O as her finger glided in and then out.

"Damn," he breathed as his cock hardened and

almost leapt in his pants, eager to offer itself up for such a cleaning.

"Hmm?" Sophie glanced at him in question, and then noted where his gaze was fixed, seemed to realize what she was doing and flushed, then pulled her hand away from her mouth.

"Sorry," she muttered as she cleaned her fingers in the bowl of lemon water provided. "Mrs. Tomlinson did her best to drum table manners into me, but three years in the group home . . ." She shrugged. "Manners weren't a priority there. Meals were mostly an 'eat as quickly as you could so no one got the chance to steal your food' situation."

Alasdair nodded in understanding, but his gaze was fixed on her mouth as she spoke, the memory of her sucking on each finger still strong in his mind so that when she suddenly fell silent, he blurted, "Dinner."

"Dinner?" Sophie eyed him with confusion as she dried her hands on the napkin.

"Tonight. You and me," he managed, and knew he sounded like the caveman she'd accused him of being, but couldn't help it just then. While he'd just been thinking they were doing fine and life mate passion wasn't an issue, now he had a raging hard-on just from watching her, and his brain seemed to be suffering for it. He could only think that all the blood in his body had rushed down to fill his cock, leaving none to supply oxygen to his brain.

Several expressions flashed across Sophie's face at his words. Surprise, pleasant surprise in fact, which was followed by an excitement that made him quite sure she would say yes. But then uncertainty and finally a small concerned frown started him worrying.

"I'd really like that, but you need to sleep," she said gently, "and I'm trying to make up for leaving work early yesterday. My plan was to work through lunch and my breaks and work until eight thirty tonight to make up for it, but now that I took off lunch to eat with you, I'll have to make that up tonight and work an hour even later than I'd planned."

"You have to eat," he pointed out.

"And you have to sleep," she argued. "I can order something in and eat at my desk."

Alasdair was shaking his head before she finished speaking. He repeated, "You have to eat. I could pick up something . . . a pizza," he added after a brief moment to think of something Bricker and the rest of the mated and eating hunters liked. Pizza seemed popular with the men. "I could bring pizza by at say . . . seven?" he suggested, and when she hesitated, he urged, "You can stop for half an hour. You do need to eat dinner."

"That's true," she said slowly, obviously swaying toward agreeing.

"And then I'll leave you alone to finish work and maybe we could meet up for coffee and dessert after you're done and before I head off to work myself." He was very satisfied with that plan. It meant he would work in three full dates today. The dessert would be the third and then . . . His slowly deflating erection perked up at the "and then" and Alasdair grimaced and turned his mind firmly from the "and then" to the now as Sophie groaned, "I'm so weak."

"Weak?" he asked uncertainly. She didn't seem weak to him. The woman had been through a lot in her life, yet seemed self-confident, smart, and mostly undamaged by it all.

"Yes, weak," Sophie said with amusement. "You're tempting, and I'm weak enough to give in to temptation and say yes."

"Yes, to dinner?" he clarified.

"Yes, to a half hour dinner break of pizza with you," she said, mapping out her boundaries on the situation. She pursed her lips before adding, "If that is acceptable. Otherwise—"

"It is acceptable," Alasdair interrupted, not wanting to hear what the "otherwise" might lead to.

Sophie nodded and then glanced at her wristwatch and muttered, "Oh shoot."

"What?" he asked, and glanced at his own watch to see that it was nearly one o'clock. Her lunch hour was almost up.

"I have to get back to the office," she murmured, and glanced at her still half-full plate, then raised her head and looked around for their waitress. Fortunately, the older woman who was their waitress had apparently been watching, because she rushed up almost at once with a Styrofoam container.

"For your leftovers?" the woman asked with a grin.

"You rock, Alice," Sophie said with appreciation as she took the container and quickly shifted her food into it.

She obviously knew the waitress, Alasdair thought as he held his hand out for the bill the waitress held. The woman hesitated, her gaze sliding from him to Sophie and back, but then she handed it over and held up a portable credit card reader in question.

"It's fine," Alasdair said, waving away the need for the machine with one hand as he pulled out his wallet with the other. He quickly counted out the cash needed, added a sizeable tip, and handed over the money, saying, "Thank you. The meal was delicious."

Smiling, Alice accepted the cash and compliment, and wished them a good day before hurrying off.

"You didn't have to do that," Sophie said when he turned back to her. "I'm happy to pay for my lunch. Can I reimburse you for—?"

"No," Alasdair interrupted when she reached to pull her wallet out of her purse. "I invited you out so it's my treat."

She eyed him briefly, but then simply nodded and slid her wallet back into her purse, gathered the container holding the remainder of her lunch, and stood up. "Well, then, thanks for lunch and I guess I'll see you around seven."

Alasdair nodded, and slid out of the booth to join her. "I'll walk you back."

It was a short walk back to the insurance company, which was no doubt part of the reason Sophie had chosen Swiss Chalet for lunch. Neither of them spoke on the way, but the silence wasn't an uncomfortable one, more a companionable one. It was nice, he decided.

Once they reached the parking lot, Sophie asked, "Did you drive here or take the subway?"

"I drove."

"Well, then, I'll leave you here," she said, offering him a smile and her hand. "Thanks for lunch."

"You're welcome," he said, taking her hand. They both then stood completely still as a consortium of sensations vibrated between their clasped hands and spread outward. He could hear Sophie's heartbeat speed up just as his own was doing, and could smell the change in her scent as excitement washed over them both. She wanted him as much as he wanted her, and Alasdair was hard-pressed not to tug her forward, cover her mouth with his, and kiss her until she was mindless with need and willing to follow him anywhere to satisfy it. But the recollection of Odan's raspy voice saying, *Three-date rule* ran through his head and he forced himself to release her hand, with a softly growled, "See you at seven."

"Seven," she agreed a little breathlessly, and immediately turned to continue to the front door, but he heard her mutter to herself, "You are so weak, Sophie Ferguson."

Alasdair smiled to himself, and then his gaze slid to the large plate glass windows along the front and sides of the building and he blinked when he spotted the people visible through the tinted glass. He could see at least half a dozen people milling around the reception area, but four of them were standing at the window staring out at him.

He suspected they were the family members she worked with, but the tableau reminded him uncomfortably of a scene in a horror movie he'd once watched with Colle. Shaking his head at the thought, Alasdair gave them a wave and turned to head to his SUV.

Twelve

Sophie found herself bombarded with questions the moment she stepped through the door.

"Ohmygod! Is that him?"

"Jan said Alasdair of the flowers showed up and you went to lunch with him."

"Good Lord, he's hot, isn't he?"

Sophie stared wide-eyed at the people crowded by the window staring out at a departing Alasdair. Megan, Bobby, and Lise were asking their questions while gaping out the window like goldfish in a bowl, while Mr. Tomlinson was just smiling faintly as he surveyed the parking lot.

"Sophie!" Megan cried with outrage when their questions weren't answered quickly enough. Giving up her position by the window, her sister rushed toward her. "Is that him? The flower guy, Alasdair?"

"Yes," Sophie said finally.

"He's a big fellow," Mr. Tomlinson commented,

moving away from the window now too. "I hope he was a gentleman."

"Definitely a gentleman," Sophie assured him solemnly. "So far he seems like one of the good ones."

"Good." George Tomlinson nodded with satisfaction. "And do you plan to see him again?"

"Yes," Sophie admitted reluctantly. "He—we're having dinner." She didn't want to get into the specifics of it. If anyone knew they were planning to have pizza here, she wouldn't put it past the whole Tomlinson clan to show up and join them so they could give Alasdair the once-over.

"Dinner. Good," Mr. Tomlinson said with a nod. "Well, then, have fun and keep me apprised if there's anything you think I should know."

"I will," she said and smiled faintly as he paused to give her a pat on the arm before moving past her to head to his office.

"So?" Megan asked as soon as her father had disappeared down the hall. "Tell us everything!"

Sophie laughed slightly and followed in Mr. Tomlinson's wake, heading for the break room to store her leftovers as she said, "There's nothing to tell, Megs. He came here, asked me to lunch. I said yes. We went to lunch. Ate, and came back. End of."

"No, not end of," Megan insisted, following her with Bobby and Lise trailing. "Where did you go? What did you talk about? What did he—"

"Swiss Chalet," Sophie interrupted.

"Oh God! No!" Megan groaned. "Not there of all places."

"Yes, there," Sophie said with amusement as she opened the refrigerator door and slid her lunch in.

"Well, that's him done, then," Megan said unhappily. "No taste or class. You can't see him again."

"*I* picked Swiss Chalet," Sophie said on a laugh as she closed the door of the refrigerator.

"Of course you did," Megan said with exasperation, and then heaved a dramatic sigh and followed her out of the break room. "Well, let's hope he picks somewhere finer for this dinner you mentioned. When is it? Tomorrow night?"

"We're having pizza," Sophie told her, knowing that would push the question of when out of Megan's mind. She was right, of course.

"What?" she squealed in horror. "*Pizza?* I thought this guy had money?"

Sophie stopped at the door to her office and swung around with surprise. "Who said he had money?"

"Well, you flew out in a helicopter to some wedding hours away, and flew back in a plane. It sounds like the family has money."

Sophie considered that and then nodded slowly. "I suppose it does. At least someone has money. Natalie owns the golf course. She inherited it from her parents. And Valerian does have a helicopter, so I suppose that suggests money," she admitted. "But that doesn't mean Alasdair has money."

"The flowers he sent you suggest he might," Bobby countered, stopping behind Megan and leaning against the hall wall with his arms crossed. "I mean, come on, Soph, he must have paid a bundle for them."

Sophie turned to peer through her door at the flowers on her desk. They *were* gorgeous, and huge and yes, they probably had cost a small fortune. Still . . . "I have no idea if he has money or his family does or whatnot and I don't care. I like him. He's nice, and interesting and I enjoyed his company so I'm going out with him again." She paused briefly, and then said, "Now I have to get back to work. I still have to make up time for leaving early yesterday so I'm working late tonight. See you at Sunday dinner," she added as a way to let them know she wouldn't appreciate interruptions this afternoon.

Sophie then slid into her office and closed the door.

"The devil ye say! Course we told 'em to put the message on the card. If they didn'y do it, 'twas no' our fault," Connor said firmly.

Alasdair scowled at his uncles as they all nodded in firm agreement. He'd returned to the house to find Sam had gone out for groceries and his brother and uncles were all abed. He'd considered waking them up as he'd planned, with a bucket of water each. However, the idea had seemed an exhausting one at that point. It meant lugging up four buckets of water and visiting one room after the other.

In the end, Alasdair had decided his time would be better served getting some rest. He had plans for the night, after all. He had to work at midnight, of course, but before that was dinner and then dessert with Sophie . . . and if things went as expected, a dessert *of* Sophie after that. The very idea had made him hard again.

Alasdair tried to tell himself that he shouldn't get his hopes up. After all, Sophie had some say in the matter. However, life mate passion was a well-known symptom, often discussed by unmated immortals, usually with envy and anticipation. Unmated immortals might tease and taunt the newly mated for the life mate brain and horndog tendencies they suffered after first finding their life mate, but it was a smoke screen to hide their jealousy. That passion was something every immortal looked forward to experiencing someday. Eagerly.

Alasdair had already experienced a little of it. Sitting beside her during the wedding ceremony and then dinner had been a sweet torture, his entire body vibrating and attuned to hers. Taking her arm to escort her from one tent to the other last night had sent sparks of excitement shivering from his fingers through his body so that it had almost been a relief to reach the table and release her. But watching her suck her fingers today at lunch had been something else. His mind had gone wild with imagining her sweet lips doing other things.

For a man who hadn't been the least interested in sex for over two hundred years, the sudden awakening of his hunger for it, and the strength of that hunger, made it hard to think of much else. That was why he wasn't surprised when he lay down to sleep and immediately found himself having sex dreams about Sophie. Sadly, she was at work and wide-awake, so he hadn't got to experience the shared sex dreams that was another symptom of new life mates, but his solo dreams were good enough to have him achy and cranky when he woke up.

A quick shower and getting dressed had done little to improve his mood. But encountering his uncles in the hall as they came out of their own rooms had at least given him a target for his temper.

"Well, there was no message about lunch, so some-one messed up and knowing you as I do, I'm thinking it was an error on your part," Alasdair said firmly, and then turned to head for the stairs, not interested in hearing their denials. He wasn't surprised when his uncles followed on his heels, protesting the whole way down the stairs.

It was when they entered the kitchen and spotted Sam that their nattering died as Connor bellowed, "Hoy! Lass! Tell Alasdair there was supposed to be an invite to lunch on the card with the flowers fer So-phie," he instructed, and then turned to Alasdair to explain, "Sam placed the order fer us."

"What?" Sam asked, casting a confused glance their way as she closed the refrigerator door and turned to set several food items on the island. She was obviously starting dinner preparations.

Connor scowled with irritation, and said, "Did we no' ask ye to invite Sophie to lunch in the card on those flowers ye ordered fer us?"

"No," Sam said as she turned away to grab a knife out of the knife block.

"What do ye mean, no?" Inan said with outrage as they watched her retrieve a vegetable peeler from a drawer, and then collect a cutting board from the cup-board, before settling on a stool at the island. "Course we did."

"No, you did not," she said with certainty, pluck-ing a zucchini from the collection of vegetables she'd retrieved from the refrigerator. "The four of you came charging into the kitchen demanding I order flowers and send them to Sophie from Alasdair. We argued over the arrangement in question until I convinced you to send the deluxe *Thinking of You* bouquet instead of the one the four of you had originally chosen, and then you all just marched out of the kitchen in a snit because I wouldn't send the ones you wanted."

"I still do no' ken why ye would no' send the ones we liked. They were prettier," Inan said with irritation.

"They were a funeral spray," Sam said with exasperation, and Alasdair's eyes widened in horror at how close Sophie had come to receiving a funeral arrangement from him.

"Well, we told ye to ha'e the *In Sympathy* banner removed," Connor pointed out with irritation. "She would no' ha'e kenned the difference without that."

"Oh, yes, she would have," Sam assured them.

His uncles all scowled at Sam, but she just scowled back.

Finally, Connor said, "I suppose we could ha'e been a might overset at the disagreement, and maybe might ha'e forgotten to ask ye to include the invite to lunch on the card."

"There's no maybe about it. You never mentioned what to put on the card so I just had them put his name," Sam informed them.

"Well, hell," Connor muttered unhappily, his shoulders slouching somewhat as he turned to Alasdair. "Sorry, lad. I guess we made a muckle mess o' that."

His other three uncles nodded, looking miserable enough to make him feel guilty.

"'Tis fine," Alasdair said gruffly. "It all worked out. She let me take her out to lunch."

All four men brightened at this. It was Inan who

said, "So, ye've the second date under yer belt. Well done, lad! One more to go."

"Second date?" Sam asked, glancing up with interest. "When was your first date?"

"They're counting the wedding," Alasdair said dryly, and Sam immediately shook her head.

"She was on a date with Tybo, how could that be a date with Alasdair?" she asked his uncles with disbelief. "And why one more to go? One more to go until what?"

Much to his relief Odart forestalled anyone explaining the ridiculous third date rule by growling, "What o' dinner?"

"Aye. Did ye ask her out fer dinner?" Connor asked.

"Aye," Alasdair said, but his tone was distracted and his gaze moved to Sam as the question reminded him that he needed to know where to get pizza. "Sam, wh—"

"Google it," Sam said before he could even finish getting the question out. She'd obviously read the question from his mind. "I know a couple of good places near here, but you want something near enough to Sophie's office that the pizza won't be cold or soggy before you get there."

"Right," Alasdair breathed, and pulled out his phone to google the best pizza in Toronto.

"Pizza?" Inan asked with interest.

"Sophie's working late, so I'm taking her dinner," he explained, going through the search. "And then after work I'm taking her out for dessert."

"Three dates," Connor crooned. "That'll be three e'en without the weddin'."

"Aye," Inan agreed happily. "It'll be a green light

night fer ye, lad, and she'll no' e'en feel like a hurdie afterward. Well done, boy!"

Alasdair grunted as his uncles each thumped him on the back. Much to his relief, they then left him alone and moved over to pester Sam about what rabbit food she was cooking for poor Mortimer tonight. Ignoring them, Alasdair quickly found a restaurant near the insurance office that had good reviews, but then he was faced with a menu that seemed to have a lot of choices.

"Who stole yer scone, lad?"

Alasdair glanced up with surprise when his uncle Connor asked that.

"Yer scowlin'," Connor told him dryly. "Can ye no' find a place with pizzas?"

"I found one," Alasdair said with a small frown. "It's just that they have a lot of choices, and I didn't think to ask Sophie what she likes. Maybe I should call her," he added, his eyebrows drawing together.

"Oh, now don'y be doin' that, lad," Connor said at once. "A lass needs to ken she can depend on her maun to satisfy her needs on his own without her input. Let's see what they ha'e on offer."

Alasdair found his phone plucked from his hand, and then was pushed out from even seeing it himself when his other uncles suddenly crowded in to look at the menu he'd pulled up.

"Oh, order this," Inan said, sounding excited.

"And this," Odart growled.

"This one sounds good," Connor murmured. "Order it too."

"What do ye mean order it?" Alasdair asked with alarm. "Ye're no' ordering online."

"Aye. Fer pickup," Connor told him. "It'll be grand."

"Crap," Alasdair breathed, and tried to fight his way between two of his uncles to get to his phone, but that was impossible. They were all large men, and they weren't moving. This, he was sure, was going to be a disaster.

Thirteen

It was five minutes to seven when Sophie saw Alasdair's SUV pull into the small parking lot next to the insurance office. Actually, it was dark out already and what she really saw was headlights as he pulled in. It was enough. Jumping up from her seat, she brushed down her skirt, tugged her blouse down a bit, and retucked it into her skirt, then bit her lips to give them color. Sophie then ran her hands through her hair as she hurried out of her office.

She was excited and nervous and relieved all at once. Excited to see him again, nervous to see him again, and relieved he was finally here. The office always cleared out quickly on Friday nights. By 5:35 she'd been alone, and then she'd spent the last hour and twenty minutes watching the clock rather than getting much of anything done.

Sophie had tried to make herself work. She'd lectured herself that she wasn't paid to sit there daydreaming about some guy she barely knew. But daydream she had. About his arriving, her leading him to the break room where he'd set the pizza down and they'd gather plates and drinks together, and then eat. But at some point, they'd both reach for the same slice of pizza and their hands would touch. They'd both freeze, then look at each other and, somehow, they were suddenly kissing over the pizza. In her imagination, it was a pretty steamy kiss that led to touching, and then—

Sophie pushed the memory of her imaginings away as she hurried to the reception area. Those imaginings had left her hot and bothered all afternoon. Now the main focus of her fantasies was here. In the flesh. She wanted to jump him like a cheetah, but that just wasn't going to happen.

She had to be calm, cool, and collected, and not the horndog she was inside, Sophie lectured herself and shook her head at the very fact that she even had to. Honestly, she'd never had this kind of reaction to a man before. Sure, she'd been all excited and squealy at the thought of seeing Andrew again when they'd first started dating, and even with John and Derek, her two fiancés. But she hadn't sat around fantasizing about ripping their clothes off and climbing their bodies like flagpoles as she had done in her mind with Alasdair all afternoon since lunch.

Giving her head a shake to push those thoughts away as she reached the front door, Sophie glanced out and then frowned slightly when she didn't find Alasdair there. Leaning closer to the door, she looked up the sidewalk toward the parking lot and saw that he had parked, and was out of the vehicle, leaning in the front passenger door.

"Getting the pizza," Sophie muttered to herself. In the next moment a frown claimed her lips again and she thought, *Maybe I should go out and help him.*

That seemed silly, though. A big man like him could carry a pizza by himself.

But what was taking him so long? she wondered, eyeing him again.

"Dear God!" she gasped with disbelief when he straightened from the vehicle and she saw the mountain of boxes and cartons in his arms. "What on earth . . . ?"

Quickly unlocking the door, Sophie stepped outside. Alasdair was standing, staring back into the vehicle as she crossed the almost empty parking lot, but turned to see her coming and smiled with relief.

"Oh good. Do you think you could grab the pop? It rolled off when I straightened."

"Yes, of course," Sophie said at once, and moved around him to lean into the car. Only to pause in surprise. She'd expected a couple of small bottles of pop. What she found were four large two-liter bottles of pop. Apparently, Alasdair was thirsty.

Shaking her head, she leaned in to gather up the four bottles. They were heavy, but she managed it by catching three to her chest with one arm, and grabbing the other by the top. She then straightened out of the vehicle and hip checked the door to close it.

Facing Alasdair, she briefly surveyed what he was holding, then headed back across the parking lot. She'd left the door unlocked and didn't want to leave it that way any longer than necessary, so saved her questions for now and led him to the front entrance. Sophie managed to get it open with some juggling and effort and held it for him to enter.

But as she locked the door once inside, she asked, "Did you think you had to feed my coworkers?"

"No," he said, and then sounding alarmed asked, "Do I?"

"No, of course not," Sophie said on a laugh as she nodded for him to lead the way out of reception. "They all left at five thirty."

"Oh. Right," he muttered before disappearing around the corner into the hall and out of sight.

"If you didn't think you were feeding a large crew, what's with the—?" Sophie's question died when she turned the corner herself and found the hall already empty. She moved to the break room door and peered in, but he wasn't there.

"What's with the what?"

That question came from farther up the hall. Alasdair was coming out of her office door. His hands were empty now and he rushed forward to relieve her of the four bottles of pop.

"Sorry about that," he murmured as he took them from her. "I wasn't sure what kind of beverage you liked, so I got a selection."

"Oh," she said with a faint smile. "That was sweet."

"I'm glad you think so. I felt stupid myself," Alasdair admitted on an irritated growl. "I should have asked you what you like to drink. And what kind of pizza you like. Not to mention salads and appetizers," he added as they entered her office.

Understanding sliding over her now, Sophie eyed the six pizza boxes he'd set on the corner of her desk and the half a dozen Styrofoam cartons on top of them and guessed, "So you got a selection? Of everything?"

"Yes," he breathed, setting down the bottles of pop

now. "Hopefully you'll enjoy something out of—
You're laughing at me," Alasdair interrupted himself
to say as he turned to see her face buried in her hands
and her shoulders shaking.

"No," Sophie said at once, her silent chuckles dying
an abrupt death as she raised her head from her hands.
Voice firm, she said, "I'm not laughing at you. I just—
You— It's— This is so sweet of you," she settled on
finally.

"It is?" he asked warily.

"It is," she assured him solemnly, and then crossed
the few steps between them and leaned up on her tiptoes to cup his face between both hands and whispered, "Thank you," before pressing a gentle kiss to
his lips.

At least that was what Sophie had intended. A nice,
gentle peck of appreciation and gratitude for the trouble and expense he'd gone to in an effort to ensure she
would enjoy this meal.

However, when their lips touched, this crazy, electric zing hit at the point of contact and zipped through
her body. Sophie's mouth opened on a soft, surprised
gasp. Alasdair's tongue immediately slid in. One hand
moved around her waist drawing her close, even as the
other delved into her hair to cup her head and shift it
to the angle he wanted, and all hell broke loose in her
body. The next thing Sophie knew she was plastered
to his chest and moaning as her body writhed against
his and her mouth tried to make a meal of him.

Or maybe he was the one making the meal. She
couldn't tell and didn't care. She was on fire and he
was the only one who could ease her need. She just
knew it, so her hands slid around his head, and her

fingers tangled in his short hair, urging him on as he explored her mouth.

Sophie felt his hand at her breast and gasped, her body shuddering as his fingers closed over the eager globe through her clothes. One of his legs pressed between both of hers, his upper thigh rubbing against her there and she broke their kiss on a cry of excitement that turned into a surprised gasp when his other hand slid down over her butt to the back of her upper thigh to tug her leg up and around his hip. It allowed him to press more tightly against the core of her excitement and drew a deep guttural groan from her when he thrust against her.

Alasdair groaned too, then muttered something in a language she didn't understand before claiming her mouth again for an almost vicious kiss as he pulled her leg even tighter around him and thrust more firmly. Releasing his hair, Sophie clutched at his shoulders instead and held on for dear life as she kissed him back. The man was magic, a wizard. He was about to bring her to the fastest orgasm she'd ever experienced, standing right there in her office and fully clothed with just kisses and dry humping for cripes sake . . . and she wanted that orgasm desperately. She also wanted to strip him naked, rip off her own clothes, and crawl all over his body, but that would have to wait because she wasn't willing to give up the sensations he was causing in her right then.

In fact, when after the next thrust he suddenly stiffened and broke their kiss to look toward the door, Sophie growled and released one shoulder to try to force his face back so that she could reclaim his mouth. Even as she did, her own body writhed against his, trying to get him to move again. It wasn't until she heard a ringing sound that she stopped and turned to look at her office door.

"Is that—?"

"The front door," Sophie managed, but she was panting like a racehorse after a race.

Trying to regain control of her breathing and her crazy beating heart, she reluctantly let her leg slide off of his hip so that she was standing on both feet again. Sophie then released the hold she had on his face and shoulder and took a step back just a heartbeat before her office door opened.

"Oh." Megan stopped halfway through the door, surprise lighting up her face as she peered from Sophie to Alasdair. She blinked at them briefly and then held up an insulated bag. "Dad told Mom you were working late so she insisted I bring you supper." The bag lowered now as her gaze slid to Sophie's desk and she smiled wryly. "Guess you don't need it, though."

"No," Sophie agreed, and then paused to clear her throat when the word came out a weak croak. She then tried again. "Alasdair brought me dinner."

"I can see that," Megan said with amusement, her gaze sliding over the numerous pizza boxes and Styrofoam containers. Eyebrows rising, she glanced back to them to ask, "Are you guys expecting company? A pizza party or something?"

"Oh! No," Sophie said with realization, and then explained, "Alasdair wasn't sure what I'd like so got a variety."

"Nice," Megan said with approval.

"You are welcome to join us," Alasdair offered politely.

"Oh no." She shook her head and backed halfway out the door. "Thank you. I already ate, and I'm supposed to be meeting a date at the 44." She paused there, though, and frowned down at the bag she held. "I suppose you don't want this?"

"Are you kidding? Pass up Mama's cooking?" Sophie moved forward at once to claim the insulated bag. "I'll have it tomorrow. Thank her for me."

"Sure," Megan said, and then gave her the once-over, grinned, and waggled her eyebrows before turning to start up the hall with a laughing, "Have fun."

Sophie glanced down at herself and almost moaned aloud when she saw the state she was in. Her pencil skirt had been pushed upward from her leg being lifted, to wrap around Alasdair. It was now a wrinkled mass around her hips and upper thighs, and her blouse was gaping open, the top couple of buttons missing. No doubt her lips were rosy and swollen and her hair possibly a mess too, she acknowledged as she quickly pushed her skirt down and tried to draw her blouse closed, but it wouldn't stay closed with the buttons missing. It still covered everything, but was just open lower than she was used to.

Sighing, Sophie gave up on it and peered out into the hall in time to see Megan disappear around the corner into the reception area. Still, she waited there for the chime of the front door that would tell her that Megan had left.

While Sophie waited, she considered what to do next. Starting up with Alasdair again was a definite no. This was a place of business and Megan wasn't the only one who might show up. Bobby had been known to drop in and check on her when she worked late, as had her foster father, George Tomlinson, or Papa as she had come to call him over the years.

Despite that, Sophie was even now fighting the urge to throw herself at the man. The passion he'd stirred in her was still there, bubbling under the surface, urging her to lock her office door and—

The sound of the door chime caught her ear, bringing an end to her thoughts. Sophie reluctantly closed the door and turned to face Alasdair, trying to think of how to politely explain that they needed to not go back to doing what she really wanted to do. In the end, though, it wasn't an issue. Alasdair wasn't facing her anymore. He'd moved to her desk and was shifting the various Styrofoam containers off the stack of pizzas and onto her desk so that he could open the top box.

"What kind of pizza do you like?" he asked.

When Sophie didn't respond right away, mostly because she was trying to adjust mentally to the situation as it was, rather than as she'd expected, he glanced around at her and offered, "I'm sorry. I shouldn't have . . ." He gave a vague wave to where they'd been standing making out before Megan's arrival. "This is a place of business. I forgot myself for a moment. My apologies."

His words made a smile bloom on her face. Sophie supposed it was because she didn't think he had any reason to apologize. The truth was she'd kissed him. True, she'd only meant for it to be a quick peck, but she *had* started it. That quick peck exploding into the passion that had overwhelmed them both wasn't his fault. Or even hers she didn't think. It had just happened.

Of course, he was right and they had no business

behaving like that here. And now that Sophie knew what could happen between them, she would just be sure to keep a safe distance from him. While they were here. She definitely wanted to explore that passion again, though. Later. Somewhere else.

"What kind of pizzas did you get?" Sophie asked, rather than address his comment.

"A meat lovers, a deluxe, a veggie, a margherita, a Hawaiian, and a white pizza with chicken that I can't remember the name of," he ended with a slight frown.

"I'll have meat lovers," Sophie decided, walking over to set the insulated bag of Mama's food on her desk.

Nodding, Alasdair began to shuffle the boxes around, presumably to move the meat lovers to the top. As he did, he announced, "There are two salads to choose from, Greek and Caesar. Then there are four appetizers: grilled shrimp, breaded mushrooms, chicken wings, and breaded pickles."

"Wow. Okay. I'll get plates from the break room," Sophie said, turning to head for the door. "And napkins. And glasses and ice."

Pausing at the door, she swung back. "Maybe we should just eat in the break room."

When Alasdair paused, and glanced around with surprise, she added, "There's a table and chairs in there and only one chair in here, so . . ." She shrugged.

Nodding, Alasdair began to stack the containers back on the pizzas again. "Good thinking, Sophie Ferguson. Let's do it."

Smiling, she opened the door and then rushed back to gather the bottles of pop again before leading him to the break room.

It was really the oddest thing, but once in the break room the atmosphere between them totally changed. All the sexual tension seemed to evaporate as they worked together to gather plates, glasses, forks, and napkins, then got ice for their drinks while they heated up the plates of pizza they chose.

While Sophie took a slice of the meat lovers, Alasdair decided to try a slice from each of three pizzas, the meat lovers, the deluxe, and the Hawaiian. They popped each plate in the microwave and then settled at the table where Alasdair shrugged out of the black leather jacket he was wearing with black jeans and a black long-sleeved shirt. They then fell into a brief silence while they began to eat.

Sophie was about halfway through her first piece when Alasdair suddenly commented, "You called Megan's mother 'Mama.'"

Pausing, she glanced over at him with confusion for a minute, and then recalled saying something to Megan about not passing up Mama's cooking. Smiling, she nodded slowly. "I call Deb and George Mama and Papa at home, and have done since I was about fifteen. I just don't usually do it at work or . . . well, anywhere else really."

"You said they didn't adopt you, though," he reminded her. "Did you want them to?"

Sophie considered the question and then slowly shook her head. "I was fourteen when they took me in, nearly an adult," she pointed out. "Besides, I already had parents. My mom and dad were good people. Great parents. The love and acceptance they gave me . . ." She shook her head. "No one could replace them."

"So you called your foster parents Mama and Papa rather than Mom and Dad as a way to . . ." He hesitated, a frown claiming his lips as he tried to find the right term to use. Finally, he said, "Differentiate them? They were Mama and Papa, not your mom and dad?"

"Yeah, that's pretty much it," Sophie admitted with a wry smile. "I love them and appreciate everything they've done for me and wanted to honor that. But I didn't want to have to replace my parents to do it," she explained slowly, and then grimaced. "Megan and Bobby were bugging me to call them Mom and Dad. They wanted their parents to adopt me even. At least Megan did. I don't think Bobby cared one way or another, but Megan was really pushing for it."

"Why wouldn't Bobby care?" Alasdair asked with curiosity.

"Well, we can hardly marry when I turn forty if we're legally brother and sister," she pointed out with amusement, and when his eyes widened incredulously, she laughed at his expression. "We made a deal as teenagers, if neither of us is married by the time I turn forty we'll marry each other. It's mostly a joke," she added quickly when his mouth began to turn down. "Neither of us see each other that way. I mean, there's no attraction between us. He really is like a big brother to me, and I can't even imagine . . ." She made a face and shook her head at the very thought of having any kind of sexual relationship with him.

Sighing, she pushed the thought away and said, "As to why Bobby wouldn't care . . ." She shrugged. "He was a boy and two years older than us. I don't think he cared much about anything as a teenager. But as far as he was concerned, I was family, with or without a piece of paper stating it. He always treated me like a 'bratty little pain in the butt' sister just like Megan."

"Huh," Alasdair muttered, and took another bite of pizza, his expression thoughtful.

A moment of silence passed as they both ate, and then Sophie said, "One of your uncles said you were born in Scotland, but then moved to America." At least that was the gist of what the man had said. Though he'd used a more colorful phrase as she recalled. Something about jumping ship to the Americas and breaking his mother's heart, or the like.

"I did," Alasdair acknowledged. "Colle and I both moved to America some years back."

"How many years back and why?" Sophie asked at once.

Alasdair was silent for a minute, but finally said, "Colle."

"Your brother?" she asked with surprise. "He wanted to come over? You didn't?"

"I did," he assured her. "But really Colle was the driving force that had us leaving home."

"Why did he want to leave Scotland?" she asked with interest.

"Mostly our family," Alasdair said slowly, and then explained, "We have a large one, with lots of aunts and uncles and great-aunts and great-uncles, very few of whom have had children of their own yet, so they were all very . . ."

When he paused, seeming at a loss for how to describe the issue, Sophie suggested, "In your business?"

"Basically," he admitted. "Although they would have called it interested and concerned."

"Right." She nodded solemnly, but thought definitely in their business.

"Besides, there were certain expectations in the family. It was intended that we would join the family business and take up jobs at one of the family golf clubs. But Colle and I weren't really interested in that. It sounded boring and sedate to us. We were more interested in adventuring."

"So, you became policemen?" Sophie asked with amusement. She doubted being a policeman in Canada was much of an adventure. It wasn't exactly a hotbed of crime here compared to New York, and she suspected his job consisted mostly of writing speeding tickets and handling calls about domestic disputes. Although, she supposed it might have been a more interesting career in New York. But still not an adventure, Sophie thought as she grabbed her plate and stood to get another piece of pizza.

"Do you want anything while I'm up?" she asked as she grabbed another slice as well as a couple of wings, two breaded mushrooms, and a deep-fried battered pickle. She didn't bother with the shrimp. She'd never cared for shrimp, so left them for Alasdair.

"No need to trouble yourself. I will get my own." Alasdair stood to pick what he wanted while she stepped away and popped her plate into the microwave.

Sophie glanced to Alasdair while she waited for her

food and smiled at his expression as he contemplated the breaded and deep-fried pickles.

"They're dill pickles," she told him, able to tell from his reaction that he'd never had them before.

Judging by his expression when he glanced her way, her explanation hadn't helped much. "Are they any good?"

"I like them," Sophie said with a shrug, and then added, "If you like dill pickles you'll probably enjoy them." When that didn't change his expression, she suggested, "Try one. They're good with the dip."

Alasdair didn't look like he was sure that was a good idea, but he did pluck one out of the container and add it to his plate before moving on to the shrimp.

"You didn't have any shrimp," he commented as he put several on his plate.

"They're all yours. I'm not a shrimp fan," Sophie said with a shrug, and then watched with amusement when he just dumped the entire container of shrimp on his plate.

Smiling faintly, Sophie turned back to the microwave and watched the digital countdown, then pulled out her plate. She closed the microwave door and turned, not realizing Alasdair had moved up next to her until she crashed into him. The collision knocked her plate up and Sophie gasped in shock and pain as the hot pizza and appetizers were crushed flat between them.

"Ow, ow, ow," Sophie gasped, leaping back and pulling the plate away. The appetizers immediately fell to the floor, but the pizza didn't. The heated cheese and toppings were plastered to her blouse and burning her through the thin material. She didn't even think, but immediately tugged her shirt up out of her skirt and then jerked it open, sending buttons flying in her desperation to get it away from her skin.

Fourteen

"I'm sorry. Are you all right?" Alasdair asked from where he'd immediately knelt to begin collecting the appetizers from the floor. When she didn't answer right away, he glanced up to see her standing there holding her blouse wide-open. His eyes nearly popped out of his head as he caught sight of her pretty white lace bra. But then his gaze dropped to the large angry red patch of skin on her stomach.

"Damn," he muttered. Setting the gathered food on the counter, he grabbed the dish towel lying there and hurried to the sink to wet it. A moment later he was back, kneeling before her and pressing the now cold and damp cloth against the red patch of skin.

Gasping, Sophie instinctively sucked in her stomach in an effort to avoid the touch of the cold cloth on her hot skin and Alasdair peered up at her with worry.

"Does it hurt?" he asked, and then scowled and muttered, "Of course it hurts. Burns hurt."

"No. It's cold," Sophie said on a half laugh. "I don't think I got burned. It was just painfully hot. But I think I got the material away from my skin in time to avoid any actual damage."

Alasdair glanced up at her, and then lowered his gaze to the wet cloth he was holding to her stomach. After a hesitation he lifted it away to examine her skin.

Sophie looked too, relieved to see that the angry redness was already beginning to fade. She hadn't sustained an actual burn, but then she'd suspected as much when all she'd felt was shock at the cold of the damp cloth and no pain.

Her gaze switched to Alasdair then and, feeling suddenly uncomfortable standing there with her shirt open, she teased, "Unless you're planning to kiss it better, I should probably—"

Sophie's words died when he suddenly leaned forward and pressed his lips to her stomach. Startled both at the action as well as the shock of excitement it sent through her, she gasped, and grabbed his shoulders for balance as his tongue came out and slid over her suddenly sensitive skin. It was the last thing Sophie had expected, but not as unexpected as the effect it had on her.

Dear God it was just her stomach and yet the gliding of his tongue across her flesh there set off a storm inside her body. Excitement had goose bumps popping up across her skin, and a torrent of warm liquid was immediately pouring down through her body to pool between legs that were suddenly shaking.

As if aware of her response, Alasdair's hands shifted to her hips, helping to hold her up as he pressed his face to her pelvis and inhaled in a way that made her worry that he could smell her excitement. When Alasdair then pressed his mouth there and blew his hot breath on the sensitive, tingling flesh through her skirt and panties, Sophie almost came on the spot.

"Alasdair," she gasped, her hips shifting into the caress with a mind of their own.

He lifted his head slightly and peered up her body with hungry eyes that looked more gold than black, and then his hands left her hips to glide up her stomach and cover her breasts on top of her lace bra. Sophie immediately shifted her hands to cover his and let her head fall back on a moan as he began to massage her aching flesh.

Sophie looked down again when she sensed movement and saw that he was rising up on his knees so that his face was level with her breasts. She held her breath and didn't protest when he tugged one cup aside to free the eager globe inside. When Alasdair then covered it with his mouth, drawing not just the nipple but a good portion of the breast itself into his mouth, she cried out and shifted her hands to his head, urging him on as he began to suckle and tug at the excited flesh.

It was a lot. Too much. And not enough at the same time and Sophie was suddenly desperate to have his mouth on hers. Unable to find her words, she instead tugged on his hair in a silent effort to urge him upward.

Alasdair responded at once, letting her breast slip from his mouth as he straightened to his feet and covered her lips with his. She opened at once, inviting him in and groaning with relief and pleasure when his tongue slid in to fill her. His hand was at her breast again, squeezing the heavy globe and then lightly pinching her nipple, and Sophie groaned into his mouth, her hips shifting against him. Wanting more, she reached her hand down between them to find the hardness she could feel pressing against her, but Alasdair caught her hand with his free one and tugged it behind her back. The move arched her more fully against him, and he broke their kiss to take advantage and lower his head to her breast once more.

Sophie's eyes popped open on a cry of excitement at the jolt that sent through her, and then screamed in shock as her gaze landed on the window over the break room sink and she saw a shadowed figure staring in at them.

When Alasdair stiffened and pulled back to peer at her with surprise, she slid from his arms and scrambled to tug her blouse closed, explaining breathlessly, "Someone's out there."

Alasdair turned toward the window, but of course the person was gone. Still, he walked over to look out, and then turned and hurried from the room. A moment later, Sophie heard the chime of the door opening, and slowly followed his path out into the reception area to keep a wary eye on the now unlocked door as she waited for him to return. She spent that time trying to do up her blouse, but there were precious few buttons left now. It was also still covered with cheese, tomato sauce, and chunks of meat that were cold and clammy against her skin through the silky material and made her grimace with disgust. She really wanted to rip the damned thing off, but she didn't have replacement clothes here. Just the sweater she'd worn on top that morning because it had still been cool.

She'd take her blouse off and pull that on, Sophie

decided. But not until Alasdair returned. That thought
had barely made it through her mind when the chime
made her look toward the door to see Alasdair returning.

"There was no one out there," he said as he locked
the door. "But I heard a vehicle engine starting up
when I looked out the break room window. They must
have pulled out before I got to the door." He raised
his eyebrows in question. "Could it have been Megan
coming back for something?"

Sophie shook her head. "I only caught a glimpse, but
I'm pretty sure it was a man." Turning, she headed toward the hall before saying, "It could have been Bobby
dropping by to check on me. Or Papa, Mr. Tomlinson,"
she corrected herself. She'd trained herself never to call
George Tomlinson "Papa" in the office. Just as Megan
and Bobby avoided calling him Dad or Father here. It
was an effort they all made to try to be professional.
"They often check on me when they know I'm working
late."

"Do they often park and look in the windows before
coming in?" Alasdair asked dubiously.

"No," Sophie admitted, but then changed the subject
and said, "I don't have any spare clothes to change into
here so I'd say my working late is done for tonight."
Pausing as she reached her office door, she glanced
back to ask, "Would you like to take the pizza and
stuff to my place to finish up?"

Even from that distance she could have sworn his
eyes began to glow golden as his gaze swept down her
body in a caress she could almost feel. "Yes."

His voice was gravel, smoke, and full of promise.
It sent a fine shiver through Sophie that had her swallowing as she nodded. Her own voice was husky and

a little breathless when she said, "I'll grab my purse then and come back to help gather the food."

She ducked into her office then and stripped off her blouse as she crossed the room. Pretty sure it couldn't be saved, Sophie dumped it in her garbage can, and grabbed her sweater off the back of her chair to pull on. It was a knee length kimono-style sweater without buttons, but she found a pin in her desk drawer that she placed at the level of her bra bottom. It left a lot of cleavage on display and the bottom flowed out to the sides as she walked, leaving a lot of stomach on show as well, but Sophie didn't care. She doubted she'd be wearing it long anyway.

Alasdair already had almost everything cleaned up and packed away when she got to the break room. He was just downing the last of his soda when she entered. He then quickly rinsed the glass and set it next to her own already in the draining rack, and they began to gather up all the food he'd packed away. Everything but the shrimp, she noticed. He must have gobbled that up while he'd cleaned too, she thought, and was kind of glad. Sophie disliked it enough that she didn't even really want it in her refrigerator at home.

They were quick about turning off the lights and locking up, then Sophie helped Alasdair load the pizzas and everything into his SUV before hurrying to her own car. She was starting the engine before it occurred to her that she hadn't thought to tell him her address. With that in mind, she kept an eye out as she drove, to be sure she didn't lose Alasdair, who was following her.

Once at her apartment building, Sophie waved Alasdair to the drive around in front of the entrance, and then drove down into the underground parking to her designated spot. By the time she parked, retrieved the foldable shopping trolley she used for groceries from her trunk, and took the elevator up to the ground floor, Alasdair was waiting at the door with the bags she'd found at work for the pops and appetizers.

"I'll bring the pizzas," he said as he helped her load the bags into the trolley so that the containers holding the salads and appetizers wouldn't get crushed.

"Don't be silly. I can set the pizzas on top and you won't have to carry anything," Sophie insisted as she straightened from arranging the bags.

"Are you sure?" he asked.

"Positive. That way if you can't find a parking spot close by, you aren't having to cart the pizzas a long distance," she added.

After a hesitation, Alasdair nodded and then hurried back to his SUV for the pizzas.

"Just buzz once you get back and I'll let you in," Sophie told him as she unlocked and opened the glass door to the lobby.

Nodding, Alasdair watched until she had crossed to the elevator and pressed the button. Fortunately, one of the elevators was on the ground floor and the door opened at once. Sophie steered her trolley onto it and then pushed the button for her floor and waved at him as the elevator doors closed.

Alasdair got back into the SUV he'd borrowed from work, and then winced and rubbed his stomach. While he'd enjoyed the pizza when he'd eaten it, it wasn't sitting well. He'd started having sharp pains shortly after leaving Sophie's workplace and they were getting worse by the minute.

Or maybe it was the shrimp, Alasdair thought as he shifted the SUV into gear. In the end, he'd had more shrimp than pizza. He'd kept popping the little morsels into his mouth as he'd worked to clean up their mess in the break room, and had ended up eating the lot of them. Alasdair had heard that seafood could go bad quickly if not kept refrigerated and by his guess there had been more than an hour between when he'd picked up the food and when they'd finally sat down to eat in the break room. Who knew how long it had been done and waiting at the restaurant for him to pick up before that.

It would be better if it was the shrimp, since Sophie hadn't had any, he thought grimly as he stopped his vehicle at the end of the curved driveway to eye traffic. There wasn't much at that hour, but there *was* a car across the street just pulling out of a parking space and driving away.

"Damn, some good luck for a change," he murmured under his breath, and quickly pulled out onto the road to claim the spot. It was as he got out of the SUV moments later that the pain in his stomach went from a growing ache to a stabbing pain. It was bad enough that it had him stopping abruptly beside the vehicle and hunching forward, both hands moving to his stomach. It felt like someone had stabbed him.

Definitely bad shrimp, Alasdair thought grimly, and staggered around to the back of the SUV, intending to grab a couple of bags of blood to help his body deal with the issue it was having. One minute he was opening the back of the SUV to access the blood cooler, and the next he was on his knees between his vehicle and the one behind it, tossing up his stomach's contents onto the pavement. He'd heard the term *projectile vomiting* before, but never experienced it until now. It was painful and nasty, made worse by the volume of blood accompanying the ejection of food from his body.

There was a lot of blood. In fact, once the food was gone, he kept vomiting up blood for several minutes before it finally stopped, but then he felt much better. At least, his stomach felt better. The pain was gone, he just felt dried out and a little crampy everywhere. He needed to top up on blood to make up for what he'd lost, Alasdair realized as he slowly got back to his feet.

Turning to the open back of the SUV, he climbed inside and pulled the door closed. He didn't need anyone witnessing him sucking back bags of blood.

In her apartment, Sophie quickly kicked off her high heels, rolled her trolley into the kitchen, and began to store everything in her refrigerator, which turned out to be something of a trial. Living alone, she didn't have tons of food in her fridge, but six large pizza boxes, four large pops, and all the salads and appetizers took up a lot of room. It required some rearranging and clever stacking to fit everything in.

The entire time Sophie was working at it, she was listening for her buzzer, sure Alasdair would be back before she finished. But he obviously had some trouble finding a parking spot, because she was just finishing when her buzzer finally sounded.

Pushing the refrigerator door closed, Sophie rushed out to the buzzer and pressed the button to let him in. Then she turned and walked to the end of the entry hall to look into her living room to be sure it was clean.

Satisfied that she didn't need to rush around cleaning up, Sophie turned and walked back toward the door. She then stood there shifting from one foot to the other as she waited, her mind replaying what had happened in her office and then in the break room between her and Alasdair. She was pretty sure they were going to pick up where they'd left off when he got here. At least, that was her plan. It was why she'd put everything in the fridge. They could warm it up and snack on it later. Unless he was really hungry, of course. Maybe he'd want to eat first.

Sophie was fretting over that when he tapped on her door. Stepping forward, she pulled her door open, took one look at his expression, smiled, and grabbed him by his shirtfront to drag him into her apartment.

It was all she had to do. Alasdair had taken her in his arms and was kissing her before the door closed behind him. Sophie kissed him back, but this time she didn't want to just clutch at his shoulders or bury her fingers in his hair. This time she slid her hands up and over his chest, moaning into his mouth as her body responded with pleasure.

Alasdair immediately walked her backward and then turned and pressed her up against her hall table. He broke their kiss then and—pinning her against the table with his hips—leaned back to unsnap and carefully remove the pin she'd put in her sweater. He closed and then dropped it, tugged her sweater off her shoulders to her elbows, then undid the clasp of her front-closing bra and pushed that off her shoulders as well. Alasdair didn't fully remove either item of clothing, but instead they somehow ended up tangled around her lower arms, so that her hands were trapped behind her back.

Sophie was trying to untangle herself when his hands closed over her breasts and his mouth covered hers. Groaning, she arched into his caressing hands and kissed him back, her hips pushing forward against him as he sent a fire rushing through her body that had her legs weak and trembling.

"I want to touch you too," Sophie groaned when he finally broke their kiss to trail his mouth across her cheek.

"Later," Alasdair growled as he nipped at her ear, then he suddenly dropped in front of her, his hands leaving her breasts to clasp her outer legs just above her knees.

Blinking, Sophie peered down to see that he was now kneeling before her. Her breath shallow and fast, she watched as his hands began to slide upward, pushing her skirt before them until her white lace panties came into view. He stopped then to lean forward and press his mouth to the delicate lace, and Sophie cried out and went up on her tiptoes in reaction as he caressed her through the delicate cloth with his lips and tongue. She didn't even notice when his hands continued pushing her skirt upward. Not until it was bunched around her waist and he slipped his fingers into the top of her panties and began to pull them down until they pooled around her feet.

"Oh God," Sophie gasped when he caught her by one foot and lifted her leg so that he could press a kiss to her inner thigh. But she lost all ability to form actual words when he continued to lift that leg until it rested over his shoulder and then buried his mouth between her thighs.

A strangled scream ripped from her throat at the first flick of his tongue over her damp flesh and then all Sophie could do was gasp and pant, head back and body straining.

Suckling with his lips and lashing her with his tongue, Alasdair drove her wild, bringing on a fierce frenzy that ended when he pushed his tongue into her, setting off an explosion in her body that brought the world crashing down on her, blanketing her mind with darkness.

Fifteen

Sophie woke up alone on her bed with one of the throws from her living room covering her. Her hands were free now, her bra and sweater gone, but she was still wearing her skirt she saw when she lifted the throw to peer down her body. The skirt was no longer tangled around her waist, but had been tugged back into place, she noted.

Releasing the throw, Sophie let her head drop back on the bed and closed her eyes as she wondered where Alasdair was. He hadn't left, had he? She worried over that briefly and then groaned as her mind concluded that he likely had. Why would he stick around? He'd given her the most mind-blowing orgasm of her life and she'd fainted like a Victorian miss and left him high and dry. Why would he stick around after that?

"Good. You're awake."

Blinking her eyes open, Sophie stared wide-eyed at Alasdair as he entered the room with a tray in hand.

He was still fully dressed, minus the leather jacket he'd been wearing earlier, and it was only then that she realized he'd still been wearing even that in the entry while he'd—

"I hope you're hungry?"

Sophie forced her thoughts away at that question, murmured, "Yes," and finally moved. She sat up, clasping the top of the throw to her chest, but it hampered her when she then tried to shift up the bed so that she could lean against the headboard. Deciding it was silly to be so concerned about covering up when he'd already seen everything, she quickly gave that up.

Letting the throw drop to pool around her waist, Sophie scooted up the bed to where she wanted to be and then hesitated when she saw that Alasdair had paused halfway across the room and was staring at her.

"Is something wrong?" she asked with uncertainty. "Have you changed your mind? Did you want to eat out in the dining room instead?"

"Nay." The word was a soft growl with a definite Scottish sound to it. "But ye may be wantin' to cover that bonnie body o' yers, lass, do you want to eat. Else I cann'y be promising no' to ravish ye again instead o' feed ye."

Sophie's eyes widened at both the sexy damned accent and his words. The combination of that and the hunger on his face had a desire rising up within her that could not be satisfied with food. Her gaze dropped to the plates of pizza and appetizers on the tray with two glasses of pop, and then moved back to his face and she briefly struggled with her decision. Alasdair was obviously hungry or he wouldn't have gone to get the food. Would it be selfish of her to delay their eating?

Her gaze shifted back up to his face. It was his expression that decided the matter for her. Sophie was pretty sure the hunger on his face wasn't for pizza. So, she didn't tug the throw up to cover herself. Instead, she tossed it aside and then stood up, unzipped her skirt, and let it drop to the floor. That was all she had to do to be completely naked and it was enough. Alasdair immediately bent to set the tray on the floor, then straightened and began to remove his shirt as he started forward. He didn't bother to undo the buttons and remove it properly, he simply tugged it open, uncaring of the buttons that popped off with the maneuver.

Sophie's eyes widened as much at the sight of his beautiful chest as the action itself, which frankly was sexy as hell to her. But then her gaze got caught on the wide expanse of his chest and the shifting of his muscles as he shrugged out of the shirt and let it drop to the floor. Alasdair's hands moved to his belt and jeans next and she watched with fascination until he stopped in front of her. He'd managed to undo the belt and the button of his jeans by that point, but then gave up on them to reach for her.

Sophie sighed as his hands closed on her hips and went willingly when he drew her against his chest. But when he bent to kiss her, she reached down to help with his zipper, eager to get him naked. However, the minute her hand touched metal, Alasdair suddenly turned her sharply until her back was to him, and then closed his arms around her as he began to nuzzle her neck.

"I want to make love to you," he growled by her ear. Sophie shivered in his arms at both the words and the feel of his breath against her ear, and then let her head fall to the side and moaned as he began to kiss her neck, then caught the tender skin between his lips and sucked as he fondled her breasts. Both felt so damned good, and she shifted her hips, rubbing her butt against his groin, then gasped out a cry when one of his hands suddenly left a breast to slide quickly down over her stomach and palm her between the legs. Cupping her there, Alasdair urged her bare bottom more firmly back against the rough cloth of his jeans and she could feel him growing and pushing back through the cloth.

"Condom." Sophie gasped the only word she could manage as his clever fingers slid between her folds to find and caress the center of her excitement.

"Aye," he growled, thrusting a finger into her even as he continued to caress her.

"Yes," she cried, thrusting into the caress.

His second hand gave up her other breast then, and she felt it between them but found it hard to pay it any attention with what his first hand was doing. She did notice, though, when the rough cloth was no longer rubbing against her bottom. Sophie realized he'd done what she'd wanted to and finished undoing and shoving down his jeans. She felt a moment's regret that he hadn't allowed her to do it, and then he used both the hand between her legs and the other now across her chest again to urge her back more firmly against him. Her back was now rubbing his chest and her bottom nestling a hardness that felt huge in this position.

Alasdair caressed her on three fronts, the fingers of the one hand between her legs, gliding over slick skin, while the other hand began to move freely between her breasts, giving first one and then the other attention even as he alternated between nuzzling her neck—sucking at the tender flesh there—and nipping at her ear.

With her arms pinned to her sides by his arms around her, all Sophie could do was moan, groan, and writhe in his embrace. But the multipronged assault soon had her moaning in frustration and twisting her head up and back toward his in search of his mouth. He gave it to her, kissing her urgently if only briefly, and then he urged her forward, bending her over the side of the bed.

Sophie had barely rested her arms on the mattress surface when he withdrew his caressing hands. He then caught her by the hips, lifted her, and thrust into her from behind and she cried out, then tried to muffle the sound by biting into the comforter on her bed as he withdrew and thrust in again. Sophie had no idea if he continued to thrust. That was as much of the ride as she could take. Her body shuddered and jerked as pleasure burst over her, lights exploding behind her closed eyes that quickly died out as she sank into unconsciousness again.

The next time Sophie woke up, she was not alone in bed and she wasn't on her back. Instead, she was lying on her stomach on top of Alasdair in her bed with the sheets and comforter covering them both.

Sophie lay completely still, her mind replaying what had happened, but then she lifted her head and eyed him narrowly. She wasn't surprised to find him awake and watching her. "Did you at least come this time?"

Alasdair's eyes widened at her forthright question, and then he grinned. "Of course."

Sophie relaxed a little at this news, but asked, "Why don't you want me to touch you?"

Apparently, that question was a little too forthright for him. Alasdair stiffened, his expression freezing briefly before it became shuttered. Finally, he asked, "What makes ye think I don'y want ye to touch me?"

Sophie's eyebrows rose slightly at the return of his accent. She'd noticed it came and went and wondered why. Before this, it had only shown up at times when she'd thought he was turned on. But she didn't think he was turned on now. Was stress bringing his accent out? She wondered over that and then gasped in surprise when he suddenly rolled in the bed, putting her on her back and coming down on top of her.

"What are ye thinkin', lass?" he asked, catching her hands and raising them over her head. Alasdair pressed them to the mattress, holding them there as he used a knee to quickly urge her legs apart. He then settled in the cradle of her thighs and shifted his hips so that his erection rubbed against her core, making its presence known. His head then dropped to her chest, and he caught one nipple between his lips, tugging on it gently once, twice, then a third time before he murmured, "Hmmm?" around her now tight, excited nipple.

Sophie moaned as pleasure coursed through her on a warm, wet wave. She couldn't believe that her body was capable of it at this point. She'd come twice already. Which might not seem like much in the normal course of events, but these hadn't been normal orgasms. Sophie had never before had orgasms so powerful that she'd fainted during them.

"Hmmm?" he hummed around her nipple again, sending another wave of heat and need through her.

"I . . ." Sophie began, but couldn't seem to remember what he was asking her or even what they'd been talking about. It was hard to think with her body throbbing and burning as it was.

"Sophie love," he growled, releasing her nipple and raising his head to look at her face. "Use me."

Her eyes blinked open with confusion at that, and she met his gaze in question.

"Rub yerself on me, or take me into ye and find yer pleasure. I'll stay completely still. Ye're in control, love."

She didn't point out that with him on top of her, holding her hands over her head as he was, she was hardly in control. Sophie simply drew her legs up, planted her heels in the bed, and lifted and shifted herself, rubbing herself against him now in search of her pleasure. They both groaned as she did, and then she shifted slightly, letting him slide into her and she began to thrust against him, using him as he'd said.

Alasdair stayed as stiff and still as a plank, their gazes locked as she used him. Sophie wanted it to go on forever, but while intercourse alone didn't normally do it for her, this time was different. Every thrust sent another wave of excitement and pleasure slamming through her, each wave growing larger than the last. Sophie barely managed half a dozen such thrusts before she was riding the waves through an explosion of light and into darkness again.

Alasdair woke up uncomfortable and cold. Frowning, he lifted his head to look around and grimaced when he saw that he was lying slumped in the open door of Sophie's refrigerator with her unconscious in his lap. It was only then he recalled their last round of loving. They'd come out in search of food and had been retrieving it from the refrigerator when he'd reached past her to grab one of the containers of appetizers. His arm had brushed her nipple, she'd gasped, and he'd bit back his own gasp as excitement and pleasure had rushed through her and echoed through him. Alasdair had then made the foolish mistake of kissing her. Once that happened, they were both lost. The next thing he knew, she was in his arms, her legs around his hips and they were going at it like bunnies right there in the open door of the fridge.

Although, Alasdair thought now, he supposed bunnies would have lasted longer than the half a dozen thrusts he'd managed before they'd both found their pleasure and passed out.

"Idiot," he muttered to himself, knowing that losing himself like that wasn't just foolish, but could have been deadly for Sophie if they'd fallen wrong. It was why he'd immediately moved her to the bed after waking up from their first encounter in the entry. He'd woken up that time with a splitting headache and blood on the floor under his head from hitting it as they'd passed out that time.

Alasdair had no idea how bad the head wound had been. It had healed by the time he woke up, so he'd carried her into the bedroom and laid her on the bed, then quickly gone back to clean up the blood on the floor. Alasdair had followed that up with washing the dried blood out of his hair before preparing the tray of food he'd taken in to her.

Fortunately, Sophie hadn't been hurt that time, and didn't appear to be injured now either. He'd apparently taken the brunt of it again, landing on the floor with her on top of him. This time there was no blood to suggest he'd sustained an injury, and no mess to clean up. Still, he wasn't sure how long Sophie would sleep, so felt it was best to get her to the bedroom quickly. Alasdair didn't want to risk her waking and starting something up again until he had a soft surface for her to land on.

Sophie didn't stir when he shifted and lifted her and then got to his feet. Before leaving the kitchen, Alasdair used a foot to push the refrigerator door closed, and then his gaze landed on the oven's digital clock and he cursed softly when he saw that it was after eleven o'clock. His shift started at midnight. He needed to get moving.

A thump and soft curse woke Sophie. Opening her eyes, she was just in time to see Alasdair bend to pick up something. It wasn't until he'd set it on her dresser that she recognized the orange-and-white container of her day serum facial cream. Obviously, he'd knocked it over on his way to the door, she realized, when he released it and then walked out of the room, pulling the door closed behind him.

He was wearing his clothes, her mind suddenly

pointed out once the door was shut. Including his leather jacket.

Jerking upright in bed, Sophie glanced to the clock on her bedside table. Her eyes widened incredulously when she saw that it was nearly eleven thirty. He had to go to work, she recalled.

Tossing aside the sheet and comforter covering her, she leapt out of bed. Her housecoat was hanging from a hook on the back of her bedroom door. Sophie snatched it as she opened the door and then shrugged her arms into it as she hurried up the hall to the living room. She had no idea why she suddenly felt a need to cover up. Sophie had been naked with the man for hours now. Perhaps it was because he was dressed, she thought as she reached the living room and started across it.

Sophie was barely halfway across the large room when she heard her apartment door close. Cursing, she rushed forward to the entry hall and ran to the door, but when she opened it and looked out, the hall was empty and the door to the stairwell was just closing. Sophie was about to charge after him in the stairwell when she realized that she didn't have her apartment keys and her door would lock automatically when it closed behind her.

Clucking her tongue with irritation, Sophie turned back into the apartment and hurried into the kitchen where she'd placed her purse on returning home earlier that evening.

Had it only been earlier that evening? It felt like a lifetime had passed since she'd pulled Alasdair into her apartment, but a quick calculation told her that little more than three hours had gone by. It was amazing how much a person's life could change in that time, Sophie thought as she dug through her purse for her keys. Heck, until yesterday evening she hadn't even known the man existed.

And now you're about to chase after him like some desperate stalker type, her mind pointed out as she finally found her keys and hurried back out to the entry.

Sophie paused abruptly at her door when that thought coursed through her mind.

"Damn," she breathed as it suddenly occurred to her that she was about to race out of her apartment in nothing more than a robe. And all to chase after a man like some pathetic—

"Shut up," Sophie muttered to herself with irritation. She had never in her life been a pathetic anything.

"I'm not going to be some pathetic simp and chase after a man," she announced firmly. Nodding, Sophie slipped her keys into her pocket and turned away from the door to walk back to her bedroom.

So, Alasdair had left. So what if he'd slunk out of her apartment like a snake while she was asleep. Taking off without waking her to say goodbye or arrange to see her again like she was some kind of cheap one-night stand. Hadn't she decided she would avoid dating and men after Derek's death? Yes, she had. This was for the best, Sophie told herself as she entered her bedroom.

Then she spotted the note on her bedside table and sprinted across the room to snatch it up.

Left for work. Didn't want to wake you. Will call in the morning.

A.

A smile curved Sophie's lips as she read the short missive. He certainly had pretty handwriting for a man. And he was going to call in the morning.

Squealing, she pressed the letter to her chest and spun on the spot. Then she stopped abruptly and headed out of her room again, this time hurrying to the sliding door to her balcony. Unlocking it, she pulled it open and stepped out into a surprisingly cold night. It had been cool when she'd left the office, but a bitter wind was blowing now, putting a chill in the air that was threatening the arrival of winter.

Tugging her housecoat more tightly around herself, Sophie retied the sash and then crossed her arms over her chest and hurried to the railing on bare feet to peer down at the street below. Her apartment looked out on the front of the building. Hopefully she hadn't taken too long and would be able to see Alasdair when he—

A smile stretched her lips when he appeared below, crossing the circular drive in front of her building. She'd made it in time. Now what, though? Should she call out and blow him a kiss? Wish him a good night at work?

She'd have to shout for him to hear her, Sophie acknowledged with a frown, and she had neighbors. A lot of them. Some of whom might be sleeping already and probably wouldn't appreciate her bellowing like some lovesick calf.

Sophie had just come to that conclusion when Alasdair suddenly glanced back over his shoulder and up and then stopped. Turning to face the building, he peered straight at her. Even from her balcony she could see the white of his teeth as he smiled, and then he pulled something out of his pocket and looked down at it briefly. It wasn't until he lifted whatever it was to his ear and she heard her phone ringing from inside her apartment that she realized what he held was his phone.

Smiling, Sophie hurried inside to her kitchen to pull her phone from her purse. She answered it as she headed back to the balcony.

"Hello, stud," she said lightly, trying to tamp down her excitement and at least not sound pathetically eager as she stepped back out into the cold.

"I'm sorry if I woke you. I tried not to, but had to go to work." His voice was a husky caress to her ear.

"Oh," Sophie breathed, and then gave her head a shake and tried to sound blasé as she said, "That was sweet. Thanks."

Reaching the railing again, she peered down at him. Alasdair had continued forward while she was gone and was now walking under a streetlight in front of the apartment building. She could see him much better there, but not well. He looked tiny from her balcony.

"You should go back to bed and sleep. I will bring breakfast by in the morning after my shift . . . if that is okay with you?" he added in question.

Sophie hesitated, and then shook her head. "No. You should sleep after your shift. Besides, I need to go in to work for a couple of hours tomorrow morning to make up the last of the time I missed for the wedding," she told him, and hesitated briefly before adding, "But I'll be free for the rest of the weekend after that."

Sophie could actually hear the smile in his voice when he spoke, so was surprised when his "I will" ended with "not."

Disappointment was just crashing down over her when he added, "I have the weekend off, but am hoping to spend it with a certain beautiful nymph who has bewitched me."

Sophie swallowed at those words, her heart suddenly pattering away in her chest. Trying for a light tone, she asked, "Anyone I know?"

"I want you, Sophie," he growled.

Her eyes closed as the words made their way into her ear and sent blood rushing straight down to the apex of her thighs.

"Go to bed. You will need your rest this weekend."

Sophie closed her eyes. His words sounded like a threat, but her body appeared to take it as more of a promise. Every inch of her flesh was suddenly tingling in anticipation. Swallowing, she cleared her throat and kept her tone light as she responded, "Stay safe, Alasdair. I have plans for that body of yours this weekend."

"I am already looking forward to it," he assured her. "Good night, Sophie."

"Good—" she began, but paused without finishing the word as movement distracted her.

At first, Sophie didn't see what had caught her attention. In fact, with its lights off as they were, the car was almost on him before she spotted the dark sedan speeding straight for Alasdair, who had stopped to peer back up to her balcony, probably because her good night had been paused midword. Sophie opened her mouth to shout a warning into the phone, but there wasn't even time for that before the car hit him.

Clutching her phone, Sophie watched in horror as the front bumper plowed into his legs. She watched him crash onto the hood, his head bouncing off the front windshield, and then his body vaulted over the hood of the car and slammed onto the pavement behind it as the vehicle sped off down the road.

Her scream finally leaving her, Sophie whirled and raced through her apartment. She didn't bother waiting for the elevator but instead ran for the stairwell.

Sophie had never taken stairs as fast as she did that night. Later it would occur to her that she was lucky to make it down the twelve flights without stumbling and breaking her neck, but that didn't even cross her mind then. She was just desperate to get to Alasdair.

Sixteen

The only thing Alasdair could think in the brief moment that he lay there broken in the road was that it was good he hadn't lost consciousness. He'd heard Sophie's scream as he'd been thrown over the roof of the car, and knew she'd be on her way down to him. Which meant that despite the injuries he'd sustained and the pain he was in, he had to get himself to the SUV and get out of there. He could not let her see that he was wounded. There was no way he could explain how quickly he would heal afterward.

That thought in mind, Alasdair forced himself to sit up and nearly passed out at the agony the move caused him. Panting, he took a second to take inventory of his injuries. Both of his legs were definitely broken, though in different spots. If the pain he was suffering hadn't already told him that, the sight of his fibula sticking out of his right leg and the way his left leg was twisted from the knee down would have clued him in to it.

Judging by the pain he was experiencing in his pelvis, hips, and lower back, Alasdair suspected one or all of those were also broken. As was his right arm, he noted, glancing down at the shattered limb. And there was something wet running down his head and neck. No doubt from a head wound. Not only had the side of his head smashed into the windshield of the car that had run him down, but he'd also hit the pavement headfirst when he'd come down hard off the back of the car that had hit him.

Knowing the exact injuries he'd sustained didn't really help or make a lick of difference in that moment. Alasdair still needed to get his ass in the SUV and quickly.

Gritting his teeth, he considered the situation. Standing was out of the question. His legs were not in working order, which meant he'd have to drag himself the rest of the way to the SUV. Fortunately, it was only about six feet away from where he'd landed on the pavement. Unfortunately, that six feet seemed like six miles in that moment.

Only the fear of Sophie seeing him like this gave him the strength and determination Alasdair needed to drag himself to the SUV. With just his left arm still in use, it was an arduous job, but he did make it to the vehicle, and even managed to open the door. He then grasped the steering wheel and pulled himself up to sit on the running board.

Panting and in agony, Alasdair paused briefly there to glance around the street and over at the apartment. Fortunately, there didn't seem to be anyone around to witness the accident, and Sophie hadn't yet made an appearance.

But she would, he reminded himself. Mouth tightening, Alasdair released the steering wheel and reached for the grab handle over the door. Using that, he managed to pull himself up onto the edge of the driver's seat. He then paused briefly to take a breath before using his unbroken arm to lift each leg inside one after the other. He then tugged the driver's door closed with relief.

The worst of it over, Alasdair sagged back in the seat and closed his eyes as he waited for the shattering pain to ease up. It wasn't going to stop, and he knew that, but he was hoping it would improve at least a little now that he wasn't moving. Sadly, his not moving didn't mean his body wasn't, at least not the damaged bones, tendons, and tissue. They were already trying to repair themselves, which was even more painful than the actual breaking had been. It didn't help that a lot of blood was being used up to do it either. He could already feel the cramping starting as the nanos in his blood mined his body for every last drop of the precious liquid they could find to use in the repairs. It was only going to get worse. He needed to get back to the Enforcer house.

There was still blood in the cooler in the back of the SUV, he hadn't used even half of it earlier. Alasdair briefly considered trying to get to it, but wasn't sure he could. It wasn't like dragging himself across the flat pavement. He'd have to maneuver into the back seat, and then over it into the open compartment in the back. That would cause a hell of a lot more pain than the cramping presently was. Besides, once there Alasdair suspected he wouldn't be able to control himself. He'd end up emptying the cooler of blood, which would make the healing kick into high gear. Badly wounded as he was, healing was not going to be easy or quiet. He had no doubt he'd end up screaming his head off once the nanos set to work in earnest, and this was no place for that.

Sighing, Alasdair opened his eyes and glanced toward the apartment building again. Sophie was just pushing through the front door and hurrying toward the street. She was barefoot, her robe flowing out to reveal that she was also bare under it as well.

Forcing himself to sit up, Alasdair ran his uninjured hand over his face to wipe away what he could of the dirt and blood that might be there. Hoping that the darkness would hide whatever he'd missed, he then reached around the steering wheel with his left hand to push the button to start the engine. When the center panel immediately lit up, illuminating him in what he suspected was gory detail, Alasdair cursed.

Working quickly now, he pushed the button to roll down his window and then turned the engine off again and tried to look natural and not like he was in agony.

"Are you all right?" Sophie's voice was high and anxious as she rushed up to the side of the vehicle.

"I'm fine," he growled. "You shouldn't be out here. It's cold and ye're barefoot. Ye're also naked under that damned robe. I want you to go right back inside and—"

"Let me see," she demanded, reaching for his door handle.

Fortunately, Alasdair was quicker than her and managed to hit the button to lock the doors before she could open his.

"Unlock the door, Alasdair. I want to make sure that

you're all right. You landed on the car hard when it hit you, and the ground even harder. You—"

"I am fine." Alasdair repeated the lie in a sharp tone. He then took a deep breath in an effort to sound less testy before adding, "It wasn't as bad as it probably looked from above. I saw the car coming out of the corner of my eye before it hit me and hopped onto the hood then somersaulted over the rest of the vehicle. I probably will not even have any bruising from it by tomorrow."

"But—" she began with a combination of confusion and disbelief.

"Sophie, love," he interrupted firmly. "I really have to get to work. I only waited here because I saw that you were no longer on the balcony and suspected you were on your way down here. Otherwise, I'd already be gone. Now go back inside. I need to get to work and you shouldn't be out here like this. I'll call you tomorrow."

Much to his surprise she stood silently for a minute, a stunned look on her face, and then gave a small nod and leaned quickly forward to press a kiss to his cheek. Before he could even react, Sophie then whirled away and rushed back across the street.

Alasdair released a relieved breath as she moved away. He watched Sophie until she was inside and stepping onto the elevator. But once the doors closed, he sagged back in his seat again and considered his situation. He needed to leave. If he didn't and Sophie came back out onto the balcony to check on him and saw that he was still there, he had no doubt she would come right back down and insist on getting a better look at him. He couldn't risk that.

Unfortunately, driving was impossible in his present condition. Neither leg was functional enough to manage the brakes and gas. Maybe he should call the Enforcer house and have Mortimer send someone out. They could control the amount of blood he took in, give him just enough to ease the cramping for the ride, then they could drive him back. They could even control Sophie if she should come back before they arrived and sorted out that he wasn't "fine" as he'd claimed. They could wipe her mind of whatever she might discover before their arrival too.

"Hey, buddy, you got any spare change?"

Stiffening, Alasdair opened his eyes to see a man in his early twenties jogging up to his open window.

"My girl got pissed and kicked me out of the car here in the middle of nowhere. I need an Uber or something to get home, but have no money," the young man explained when Alasdair didn't immediately respond. "I'd pay you back."

Alasdair considered the fellow, an idea taking shape in his head.

"What's your name?" he asked, not wanting to expend the energy it would take to read him.

The kid's eyebrows rose at the question, but he answered, "Eddie."

"Okay, Eddie," Alasdair said, hitting the button to unlock the doors. "Hop in. I'll give you a lift."

"Thanks, man," Eddie said with relief, and hurried around the front of the SUV to get to the passenger door. He had it open and was sliding in when he suddenly froze.

Alasdair had no idea if Eddie could smell the blood, or if he saw something that spooked him, but didn't wait to find out. He immediately slid into his mind, took control, and had him finish getting in and close the door. He then made him shift over to sit right next to him, straddling the center console. Much to his relief the kid had long legs and was able to reach the brake and gas pedals, so he had him start the SUV engine.

Handling the steering wheel himself, Alasdair had Eddie press down on the brakes and shift the SUV into gear, then ease his foot off the brakes and onto the gas so that Alasdair could steer them out of the parking space. It was a tricky business, much harder than it would have been had he been able to handle everything himself, but they managed it.

Alasdair relaxed somewhat once they had driven away from Sophie's apartment building. Mostly because he figured he could handle anything else that came at him that night. He could control mortal police officers if they got pulled over, just as he was controlling Eddie. But he could not control Sophie. That was part of what made her his life mate. But it was also what made certain things difficult.

Once they'd turned off Sophie's street, Alasdair had Eddie place his wrist near his mouth and then bit into the vein there and fed as he peered over his hand and steered. He made sure not to take too much, not just for Eddie's sake, but also for his own. He only wanted enough to reduce the cramping he was experiencing, not enough to have the healing start in earnest. Alasdair was pretty sure he wouldn't be able to drive while suffering the kind of agony that could bring on.

When he felt he'd had enough to meet the precarious

balance he was aiming for, Alasdair let Eddie have his hand back and concentrated on driving.

They were twenty-five minutes from the Enforcer house. Twenty-five minutes until he could blood up and heal. Alasdair kept telling himself that over and over during the long drive as he felt the crushed bones in his knee trying to reknit, and felt his fibula slowly pulling back into his body. He was having similar pains in his skull, pelvis, and arm, but knew the repair work was going slowly and wouldn't get far until he could feed properly. It was just something he was going to have to suffer for now.

"Sophie, love." The words played through her mind as she stared down at the spot where Alasdair's SUV had been. She had rushed out to her balcony the minute she'd hit her apartment after he'd insisted she go back inside, but he'd already left. Now she just stood there in the cold night air, his words playing through her mind. *Sophie, love.* She'd been so stunned at his use of the endearment that she'd allowed him to convince her to go back inside.

But those weren't the only words she kept hearing in her head. *I have the weekend off, but am hoping to spend it with a certain beautiful nymph who has bewitched me.*

Had she bewitched him? He'd certainly bewitched her. Sophie's body was still tingling from the things they'd done that night, and in anticipation of the weekend ahead.

Although, she was also a little concerned about

that fainting business. Sophie had passed out during every one of their half dozen lovemaking sessions. Well, they hadn't made love every time. The first time she'd orgasmed had been in the entry, and then the fifth time had been in the shower. Both of those had been purely oral not intercourse. And both times Alasdair had pleasured her and gone without her reciprocating, she thought guiltily. Irritation at feeling guilty was quick to follow, because she'd tried to reciprocate a couple times on waking, but he always managed to keep her from even touching him. Alasdair was always either holding her hands over her head, or tangling something around her hands or arms, hampering her ability to even caress him. She was beginning to think he had some kind of bondage fetish.

Sophie didn't know whether to be annoyed at the possibility or not. The truth was what he'd done to her felt so damned good she thought she might have a little leaning toward that fetish herself. Aside from a bit of guilt that she hadn't done for him what he had for her, she'd really enjoyed the night, and was sad that he had to work and it had had to come to an end.

Well, guilt, irritation at feeling that guilt when she didn't think it was her fault, and some concern about her repeated fainting. Maybe she should start taking iron supplements or something, Sophie thought, and then tried to recall how long it had been since she'd last been to the doctor for a checkup. Too long, she supposed. Sophie had always hated going to the doctor and avoided it at all costs. She should probably call and make an appointment. Just check to be sure everything was all right.

Sophie, love.

Alasdair's voice whispered through her mind again, sending another shiver through her body.

What a man, Sophie thought on a sigh, and then frowned as she recalled watching him catapult over the car that had hit him. That had scared her to death. She'd thought her curse was kicking in and she was watching yet another loved one die in front of her. It was enough for her not to want to see the man again. First her parents had died in a fire when she was a child, then her best friend had died from anaphylactic shock when she was a teenager. Those deaths had been followed by the accidental deaths of two fiancés she'd had . . . Sophie could not watch another person she cared for die. Not that she cared for him, she quickly assured herself. But her panic and agony when she'd watched him tumbling over that car and slamming to the pavement belied that.

"I can't believe he wasn't even hurt," she muttered to herself. It had been dark and she hadn't been able to see him very well, but he'd seemed fine, she acknowledged and murmured, "Crazy," as she let the scene play out in her mind again.

The driver hadn't had his lights on. He'd also been speeding and hadn't even tried to swerve around Alasdair. It had looked deliberate to her.

They really should have called the police, Sophie thought impatiently. And Alasdair knew that. The man was a police officer. He should have been calling 911 before she'd even got downstairs.

Maybe he'd report it when he got to work and have them put out an APB on the car or something, she thought next. Had he got the license plate number of the vehicle? Sophie had been too far away and viewing it all from the wrong angle to see it herself. Maybe she should call him.

"Girl, you're just looking for an excuse to hear his voice again," Sophie said to herself as soon as that thought cropped up. "You should go to bed before you do something pathetic and stalkerish."

That seemed like a good idea. Better than standing out here in the cold, at least. Maybe getting some sleep would help clear her thoughts. Right now, her mind was hopping from thought to thought like a mad bunny, taking her emotions along for the ride. Sleep seemed the smartest thing.

Nodding at the decision, Sophie turned and headed back inside to find her bed. It still smelled of Alasdair when she cuddled into it.

Seventeen

"Hey, Alasdair! You're late. Colle's been— Ohmygawd! What happened to you?"

Alasdair grimaced at that bellow from Francis, one of the guards that manned the gate at the Enforcer house. The man's voice, higher pitched in his shock, was piercing and just adding to the pain Alasdair was suffering. His head was pounding and had been for what felt like forever.

"Accident," Alasdair growled in response to the man's concerned question. "Need blood."

Francis nodded, his gaze skating first to Eddie, who was sitting still, his face vacant as they waited between the inner and outer gated entry to the Enforcer compound, and then to his partner, Russell, who had been running a mirror on a long stick under the vehicle to ensure there were no unwanted visitors clinging to the bottom of the SUV. Finished with that, Russell had now come up to peer in the passenger side window, drawn by Francis's shocked exclamation.

"Call it up to the house and open the gate," Russell instructed after a quick examination of Alasdair. Unlike Sophie, Francis and Russell had incredible night vision, as did all immortals. They could see the wounds and blood and didn't hold him up any longer than necessary.

"Do you need one of us to drive you up to the house?" Russell asked as the gate began to open.

Alasdair shook his head. "We can manage." He started then to have Eddie shift them back into drive, but paused to say reluctantly, "But tell 'em I'll need help getting inside. Both my legs are broken . . . and possibly my pelvis."

"And your arm, plus your skull is partially caved in," Russell added dryly, and then assured him, "Francis will tell them."

Alasdair grunted his appreciation and had Eddie shift gears and ease down on the gas to send them forward. Moments later, they were parked in front of the Enforcer house. Several people immediately converged on the vehicle, including his brother and uncles, who were the first to get to him.

"Damn me, lad. It looks like ye were tusslin' with a rhino," Uncle Connor growled as Inan opened the passenger door and took control of Eddie. He had the young man slide out on the passenger side of the vehicle to make room for Colle to climb in and get a better look at Alasdair.

"What happened?" his twin asked, reaching up to urge Alasdair's head to the side so he could get a look at the damage he'd taken there.

"Run down," Alasdair growled.

"Your arm looks broken," Colle said with a frown, shifting his attention from his head to the rest of his body.

"It is. So are me legs."

"Both?" Colle asked with alarm.

"Knee o' one. Fibula o' the other," he said, his words sharper than he'd meant because of the pain. After a hesitation, he admitted, "I can'y walk until they heal. If ye could just bring me some blood and give me a few minutes—"

"Screw that," Colle interrupted with disgust. "I'm not bringing you blood out here and leaving you to writhe in pain in the SUV so you can walk in under your own power. I'll carry you."

Colle was getting out of the passenger side, probably with the intent to walk around and grab him, but Uncle Ludan beat him to it. Opening the driver's side door, the older man didn't wait for Colle to make his way around the SUV, he simply leaned in to scoop him up like a bairn.

"I can walk," Alasdair protested, knowing that was a stupid thing to say since he very clearly could not walk.

"Shut it," Ludan ordered. "Ye'll be carried and ye'll like it."

Alasdair scowled at him for it.

Colle came up on Ludan's side as they headed for the house, and asked, "Who ran you down?"

Alasdair shook his head.

"You didn't see?" Colle asked with surprise.

"No," Alasdair sighed. "It was dark. I was on the phone with Sophie as I crossed the street. There was no traffic when I started across, and there was no warning. The car didn't have its lights on and came out of nowhere. I didn't even hear it or get a chance to jump out of the way."

"Must ha'e been one o' those new electric jobbies," Connor commented from Ludan's other side. "I hear they're quiet."

Alasdair was considering that when Inan crowded up between Connor and Ludan to ask, "Ye were at Sophie's?"

"Aye," Alasdair sighed.

"So ye did fit in the three dates, then? Did ye get to bed the lass?" Inan asked excitedly, and then answered his own question with, "Ye must ha'e if ye were coming from her place. Ye lucky dog!"

"Oh, aye, first food poisoning, and then getting hit by a car, I'm feelin' lucky all right," Alasdair muttered, but despite his sarcasm he did feel lucky on the Sophie front. Between the food poisoning and before being taken out by four thousand pounds of scrap metal on wheels, it had been a glorious night. Sophie was a wonder. There wasn't a shy or inhibited bone in her body.

Alasdair hadn't been sure what to expect as he'd waited for her to open her apartment door. He'd worried that, if it hadn't been the shrimp that had caused his stomach issues, she too might be suffering from their meal. If she hadn't, though, he'd thought they might eat, talk some more, and then perhaps—if there was an opportunity—he might lure her into his arms again. What he hadn't expected was for the woman to open her door, literally grab him by the shirt, and drag him into her entry, which had been redolent with the aroma of her body's excitement and need.

He didn't know who had moved first to kiss, perhaps they'd both done so at the same time, but they'd suddenly been kissing, and Alasdair had pretty much lost his head. That, added to the uninhibited way she'd responded to him, had made him lose his common sense and feast on her right there in the entry where she could have been severely injured when they found completion and lost consciousness.

But damn, it had been hot. Alasdair could still feel her quivering body in his hands, hear her moans and cries in his ears, and taste her passion on his tongue. He couldn't wait to see her again. There were so many things he wanted to do to and with her.

"I'm thinkin' yer gonna ha'e to wait until ye've healed a bit fer that, lad," Connor said, obviously having intruded on his thoughts.

His uncle's words brought Alasdair down to earth with a rather painful thump as he was forced out of his mind and back into his pain-racked body.

"But I'm glad we were able to help ye bed yer woman," Connor added.

Alasdair stiffened at those words, but before he could respond, Inan put in, "Aye, and from those memories in yer noggin', it's lookin' like ye did us proud with her, boyo. Good on ye, lad."

Alasdair merely scowled over Ludan's shoulder as he was carried into the house like a damned baby.

"We handled Eddie's memory and Bricker and Decker are taking him home."

Alasdair nodded at Colle's announcement and grunted

his version of a thanks around the bag of blood at his mouth. It was the first bag of a second round of four that he'd been offered since being carried up to his room and placed in bed. There hadn't been many questions once they'd got him inside the house. Instead, they'd read his mind while he'd consumed those first four bags of blood.

Alasdair had barely finished the fourth bag when the healing had started in earnest. The pain, or perhaps the healing itself, had sent his body into convulsions that had left him writhing and shuddering helplessly on the bed until the agony he was suffering had finally driven him into the dark oblivion of unconsciousness.

Alasdair didn't know how long he'd been out, but he'd woken up just moments ago to find Sam and his four uncles at his bedside waiting. When Sam had asked how he felt, all he'd been able to do was give a miserable grunt. He was still in terrible pain, but it seemed worse than before. Now he wasn't just in pain damned near everywhere, but he also felt dried out, as if every last drop of liquid in his body had been sucked from him.

Nodding as if he'd spoken all of that aloud, Sam had stood to move to a cooler on his bedside table and had retrieved four bags of blood from it. She'd then slapped the first to his fangs and sat down with the other three bags to wait. That's when Colle had entered.

His twin brother paused beside the bed, eyeing him with a combination of concern and discontent, and then shook his head. "It's hard to tell from your memory whether your stomach issue was food poisoning or just poisoning, or if the car hitting you was a deliberate attack, or just a case of bad luck."

Alasdair's eyebrows rose at the comment. He was pretty sure his stomach issue had just been bad shrimp. Sophie had eaten everything else he had and not suffered for it. As for the car hitting him, he'd been thinking that was just a case of bad luck. He'd been having a run of that lately. Besides, neither poison nor running an immortal down were likely to kill them, so it had probably been bad shrimp and a drunk mortal or some such thing. Just bad luck.

"We're not sure the stomach thing was bad shrimp," Colle said as if he'd spoken his thoughts aloud. "The amount of blood you vomited up suggests poison." He frowned and then added, "Although, you're right, poison wouldn't have killed you either."

"Maybe killing him wasn't the intent behind the attacks," Uncle Connor suggested.

Alasdair shook his head at once. A deliberate attack didn't seem likely, even if it had only been meant to hurt him. He didn't know anyone in Canada aside from his family and the few hunters he'd met since arriving. Why would anyone target him?

"Well, that's something we'll have to think about later," Colle said abruptly, and then added, "But right now, I have to get to work. Tybo and I are going to take the shift alone tonight."

When Alasdair grunted a protest around the bag at his mouth, Colle grinned at him. "You, brother, are in no shape to work. Besides, two of us will do, and you need to rest up and regain your strength for Sophie now that you've moved your wooing to the bedroom. We'll see you Sunday night if you can drag yourself from her bed."

Alasdair watched him go, troubled by something in

Colle's voice. His words had seemed light and teasing, but the tone itself had been more short and annoyed or something.

"He's hurtin' a bit is all," Inan said quietly once the door had closed behind Colle. "Yer findin' yer life mate changes things between the two o' ye. He can read ye now which is new, and definitely alters the dynamics o' yer relationship. He's tryin' to navigate that."

Alasdair frowned at this surprising bit of wisdom from his uncle, and then stiffened in surprise when Sam suddenly ripped the now empty bag away from his fangs and slapped on another. He tried to relax then, but he was thinking about Colle and the change in their relationship. As twins, they hadn't been able to read or control each other. They'd definitely enjoyed the benefits of not needing to shield their minds from each other. It had allowed them to be friends and companions and prevented the loneliness most immortals suffered until they found their life mate.

Now, if he was very lucky, Alasdair would be sharing that companionship and much more with Sophie, but Colle would lose that same companionship they'd enjoyed all these centuries. At least until Alasdair got past this first stage of finding a life mate where he was easily read by everyone. Hopefully, once that passed and he was no longer an open book, he and Colle could return to the companionable friendship they'd always had.

"While we ha'e ye here," Connor said suddenly. "We're thinkin' we need to come up with a plan fer ye to win yer lass's heart."

Alasdair's alarmed gaze flickered to his uncles.

Seeing them all nodding solemnly, he immediately shook his own head. He did not want their interference. He was wooing Sophie and doing just fine, thank you very much.

"Ye've got under her skirts, lad. But ye'll no' find her heart there," Connor said dryly. "And her heart's what yer needin' to win if ye're ha'e any hope o' convincin' her to be yer life mate."

Alasdair grimaced around the bag of blood at his mouth and slumped back against the headboard of his bed, resigned to listening to their advice. It wasn't like he could avoid it at the moment. So he waited for them to start telling him how he should lay siege to Sophie's apartment, or club her over the head, drag her somewhere remote and unescapable, and keep her there until she agreed to be his life mate.

"Damn me! We're no' cavemen, boyo!" Ludan snapped, obviously offended by his thoughts.

"Aye," Inan agreed with a frown. "Ha'e ye ne'er heard o' courtly love? That's what we were raised with, lad. And it didn'y include clubbing or laying siege."

Tearing the now empty second bag from his mouth, Alasdair snapped, "Well, what did it include, then?"

His uncles were old relics. Hell, he was an old relic, they were ancient. He found it hard to believe they knew anything useful about gaining the heart of a modern woman.

"In our day ye'd learn to play the lute and serenade her," Inan told him. "I won many a heart that way. No' a life mate's o' course. I've no' been lucky enough to encounter mine yet. But I did win hearts," he assured him, and then asked, "Do ye play any instruments, lad?"

Alasdair traded Sam the empty bag for a new one

and popped it to his fangs before shaking his head. He'd never been musically inclined.

"Hmmm," the four uncles muttered as one, and then Connor brightened and said, "Love poems."

When Alasdair's eyebrows flew up in horror at that, he nodded firmly.

"Many a warrior would write love poems to the lady they were enamored of. That worked a treat too. At least it did fer me," he added with satisfaction.

"Do ye think ye could write a—?" Inan began to ask, but paused when Ludan nudged him and pointed out, "The lad can barely speak. Ye can'y be thinkin' he'd be any good at writing poetry."

Alasdair scowled at his uncle over the bag of blood at his mouth, offended despite the fact that the man was probably right. He didn't speak much, and wasn't much of a letter writer either. It was doubtful he'd be much good at writing love poems, even for Sophie, who certainly deserved them.

"Hmmm," his uncles said as one again, and took a moment to think.

"Love tokens," Odart said suddenly.

Inan immediately began to nod and explained, "We used to exchange love tokens durin' courtship. Things like mirrors, girdles, rings, washbasins—"

Alasdair couldn't help himself, ripping the now only half-empty bag of blood away from his fangs, he squawked, "Washbasins!"

"Alasdair!" Sam snapped, leaping up to take the bag away from him as the blood sprayed everywhere.

"Sorry," he muttered, and scowled at his uncles for causing him to make the mess he had. "A washbasin as a love token?"

"Well, it was at the time," Inan said with a scowl of his own.

"Well, now we have sinks instead. Shall I send her one of those?" he asked sarcastically, a little frustrated because he was starting to worry that winning Sophie's heart was going to be harder than he'd feared.

"Out," Sam said suddenly, dumping the torn blood bag in the cooler where it couldn't damage anything. Straightening, she scowled at all of them and then directed her attention to his uncles and said more kindly, "I know you're trying to help Alasdair, but right now you're just upsetting and distracting him from feeding. He needs to feed, so he'll heal, and I need him to heal so that I can get back to the things I need to do, so you four need to leave."

"Or," Inan said, "ye could go do what ye need to do and we could make sure he feeds."

"Or, you can all go and leave me to deal with him," Marguerite said from the door, making them aware of her arrival. Smiling sympathetically at Sam, she moved farther into the room and added, "I came to see if you knew how Alasdair and Sophie were doing and Mortimer told me what happened. I'll sit with him while you get back to work. I know you're busy right now with various legal issues for Mortimer and Lucian. I'm happy to stay and help so you can get back to it."

"Thank you," Sam said with obvious relief. She gave the other woman a quick hug of gratitude, then turned to Alasdair's uncles. "Come on, you four. I've got some raw steaks in the fridge you can gnaw on for a bit while you think of more modern ways for Alasdair to win Sophie's heart."

The four men got reluctantly to their feet, but Inan said, "We had meat at the wedding, lass. We're good for a bit."

"Well, then, maybe you could go to the Night Club and try some of their specialty blood drinks while you think," Sam suggested as she walked to the door. "I hear sweet tooths are nice."

"The Night Club?" Connor asked with interest as the men followed her. "I heard G.G. owns it over here now too and has set up one o' the rooms like a good old-fashioned pub."

"I believe he has," Marguerite told them. "He's made several themed rooms. It's quite nice."

"Hmmm," the men said as Sam ushered them out of the room.

Marguerite smiled with amusement as she turned back to peer at Alasdair. "They are going to the pub."

Alasdair raised an eyebrow at her confidence, wondering if she could read his uncles.

"They are all younger than me," Marguerite said, answering his silent question.

He nodded in understanding, knowing that meant she could read them.

"Your uncles may be gruff and rough around the edges, Alasdair, but they love you and Colle," she said now as she settled on the chair Sam had been occupying. "I doubt you'll recall this, but they used to babysit you and Colle when you were bairns.

"Your mother, Marsle, was very young, just eighteen, when your father found her. Then she became pregnant with you and your brother almost right away. Your grandmother, Margareta, thought it would be best if she let that pregnancy go."

That was surprising. His father's mother had been nothing but a loving grandmother to him and Colle. Hearing that she'd wanted his mother to "let that pregnancy go" was more than a little shocking, and even hurtful.

"Margareta loves you both dearly," Marguerite said firmly. "But at the time she was concerned. Your mother and your father were still newly mated and in the fog that all newly mated go through. She was afraid that any child born at that time would be neglected. However, your uncles stepped up and took over caring for the two of you until the new life mate fog passed and your parents could be there for you both properly."

Alasdair relaxed and nodded in understanding. He couldn't imagine having a child with Sophie at this point. His mind was already so full of her, he found it hard to think of much else. Having a child to worry about would be difficult at best. He could easily envision a child being left by the wayside as they pored over each other's bodies in an orgy of need. And while they were unconscious afterward.

Marguerite nodded as if he'd spoken those thoughts aloud. "It's something Natalie and Valerian are struggling with right now. They both love little Mia dearly, but . . ." She shrugged, not needing to point out how powerful life mate sex was. "It's why they've decided to hire an immortal nanny. So that there is someone keeping Mia safe and well until the life mate fog passes. And that is essentially what your uncles were for you and your brother. Even after the fog passed for your parents, your uncles continued to spend a great deal of time with you both. I think they all think of you and Colle as more like sons than nephews. It's why they've always been in your business over the centuries, and why they were as hurt as your parents when you and Colle decided to leave for the Americas."

Alasdair grimaced as guilt pinched at him. Everyone had been upset when he and Colle had set out to sail to the Americas, but his parents and uncles had taken it hardest. Now he knew why.

"That is also why they are so determined to help you gain your Sophie," she added now with a faint smile. "So, try to be patient with them. Hmm?"

Alasdair nodded. He would try.

"Good. Now," she said, taking the empty bag from his fangs and slapping the last bag on. "You do not need to serenade or write love poems for Sophie to win her. In fact, just being you will win her over more than anything else, and that includes the fact that you are immortal."

When Alasdair showed his surprise at that, she nodded.

"I spent a good deal of time reading her mind during the wedding ceremony and that child has lost nearly everyone she has ever loved," she told him solemnly. "Her parents along with her beloved dog died in the house fire, then she lost her best friend to death as well, and her first love—well, he's still alive but in a coma, but two of her fiancés after that did die. She will not admit it easily, but Sophie is terrified that she is cursed, and that anyone who loves her will surely die. That fear may be taking a second seat to the passion and need she feels for you now, but when she starts to really care for you, it will surely pop up to cause issues. Telling her that you are immortal would go a long way to easing those fears."

Alasdair was considering that when Marguerite added, "But I must say, all these deaths in her life trouble me. I was only catching bits and pieces of memory that cropped up whenever Sophie observed Natalie and Valerian's happiness and thought on her own chances of love. From what I gathered, none of these deaths were from natural causes." She fell silent for a minute, her expression troubled, and then said, "I am not saying that foul play was involved, but . . ." She shook her head. "It just troubles me. I think you should try to get her to talk to you about these losses. Perhaps you can get a clearer picture and sort that out."

Alasdair nodded solemnly. He would ask Sophie about her childhood and past and try to get her to talk about the people she'd loved and lost. It was not going to be an easy task. Life mate sex was addictive and overwhelming. It would be hard to think of much else when near her. But he'd find a way, he decided.

"Maybe you should take her away on an overnight trip," Marguerite suggested. "Somewhere out in public where you would be unable to indulge in life mate sex. In fact, I think that is probably for the best if you want any chance of actually talking to her."

Alasdair was just nodding at that when the effects of the blood he'd been consuming kicked in. The pain he was feeling suddenly increased a hundred-fold as the nanos in his body set to work again with a fury. Ripping the now empty last bag from his fangs, he ground his teeth to keep from shouting out in agony, and then couldn't even do that as his body began to convulse.

Eighteen

"Wow, woman! Have you moved in or something?
You don't work Saturdays."

Sophie glanced up from her computer screen and
smiled at Megan as her friend breezed into her office
and plopped herself on the corner of her desk.

"Neither do you," Sophie pointed out rather than
answer.

"I just dropped off Dad's lunch. He forgot it when
he left this morning," Megan explained, and then gave
her a meaningful look and asked, "So? What are you
doing here?"

"I just came in to finish making up the hours I
missed on Thursday," Sophie said finally.

Megan sat up a little straighter and peered down her
nose suspiciously at Sophie. "I thought you were doing that last night?"

"I was," Sophie agreed.

Megan's eyebrows rose. "I'm gonna guess that

means that you left early? Or did work time become playtime last night when Alasdair showed up? Maybe instead of eating and going back to work, you ended up eating and then polishing your desk with your bare butt while he did dirty little things to you." Her eyes widened even as she said that, and Megan suddenly jumped off the desk with a loud, "Ewww. You did, didn't you? And I just sat where you two got busy."

"No, we didn't," Sophie said on a laugh. "Good Lord, you know me better than that. I'd never have sex in the office," she assured her, and then paused as it occurred to her that she damned near had had sex here. Twice. Once in her office and once in the break room, and the only reason they hadn't was because they'd been interrupted.

Shaking her head to remove the memories of what had happened, Sophie said, "Actually, I ended up with burning-hot pizza on my blouse and didn't feel like working covered with pizza sauce and mozzarella so I called it a night and went home."

"Ohhhhh," Megan said meaningfully. "I bet Alasdair could have helped you with that. Did he offer to accompany you home and lick it off for you?"

Sophie pressed her lips together. She really wanted to tell Megan all about what had happened with Alasdair. She usually told her everything. But this was so new, and Alasdair wasn't like anyone else she'd ever dated. And—

"Ohmygawd he did," Megan squealed, eyeing her with amazement. "Did you take him home with you?"

"I—"

"Ohmygawd, you dirty ho, you took him home and had sex with him," Megan accused with shocked glee.

"Don't deny it, it's written all over your face. There's even the impression of a penis on your forehead."

Sophie burst out laughing at that, and grabbed an eraser off her desk to toss at her friend. "Idiot. There is not."

"I don't know," Megan said, straightening from ducking the eraser. "It looks like a penis to me."

"There is not an impression of a penis on my forehead," Sophie said with exasperation.

"Did I say forehead? I meant neck," Megan taunted. "Great big honking penis-shaped hickeys on your neck in a lovely purple red."

Groaning, Sophie reached to tug up the neckline of the turtleneck she'd changed into that morning after spotting the hickeys Alasdair had given her last night. They were not penis shaped, but they were biggish and all over her body. On both sides of her neck, several on her breasts, and even her hips. Probably on her butt too. She hadn't checked but did recall him nipping and sucking on one butt cheek at some point. The man's mouth had been everywhere.

"Okay," Megan said abruptly, dropping to sit on the corner of her desk again. "I need deets. The man must be good, because you just don't sleep with guys on the first date. I do," she added with a grin, "but you have always been more conservative. The relationship type rather than the party girl. So come on, spill. I want to hear it all. How did he break through your good girl barriers and hustle you into bed so quickly? Did he roofie you? Did he do a sexy little striptease? Did he go down on you?" She paused and narrowed her eyes. "He better have given you at least one orgasm."

Sophie was laughing by the time her friend finished

and said, "I love you, Megan. You always make me laugh."

"Screw that, of course you love me. We're sisters. Now tell me what happened," she insisted. "He did give you an orgasm, didn't he?"

Giving in, Sophie grinned and admitted, "He gave me six."

"Whaaaat?" Megan gaped briefly and then her mouth snapped closed and she asked, "Seriously?"

Sophie nodded. "Seriously. Six mind-blowing, 'leave me in a swoon' orgasms. And as to your earlier questions, he didn't roofie me, but he did go down on me. Twice."

"Daaaamn," Megan breathed, beginning to fan herself. "Oh, he's good. A keeper. Does he have a brother?"

"A twin."

"Really?" she asked, perking up with interest.

"Really what?" Bobby asked, poking his head into her office. "And what's all the squealing going on back here? I could hear you all the way from the reception office, Megan. And if I could hear you from there, you know Dad could hear you from his office. You're lucky he didn't come in and give you hell."

Megan waved that possibility away with unconcern and happily announced, "Sophie got mega-laid last night."

"Really? Do tell!" Bobby said with a grin, entering her office now. "Was it that big guy you had lunch with yesterday?"

"His name is Alasdair," Sophie reminded him with exasperation.

"Alasdair, Shmalister," Bobby teased. "Was he any good?"

"She had six orgasms," Megan told him.

Bobby's eyes and mouth went round and then he shook his head. "No way."

"Way," Megan told him. "And he has a twin. Sophie is going to introduce me to him."

"You mean he's still alive?" Bobby asked with amusement. "You didn't kill him with your crazy sexual demands?"

When Sophie just shook her head at his teasing, Megan snorted and said, "Well, someone's obviously never given his girlfriend Elizabeth six orgasms in one night."

"In less than three hours," Sophie corrected, and then added, "Including naps."

"Whaaat?" Megan gasped and then her eyes narrowed. "Wait. He didn't spend the night?"

"He had a shift at midnight, so left a little after eleven," Sophie said defensively.

"And he was able to walk when he left?" Bobby asked, sounding more serious this time.

"You are really wrecking my image of you as a sexual stud, brother," Megan told him dryly.

"Have you never heard of chafing?" Bobby asked. "Heck, I'm surprised Sophie's walking today after a three-hour marathon of sex. Speaking of which, the guy must be Mr. Quick-Release to pound it out six times in three hours with naps included. What is he? A three-minute-egg kind of guy?"

"No," Sophie said, but didn't add that she doubted they'd lasted three minutes most of those times. Megan and Bobby probably wouldn't believe it was because it was so damned good.

"All right," she said, standing up. "It's ten. That means I've been here two hours. I have now *finally* finished working off the time I took off Thursday. I have things to do. I'm outta here."

"What things?" Megan asked with interest, sliding off her desk.

"Oh, some shopping and housecleaning," Sophie said airily.

"I thought you went grocery shopping on Wednesday," Megan said suspiciously.

"Did I say grocery shopping?" she asked lightly as she bent to grab her purse out of her bottom drawer.

"You're going to get pretty lingerie, aren't you?" Megan said, waggling her eyebrows. "You're seeing him again."

"I am, and I am." Straightening, Sophie grabbed the jacket she'd worn in to work from the back of her chair. She then walked around her desk, headed for the door.

"Where's he taking you?" Megan asked as she and Bobby trailed her out into the hall.

"I don't know. He's calling after he catches some sleep." Sophie didn't mention that she was hoping they were going straight to her bedroom. Although, really, anywhere in her apartment would be fine. She just wanted to rip the man's clothes off and explore every inch of his body. Sex with him was addictive despite the worrisome fainting. She couldn't stop thinking about last night and what might come next. Sophie was even considering finding a sex shop after she hit the lingerie store, and seeing if she could find handcuffs or something. Lying in bed last night after he'd left, she'd developed something of a fantasy of handcuffing him to her bed and having her way with him. Just thinking about it now had her nipples hardening and wet heat developing between her legs.

"Make him take you to someplace fancy for dinner. Like La Bonne Vie," Megan ordered. "Or—" She stopped abruptly as the sound of a phone ringing came from the depths of Sophie's purse. "Oooh, I bet that's him."

She gave a distracted shake of the head. "He worked all night. He'll be sleeping."

The words had barely left her lips when she pulled her phone out and saw that it was indeed Alasdair.

"Oh," she breathed with surprise, staring at his name on her display as her phone rang again.

"Told you," Megan said with glee.

"What are you waiting for? Answer it," Bobby said now, and then grinned and added, "We need to know what your plans are for tonight so we can show up and grill him about his intentions."

Sophie snorted at that, and tapped the phone to answer it, then lifted it to her ear. "Hello?"

"Good morning, beautiful. Are you still at work?"

Sophie smiled at the sound of his deep voice across the phone lines. "You're supposed to be sleeping."

"I slept all night. Been up for hours. Just waiting to call you."

"What?" she asked with surprise. "I thought you had to work all night?"

"My schedule changed. I will explain when I see you," he promised, and then immediately asked, "When will I see you?"

Sophie hesitated, the plans she'd had for finding

sexy little silkies and handcuffs then cleaning her apartment running through her mind and right out the window. "How about now?"

"Perfect. Then we can get an early start," he said at once.

"An early start for what?" Sophie asked with interest.

There was a pause, and then Alasdair asked, "How do you feel about packing a bag and getting out of town for the rest of the weekend?"

Sophie's eyebrows rose. "Where?"

"Niagara Falls. One of the men said it was nice. We could take the trolley, visit the Old Fort, see what's playing at the theater tonight . . ."

"And stay in a hotel with a heart-shaped Jacuzzi?" Sophie teased because that's all she knew of the area. She'd never been to the falls herself, but a friend of hers from university had been proposed to in a heart-shaped red Jacuzzi that had apparently taken up a good portion of their hotel room.

"A room with a heart-shaped Jacuzzi could be interesting if it's big enough for two," Alasdair said, his voice deepening and sexy as hell. "What do you say? Can I take you away for a bit?"

"Yes," she breathed.

"Then I'm on my way," he said promptly.

"I'm just leaving work."

"I'll meet you at the apartment," he said. "See you soon."

"Soon," Sophie agreed, and ended the call with a smile.

"Ohhhh, look at that smile. You've got it bad, sister," Megan teased as Sophie slid her phone back into her purse.

"He is not taking you to Niagara Falls, is he?" Bobby asked with disbelief.

Sophie glanced at him with a start. "How did you know?"

"Where else would you find something as tacky as a heart-shaped Jacuzzi?" he asked dryly.

Sophie grinned at his disgusted expression. "He's taking me there for the rest of the weekend."

"So, I should tell Mom you won't be around for Sunday dinner?" Bobby asked, eyebrows raised.

"Oh yeah," Sophie said with a small frown. She always had Sunday dinner with the Tomlinsons. It was something of a tradition, becoming more important once she, Megan, and Bobby had moved out to their own homes. Mama made a big meal and they all got together to talk about the week and what was going on in everyone's life. It was family night and something everyone made an effort to attend.

"I'm not sure when we'll be back tomorrow," she admitted finally. "I'll call when I know one way or the other."

Bobby nodded, but Megan scowled and said, "Well, that sucks. No family dinner and—if he's taking you out of town to some tacky love hotel—the Six Orgasm Man won't want his brother and I tagging along, so no chance for me to meet the twin."

"No," Sophie agreed. "I'd say not."

Megan clucked with irritation. "I *need* to meet his brother, Soph. I need me some six orgasm nights."

A soft laugh slipped from her lips when Megan gave her puppy dog eyes, but she said, "Sorry, love, I guess it's not in the cards this weekend." When Megan began to pout, she added, "But I promise that while we're there I'll talk to him about getting you two together. Maybe we can do something next week."

"But that's sooo far away," Megan whined.

"That's okay, Megan Muffin," Bobby said sympathetically, throwing an arm around her shoulder. "I still love you and I have a couple of buddies I could set you up with."

"Ugh!" Megan shrugged his arm off. "I've met your buddies, Bobby. Soooo not interested."

"Hey! My buddies are cool," Bobby protested.

Sophie left them to bicker and hurried the rest of the way to the front door. Her mind was already on what she should pack. It was a little cool today, more like the fall temperatures it should be, and she thought tomorrow was supposed to be the same. She'd need to listen to the weather forecast on the way home, Sophie thought as she reached her car.

"Hey! Wait!"

Sophie glanced around, eyebrows rising as she watched Megan hurry toward her across the parking lot.

"What's up, buttercup?" she asked when Megan reached her.

Panting, Megan put up a hand, requesting a second to catch her breath, and then got out, "Your car."

"My car?" Sophie asked.

Megan nodded. Her breathing less labored, she said, "Since you'll be out of town today and tomorrow and won't need it anyway, can I borrow it?"

Sophie's eyebrows flew up. "What's wrong with your car?"

"It's in the shop," she said with annoyance. "It was making this weird ticking sound so I dropped it off at the mechanics this morning on my way in, and Ubered from there. The mechanic said it would definitely be in all weekend, so I was going to look into renting something until it's ready, but if you aren't using yours . . . ?" She gave her a pleading look.

"All right. Fine," Sophie said at once. "But I need to pack. You'll have to drive me home. Right now. And straight there," she added firmly. "None of your famous 'I just have to make a quick stop here' detours."

"No stops," Megan promised, a grin replacing the pleading look. Throwing her arms around Sophie, Megan gave her a bear hug. "You're the best sister ever."

"Yeah, yeah," Sophie said with amusement as they separated. Shaking her head, she walked around the car to the passenger side saying, "You might as well drive."

"Okey-dokey." Megan was in the car before Sophie had reached her own door.

Getting in, she quickly pulled out her keys and unclipped her car key fob from the ring as Megan started the engine. She then dropped it in Megan's purse. "No drinking and driving this weekend."

"I never drink and drive," Megan assured her, backing out of the parking spot.

"And no sex in my car," Sophie warned, knowing Megan avoided taking men she didn't know well to her apartment and wouldn't go to theirs in case they were serial killers or something. Instead, if she found them really attractive and irresistible, she just had her way with them in her car. It didn't happen often. Megan wasn't out jumping men left and right. But it had happened.

"Oh, now that's just mean," Megan muttered as she shifted gear and headed for the exit. "It's bad enough I'm not going to meet the Six Orgasm Man's brother, now you expect me to forgo sex altogether this weekend?"

"You can have sex. Just not in my car," Sophie said, but she was grinning at Megan's chosen nickname for Alasdair. The Six Orgasm Man. It made her think of an old show she used to watch in reruns at the group home. *The Six Million Dollar Man*. She decided the two names were probably interchangeable. Any man who could give her six orgasms in such short order had to be worth at least six million. Though, she probably shouldn't tell Alasdair that, or about the nickname Megan had given him. She just had to hope Megan never called him that in person.

Nineteen

"Damn."

Sophie glanced over from doing up her seat belt to look at Alasdair. They were in his SUV. He hadn't been here when Megan had dropped her off, and by the time he'd arrived fifteen minutes later, Sophie had just finished packing. She'd buzzed him in, rushed back to her room to zip up the small suitcase she'd packed with everything she thought she might need.

Sophie had been coming out of her apartment by the time the elevator expelled him onto her floor.

Spotting her, he'd stopped at once and held the elevator door open to keep it from leaving. He'd then smiled as he'd watched her approach.

"That rare woman, one who can pack fast," he'd teased as she'd reached him. Kissing her on the cheek, he'd relieved her of her suitcase, and urged her into the elevator. "I expected to be sitting in your living room waiting while you agonized over what to take."

"Nah," Sophie had responded. "We're only going overnight, so I just packed the essentials: jeans, dress pants, a casual shirt, a dressier top, a dress, running shoes, and high heels."

"No pajamas?" he'd asked lightly.

"I sleep nude," she'd told him with a grin and then had raised her eyebrows. "Hope you don't mind?"

Eyes flaring gold with hunger, Alasdair had merely groaned in response and leaned against the wall next to the elevator buttons, about as far away from her as he could get.

"Why so far away? Scared of me?" she'd taunted.

Rather than chuckle as she'd expected, Alasdair had nodded solemnly. "Get too close and I won't be able to keep my hands to myself. Better I keep some distance between us. At least until we get to Niagara and check into the hotel."

Sophie had felt herself flush at those words. Not with embarrassment, but with the feelings the words stirred in her. She'd immediately begun to imagine what could happen in that elevator if he didn't keep his hands to himself.

The small fantasy had kept her busy for the rest of the ride down to the ground floor. In fact, it had almost made her forget to check the mailbox on her way out. Sophie had realized as she was packing that she'd forgotten to do that the day before and had planned to check before leaving in case there was anything important.

There hadn't been, just flyers and junk mail. Sophie had dumped everything in the recycling bin kept in the mail room for just that purpose and then had been stopped by an elderly tenant she often chatted with in the elevator, Enid. Enid had insisted on being introduced to her "beau," and then had chattered happily away for several minutes before Sophie had managed to extricate herself and Alasdair to hurry out to the SUV, which he had again parked across the street.

Now they were in his vehicle and he was scowling as he tried to start it and got no response. It wasn't turning over at all. The SUV seemed dead.

"Problem?" she asked.

Alasdair was silent as he tried to start the engine again and then gave up with disgust. Dropping back against his seat, he stared out the windshield for a moment, and then asked, "How would you feel about taking your car?"

"Oh." Sophie bit her lip, and then admitted apologetically, "I lent it to Megan for the weekend. Sorry."

"Damn," Alasdair breathed, and then undid his seat belt. "We might as well go back up to your apartment while I figure out something else then. I'll have to call the office and have someone come pick up this SUV and take it in to see what the problem is. Maybe they'll have another one we can use that they can bring with them."

Nodding, Sophie undid her seat belt and grabbed her purse, then opened her door to get out.

Alasdair retrieved their luggage from the back, and she led him into her building and up to her apartment.

While Alasdair made his phone call, Sophie moved into the kitchen to give him privacy. After standing there for a moment, though, she decided to make coffee. It looked like they had some time to kill.

"Mortimer's going to see if he has anything available,"

Alasdair announced, entering the kitchen as she was filling the coffeepot with water from the tap. "If he can't, I'll rent something, but either way we have to wait here for someone to collect the SUV."

Sophie nodded, and then sucked in a startled breath when his arms slid around her from behind to wrap around her waist.

"Coffee?" he growled by her ear.

"Yes," she breathed, immediately excited. Leaning back into him, she pressed her bottom against his front, and deliberately rubbed back and forth.

"Sophie, love," Alasdair groaned, his arms tightening around her to hold her still.

"What?" she asked breathily, trying to keep an eye on the water so it didn't overflow, but very much distracted by the heat, feel, and scent of Alasdair. She couldn't rub from side to side anymore the way he was holding her, but she could press back more firmly against him and did, her back arching and thrusting her breasts forward and up as she did.

"Yer naughty," Alasdair growled, stiff as stone around her now. "And if ye don'y behave yerself I cann'y promise no' to ravish ye."

"God, I love your accent," she breathed, and thrust back against him again. "Ravish me."

The words had barely left her lips when he released her to take the coffeepot from her hand, set it aside, turned off the tap, then spun her around and began to tug her T-shirt out of her jeans as he kissed her.

Sophie kissed him eagerly back, her own hands moving to the top of his pants. She'd managed to get his belt undone before she had to stop and lift her arms so that he could tug her T-shirt off over her head.

While he then set to work on her bra, a pretty pink one this time that she'd picked purely for him, her own hands returned to his jeans. Sophie quickly undid the button and managed to lower his zipper before she had to stop for him to slide the now undone bra off her.

She reached for him again while he was tossing that aside, slid one hand into his open jeans, and found his already burgeoning erection. Sophie clasped and squeezed eagerly and then gasped into his mouth in surprise when a sharp shaft of pleasure and excitement charged through her.

Alasdair broke their kiss on a curse, took one look at her confused expression, and dropped to his knees before her. He undid and peeled her jeans and panties away so swiftly she was left gaping, until he pressed his mouth to what he'd revealed. Gasping as another jolt of pleasure tore through her, Sophie reached for the counter behind her and ended up grabbing the side of the small dish drying rack she kept there. She immediately released it, but must have pulled it forward as she did because the whole thing crashed to the floor, taking the coffee cup, knife, and plate she'd used for her toast that morning with it.

Alasdair stopped what he was doing at once to look at the mess on the floor. Muttered what sounded like, "Dangerous," and then he scooped her up and carried her out of the kitchen.

Sophie thought he would take her to the bedroom, and began to nibble on his neck and ear as they went. Startled again when her caresses caused pleasure to roll through her own body, she stopped what she was doing and opened her mouth to say something about it. But before she could, Alasdair turned his head and kissed her again, silencing and distracting her. By the time he stopped and dropped to sit down with her sideways in his lap, she'd forgotten all about it.

They were on the couch in the living room, she saw when he broke their kiss and ducked his head to claim one nipple. Sophie just caught a glimpse of his jeans lying on the floor outside the kitchen before he began to draw on the nipple he'd claimed and her eyes closed on a moan of pleasure. But she knew that his pants—that she'd undone in the kitchen—must have slid down his legs as he'd carried her and he had just stepped out of them as he walked and carried her bare-assed in his T-shirt to the couch.

Winnie the Pooh style, Sophie thought, clutching his shoulder and head as Alasdair suckled, and then her eyes popped open and she jerked in his lap when his hand slid between her legs and began to caress her.

Gasping for breath now, she stared blindly at the top of his head, her hips shifting and wiggling over his hard shaft beneath her as his fingers played over her slick skin, and then he suddenly removed his hand from between her legs. Letting her nipple slip from his mouth, he raised his head and lifted and turned her, then set her down to straddle his hips.

Sophie groaned as he eased her down, his cock sliding into her as he did.

"God, love, yer so hot and tight," he growled, his fingers shifting to her bottom and squeezing her buttocks as he raised and lowered her again.

Sophie just shook her head, unable to speak at that point. He was filling her to bursting, and sending wave after wave of unbearable excitement and need through her with each maddeningly slow stroke. She couldn't stand it. She didn't want him to stop. He was driving her crazy. She was going to lose it.

His mouth clamped on her breast in passing, his lips and tongue working the hard little nipple he'd claimed, and Sophie threw her head back on a scream that was choked off when the explosion of pleasure that had claimed her washed over her, taking consciousness with it.

"Well, I guess Niagara is out."

Sophie glanced around with surprise at those words to see Alasdair entering the kitchen. He was fully dressed again for the first time in hours, while she was naked under the robe she'd pulled on before leaving him asleep in her bed to find something to eat.

"You're awake," she said with a smile and then turned back to the stove and the steak she was cooking. She'd woken up hungry after their last sex-capade. Number eight so far that day if she recalled correctly. It was all they'd done since coming back up to her apartment. Sex, sleep, wake up and have sex again only to sleep again. Or faint, really, Sophie thought with a small frown. She assumed Alasdair slept while she was unconscious. For all she knew, he could have been wandering her apartment poking his nose into everything. She doubted it, though. He was usually right there beside her wherever she woke up, whether it was on her couch, the living room floor, or her bed.

Although, the second time she'd woken up on the couch he'd been coming back into her apartment. The men had arrived to tow the SUV away and he'd run the keys down and found out that there were no other vehicles available for them to use.

Seeing that she was awake, Alasdair had announced that he would call and rent a car for their journey to Niagara Falls, but then she'd stood and crossed the room to him. His gaze had slid hot over her naked body and then he'd met her halfway and taken her into his arms. Neither of them had thought about Niagara Falls since.

Until now, and it was well past dinnertime. They hadn't had lunch, which was probably the only reason she'd left the bedroom. She'd woken up too hungry to even consider waking up Alasdair for another round. Besides, she was actually getting sore. Really sore. Her poor body wasn't used to so much pleasure. She now understood what Bobby had meant by chafing and thought a break would be good.

"I don't mind," Sophie told him. "We can always go another time. Besides, it would have been a waste of money at this point."

"Why?" he asked with surprise.

"I doubt we would have made it out of the room to see any of those things you mentioned, the theater and whatnot," she pointed out. "And if that's the case, staying here and enjoying each other is just as good and costs us nothing."

"We would not have stayed in the room," Alasdair assured her, moving to the sink to get a glass of water.

"No?" Sophie asked dubiously. It seemed to her they had trouble keeping their hands off each other. She couldn't imagine it would have been any different in Niagara Falls.

"I had plans to wine and dine you, and show you the sights," Alasdair announced, turning to lean against the counter with his water.

"Yeah?" she asked, glancing over with a smile.

Alasdair nodded. "I was hoping it would give us a chance to talk and get to know each other better if we were somewhere we couldn't . . ." His gaze slid down her body in the red silk robe she was wearing and his mouth quirked up in a crooked smile. "Where you could not distract me with your luscious body."

"Hey, you're pretty distracting yourself, so don't blame me for the problem we have keeping our hands off each other," Sophie said lightly, deliberately avoiding the subject of his desire for them to talk and get to know each other better. That idea made her extremely uncomfortable. That suggested a relationship, and Sophie had sworn off those after the death of her last fiancé. Dating and having fun was fine, but she didn't expect or want anything deeper than that. Maybe.

Scowling at her own thoughts, she asked, "How do you like your steak?"

"Rare," he answered at once, and then asked, "What was life like in the group home?"

Sophie stiffened briefly, but then decided she could answer that without getting too personal, so told him, "Pretty grim."

"How so?" Alasdair asked.

The scrape of a barstool across the tile floor had her glancing around to see that he'd sat down at one of the chairs at the island and was even now pulling the cutting board and vegetables she'd set there in front of himself. When he picked up the knife lying there and began to slice up the cucumber she'd intended to use as part of the salad, she turned back to the stove.

It was another minute before Sophie answered him. "I don't know what most group homes are like, but the one I was at was a big, old house. It was kind of a spooky place and all the kids swore it was haunted." She chuckled faintly at the memory.

"Was it?" he asked.

She shook her head. "Only by the caregivers who were supposed to look after us."

"What were they like?" Alasdair asked.

Sophie's mouth tightened as she thought back to those days. "Most of them were okay. They were nice and really wanted to help us, I think," she admitted. "But there were a couple of others who were just bullies. They'd yell and verbally abuse the kids over nothing. We all knew they were just trying to push someone to react physically by either shoving or striking out at them. But we also knew that if that happened there'd be hell to pay."

"How?"

Sophie turned the steaks over. "Staff was allowed to restrain the kids if they got physical, but the bullies did more than that. They'd punch and choke them and call it restraining."

"Did that ever happen to you?" Alasdair asked, his voice concerned.

"Oh, heck no. The bullies usually went after the boys, not us girls," she told him. "We girls didn't have to worry much about them, just the perverts."

"The perverts?" Alasdair asked, sounding shocked.

Sophie gave him an amused smile over her shoulder.

"You're surprised that predators would tend toward jobs where vulnerable children were easily accessible?"

Seeing the concern that filled his face, she returned her attention to the steaks and said, "One of the pervs took an interest in me. But I got lucky."

"How so?" Alasdair asked, his voice sounding grim.

"When I first moved there, I was given a room with a girl my age named Beverly." Sophie smiled at the memory. "She was a sweetheart. We became best friends pretty quickly and she warned me about the two pervs on staff, Chester the Molester and Sicko Steve," she said, recalling the nicknames the kids had given the two men. Shaking her head, she continued, "Beverly told me never, under any circumstances, to allow them to get me alone.

"That was hard to do, of course. I mean those two were slick and tricky, skulking the halls and looking for any opportunity to trap you in the bathroom or somewhere else. And Sicko Steve seemed to constantly be trying to catch me unawares. But Beverly and her brother, Andrew, kept an eye out for me, and I did the same for them."

Sophie smiled again as she thought of them. "The three of us became pretty tight. I don't think I would have survived the group home without them."

Alasdair watched Sophie smile blindly down at the steak she was cooking. It seemed obvious she was in her memories, back in the past in that group home.

With her best friend and the girl's brother. He frowned as he recalled Marguerite listing off all the people Sophie had lost and mentioning a childhood best friend. Obviously, she hadn't been talking about Megan. She still lived. Was Beverly that best friend lost to an unnatural death?

"Are the three of you still friends?" Alasdair asked, hoping to find out. "Where are Beverly and Andrew now?"

Sophie jerked as if waking from a dream and turned the stove off before saying flatly, "Gone. Beverly is dead. Andrew's still alive but in a coma in the hospital."

"What happened?" Alasdair asked gently.

Sophie opened the oven and slid the steaks onto a plate waiting inside, already warmed up. Closing the door, she carried the frying pan to the sink. He watched and waited as she started to clean the pan. It wasn't until she'd finished and set it on the drying rack that she spoke again.

Picking up a towel, she dried her hands and said, "Andrew was into skateboarding big-time. He was always doing tricks and stuff. Hardflips and backside tail slides, stuff like that. And he never wore a helmet," she said, sounding angry. "I don't know what he was doing that day. Beverly and I usually stopped at the park with him on the way home to watch him mess around and try new tricks, but we were doing a group project with Megan for history and didn't stop with him like usual. We walked him there and then Beverly and I went to the library instead. Megan had to stay late for getting lippy with our economics teacher, so she followed us a little later. We were all at the library for at least an hour, and then Beverly and I parted ways with Megan and headed back to the group home. We expected Andrew to be there when we got back, but he wasn't. We went looking for him."

Giving him her back, she carefully folded the dish towel and said, "We found him lying in a pool of blood, his skull caved in on one side. He must have been trying one of his new tricks and wiped out."

"And he's in a hospital, still alive but in a coma all these years later?" Alasdair asked slowly, finding that hard to believe. "They haven't pulled the plug on him?"

"His mother won't let them," Sophie said. Setting down the towel, she faced him again and leaned against the sink as she explained, "Beverly and Andrew weren't in the group home because their parents were dead like mine. Their mother was a drug addict and they were taken away for neglect or something. But she came from a wealthy family. She was fighting to get them back the whole time we were in the group home, and she was finally clean. I think she was about to get them back too, but then Andrew had his accident, and Beverly . . . died."

"How?" Alasdair asked softly.

Sophie paused, obviously reluctant to tell him, but after a moment she finally said, "Beverly was allergic to nuts. Two weeks after Andrew's accident, she somehow was exposed to nuts, or nut oil or something nut related. We never figured out what, but she went into anaphylactic shock and died."

Alasdair blew out a breath at this news. Two tragedies in a couple of weeks.

"I still don't know how it happened," Sophie added with a troubled frown. "Beverly was always super careful to avoid nuts. We all were. Andrew and I wouldn't even go *near* nuts for fear we'd somehow transfer it to her." She shook her head unhappily.

Alasdair was silent for a minute, and then said, "You were alone at the group home after that? With no one to watch your back?"

Sophie met his gaze and shrugged. "Not for long. I went to foster at the Tomlinsons shortly after that. They'd already applied and been doing the courses to take me when that all happened." She smiled crookedly. "Beverly was upset about it at the time. Afraid I'd move out and forget about her. I promised her nothing would change. We'd still be best friends. We'd have sleepovers and stuff and she could hang with us at the Tomlinsons' as much as she was allowed." Sophie bit her lip and admitted, "That didn't help much. She was still upset, even more so after Andrew's accident. I began to feel guilty about it and decided it might not be a good time to leave her. Especially with Andrew in the hospital. But in the end, I wasn't the one who left first."

Sighing, she straightened and moved to the cupboard to pull out a package of something he couldn't see the name of.

It turned out to be some kind of garlic pasta you just added to boiling water, then stirred butter into. It smelled really good while it was cooking, and they were both quiet as they finished prepping their meal, her handling the pasta while Alasdair continued cutting up tomatoes and green onions to add to the salad he'd taken over preparing.

It wasn't until they were sitting down to eat that he continued their conversation by asking, "Why have you never been married?"

Sophie glanced up with surprise. "Who said I'm not?"

Twenty

Sophie watched the shock spread across Alasdair's face, and couldn't hold back her grin. "Of course I'm not married. I'd hardly be having crazy monkey sex with you if I was."

Alasdair sat back in his seat with relief, and shook his head. "Ye've a mean streak, lass. Ye near to gave me a heart attack with that."

"I do love your accent," Sophie said, her grin widening. "It turns me on."

"Does it?" he asked with interest, a smile now curving the corners of his mouth.

"Mm-hmm," she said. "In fact, if I weren't so sore, I'd jump you right now."

His smile died at once, concern replacing it. "Ye're sore?"

"Aren't you?" she asked dryly.

Alasdair opened his mouth to respond, but then

paused as her buzzer sounded. They both glanced toward the hall with surprise.

"Were you expecting company?" he asked.

Sophie shook her head. "I'm not even supposed to be here, remember? We were going to be in Niagara Falls, and my family knows that. Megan and Bobby were with me when you called."

Alasdair nodded and then scowled when the buzzer sounded again.

"I better see who it is," Sophie said, standing up. "It's probably someone buzzing the wrong apartment, but if they aren't told, they'll just keep trying."

Alasdair didn't comment, but he did stand to follow her out to the hall.

The building was a nice one, but it was older, with an old-fashioned intercom system with a button you pressed to speak, another to hear, and a third you pushed to open the door downstairs. Sophie had considered updating it when she moved in, but in the end hadn't bothered. Mostly because she didn't have a lot of company other than Megan and Bobby, who both had keys.

"I noticed a camera down in the entry, but I don't see a screen you can check to see who's at the door," Alasdair commented, peering at the speaker built into the wall with the buttons above it.

"I could see the camera view if I turned on the TV to channel one, but why bother?" she said, and pressed the button to speak. "Yes?"

"Sophie? This is Alasdair's brother, Colle. Can I come up? It's important."

Sophie immediately pressed the button to open the

door in the entry and glanced over at Alasdair to see the surprised and disturbed expression on his face.

"I hope it's not bad news," she murmured, and then glanced down at herself and clicked her tongue. "I better go get dressed."

Alasdair nodded. "Take your time. I'll let him in when he gets here."

Sophie didn't respond, but hurried off to her bedroom. It wasn't until she reached it that she realized the clothes she'd been wearing earlier were still out in the kitchen. She'd picked them up, folded and set them on the counter when she'd first gone out to make supper. She didn't bother going back for them now. The building might be older, but the elevator was pretty fast and she was afraid Colle might arrive while she was out there.

Hurrying to her closet instead, Sophie opened the doors and considered her options. In the end, she settled on a fresh pair of jeans and a T-shirt. Taking them with her, she went to her dresser to fetch a bra and panties and took everything with her into the en suite bathroom to dress.

At least, that was the plan before she saw herself in the bathroom mirror. Sophie moaned at the sight of herself.

Her hair was a crazy mess around her head, tangled and standing up in different directions. But she could fix that. It would take scads and scads of hair conditioner to do it, which meant a shower, but she *could* fix it.

What she couldn't fix were the huge honking red-and-purple hickeys. Dear God, she had even more of them now than she'd had that morning. Alasdair obviously had a serious thing about sucking on her skin.

She'd have to talk to him about that, Sophie thought as she turned around to head back into her room to find a turtleneck. She enjoyed what he did to her, but didn't need everyone getting a visual of it.

Alasdair was waiting in the open door of Sophie's apartment when the elevator arrived. Colle stepped out the moment the doors opened, but he wasn't alone. Tybo and the uncles were on his heels and Alasdair felt apprehension slide through him at the sight of the large group. He knew Colle wouldn't bring them unless something serious was up.

"What's going on?" he asked with concern as they approached.

"Are you good?" Colle asked rather than answer his question.

"Yes. Of course. Why? Has something happened?" Alasdair asked with confusion.

"I'll say," Inan muttered.

"Inside," Ludan growled.

When Alasdair opened his mouth to demand to know what was happening, Ludan held up one hand and peered meaningfully toward the apartment door directly across the hall. Alasdair followed his gaze, suddenly aware that he could hear what sounded like some sort of action movie muffled through the door. Which meant any conversation they might have in the hall would probably be heard on the other side.

Nodding, he turned to lead the men inside, and then

continued on into the kitchen when the entry got too crowded. It seemed the smarter choice than the living room, since he wasn't sure what was happening and if Sophie should hear it. The kitchen would at least give them some privacy.

Stopping by the sink, he turned to survey the men now crowding into the room. It was a good-sized kitchen, but this group made it seem small with their very presence. Raising his eyebrows, Alasdair asked, "What's going on?"

There was a moment of silence as the men exchanged glances, and then Colle said, "Russell checked your SUV. The problem was with the battery."

Alasdair frowned slightly at this news. They could have told him that over the phone. It didn't seem that urgent or even important. "Okay. So did he change the battery?"

"He didn't have to," Tybo told him, his voice un-usually solemn. "The problem with the battery was that it was no longer connected. The cables had been detached."

Alasdair's head went back a bit in surprise. "How could that be? I drove it here. They had to have been connected."

"When ye drove here, aye," Inan said.

"Well, then, how . . ." Alasdair paused as understand-ing sank in. "Someone detached the cables in the few minutes between when I parked and came into the building, and when Sophie and I went back out?"

All six men nodded.

Alasdair considered that. He hadn't been inside long. He'd had to wait a couple minutes for an elevator to arrive on the ground floor to take him up. Maybe a little more than a couple minutes, he realized thinking back. Long enough for four or five people to arrive and join him at the elevator, which had then stopped at three different floors on the way up before he'd ridden the last couple of floors alone. But Sophie had been coming out of the apartment as he'd arrived. He hadn't had to wait for her, and he'd held the elevator for her so they hadn't had to wait for its return to ride down. All told it had probably been between eight and twelve minutes.

No, Alasdair thought suddenly. He was forgetting the stop in the mail room and the chat with her elderly neighbor. He might have actually been inside for twenty minutes or more. And he hadn't bothered to lock the SUV because he'd known he wouldn't be long.

Still, twenty minutes wasn't that long. How long would it have taken for someone to—

"It wouldn't have taken more than a minute, maybe two to pop the hood, loosen the nuts, and remove the cables," Colle said dismissively, making it obvious he'd heard his thoughts.

"But the engine would have been hot if he'd just driven all the way in from the Enforcer house," Tybo pointed out.

Colle nodded. "Then whoever did it must have had heat resistant gloves or something with them."

"It was well planned, then," Alasdair commented.

"Aye," Inan agreed. "Most people don'y carry around wrenches and heat resistant gloves."

The men all grunted agreement, including Alasdair, and then he sighed and said, "So . . . someone didn't want Sophie and I to go to Niagara Falls."

There was silence as many glances were exchanged and then Colle said, "I think it's a bit more than that."

"More how?" Alasdair asked at once.

"Someone T-boned the passenger side of the tow truck on the way back to the Enforcer house," his twin announced.

Alasdair's gaze sharpened on Colle. A tow truck had been needed to tow the SUV back to the Enforcer house. Unfortunately, that wasn't something the Enforcers had in their garage. A mortal tow truck service had had to be called in. But since there was both blood and weapons in the SUV, as there was in every Enforcer vehicle, someone had been needed to keep an eye on the driver during the process to ensure he didn't snoop.

Alasdair had expected to do it himself, but Mortimer had said no, he didn't have a vehicle for him to use to return to town until the SUV had been repaired, which would ruin his planned trip. He'd said he'd send one of the guys to ride with it instead.

Apparently, Colle had had trouble sleeping and had gone downstairs just as Mortimer was trying to decide who to send. His brother had volunteered for the job. He'd then caught a ride to Sophie's apartment with Bricker, one of the other Enforcers who had been on his way home after his shift.

Colle had told him all of that when Alasdair had taken the keys down to him. Alasdair had then kept him company in the lobby for a few minutes until the tow truck had arrived. When Colle had headed out to join the driver at the SUV, Alasdair had returned upstairs to Sophie's apartment, thinking it was all good and the SUV was taken care of. Obviously not, though. They'd been T-boned, Colle said, and on the passenger side, where Colle would have been seated.

"How bad?" he asked with concern.

"The driver's dead," Colle said solemnly.

Alasdair sucked in a breath, his gaze now sliding more carefully over his brother. If the driver had died, Colle had no doubt been one hell of a mess and only alive now because he was immortal.

"Yeah, it was bad," Colle said grimly, obviously picking up on his thoughts.

The men all nodded, and Inan said, "He was in e'en worse shape this afternoon than *you* were last eve. He was half-encased in metal, but somehow managed to call the house fer help."

"And thank the sweet Lord fer that," Connor said grimly. "If there'd no' been Enforcers in the area and mortals had come upon him first . . ." He shook his head.

"He only finished healing an hour ago," Tybo told him grimly.

The simple words told Alasdair all he needed to know. It had taken Colle twice as long to heal as he himself had needed after the hit and run. It had been really bad.

"By then Russell had checked the SUV engine and found the battery cables had been detached," Connor told him, and then explained, "The SUV was no' much hurt in the crash. The front passenger side of the tow truck took all the damage."

Alasdair shook his head, thinking about the unknown tow truck driver. Now dead. And Colle must have suffered terrible pain after the accident. "What about the driver of the vehicle that hit you? Surely their vehicle wasn't drivable after that?"

"Apparently it was, because it was gone by the time I recovered enough to look around," Colle said grimly.

"You didn't see who hit you?" Alasdair asked with surprise.

Colle shook his head. "I was concentrating on the tow truck driver at the time. The kid was young and pretty new on the job. It was a flatbed tow truck. We had to put the SUV in neutral and steer it out of the parking spot and onto the street so the tow truck had room to do what it had to do.

"Everything was fine at first. He got the flatbed tilted into a sort of ramp, and got the SUV up on the flatbed using the winch, but when he started to untilt the bed back to the flat position, the chains popped off the SUV and it went sliding backward. The back end of the flatbed was already about a foot off the ground when it happened. The SUV rolled off and hit the road hard. Not hard enough to do damage, but enough I could hear things crash around inside. We both rushed to the SUV to try to stop it, but the kid got to the driver's door before me. I thought he glanced into the back as he rushed to get the door open and get inside to stop the SUV from rolling down the road. But I wasn't sure.

"When I looked in the back after he stopped the SUV and went around to hook it up again, both the cooler and the weapons locker had been knocked over by the jolt, and blood bags and guns were strewn all over the floor of the back of the SUV."

"So, you were reading his mind to see if he had actually seen that and needed a memory wipe," Alasdair said quietly.

Colle nodded. "I was searching his memories when we were hit. As far as I can tell, some kind of large vehicle came out of a side street at speed and plowed into us, slamming into the passenger side door." He shook his head. "Fortunately, it happened in an industrial area between two huge parking lots. I don't think anyone even noticed it had happened. At least no one came up to check that we were okay before Eshe and Mirabeau arrived to help."

"The driver was dead when they got there," Connor told him. "And the lasses had to peel the metal away to get Colle out. Other than his head and one arm, he was just a sliced-up body bag with shattered bones and crushed organs rattlin' around inside. It's why it took so long fer him to heal and us to get here. He's been frettin' o'er ye in the meantime."

"I'm fine," Alasdair assured them, and then scrubbed his hands over his face before considering the men and what they'd told him. "So, you think the detached battery cables and the car accident are connected. That the battery was disabled so that the vehicle would have to be towed, and someone could—"

"Kill you," Colle said quietly, and when Alasdair glanced at him sharply, said, "I think I was mistaken for you, and someone rammed into the truck intending to kill you. Probably a mortal who thinks you're a mortal, since an immortal would know better than to think these pesky little attempts would be anything more than a painful annoyance," he said grimly.

"You think the shrimp wasn't bad and the hit and run wasn't an accident," Alasdair said solemnly.

Colle nodded. "From what we got from your memories while you were recovering, there was too much blood with your vomit for it to have been a simple case of food poisoning. It must have been a serious poisoning for that much blood to be needed to remove it. That means, the hit and run probably wasn't an accident either. There must be a mortal out there trying to kill you, brother."

Alasdair was silent for a minute, thinking about that. There was no real proof that what Colle was suggesting was true. The evidence was all purely circumstantial. But it was compelling enough that he didn't try to argue that the poisoning, the hit and run, and Colle's "accident" were all just bad luck. Instead, he simply asked, "Why?"

"Sophie," Ludan answered abruptly.

When Alasdair just stared and didn't respond at first, Colle said, "Marguerite told us that there has been a lot of death around Sophie. That she's lost a lot of people she cared about."

"Yes. Marguerite mentioned that to me too," Alasdair admitted. "She suggested I get Sophie to talk about these deaths to see if I couldn't figure out if she's just unlucky enough to have suffered so many tragedies, or if there was something hinky about their deaths."

"And?" Uncle Connor asked. "Did you?"

"I'd just got her talking about that while we were making dinner."

"Did you learn anything?" Tybo asked with interest.

Alasdair hesitated, and then admitted, "We hadn't got very far. She did tell me about a brother and sister she was close to while living in the group home after the fire that killed her parents. The brother suffered a head trauma and is in a coma to this day, and the sister died from an allergic reaction. There's nothing to suggest either was anything other than accidental, like the fire that killed her parents."

The men were silent for a minute and then Tybo said, "After Marguerite told us about Sophie's history, Mortimer sent Eshe and Mirabeau out to look into the parents' deaths."

"And?" Alasdair asked with interest.

"Turns out the fire was arson," Tybo told him quietly.

"Arson?"

Alasdair glanced to the door with a start at that strangled cry to see Sophie standing in the doorway, a stunned expression on her face.

Twenty-One

"Sophie, love," Alasdair murmured, moving through the other men to get to her. He'd intended to take her in his arms and comfort her, but she pushed past him to confront Tybo and demanded, "Who said it was arson?"

"I'm sorry, Sophie," Tybo said with regret. "I never would have said that if I'd realized you were close enough to hear. You shouldn't have learned it this way."

Sophie waved away his apology. "Who said it was arson? It wasn't. It was just a fire, electrical or something," she said vehemently.

Tybo shook his head. "I'm sorry, but it wasn't an accident, Soph. An accelerant was used and—"

"Lies," she snapped.

"It was in both the police report and the fire investigator's report," he told her firmly. "It was even mentioned in your caseworker's files and your medical files from the psychiatric hospital. It was arson, I promise."

Sophie stiffened, dismay and confusion filling her face. "The psychiatric hospital shut down years ago. How could you even know I—?"

She paused abruptly when Alasdair put his hands on her shoulders. He wanted to offer her comfort, but she stiffened and then lowered her head in what looked like shame and whirled away to rush out of the room.

Alasdair hurried after her. He could have caught up to her easily, but didn't and gave her space until she reached the bedroom and started to close the door. Afraid she'd lock it and he'd have to break through, he rushed forward and caught the door before it was shut. When he pushed it open and stepped into the room, Sophie quickly backed away until she came up against the bed, a trapped expression on her face.

She looked around almost wildly, as if seeking escape, but when there wasn't one, Sophie suddenly went strangely calm and Alasdair watched the transformation with fascination. It was honestly impressive how quickly the change came over her. She breathed out a small, resigned sigh, then straightened, her expression turning cold as she faced him. Her voice was expressionless when she asked, "How long have you known?"

"Known what?" he asked cautiously, feeling as if he'd suddenly found himself in a minefield.

"That I was in a psych ward."

Alasdair stilled. She was trying to seem uncaring, but this façade she'd pulled on wasn't without cracks, and he didn't miss the shame that slipped through in her voice. He took a breath to think before finally saying, "About a minute . . . if it's even been that long since Tybo mentioned it just now."

Sophie closed her eyes, unhappiness in every line of her body. It was also present in her voice when she said, "Well, now that you know, you can take off if you want. I'll understand."

That brought a scowl to his face. "Sophie, I'm not taking off. I don't care if you were in a psychiatric hospital as a child."

Her eyes flashed open and just like that she was on the defensive again. "How did you know it was when I was a child if you didn't know about it before Tybo mentioned it? He didn't say when it was."

Alasdair smiled faintly. "Sweetheart, they started shutting down mental hospitals in the US back when Ronald Reagan was president. I'm sure Canada wasn't far behind. But aside from that, it's my job to know about such things, and I'm aware that there haven't been any here for at least a decade, probably more. You had to have been a child or young teen."

When Sophie just eyed him warily, he said, "I'd guess that your stay had something to do with the deaths of your parents when you were eleven? I'm sure it couldn't have been easy losing them at such a young age. You didn't have anyone else. They were your whole world. No one would judge you for needing help to cope with a major loss like that."

Sophie's shoulders suddenly sagged, and she dropped to sit on the end of the bed.

After a hesitation, Alasdair moved cautiously forward. When that didn't spook her, he continued until he'd reached the bed. Alasdair then sat down next to her and took her hands in his. That's all he did at first, sat holding her hands, but after a moment he asked, "Will you tell me about it?"

Sophie seemed to struggle with the request. He watched several expressions flicker across her face, before she finally said, "I thought it was morning when I woke up."

Alasdair blinked. He'd meant tell him about her incarceration in the psychiatric hospital, which is what he'd thought was bothering her, so her lead-in was somewhat confusing. He didn't realize she was talking about the night her parents died until she continued.

"Bright light was pouring through the open window where Megan was standing. She was looking out with the oddest expression on her face, so I got up to see what she was looking at. That's when I saw the light wasn't from the sun, but from fire. My house was on fire."

Sophie took in a deep breath and then went on, "I remember seeing Megan's mom and dad running across the lawn in their pajamas, heading for my house, and then I heard the sirens and looked up the road. I could see the lights from the fire trucks in the distance. Then someone screamed." She paused and swallowed. "It was . . . so agonized. A nightmare scream. I looked back to my house and my mother was stumbling out the front door. She was on fire." Sophie shook her head. "It must have been her nightgown that was on fire, but the flames seemed to be engulfing her. She looked like she'd stepped out of hell, and she was just screaming and screaming."

Her voice broke and Alasdair tightened his hands on hers.

"I don't remember much after that. I guess I was in shock. I was told that I started screaming and just wouldn't stop. I had to be sedated, and was taken to the hospital for observation. I was told that when I woke up there, I wouldn't talk to anyone, not the nurses, doctors, the police, or the caseworker who had been assigned my case when it was realized I had no family. Although I don't remember any of that either.

"The doctors called it traumatic mutism, because while I didn't let out a peep while awake, I woke up screaming every night. The doctors labeled that night terrors," she announced, and added dryly, "They had labels for everything."

"Doctors always do," Alasdair murmured. "I suspect it makes them feel more in control."

Sophie grunted a half laugh at that, then sighed. "I was transferred to a psychiatric hospital for treatment to help me deal with my trauma and night terrors. They tried a wide selection of drugs one after the other, hoping to find one that would get me talking again. I saw various counselors, psychologists, and psychiatrists almost daily."

"Why?" Alasdair asked with surprise. "Doesn't counseling usually need the patient to talk? How does that work with someone suffering traumatic mutism?"

"It doesn't," Sophie told him with a hint of a smile curving her lips. Shrugging, she added, "Mostly they did all the talking at first, reassuring me that I was safe, and would be taken care of and stuff. Then they started having me draw and paint during my sessions." Pausing, she looked at him, and with a wry smile curving her lips, she said, "They called that art therapy."

"Of course they did," he agreed, smiling in return.

Seeming suddenly exhausted, Sophie leaned into his side to rest her head against his arm. Alasdair immediately shifted that arm and curved it around her, drawing her against his chest instead.

She settled there, one hand and her cheek on his chest, and said, "It took three months for me to start talking again, and another three months before they decided I was recovered and could return to the world." Lifting her head so that she could look up at him, Sophie added, "I think they only waited that long after I started talking because they were cowards."

"Cowards?" he echoed with confusion.

Sophie nodded and lowered her head to rest it against him again. "They were afraid of discussing what they called my 'situation' and possibly causing a setback. So, they kind of did it in increments. They informed me gently that my parents and Blue—my dog—had perished in the fire." Her mouth twisted slightly. "As if I hadn't figured that out from what I'd witnessed and the fact that I hadn't seen any of them since that night."

Shaking her head, she continued, "Then they spent weeks watching me like a hawk and making me talk about how that made me 'feel,' before dropping the next bit of info they feared might be triggering."

"What was that?" Alasdair asked when she fell silent.

"That my father's family wouldn't take me in and wanted nothing to do with me," Sophie admitted. "That was invariably followed by more talk sessions about how it made me feel before they moved on to telling me that my aunt, my mother's sister, who lived in Nova Scotia and who I'd never met—was a single parent to several children and didn't feel she could take me on."

Sophie began to toy with the buttons on his shirt. "After several more talk sessions about how that made me feel, they then told me that, sadly, while they'd searched for foster families willing to take me in, my 'issues' were making it hard to find a placement and they feared they'd have to place me in a group home."

Alasdair was peering down at Sophie and saw her roll her eyes before she added, "Of course, then it was weeks more of asking how I felt about no one wanting to take the kid from the loony bin. Mostly because they had trouble accepting that it didn't bother me."

"It didn't?" Alasdair asked, unable to hide his surprise.

"See!" she exploded with exasperation, abruptly sitting upright to glare at him. "That's exactly how all those doctors and counselors reacted,"

"Sorry," Alasdair said quickly. "I just can't imagine not being crushed if my parents had died when I was young, and Uncle Ludan and the others had all refused to take Colle and I in."

Sophie relaxed at his explanation, and then nodded slowly. "Hmm. Well, that's where you're making your mistake. The same one they were making, I guess."

Alasdair's eyebrows drew together. "I don't understand."

Shifting to sit sideways on the end of the bed so that she faced him, Sophie crossed her legs and explained, "You know your uncle Ludan . . . and your uncles Connor, Inan, and Odart too, of course. You have history with them, and love them and they love you. Right?"

"Yeah," he said slowly.

"Well, I didn't know these relatives they were talking about. My father never spoke of his family, and while I think my mother mentioned that she had a much older sister living out East, that's basically all I knew about her. I'd never met her, or even heard anything about her." She raised her eyebrows. "Do you see? Like the unknown foster families, they were strangers who wouldn't take me in, not *family* who wouldn't take me in. My mom and dad were the only family I knew. So"—she shrugged—"it was kind of an 'oh well' situation to me."

"But surely you didn't want to go to a group home?" he asked, trying to understand.

"I was eleven years old," she pointed out. "I'd never even heard of group homes, so had no idea how bad they could be. They were just another group of people I didn't know. So, in my head, it was this stranger won't take you, that stranger won't take you, these strangers won't foster you, but these strangers will take you in."

"I see," Alasdair murmured, nodding now because he did see. No matter where she'd ended up, it would have been with strangers. Because, related or not, even the members of her mother's and father's birth families had been strangers to her.

"Besides, I was sure anywhere had to be better than the psych hospital," Sophie told him with amusement.

When he raised his eyebrows in question, she hesitated and then asked dryly, "Have you ever eaten hospital food?"

Alasdair smiled, but suspected that comment was just a deflection. He was sure time in the old psychiatric hospital hadn't been fun. Sophie might have been there because of the trauma caused the night her parents died, but he knew there would have been patients in there with her who'd had more serious ailments than mutism and night terrors. Patients who had more than likely been terrifying to a young eleven-year-old girl who had just lost everything.

"Speaking of food," Sophie said lightly, standing up. "We should go back out to the kitchen and see if your uncles have eaten ours."

"Wait," Alasdair said, getting up as well. When she paused and turned back to him, he examined her expression, and then sighed and said, "They're going to want to talk about your parents' deaths and what they found out."

"You mean the arson they claim happened," she said, her smile fading.

Alasdair nodded. "And probably about the other people in your life who have died, like your fiancés and your first love."

Sophie gave a start at that, her gaze flying to his face. "What? Why?"

Alasdair took a moment to marshal his thoughts, and then spoke carefully. "Because their deaths were all . . . You've lost a lot of people in your life."

"Yeah," Sophie acknowledged. "Bobby calls me the Black Widow and teases me that I'm cursed," she admitted with a bitter twist to her lips, and then noting his concern, she offered a brittle smile and said, "Don't worry, you should be safe as long as you don't give me a ring."

Sophie turned toward the door again, but then immediately swung back, her eyes suddenly narrowed. "How do you guys know about my fiancés? I told you about my parents, Beverly, and Andrew, but I didn't mention that I even had fiancés, let alone that they had died."

Alasdair took a moment to acknowledge that Andrew *had* been her first love, and then realized she was glaring at him now with suspicion. Unfortunately, he had no idea how to explain how they'd known. He could hardly tell her that Marguerite had read her mind at the wedding and plucked out all this information, but he didn't want to lie.

"Marguerite told me," he admitted, feeling bad even as the words left his mouth. It didn't make him take them back, though. First of all, that was actually the truth. Secondly, he could smooth over the Marguerite business later. But most importantly, right now he needed Sophie to trust him.

"Well, how the hell did she know?" Sophie asked, amazement on her face.

When Alasdair gave a helpless shrug, unable to explain without revealing everything to her, she huffed with exasperation and turned to hurry out of the room.

He followed, worried about what was coming and how they were going to handle this without telling her who and what they were.

Twenty-Two

Sophie entered the kitchen to find Tybo, Colle, Ludan, and Connor sitting in the tall chairs at her island. Without any other options, Inan and Odart had hefted themselves onto the kitchen counter. Her gaze slid slowly over the uncles, noting that they were wearing kilts again. Although, not really kilts. These ones had large swatches of cloth drawn up over one shoulder and across the chest. Plaids, she thought they were called, before she turned her attention to the men as a whole. She'd heard them talking as she'd approached, but their voices had all died immediately at her appearance.

Crossing her arms, Sophie surveyed them, her gaze running over each one in turn before shifting back to Tybo and halting there. She arched one eyebrow.

Tybo kind of froze under her gaze, then glanced down at the steak he'd been cutting into when she entered. Setting down the fork and knife, he muttered, "Sorry. It smells good and I was only going to try a bite."

Sophie scowled and said, "Why were you looking into my parents' deaths? And how did Marguerite know about my fiancés?" She paused a beat, before the final question burst out of her almost against her will. "Was it really arson?"

Tybo hesitated, and then simply turned to hold out a hand to Inan. Alasdair's uncle immediately picked up a black valise she hadn't noticed on the counter beside him. He handed it silently to Tybo, who held it out to her.

Sophie stared at the valise for a moment as if it were a snake, but then reluctantly reached out and took it. Clasping it in both hands, she glanced to Alasdair as he shifted beside her. Meeting her gaze, he nodded encouragingly, and she sighed unhappily and carried the valise to the bit of free counter next to the refrigerator to set it down and open it.

Everyone was silent as she pulled out several files and laid them out side by side. There were copies of the police and fire investigator's reports on the death of her parents, as well as copies of both her medical files and her files from the caseworker who had been assigned to her on her parents' deaths.

Swallowing, Sophie started with the easiest and opened the caseworker's file. There wasn't much there that surprised her, except that from her caseworker's notes, the woman had seemed to like her. In her memory, the woman had always seemed busy and harried, with little time for her, but her notes showed that she'd kept a close eye on Sophie and had found her sweet and intelligent. She'd thought she would do well in life despite the traumas she'd suffered.

Smiling faintly, Sophie closed that file and moved on to the medical file. That was much thicker, and she really just leafed through it quickly with only a brief stop here and there if something caught her eye. Again, there were no surprises. Most of it was just medical jargon for "this kid is traumatized by watching her parents die," and then more medical jargon on the different medications and methods they'd used to help her through it.

Setting it on top of the caseworker file, Sophie debated over the last two files. The police report on her parents' deaths, or the fire investigator's report. Which to read first? Finally, she selected the file holding the copy of the fire investigator's report and opened it. Words immediately started jumping out at her. Catastrophic level fire. Incendiary cause. Pour pattern. Accelerant.

Sophie flipped through the pages more quickly, freezing when she came to copies of photos. The first was of a burnt-out husk of a room that she presumed was in the home she'd grown up in. But she couldn't even tell which room it was. It was just a blackened wall on one side and charred two-by-fours on the other two visible walls where the drywall had apparently burned away. Other than that, there was just black debris everywhere, the burnt ashes and remains of whatever furniture had filled the room.

Afraid of what the other photos might hold, she didn't look further, but closed the file and then just stood there trying to absorb that the fire that had killed her parents and the family dog, Blue, and that she'd always thought was accidental, had been arson. Someone had deliberately set their house on fire, resulting in her parents' deaths. Murder.

Why had she never been told? How could this have been kept from her? Sophie wondered if the Tomlinsons had known, but even as she did she realized they must have. Surely it would have been in the news at the time. As for why she'd never been told, she knew the answer to that too. They all—the Tomlinsons, the police, and her doctors—had no doubt felt it better not to tell her for fear she'd have a "setback" and wind up in the hospital again.

Her gaze slid to the medical file and her eyes narrowed, then she snatched it up and opened it again. This time she read more carefully and found her answer. It had been deemed "inadvisable" to inform her at that time that the fire that killed her parents had been arson. Perhaps when she was older, more stable and better able to cope with the information, it could be shared with her, but as of the date of her release from the psychiatric hospital, it was considered more prudent to withhold that information.

Sophie's mouth tightened, and then she shifted the medical file aside again and reached for the police report, only to pause when a hand was suddenly on top of it, keeping her from opening it.

Turning sharply, Sophie scowled when she saw that the hand belonged to Tybo. He now stood beside her, his expression solemn.

"There are pictures of your parents' bodies, Sophie," he warned gently. "You don't want to see that."

Sophie released her hold on the file at once and stepped back as if it might bite her. Because he was right, she had no desire to see her parents' charred bodies. Her memory of her mother on fire had been hard enough to live with. She just couldn't . . .

"Come sit down, lass."

Sophie turned to see Connor getting up from the chair he'd been occupying and gesturing to it. Suddenly aware that her legs were shaking, she nodded faintly and crossed to the chair, relieved when Alasdair followed and took the seat next to her, his original seat and the one Tybo had been sitting in just moments ago.

"Right." Connor walked around to stand on the opposite side of the island and leaned against the range on that side as he met her gaze. "Ye'll be wantin' some explanations."

"Please," she said, her voice raspy and throat dry.

"Fetch 'er a drink," Ludan growled.

Inan sprang off the counter and hurried to find a glass.

"Lass," Connor said, drawing her attention away from Inan. "I'm jest goin' to lay it out fer ye."

Sophie nodded and waited.

"The fire was deliberate. Yer parents were murdered."

She already knew that, so simply waited for him to tell her more.

"The police report'll no' tell ye more than that. They never sorted who was behind settin' the fire."

Sophie sank back in her seat unhappily at this news, only realizing then that some part of her had hoped that the culprit had been captured and that too had just been kept from her.

"We ken ye were young," Connor said now. "But do ye remember anyone yer ma or da had problems with? Someone ye may ha'e heard yer ma or da arguing with?"

Sophie shook her head at once. She didn't recall anything like that. As far as she remembered, everyone had loved her parents. Her gaze flickered to Inan as he set a glass of soda before her and she murmured, "Thank you."

Inan gave her a wink and moved back to sit on the counter again.

"Okay," Connor said as she reached for the glass. "Did ye ever hear yer parents talking about maybe someone at yer da's workplace? A jealous coworker or something o' the like?"

Sophie set the glass back down and turned it idly as she thought about that, but after a moment she shook her head again.

Connor was peering at her hard, his gaze concentrated, but then he sighed and relaxed. "Can ye tell us who in yer life died next, after yer parents?"

Sophie blinked in surprise at the question, and it was Alasdair who said, "Andrew."

"Andrew isn't dead," she pointed out at once.

"He's been in a coma for—" He paused and raised his eyebrows. "How long?"

"Nearly seventeen years," she answered quietly.

"That's as good as dead," Connor decided and asked, "Who was he? Was he important to ye?"

Sophie gave up arguing about whether Andrew should be considered dead or not and admitted, "He was my best friend's brother . . . and my first love."

All the men but Alasdair nodded now, as if expecting the words.

"How did he die?" Inan asked.

Sophie quickly ran through the story she'd told Alasdair earlier, ending with finding him in the park.

"Did anyone witness this accident?" Tybo asked when she finished.

"I don't think so," she said quietly.

"Surely there were others in the park?" Connor pressed. "Or houses or buildin's around it where someone could ha'e looked out and seen it?"

Sophie grimaced, realizing she'd left out a bit of information. "It wasn't really a park. We just called it that. It was really an old shopping mall that had been shut down years earlier. It was boarded up, but someone had pulled off one of the big wide panels of wood in back where a delivery door was. They'd forced the door. You could just move the panel and slip inside, then replace the panel so it looked to be still secure."

"And Andrew liked to skateboard in there?" Alasdair asked with surprise. "An old mall?"

"It was cool," she said defensively. "It was two floors with the stores and a walkway all around the outside. On the main floor, the center was taken up with a large open area with a huge multileveled fountain in the middle. Of course, there was no water in it by then," Sophie said. "The second floor was set up the same way, only the center had been left open with railings around it so that you could look down on the fountain. The boys loved skateboarding in there, they could use the stairs and the rim around the fountain to do tricks."

"But with the windows and doors boarded up, it must have been dark in there," Alasdair protested. "How did they see to do their tricks?"

"It wasn't dark. Not in the center area. Well, not during the day anyway," she added. "There were huge honking skylights in the roof over the center area, which were actually still intact. They were dirty, but still allowed in a lot of light."

"Ah." Alasdair nodded, but then asked, "Why did you call it 'the park'?"

"It was kind of a code name. We weren't supposed to be there," she pointed out. "If anyone at the group home had realized we were in and out of that place, they'd have freaked. So we called it the park. The kids all knew what it meant when you were 'going to the park.' The adults didn't, though, and just thought we were literally at a park," she explained. "Besides, we considered it our version of a skateboard park anyway."

"So, no one from the street would have seen Andrew's accident, only someone actually inside the building. Another skateboarder," Tybo said thoughtfully.

Sophie nodded. "But I'm guessing there weren't any skateboarders there when he had his accident or someone would have gone for help," she reasoned. "There was no one there when we found him."

"Then there was no one to tell if it wasn't an accident," Connor said solemnly.

Her gaze shot to the man with surprise. "You don't believe it was an accident?"

He shrugged and shook his head at the same time. "It's hard to say now all these years later."

"We might be able to tell from the incident report the police would have made at the time. It should have the medical report in it," Tybo pointed out. "Or if someone went to the hospital now and read his mi—"

"Medical report," Alasdair interrupted quickly. "You should have someone read his medical report."

Tybo had paused with his mouth open, but now closed it, chagrin on his face as he glanced to Sophie. "Right. Medical report. I'll call Mortimer and suggest he send someone over to read him—I mean, his medical report." He withdrew his phone and stood up, only to pause and ask, "What is Andrew's last name?"

"Hillbrook," she answered quietly.

Nodding, Tybo started punching numbers into his phone as he headed for the door.

"Who in your life died next?" Connor asked abruptly, drawing Sophie's attention away from the departing Tybo.

Sophie scowled at their insistence on acting as if Andrew were dead, but answered, "Beverly. She was Andrew's sister and my best friend. She died two weeks after his accident."

"What happened to her?"

Sophie quickly explained about her peanut allergy, and ended with the point that had bothered her for seventeen years. "I still don't understand how it happened. She was always careful and hadn't even eaten anything."

"Ye mean she didn'y eat anything ye thought would have nuts?" Connor asked, his gaze narrowing on her, somewhere in the vicinity of her forehead. Although, he appeared to be staring there a lot. But then all the men were except for Alasdair. It kind of made her uncomfortable.

"No. I mean, I don't think she ate anything at all. We were at our lockers, putting our coats away and collecting our books and stuff. I doubt she'd stopped for a snack. We were running a bit late that morning because we'd had to drop off our project to the history class." Sophie paused, her lips briefly pursing as she recalled it. "Megan and I had lockers side by side, but Beverly's was a little way down the hall, so I didn't realize she was in trouble right away. It wasn't until people started exclaiming and freaking out that I realized something was up.

"I ran down and pushed my way through the group of kids gathering around her to see that she was on the floor, gasping for air and clawing at her neck. Her backpack was open on the floor beside her like she'd been searching it. I knew right away what the problem was. I dropped to my knees beside her and started searching for her EpiPen, but it wasn't in the inner pocket that she normally kept it in. It was at the bottom of her bag. By the time I found it and gave her an injection . . ." Sophie sighed. "I guess it was too late. The ambulance attendants arrived shortly after I gave her the injection, but she was gone. They tried CPR but . . ." She shook her head.

A moment of silence passed, and then Inan said, "She *must* have eaten something with nuts in it. Maybe someone gave her a candy or cookie or—"

"No," Sophie said firmly. "While the ambulance guys tried to resuscitate her, I asked everyone what she'd eaten. Everyone said she hadn't eaten anything, she'd undone her lock, took off her coat and gloves, tucked them into her locker, and then started to gasp for air."

After a brief pause, she added, "Besides, they did an autopsy on Beverly to find out what had caused the allergic reaction. I heard a couple members of our staff talking about it. They said that while they found traces of peanut oil on her lips, the only thing in her stomach was the banana she'd eaten that morning." She frowned, and then told them, "They swabbed her lock and locker door to see if peanut oils had somehow got on one of them, but there was nothing. They couldn't figure out how she'd come in contact with peanuts."

They were all silent for a minute. Sophie didn't know what the men were thinking, but she was wondering if Beverly, like her parents, had been murdered. She'd never even considered that before this. She'd always thought it had just been bad luck or a fluke. But now that she knew her parents had been murdered, she was examining Beverly's death from a different perspective.

"Who died next?" Connor asked abruptly, interrupting her pondering.

Sophie shook off her thoughts and said without having to think about it. "John. My first actual fiancé."

"First actual fiancé?" Inan asked.

"Well, Andrew was sort of—" she started, and then said, "A week before he died, Andrew gave me a ring. But he called it a promise ring. He said he'd get me a real ring once he had a job and could buy a proper engagement ring. He said we were engaged to be engaged," she added with a faint smile.

"Right," Connor said on a weary sounding sigh, and then cleared his throat and said, "Tell us about John, then."

"John," she murmured, shifting gears in her mind. "We met first year of university and were engaged near the end of second year. A few weeks later, during exams, he was hit by a car on his way back to his dorm from my place. It was late, one or two A.M., I think. It was a hit and run. He was just left there to die by the side of the road. The police figured it was a drunk driver because of the hour. He wasn't found until the next morning."

"John's last name?" Tybo asked, drawing her attention to the fact that he now stood in the doorway, his phone still pressed to his ear.

"Houghton," she answered.

"Who was next?" Ludan asked, and Tybo, who had started to turn away, talking into the phone, paused and swung back and waited.

"Derek Winston," Sophie answered unhappily.

Tybo immediately turned away again and she heard him repeat the name into the phone.

Sophie lowered her gaze and shifted unhappily in her seat. She'd lost so many loved ones over the years. She'd known that of course. But now that she was having to list them out . . . there were so many, and not one of them had been by natural causes.

"Tell us about Derek," Connor requested gently.

Sophie forced herself to sit up and said, "He was an agent at the insurance company where I work. We hit it off and started dating. But we kept it quiet at first because . . . well, office romance, hello? I was afraid Papa—Mr. Tomlinson—wouldn't approve," she explained. "We dated for nearly a year, and things were going great, and then Derek proposed."

She lowered her head unhappily. "I said no at first because I was afraid everyone would be upset, not just that I'd dated someone in the office, but that we'd snuck around to do it. We fought about it. He wanted to come out in the open with our relationship. I didn't. Finally, he convinced me to accept his proposal and the ring with the caveat that I'd wear it on a necklace under my blouse until he figured out a way to make our relationship public without upsetting everyone."

Her hand moved automatically to her chest where the ring used to lie nestled between her breasts. It wasn't there anymore. She'd stopped wearing it last year, a year after his death.

"Derek's figuring it out was to look for a job elsewhere," Sophie continued finally. "About a month later he'd found one, and gave notice at the insurance company." She smiled faintly at the memory. "We were going to wait a couple weeks and then 'start dating,' or at least let everyone think that was when we started dating. The plan was to 'date' for a couple of months and then come out as engaged. We felt that shortened timeline would be accepted because we'd known each other for so long before supposedly starting to date."

Her hand dropped from her chest. "But none of that happened. The day after Derek gave notice, he was in a car accident on the way home from my apartment. He was T-boned. It was early morning. No witnesses."

"The killer's developed a pattern," Connor commented thoughtfully.

The men all grunted, but Sophie raised her eyebrows and shook her head. "Other than their all ending up dead, I'm not seeing a pattern."

"Because ye're no' includin' Alasdair and Colle," Inan told her.

Sophie stiffened, her gaze shooting to Alasdair. He peered back silently and covered both of her hands in her lap with one of his to squeeze reassuringly. It was Connor who pointed out, "Alasdair was hit by a car last night while leaving your apartment. A hit and run."

"Oh yes," Sophie murmured. She hadn't forgotten about that exactly, but he hadn't been hurt in the accident. He hadn't even had any of the bruising he'd suggested he'd got away with. She knew that for a certainty, she'd seen the man naked. There wasn't a mark on him. That being the case, she hadn't thought to include him in the count.

"And then today, the tow truck Colle was riding in was T-boned when they left here," Inan added.

"What?" Sophie asked with shock. She knew he'd got the keys from Alasdair and had accompanied the tow truck towing the SUV back to work for him. Alasdair had told her that. But this was the first she was hearing of a crash taking place. She turned to look at Colle, who was sitting on the other side of Ludan in one of the chairs along the end of the island. From what she could see he looked fine. There was no sign of injury.

"You were in an accident?" she asked with a frown.

"There was nothing accidental about it," Colle said grimly. "Someone came out of a side street and plowed into my side of the tow truck on purpose."

"How bad was it?" Sophie asked with concern, her gaze sliding over what she could see of him again.

"The driver was killed," he said quietly.

That just confused her. If they'd been T-boned on the passenger side, Colle should have been the one killed, yet he seemed unharmed. Besides—"Why would anyone try to kill Colle? I mean, if someone is killing off people in my life, why go after Colle? I barely know him."

"We think whoever 'twas mistook him fer Alasdair,"

Connor explained, and pointed out, "They're identical, ye ken."

Sophie's eyebrows rose. She wouldn't say they were identical. They were close, but Colle smiled too much and Alasdair . . . Well, there was just something different about him. The way she felt when he was near . . . She didn't experience anything close to that around Colle.

"Maybe it was just an accident. A coincidence," she suggested.

Inan shook his head. "There was nought accidental about it, lass. The SUV wouldn'y start when ye two were goin' to leave because the cables on the battery had been detached. It was deliberately disabled, which forced it to be towed." He let that sink in and then said, "And the vehicle that T-boned the tow truck was able to drive away. We think it must ha'e had a reinforced front, or that it had a snowplow blade or somethin' o' the like on the front that took the impact."

"Ye've got a murderin' bastard on yer tail, lass," Connor said grimly. "They're goin' after anyone ye love, and Colle took an attack meant for Alasdair."

Sophie gave a start and protested, "I don't love Alasdair."

Twenty-Three

Sophie's own words echoed in her head in the silence that followed.

I don't love Alasdair.

Aware that everyone was staring at her, she shifted uncomfortably and then glanced at Alasdair. His expression was inscrutable. She couldn't tell how he felt about her statement. Still, discomfort moved her to say, "I mean, I like you. A lot. Even a lot, a lot. But we only met the day before yesterday. It would be crazy to say I love you already. Not that I can't see myself loving you, but not yet. Not after forty-eight hours and two dates."

Sophie shut up then, and silently berated herself for letting her mouth run away on her. She didn't need to explain why she couldn't possibly love him yet, and doing so just made her think of that old saying, The lady doth protest too much.

"It's been more than two dates. At least three or

four," Inan said now, and then counted off, "Lunch and dinner yesterday, and then back here for dessert afterward. Then there's today too. Well, yesterday now," he added with a glance at the clock.

Sophie looked to it now and was surprised to see that it was after midnight. So, Sunday now. It had obviously been later than she'd thought when she'd woken up and decided to cook supper.

"So, really, it's been four dates," Inan continued. "Five if ye count the wedding."

"The wedding?" she asked with disbelief.

"Aye. Well, I ken ye were on a date with Tybo, but ye spent half o' it sat next to our Alasdair, so I'm thinkin' it was as much a date with him as Tybo."

An irritated sound drew their attention to a scowling Tybo. He'd put his phone away and was now leaning against the doorframe, arms crossed and looking obviously annoyed at Inan's words.

Sophie gave him a sympathetic smile, and then turned back to Inan. Trying for a lightly amused tone, she said, "Three dates or five, it still isn't long enough to think I've fallen in love with him."

"Ye keep tellin' yerself that, lass," Connor said with real amusement, and then his expression sobered as he continued, "But apparently the murderin' bastard who's been plaguing ye fer nigh on twenty years thinks ye do love Alasdair. And he's determined to remove him from yer life. Ye can see we need to sort out who it is and stop him."

"Aye." Inan slid off the counter again and moved forward to stand next to Connor. "Who's been in yer life for the last twenty years since yer ma and da died?"

"The parents' death might not be part of this," Alasdair pointed out. "Maybe you shouldn't include it."

"It was arson. Murder," Connor argued. "O' course we ha'e to include it."

"But twenty years is a long time," Colle pointed out, backing up his twin. "Her parents' murder might be separate from all the rest of the deaths. A different killer."

"Ye think there're murderers hidin' around e'ery corner?" Connor asked with amusement.

"No, of course not," Colle said with irritation. "But—"

"Besides," Connor interrupted him, "the brother and sister, Andrew and . . ."

"Beverly," Sophie supplied when Uncle Connor hesitated.

"Aye, Beverly," he said with a nod to her. "They both died just three or four years after the parents, and two weeks apart."

"True," Alasdair allowed. "But the parents' death was arson, Andrew's cause of death a head wound, and Beverly died from anaphylactic shock."

Colle nodded. "Serial killers don't usually change their MO. It's possible Andrew and Beverly weren't murder, but just accidental deaths, and the murder of Sophie's mom and dad has nothing to do with the deaths of her fiancés and the attacks on us."

Sophie stiffened at Colle's words. *Serial killers don't usually change their MO.* Serial killers? She had a serial killer running around bumping off the people she loved? Her gaze moved to Alasdair with alarm. Someone was trying to kill him because of her.

"I ken that's the general consensus," Connor growled

with irritation, "but what if it's no' true? What if serial killers try different methods until they find the
one they like best? The arson could ha'e been a first
try. Expedient. But mayhap they didn'y like usin' fire.
Mayhap it wasn'y personal enough. They couldn'y
watch them die, so mayhap the next time they tried
bashin' in the boy's head."

"And they didn't like that way either?" Colle suggested dryly.

"Mayhap no', or mayhap it was too risky to use on
the sister, when the brother had jest died that way. So,
he used the lass's weakness, her peanut allergy, to do
'er in."

"And they didn't like that either so switched to ve-
hicular manslaughter?" Alasdair asked, obviously not
believing it.

The men continued to argue the matter back and
forth, but Sophie stopped listening. Instead, she tried
to wrap her mind around the possibility that she might
have a very sick individual killing the people she cared
about. A serial killer, they'd said, but she didn't think
that was the right term. Serial killers didn't usually
have a motive to kill their victims. Often, it was just a
matter of opportunity and the victim perhaps having a
certain trait. But if they were right, this killer had a motive, even if it was only to remove the people she loved.
So, she supposed that made the motive hurting her.

Sophie frowned at her own thoughts. Someone was
killing people she loved? Her gaze slid to Alasdair. He
was a beautiful man. He was also sweet, thoughtful,
and kind. He'd brought a selection of pizzas, salads, appetizers, and sodas to their dinner that must have cost
him an arm and a leg, yet he'd done that rather than risk

getting something she didn't like. He had helped with cleaning up at the office before leaving, helped prepare dinner tonight, and was always insisting on carrying things for her, opening doors for her, making sure she was safely inside before leaving.

And then there was the sex. The man was not only amazing at it, but considerate. He saw to it she found her pleasure first. And often last, Sophie thought wryly, since she'd developed a penchant for fainting every time she came.

In truth, Alasdair was a wonderful man. Any gal would be lucky to have him, and she didn't doubt for a minute that she could love him. She just wasn't comfortable saying she did love him already. They just hadn't known each other long enough to claim those feelings.

But whether she loved him or not didn't really matter. If someone thought she did and was trying to kill him because of it . . .

She needed to break up with him, Sophie realized. She had to end their relationship, kick him out of her life and make sure everyone knew it. She'd have to tell everyone at work and—and who else? All of her friends from university had kind of fallen by the wayside. Most had been from other towns and cities other than Toronto and had moved back to their hometowns. Others had chased jobs out to western Canada or the States. Her friends and family at work were pretty much the only people she knew. And among them, the Tomlinson family were the only people who had been in her life all the way back to the death of her parents.

Sophie did not like the direction her thoughts were taking. Megan, Bobby, and their parents were family.

The only family she had. But they *had* been there when it had all started. Living right next door. They'd even had an emergency key to their house, and her parents had had an emergency key to the Tomlinsons' too. It would have been easy to slip out, slink next door, creep inside, set the fire, and get back to their own home before the flames got big enough to draw attention.

Sophie ground her teeth together. She didn't want to think about that right now. She would sort it out later, but of paramount importance right now was making sure Alasdair was safe. She'd never forgive herself if anything happened to him. In fact, Sophie didn't think she could survive losing him like that. Her gaze focused on Alasdair as she tried to sort out how to go about it. She had just decided to simply tell the men to leave and ask Alasdair never to return, when Ludan suddenly spoke.

"Allie, lad. Ye need to tell the lass about us."

Alasdair stopped arguing with Connor and Inan and turned to his uncle with surprise. "What?"

"Tell her what we are," he growled.

Alasdair was shaking his head before Ludan had finished speaking. "She's not ready."

"Ye'll lose her do ye no' tell her," Ludan insisted.

Alasdair shook his head again and turned back to the other men to say, "I just think we should consider that the deaths are not necessarily all connected. Some could have been actual accid—" His words died abruptly and Sophie screamed in shock when Ludan suddenly lunged to lean past her across the island top and stab Alasdair in the chest.

For a heartbeat, all Sophie could do was gape. She couldn't believe Ludan had just stabbed his own nephew. But when he withdrew the knife and straightened to move away from the island, Sophie jumped from her chair and grabbed a dish towel off the counter, then wadded it up as she hurried back to press it against Alasdair's wound.

Alasdair glanced at his uncle and roared, "What the hell?"

"I was doin' ye a favor," Ludan growled mildly, walking over to rinse the knife under the tap. "She was going to break up with ye, it's why I told ye to tell her what ye are. But ye refused, so I decided to show her. Now she'll no' need to break up with ye."

"I think we can all agree there was an easier way to handle it than stabbing Alasdair," Tybo said with exasperation. Heading for the door, he added, "I'll go get the cooler."

Sophie stared after Tybo, amazed at his calm reaction to this. Then her gaze slid to the other men in the room. None of them seemed terribly upset. Like Tybo, Colle seemed more exasperated than anything, and the other three men, the uncles who hadn't stabbed Alasdair, were just watching with interest. None of them were reacting as she would have expected.

Ludan had stabbed Alasdair, for God's sake, and so damned close to his heart that the only reason she thought he'd missed it was because Alasdair was still alive.

"You were going to break up with me?" Alasdair asked, and she glanced to his face with amazement.

"Are you kidding me?" Sophie asked with disbelief. "Your uncle just stabbed you, and you're worried about my possibly breaking up with you?"

"Were you?" Alasdair asked insistently.

Scowling, she pressed harder on his wound and growled, "Yes. To save your life. If we aren't seeing each other, my murderous stalker won't have any reason to kill you. I thought it would keep you safe. I had no idea your crazy uncle would stab you for it," she added testily, and then suddenly stiffened. "Wait." Glancing over her shoulder at Ludan, she demanded, "How did you know I was going to break up with him?"

Drying off what turned out to be her steak knife, Ludan shrugged. "I read yer thoughts."

Sophie's lips twisted with disgust. "Will you just tell me, please, and not make up nonsense stories." Shifting her attention to the other men just standing around, she snapped, "Will one of you please call 911? Alasdair needs an ambulance and—" Her words ended on an alarmed gasp when Ludan returned to her side and jerked her hands off of Alasdair.

"What are you doing? I need to stop the bleeding," she cried, trying to place her hands back over the cloth. But Ludan held both of her hands in one of his and used the other to whip the cloth away from Alasdair's wound. Dropping the bloodstained cloth, he then used the same hand to jerk Alasdair's shirt open to reveal the wound and ordered, "Look."

Sophie scowled at the man and then turned a helpless gaze to Alasdair's wound. A two-inch slit in his skin that must have stretched a good five inches deep since the knife had been in up to the hilt. Despite the depth of the wound, there was no longer any sign of blood. Not on or around the wound. For a heartbeat she assumed that it was because the blood had been wiped up by the cloth as he'd whipped it away, but then she realized that there was no new blood bubbling up to leak from the wound. In fact—was the wound getting smaller?

"He's healin'," Ludan said, his tone matter-of-fact. "He's an immortal."

"He's a what?" Sophie asked on a disbelieving laugh as she turned to Ludan.

The man nodded, and growled, "We all are. And that makes us damned hard to kill," he assured her. "I should ken. I'm more than seven hundred years old and can'y count how many men ha'e tried to kill me o'er the centuries. It just doesn'y take."

When Sophie just stared at him, sure from both his words and actions that he was completely insane, Ludan caught her by the chin and turned her face back to Alasdair. "Look at his wound, lass. It's already sealin' up. That little stab I gave him was just a scratch for an immortal. Nothin' like the injuries he took when he was run down in front o' yer apartment. Those took hours to heal. But this here? It would ha'e killed you and any other mortal, but in an hour there won'y e'en be a scar on Alasdair's chest. Because he's immortal."

Sophie frowned as she peered at the closing wound. But then Ludan's words sank through and she shifted her gaze to Alasdair's face and accused, "You said you weren't hurt when the car hit you. That you saw it in time to hop on the hood and somersault safely away."

"I—" Alasdair began.

"He lied," Ludan snarled.

Alasdair cast a glare his way, and peered back at Sophie to add, "Only so you wouldn't worry."

Sophie frowned slightly, and then asked, "How badly were you hurt?" But even as she asked the question, she wasn't sure what to believe. Could he have been hurt? He'd been in the SUV when she got down there. He couldn't have been hurt that bad, and he hadn't looked hurt at all. Although, it had been dark.

"Lass," Inan said, "his right knee was nothin' but bone fragments, his fibula was snapped and stickin' out o' his left leg, his pelvis was shattered, his right arm was broken in three places, and his skull was caved in both on the right side o' his head from hittin' the windshield and the top back from when he came down on the pavement." He nodded solemnly. "Were he human, he would ha'e died there on the street. But because he's immortal, he dragged his sorry arse to the SUV and got in, then waited fer ye to reach him so he could reassure ye he was fine before makin' his way back to the Enforcer house for the blood he needed."

"Blood?" she asked with a start.

"Got it!" Tybo breezed into the kitchen with a cooler in hand and set it down on the counter to open. "I didn't think to grab your apartment keys on the way out. Fortunately, someone was entering as I returned so I just convinced them to hold the door for me."

Pulling out a bag of what looked to her like blood, Ludan turned and walked over to crouch on the other side of Alasdair.

"Open yer mouth," Ludan ordered.

"Uncle," Alasdair got out between clenched teeth. "Let me handle this."

"Allie, lad. I've been alive four hundred years longer than ye. Will ye just trust me? Marguerite is right, the lass needs to ken ye're no' goin' to die and break her heart. Open up and show her yer damned fangs."

Alasdair hesitated, his gaze locked with his uncle's for a minute, and then he sighed and opened his mouth.

As Sophie watched, his upper incisors shifted and slid down to become fangs, and Tybo popped the bag of blood onto them with one quick flick.

Dropping back onto her haunches, she stared silently as the bag began to shrink, pulling upward as the blood disappeared, apparently into his fangs.

"Vampires," Sophie whispered.

"Och, no!" Ludan barked. "Do no' even say that word in me presence. We're immortals, no' vampires."

Sophie turned to eye the man dubiously. "Which would be another word for vampires?"

"Lass, vampires are dead, soulless beings," Connor told her patiently. "They're also fictional characters. Immortals, however, are alive and we definitely have our souls."

When Sophie stared at him, unspeaking, Connor said, "Now, I ken it'll take a minute fer ye to accept this and understand, but the fact o' the matter is we're people just like you."

"Oh right. Except I don't have fangs and drink blood," she said sarcastically, and stood up to back a step away from Alasdair, and really all of them.

Ludan scowled and said, "She's frightened, Alasdair. Explain matters to her."

When Alasdair eyed the man with disbelief over the bag at his mouth, it was Colle who said, "I don't know that he should have to. After all, you started this by stabbing him and making him bring out his fangs."

Mention of Alasdair's fangs made Sophie glance his way to see that the blood was nearly gone, the bag a shriveled mass at his mouth with a lollipop-sized portion of blood still in it. She watched that quickly disappear with fascination and suddenly thought that this gave a whole new meaning to her earlier notion that Alasdair had an issue with sucking. Her next thought, though, was to worry over whether he'd ever sucked her blood. Were the hickeys hiding fang holes? She hadn't really looked at them too closely. She'd just acknowledged them and done her best to cover them up or hide them. But they were all over her body. Dear God, was that why she was fainting? Were all of those hickeys covering her body, hiding bite marks?

It was possible, Sophie realized. She hadn't really examined them closely, mostly because she'd been embarrassed. Now she stood up abruptly and rushed from the room, muttering, "I need to use the bathroom."

Twenty-Four

"Well?" Uncle Ludan barked.

"Well what?" Alasdair growled.

"Are ye no' goin' to chase after the lass?" he demanded with exasperation.

"She's going to the bathroom. I'm pretty sure she does not want company for that," he pointed out testily.

"Lad, I realize you can'y read her so I'll just tell ye, she's goin' to the bathroom so she can check to make sure that she hasn'y got bite marks hidden in all those hickeys ye've given her."

"Speakin' o' which," Connor interjected, "from readin' her mind, it would seem that ye tried to make a map on her body o' all countries in the world using hickeys."

"That's what comes o' weanin' a bairn too early," Inan opined, and then shook his head. "I tried to warn Marsle when she decided 'twas time to take the pair o' 'em off the teat, but she wouldn'y listen."

"Dear God," Alasdair growled, and launched himself out of his seat, but then winced as his not quite fully healed chest complained at the movement. As he waited for the pain to pass, he scowled at Ludan. "You couldn't think of a less painful way to reveal what we are to her?"

Ludan considered that briefly and then nodded. "I suppose I could've stabbed Colle." Both brothers gaped at the man as he continued, "But that didn'y seem right since he's just finished healin' from getting T-boned in yer stead."

"You could've stabbed yourself," Alasdair pointed out grimly.

"Now, why the devil would I do that?" Ludan asked with surprise. "She's *yer* mate."

Expelling an exasperated breath, Alasdair left the room and headed for the bedroom in search of Sophie. He gave a glance back at the end of the hall and saw that his uncles as well as Colle and Tybo were following. Alasdair glared at them, expecting that would be enough to tell them they weren't welcome, and then entered the bedroom and crossed to the bathroom door.

Alasdair paused there, reached for the doorknob, hesitated, and then raised his hand to knock.

"Sophie?" he called, tapping on the door. "Are you all right?"

"I'm fine," she snapped. "Go away."

Alasdair grimaced and shifted his feet. "Sophie, love, I know this is a bit of a shock—"

"A shock?" she asked on a disbelieving laugh. "A shock would be finding out you were married. I just watched fangs pop out of your mouth and you suck blood through them. That's not a shock, that's some horror story shit there, Alasdair."

Alasdair grunted. He could hardly argue with that. Scratching his head, he took a moment to figure out what to say next, and then tried, "There is a bright side to this."

"A bright side?" she echoed with disbelief.

"At least you don't have to worry about me dying on you like your past fiancés."

A choked sound came through the door and then she growled, "You are *not* my fiancé. As for your not dying . . . well, frankly, right now I'm not thinking that's necessarily a good thing. For God's sake, Alasdair, you're a vampire!"

"Honey, like Uncle Ludan told you, we're immortals, not vampires."

A very unamused snort came from the other side of the door. "Well, Alasdair, *honey*, you can call it what you want, but if it looks like a duck and quacks like duck, it's a damned duck."

"We're not ducks!" he protested, and then cursed. "I mean vampires. We're not vampires. We're immortals."

"Did you bite me?" Sophie asked sharply, and he could hear the sound of rustling clothing. She was obviously examining her body for bite marks.

"I have never bitten you, I swear," Alasdair said solemnly. "I would never bite you." He paused and then admitted, "At least not without your permission."

Alasdair barely heard her words when she muttered, "Like that would ever happen."

Ignoring it, he said patiently, "Sophie, you saw me consuming that bag of blood in the kitchen. That's

how we feed now. We do not feed on people anymore."

Alasdair only realized his mistake when she
squawked, "*Anymore?*"

Groaning, he leaned his forehead against the door.
"Before blood banks, we did have to feed off of
people. But we never killed them," Alasdair added
quickly. "We just took what we needed to stay alive.
Think of it like milking a cow . . . without the involve-
ment of teats. Well, usually anyway," he muttered to
be completely honest. "The point is, you don't need
to kill a cow to get milk and we don't have to kill
mortals to get blood. In fact, it's inadvisable. It re-
duces the herd you can milk in future."

"Did you seriously just compare me to a cow?" Sophie sounded pretty outraged. "And what the hell do
you mean it *usually* doesn't involve teats? Have you
been running around for the last however many years,
just biting women's boobs for blood? Like their wrist
or neck wouldn't do the job? You just had to bite a
boob? I'm really starting to think you have some kind
of oral fetish there, buddy."

Alasdair was staring at the door at a complete loss,
wondering how it had all gone so wrong, when he was
suddenly pushed aside. Glancing around with surprise, he saw that his uncle Ludan had pushed him
out of the way and was now taking his place in front
of the door.

A glance around the room then showed him that every one of the men had followed him inside despite his
glare and had no doubt witnessed the entire conversation so far. That was obvious from the fact that Colle
had his forehead in his palm, and the rest of them

were staring at him with a combination of horror and accusation, telling him he was making a mess of this.

As if he didn't already know that, Alasdair thought with a sigh. There was a reason he didn't like to talk much, and it wasn't just that he didn't like people.

"Eeejit," Ludan growled at him, and then faced the door. "Lass, I promise ye, Alasdair has no' been bitin' lass's boobs for blood for his three centuries," he assured her in a raspy voice, and then frowned and glanced to Alasdair with narrowed eyes. "Have ye?"

"No. Of course not," Alasdair snapped.

"Right." He turned back to the door. "See. He hasn'y."

There was silence for a minute, and then Sophie asked, "I'm sorry, did you say three centuries?"

"Aye," Ludan grunted.

"He's three hundred years old?"

"Nay," Ludan said at once. "Older. He and Colle were born in 1699."

A high keening sound came from the bathroom and Ludan frowned, then turned to him in question.

Alasdair shrugged helplessly. "Sophie? Are you okay?"

"Okay?" she echoed faintly, and then roared, "No, I'm not okay. I've spent the better part of the last twenty-four hours bouncing around on a penis that's more than three hundred years old. How many other women have bounced on it, Alasdair?" she demanded, and then when he was slow to answer, said, "If it was only one a year, that's still three hundred. But there are—how many days is that? Three hundred multiplied by three hundred and sixty-five days is . . . 109,500. *One hundred and nine thousand, five hundred days*, and you had me in bed the first night we went out. If you did that with all the women in your life, that could be 109,500 women who have bounced on your cock! More, because you're more than three hundred years old. How many diseases could you have? How much—?"

"Lass," Ludan interrupted her diatribe with a frown. "I guarantee ye it's no' been that many. He can'y ha'e bedded more than . . . oh . . . say thirty-five thousand. Fifty thousand tops," he added judiciously, and ignoring Alasdair's moan, explained, "Most immortals lose interest in sex after the first century or so o' living."

"Oh, do they?" she asked sarcastically.

"Aye," Ludan said firmly. "I meself ha'e no' bothered with it since I was one hundred and twenty."

"Well, I hate to tell you this, Ludan," Sophie said dryly, "but that's definitely not the case with your nephew. Alasdair's been hella into sex since we met. Like I'm sore from how into it he's been and— Oh dear God, what if I'm sore because he's given me one of any number of STDs he's probably carrying?" she asked suddenly.

Ludan frowned and glanced to Alasdair. "What's an STD?"

"A sexually transmitted disease," he answered on a sigh.

Ludan nodded and turned back to the door. "If ye're sore, lass, it can'y be because o' an STD. The nanos wouldn'y allow him to ha'e any."

"What?" Sophie sounded confused. "Nanos? What are you talking about?"

"There! Ye can explain now," Ludan told Alasdair with satisfaction as if somehow he'd helped him out.

Shaking his head with disgust, Alasdair pushed his

uncle out of the way and took his place at the door again. "Sophie?"

"What?" She sounded wary again.

"Will you please allow me to explain?" he asked gently.

"Explain what?" she asked, her voice grim now.

Alasdair didn't bother to answer that, but simply launched into his explanation. "We really are immortals, and not soulless, dead vampires. Uncle Ludan wasn't lying about that."

"Uh-huh," Sophie said, not sounding convinced. "And yet you have fangs, drink blood, and can't be killed," she pointed out. "Apparently, none of you age either because you all look twenty-five to thirty years old, including your *seven-hundred-year-old uncle Ludan*," she emphasized and then muttered, "You're over three hundred yourself. I guess this explains why everybody at the wedding looked so young."

"Yes, but it's not because we're dead and soulless vampires," he insisted. "Look, I'm going to give you the short version to help you understand," Alasdair said, and paused briefly to think, then started with, "Our ancestors come from Atlantis."

"Oh boy, here we go," Sophie moaned. "Now you're going to tell me you have webbed feet and gills to go along with those fangs, aren't you? How could I miss that?" she asked with dismay, and then answered in a near whisper he suspected none of them were supposed to hear, "Because I wasn't looking at his feet. I was hypnotized by his penis. Lord help me, my boyfriend's a vampire fishman from Atlantis with a magic penis."

Alasdair pulled his head back and looked at the

door with disbelief, and then grunted in pain when his uncle punched him in the arm.

When Alasdair turned to scowl at him, the man grinned encouragingly and said, "Good on ye, lad. The lass thinks yer tadger is magic."

Alasdair glowered at him and then faced the door again. "I am not a vampire fishman, and I do not have gills or webbed feet," he said irritably. "People from Atlantis were just like everyone else on the planet. The only difference was that my ancestors' home country was isolated from the rest of the world by mountains, and the ocean."

He paused, but when silence reigned in the bathroom, Alasdair continued, "Left to their own devices, they developed faster than people in the rest of the world. Their technology grew swiftly, until they were not just years ahead of the rest of the world technologically, but by at least a millennium. Nanos were one of their inventions. They were created by a scientist who hoped they would be a noninvasive way to heal every illness and injury, removing the need for surgery."

"How?" Sophie asked, at least sounding interested, he noted, feeling a little hope creep up inside him.

"The nanos would . . . well, they repair injuries using blood, and when it comes to illness, they surround any virus or bacteria that doesn't belong and remove it from the body."

"Nanos," she murmured on the other side of the door.

"You've heard of those, right?" he asked.

"Well, yeah. But Atlantis is supposed to have existed like thousands and thousands of years ago."

"Yes, it did," Alasdair agreed.

"Huh," Sophie muttered. "And you're trying to tell me that they developed nanos way back then?"

Alasdair grimaced at her open disbelief. "Yes, they did," he assured her. "And they probably would've improved their technology even further except that earthquakes and whatnot struck and destroyed Atlantis. Most of our people died. Only the ones who had the nanos survived, and they moved out to join the rest of the world."

"That doesn't explain the fangs and blood thing," she pointed out, sounding suspicious.

"Well, that came about because of the fall of Atlantis and the directive the nanos had been given." Alasdair stopped, frowned, and then backtracked. "I should've mentioned the nanos are bioengineered, which means they use blood to make copies of themselves and to make all the repairs. Of course, that takes a lot of blood, sometimes more than the human body can produce, depending on—you know—what they're having to repair." He paused and then sighed unhappily and pointed out, "Sophie, this would be easier if I could talk to you face-to-face."

"Well, Alasdair, this would be easier for me if we didn't have to discuss it at all," she countered, and then muttered, "Only I could end up dating a deranged bloodsucker."

"I'm not deranged!" he protested, and then tried for calm and asked, "Sophie, seriously, do we seem dangerous to you?"

"Do you seem dangerous?" she asked with disbelief. "Your uncle just stabbed you in the kitchen."

"Actually, he stabbed me in the chest," he countered, trying to lighten the situation, and earned only silence. Apparently, she wasn't in the mood for humor, he thought, and sighed. "Yes, he stabbed me. It was to show you that I will heal so you don't have to worry about my dying. I can handle anything that your murderer throws at me, Sophie."

"Don't call him *my* murderer," she snarled, unlocking and yanking the bathroom door open to glower at him furiously.

"I'm sorry," Alasdair said soothingly. "I didn't mean it that way, sweetheart."

He reached out for her, but she jerked back away from him and he let his hands drop. "Sophie, I'm a human being with some nanos inside me that make me immortal. Age, like illness and injuries, is seen as something that they have to fight. So, yes, we all look about twenty-eight years old, which is when mortals are at their peak condition. And yes, I'm over three hundred years old, my uncle Ludan is over seven hundred years old, and my great-great-great . . . I'm not sure how many *great*s fit in there, but Nicodemus Notte, the head of our clan, is thousands of years old. But all that means is I'm not gonna die easy. It doesn't mean we're a danger to you. Especially me," he added firmly. "I would never hurt you. Never ever. In fact, it's impossible for me to hurt you, because you're my life mate. And immortals simply cannot harm their life mate."

Sophie's eyes narrowed. "What do you mean I'm your life mate?"

When Alasdair hesitated, trying to decide how to explain life mates, she added, "You still haven't explained the blood and fangs thing either. I mean I understand that the nanos mean you need blood, but where do the fangs come in?"

Deciding that was an easier thing to explain, Alasdair dropped the subject of life mates for now, and said, "While in Atlantis, if we needed to top up our blood levels, they simply gave us transfusions. But once Atlantis fell, we were suddenly in a world where there were no more blood transfusions." He paused a beat, and then continued, "Unfortunately, none of the scientists survived, and none of my ancestors who got out thought to drag out any of the paraphernalia needed for transfusions. They were too busy trying to survive. So, they suddenly found themselves in a much less developed world, with no way to get the blood they needed.

"But the nanos were programmed to ensure the survival of their hosts. They needed blood to do that. We believe they forced a sort of evolution, bringing on the physical attributes needed to ensure they could get the blood they needed to ensure their survival."

"By 'physical attributes' you mean fangs," she said slowly.

Alasdair nodded. "That and strength, speed, night vision, and anything else that would help us get the blood the nanos needed."

"What are the anything else's?" Sophie asked suspiciously.

Alasdair grimaced, knowing she wasn't going to like this, but admitted, "We developed the ability to read and control non-immortals. Mortals."

"Oh my God." Sophie turned and walked to the

sink, then turned around and asked with horror, "So do I even like you? Am I really attracted to you? Is the sex really that amazing? Or am I just enjoying it because you're making me think I am?"

Alasdair started shaking his head even before she finished speaking. "I cannot read or control you."

"What? You just said—"

"Immortals can control almost all mortals, and yes, we can read the minds of almost all mortals. But there are exceptions," he said.

"What kind of exceptions?" she asked abruptly, her eyes narrowed.

"Immortals can't read or control mortals who are insane. Their minds are too scrambled to be able to read," he explained.

"I'm not insane!" Sophie snapped, and he realized that she was afraid that he thought she might be because of her short stint in the hospital after her parents' death.

"I know you're not, love," Alasdair assured her solemnly. "I'm just listing off the mortals that immortals can't read."

Crossing her arms, she glared at him and waited.

"We also sometimes can't read people with brain tumors," he told her. "It depends where the tumor is."

"All right," Sophie growled when he paused.

Alasdair nodded, and then licked his lips and finished, "And immortals cannot read their life mates."

"Which are?" she asked grimly.

"Life mates are mortals or even immortals who can't be read because—well, we think the nanos recognize, or decide, the individual would be a perfect mate for the immortal to live happily with for the duration, and so make it impossible for each to read or control the other."

"For the duration of what?" Sophie asked at once, her eyes narrowed with suspicion.

Alasdair shrugged. "Life? Existence. As long as you both shall live."

"So, the nanos make it so that you can't read life mates? And that's what makes them life mates?" she asked with a small frown.

"That's the conclusion we've all come to," he admitted.

"And I'm that, this life mate business, to you?" she asked warily.

He met her gaze solemnly. "I can't read or control you, Sophie. I know you're not insane, and the fact that everyone else can read you means you don't have a brain tumor. That means you're my life mate."

When she just stared at him, looking uncertain and somewhat dissatisfied, Alasdair added, "And since meeting you, all of my appetites have returned, which is another sign of meeting a life mate."

"Appetites?" Sophie queried dryly. "Are we talking sex here?"

"Yes. Sex . . . and my appetite for food. Before yesterday, I hadn't had sex since 1820. I lost my appetite for food around the same time. Colle and I still ate, but it was purely to keep up body mass without having to drink tons of blood. And we only ate once every week or so, and not for pleasure," he told her, and then emphasized, "But I had no interest at all in sex from the last time I indulged in it in 1820, until the night I met you."

Sophie's expression softened, but then she closed

her eyes and lowered her head unhappily. "How can I be sure that's true? You could be controlling me right now."

"Sweetheart, if I were controlling you, we wouldn't be standing here talking," Alasdair said, and eased closer to slide a hand up her arm. He almost sighed with relief when he felt the shiver it sent through her, echoing through his own body. She wasn't so angry or scared she was shutting him out. "This is another sign of life mates."

Sophie lifted her head in question. "Great sex?"

"Great sex that makes you both pass out at the end," he told her, and her eyes widened incredulously.

"You've been fainting too?" she asked with surprise.

Alasdair nodded. "Life mates share their passion. Every time I touch you, I feel your pleasure like an echo in my own body."

He let his knuckles brush over one breast through her clothes and shuddered a heartbeat after she did as her nipple hardened. "That pleasure mounts in growing and repeating waves, bouncing between us until we orgasm and it overwhelms the mind, causing us to pass out."

He took her hand then and placed it on his bare chest where his shirt still gaped open. He then urged it down his own body. Alasdair stopped at his waistband, but her hand continued under its own power to cup him through his black jeans and he sucked in a breath at the excitement and pleasure it sent through him.

Sophie's eyes widened and she moaned as it echoed through her as well.

Alasdair smiled. "That's why—despite your complaints—I wouldn't let you touch me. I could never explain how touching me would cause pleasure inside you. I—" His words died abruptly as she squeezed again. When she then ran her hand up and down his quickly growing shaft through his jeans, he closed his eyes and nearly snapped his own teeth he was grinding them together so hard. He hadn't forgotten that his uncles, brother, and Tybo were behind them, privy to all this.

Sophie apparently had, though, he realized when she moved closer and began to work on the button of his jeans.

Eyes blinking open, Alasdair caught her hands at once to stop her.

When Sophie's head immediately jerked up, he nodded over his shoulder. She tilted to the side to look around his arm, and scowled when she saw their audience.

Sighing, Sophie retrieved her hands and stepped back to stare at him with an expression he couldn't quite unravel. He wasn't sure what she was feeling, mostly she appeared conflicted. Finally, she admitted, "I'm not sure how I feel about this at all."

"Well, lass," Connor said, standing up. "What ye've got here is a life mate, if ye want it. A man who'll ne'er cheat on ye, because life mate sex simply can'y be beaten. Who'll treat ye like gold and ne'er hurt ye, because he kens how lucky he is to ha'e ye and'll no' want to return to the misery and loneliness the rest o' us unmated immortals experience e'ery day. Who'll ne'er leave ye, because there is no' likely to be another one out there for him. And who'll no' be easy to kill."

Walking toward the door, he added, "Speakin' o' that, ye can think on yer feelin's all ye like later. Right now we need to discuss who's tryin' to kill the people ye love, so we can stop it from happenin' again."

Pausing at the door, Connor swung back and added solemnly, "Aside from the fact they've already killed yer parents as well as several people who mean a lot to ye and should be brought to justice fer it, if ye do decide no' to accept becomin' Alasdair's life mate, presumably ye'll eventually come to care fer another man whose life would be in jeopardy jest by virtue o' lovin' ye. Or mayhap it'll be another female friend, like Beverly, who'll be killed. Either way, we need to solve this." He raised his eyebrows. "Will ye come out to the kitchen and help us narrow down the suspects?"

Alasdair glanced back to Sophie in time to see her sigh and nod unhappily. She then slipped around him to head for the door. He followed, worrying about what she would decide. The fact was that he already loved her and could admit it. He was sure of his feelings, partially because she was his life mate so he trusted that they would suit, but also because of what he'd experienced with her so far. He loved her strength and adaptability. She'd been through so much, yet had pushed through it. Even so, he knew the hard shell she presented was to protect a soft center. But she also had a wicked sense of humor. He'd smiled so much the last two days that were he not immortal, he knew his facial muscles would ache from it. Aside from that, though, what his uncle had said was true. Life mates were rare treasures. If Sophie refused him, he wasn't likely to find another for some time. If at all. He needed to convince her to be his mate. But it would have to wait until they'd sorted the issue of her stalker.

Twenty-Five

"No one but the Tomlinsons?" Alasdair asked with a frown. "Are you sure?"

Sophie grimaced at his expression. He looked as concerned as she felt at having to admit that the only people who had been in her life from the time of her parents' death were the Tomlinsons. But then, one of the things they'd talked about during their dates was her connection to the Tomlinsons and how they were her only family. He would know how hard it would be for her if it was one of them.

"They are the only people I know of who have been in my life that long," she said solemnly, but then added, perhaps a little too eagerly, "Maybe someone's been stalking me that I don't know of, though."

The men all grunted over that possibility and then Connor said, "Well, it's easy enough to find out. Someone just has to go read them. See if it's one of them."

"It would have to be the father if it's one of the Tomlinsons," Tybo said.

"Why?" Sophie asked him with surprise. Papa was one of the mellowest men she'd ever met. He was kind and sweet and as concerned for her as her father ever had been. She couldn't picture him committing any of the murders.

"Well, the kids were too young," Tybo pointed out. "And it's more likely to be a man than a woman. So, he's more likely than his wife."

Inan rolled his eyes at that explanation, and asked, "And what possible motivation could he have?"

"Maybe he secretly hated Sophie's father. Or was jealous of him," Tybo suggested, and then countered, "What possible motivation could any of the Tomlinsons have?"

"Bobby thinks he'll get to marry Sophie if they both reach forty unwed," Alasdair said suddenly, and Sophie glanced at him with interest. He'd actually sounded a bit jealous when he said that. That surprised her almost as much as the fact that he actually remembered her mentioning that. She'd certainly forgotten she'd told it to him in all the rush and excitement of the last two days.

"Lass?" Connor asked. "Could Bobby secretly love ye and want ye fer himself?"

"No," she said with certainty. Bobby was just too much a big brother to her. The very idea of being intimate with him was icky, and she was sure he felt the same way.

Connor nodded. "Then could yer Mr. Tomlinson have hated yer father?"

Sophie shook her head at once. "Mr. and Mrs. Tomlinson were great friends with my parents. They often went out together to dinner and stuff, leaving Bobby to watch Megan and me. And they were terribly upset about our moving," she added firmly. "Which is another thing. Even if there had been some secret beef or something I didn't know about, why kill them when we were moving soon and would be away from them without the risk of a murder sentence?"

"Moving?" Inan asked with interest.

Sophie nodded. "Dad had got promoted. We were supposed to move to British Columbia in June after school ended. It's where the head office of his company was," she explained. "Mom had already managed to get a new position out there in a private school for the following fall. They were always talking about how the Tomlinsons would come out to visit, and we'd show them the area. We were supposed to come back to visit as well."

"But ye didn'y really believe ye would," Inan murmured, his gaze concentrated on her forehead.

Reading her mind, she realized, now understanding that's what they'd been doing all those times they'd stared at her forehead so hard. Now that she thought about it, Alasdair was the only one who didn't do that. Perhaps he really couldn't read her.

"What are ye thinkin', Inan?" Odart asked in a low growl. It made everyone look at his twin with interest.

Sophie did as well and noted the contemplative look on Inan's face. He definitely seemed to be thinking hard about something.

"I'm thinkin' wee Megan may ha'e no' believed it either, and may ha'e been desperate to keep her best friend with her."

Sophie shook her head in rejection. "Well, killing my parents wouldn't have done that. It landed me in a group home."

"But she may no' ha'e thought that would happen," Inan pointed out. "In her child's mind, she may ha'e thought her parents would take ye in, adopt ye, and ye'd be real sisters."

Sophie gave a start at that comment. He'd obviously read from her mind that she and Megan had always called each other sister, even before the Tomlinsons had fostered her. Still, she shook her head. "She was a child. We were both only eleven years old."

Inan shrugged that away as inconsequential. "An eleven-year-old can strike a match as easy as an adult."

"Hmm." Connor nodded. "And she wouldn'y be the first eleven-year-old mortal to commit murder. There was e'en an eleven-year-old lass who was a serial killer a few years back in the UK."

While Sophie's eyes widened at that tidbit of news, Tybo asked skeptically, "But why would Megan kill Andrew and Beverly?"

"Well, let's think on that," Inan said, leaning back in his seat.

They were seated in her dining room, rather than in the kitchen. Mostly because her dining table sat eight and allowed them to see each other without having to crane around to look over their shoulder at anyone sitting on the counter in the kitchen.

"So," Inan said slowly, drawing out the word, "she set the fire to prevent Sophie's parents from takin' her away from her . . . But, things didn'y work out as she'd hoped, and Sophie was taken away to the hospital." Eyeing Sophie, he said, "She probably had no idea where ye went after that. Did she visit ye in the hospital?"

Sophie shook her head. "She said no one would tell her parents where I'd gone because they weren't family."

"Right." He nodded as if that was to be expected. "And ye lived three peaceful years in the hospital and then the group home. But then she found ye again in high school, when fate threw ye together again."

"Nearly three and a half years," Sophie corrected quietly. "The fire was in March and we found each other again when high school started, so September."

"Three and a half," Inan allowed, and continued, "Only, now things ha'e changed. Ye've made new friends, a new family o' yer own. Andrew and Beverly."

Sophie swallowed, but nodded.

"Had Megan made friends while ye were apart?" he asked now.

She shook her head reluctantly. "Mama—Mrs. Tomlinson—once said she was so glad Megan found me again. She'd been lonely since the fire and hadn't really made other friends. She just wanted me."

Inan nodded as if he'd expected that. "So, I doubt she was pleased to find ye had new friends o' yer own."

Sophie frowned at the suggestion. "Beverly and I included Megan in our friend group at once. The three of us did everything together."

"In me experience, friend threesomes rarely work," he said solemnly. "One o' the three always feels lesser than or left out. Since you and Beverly lived in the group home together, Megan would ha'e been the one left out, no matter how unintentionally it happened."

Sophie swallowed, knowing that was true. It had

been obvious more than a time or two that Megan had felt left out. Mostly when they parted ways at the end of the school day and Megan headed home with Bobby, while Beverly and Sophie walked back to the group home together.

"Okay, but if it was Megan, why kill Andrew?" Alasdair asked now. "Bobby seems more likely when it comes to Andrew."

"And if it was Bobby, why would he kill Beverly?" Inan countered.

"Maybe he felt bad for his sister, Megan," Alasdair suggested. "He wanted Sophie for himself, but wanted her as a friend for Megan too."

"Or mayhap Megan wanted Sophie fer her sister, and marrying her brother, Bobby, would make it official which would mean that Andrew would ha'e to be got out o' the way," Inan pointed out. "Or mayhap Andrew jest took up a lot o' Sophie's time that Megan wanted to lay claim to. Boyfriends often draw girlfriends away from each other, causing resentment and such. So, getting rid o' Andrew and Beverly—" He stopped, and turned sharply to Sophie. "Ye were refusin' to move in with the Tomlinsons after Andrew was injured?"

Sophie stiffened. It had just been a fleeting thought through her head, but he'd obviously caught it. Her mouth compressed briefly, but then she sighed in resignation and admitted, "The Tomlinsons were taking all the courses to foster me. It was all supposed to be set and as soon as they finished, I was going to be moved to their house. But after Andrew . . ." She shook her head unhappily. "Beverly and I were both so upset, we both loved him. We clung to each other, comforting one another. If I'd moved to the Tomlinsons', Beverly would have been alone." She shook her head. "I couldn't leave her. I didn't want to move to the Tomlinsons' anymore."

"And then Beverly died and ye did go," Inan said, his gaze concentrated on her forehead.

Sophie didn't respond. Why bother? They could just read the answer.

"Is that true?" Alasdair asked with concern.

Sophie gave a reluctant nod.

Inan sat back. "So once Beverly died, ye moved in with the Tomlinsons and became almost a real sister to Megan . . . as she wanted."

Alasdair's mouth compressed, and then he shook his head. "I still say it's Bobby."

"That's just your jealousy, brother," Colle said solemnly. "I know you're thinking of the fact that Megan just happened to borrow Sophie's car this morning. Otherwise, when you found your SUV didn't work, you would have just hopped in her car and left, leaving the SUV to be dealt with when you got back. Not having her car meant you had to stay and take care of the SUV right away . . . which allowed for the crash with the tow truck."

Alasdair sat back with irritation. "Fine. All right. I don't like Bobby because he thought he should marry Sophie at forty. And, yes, Inan is making some sense, and there is an argument to be had that Megan could be behind everything. But . . ." He shrugged. "I've met her. Unfortunately, I didn't take the time to read her in the brief meeting we had when she interrupted us in Sophie's office Friday night, but she seemed nice."

Sophie smiled at him, relieved to have someone else

back her up. Megan was her best friend in the world. She didn't want to believe she'd done it.

"I still think it is more likely to be one of the parents," Tybo said suddenly. "Mr. Tomlinson or even Mrs. Tomlinson. We haven't even considered her."

"Motive?" Inan asked.

Tybo considered the question and then shrugged helplessly. "Without knowing them, it's hard to say."

"That's true," Connor said heavily. "The truth is we're jest indulgin' in conjecture here. We need to read the Tomlinsons."

Sophie stiffened. "You mean read their minds?"

"It's the easiest way to get to the bottom o' this, lass," Connor said.

"What if you read their minds and it's none of them?"

The men were silent for a minute as they exchanged glances, and then Ludan said, "Then we'll ha'e more work to do. But I vow, we'll stay here in Canada until we sort it out. We'll no' leave you and our lad here in peril."

"Although," Connor added, "if that turns out to be the case, I suggest ye let Alasdair turn ye at once. I wouldn'y want to risk yer accidentally bein' injured or killed if the murderer tries to kill Alasdair again."

"Wait. What?" Sophie asked with shock. "Turn me?"

"Give ye some o' his nanos, lass. Make ye an immortal. As his life mate 'tis yer right."

Sophie turned wide eyes to Alasdair, but before she could ask anything, Inan spoke again.

"In the meantime, we need their addresses. I presume Megan and Bobby do no' still live with their parents?"

Sophie tore her gaze away from Alasdair and shook her head. "No. They both have apartments of their own too. But there's no guarantee either of them will be home. Bobby's often at his girlfriend's, and Megan was going out last night. She could be anywhere."

The men were all scowling at that. After a hesitation, she said, "But they'll all be at Mama and Papa's tonight. We have Sunday dinner there every weekend. It's considered . . . family time."

"Ye're uncomfortable calling them that now," Inan commented solemnly. "I'm sorry, lass."

Sophie didn't respond other than to shrug. What could she say? The suspicions these men had raised in her about one of the Tomlinsons possibly being behind the deaths of so many of her loved ones did make her uncomfortable calling them family. Not that she believed for a minute that either parent was behind the deaths in her life, but—

"It's nearly dawn. I suggest we all get some sleep," Ludan said, standing up abruptly.

His words made Sophie glance with confusion out the large window next to them to see that the sky was starting to lighten. The sun would be up soon. Where had the time gone?

"We'll visit the Tomlinsons at the parents' house at dinnertime when they're all together," Ludan added, moving toward her living room.

When the others immediately got up as well, she did too, thinking to walk them all to the door. Only, none of the men headed for the door. Instead, everyone but Alasdair was heading into her living room.

"We'll need to close the blinds," Alasdair said quietly. "To keep the sun out."

"Keep the sun out?" she asked weakly, watching with disbelief as Tybo claimed her couch, and Colle took her reclining chair while the uncles all started unraveling their plaids and huddling into the material as they each claimed a patch of her living room floor and settled in. Eyes wide, she whispered, "They're staying?"

"Lass, we're no' leavin' yer side until we've solved this," Connor said around a sleepy yawn.

"Aye," Inan agreed. "This killer has to be mad. They're definitely dangerous. They've already taken six lives that we ken o'. We'll no' see them add ye or Alasdair to that number."

Sophie stared at the men, glanced at Alasdair, and then back to the men, then let out the breath she hadn't realized she'd been holding. "Well, there's a guest bedroom up the hall. At least two of you could sleep there."

"Then let the young lads take it," Odart growled.

"Aye. Soft as they are, they'll sleep better," Inan commented.

That had both Tybo and Colle scowling at the older men. But it apparently didn't annoy them enough to keep them both from getting up and heading down the hall. It was only then that Sophie realized she'd set it up so that Alasdair would be sleeping with her. Not really a good thing. She had some thinking to do, but that would be hard with him there in her bed with her. Hell, she wasn't even sure she could keep her hands off him, even with his relatives here.

"Go to bed, lass," Connor said soothingly. "Ye've a stressful day tomorrow. And we all sleep like the dead. We'll no' hear anything."

Sophie met the man's gaze, surprised to feel a soothing sensation slipping through her, and then suddenly decided everything would be fine. She should go to bed. She barely heard Alasdair growl a warning, "Uncle," at the man as she headed across the living room to the hall.

Twenty-Six

"Your uncle controlled me to send me to bed, didn't he?" Sophie asked when Alasdair finally entered the bedroom several minutes later. She supposed he'd stopped to close all of her blinds to keep his uncles safe from the sun. He had probably also spoken further with his uncles, because he'd been gone long enough that the calm, agreeable sensation that had cloaked her as she'd come to her room had dissipated, leaving her to suspect she'd been controlled.

"I'm sorry," Alasdair growled, pausing by the door. "Do you want me to sleep in the living room?"

Sophie considered the offer, but then shook her head and dropped to sit on the side of her bed. "We need to talk anyway."

Alasdair nodded, and closed the bedroom door, then walked over to sit next to her, but a foot away.

"I guess you're wondering about the turning that my uncle mentioned."

"That too," Sophie murmured. "But really I wanted to ask about being life mates." Glancing at him, she asked, "Have you really not had sex since 1820?"

Alasdair smiled faintly. "Really."

"But that's like two hundred years."

"More," he pointed out.

"Hmmm." She turned to peer down at her feet. "So, you didn't meet a single woman in all that time who you were interested in sleeping with?"

Sophie glanced over to see Alasdair shrug. "I just wasn't interested."

"In sex?" she clarified.

"Yes, in sex, Sophie," he said with amusement.

She shook her head. "Crazy. I can't imagine not wanting sex for two hundred years."

"Well, I didn't. Until I met you," Alasdair added solemnly.

"Or food, for that matter. I couldn't live without cheese and ice cream," Sophie told him seriously.

"Everything gets boring if you live long enough," Alasdair said. "It's part of the reason life mates are so important to an immortal. They reawaken appetites and help keep them alive."

Sophie nodded silently.

"For most, they also offer a companionship they can't otherwise experience," he added.

She peered at him with curiosity. "How's that?"

"Well." Alasdair considered it briefly and then said, "You have to understand, immortals can't only read mortals, they can read other immortals that are younger than them too. So, most immortals spend a great deal of time when around others having to guard their thoughts, both incoming and outgoing, depending on whom they are around."

"Incoming?" she asked.

Alasdair shrugged. "It can be tiresome to constantly hear the thoughts of those younger than yourself. Especially if there are several in the vicinity, so you'll want to block them. Unless you want to know what they're thinking."

"Wait, so you don't actually have to try to read their thoughts?" Sophie asked with surprise.

"Sometimes you do," he admitted. "But sometimes, with very young immortals—" Alasdair paused briefly, as if struggling to explain. "You know how sometimes young mortal children go through a stage where they don't know how to control their volume?"

"They forget to use their inside voices when excited," Sophie suggested.

Alasdair nodded. "Well, it can be like that for younger immortals."

"You mean immortal children? Are there immortal children?"

"No, I don't mean just immortal children. But of course there are immortal children," he said with amusement. "We have babies like everyone else. The nanos are passed down through the mother."

"So, if we had children, they wouldn't be immortal even though you're immortal?" she asked with interest.

"Not unless you were turned first," he said solemnly.

"Right," Sophie muttered, and then cleared her throat. "So back to young immortals having trouble with inside voices."

He smiled faintly, and Sophie suspected he knew she was avoiding the subject of turning for now, but after a moment, he said, "Well, it's a similar thing. They can broadcast their thoughts without intending to. That's also a real problem for new life mates."

When she raised an eyebrow with interest, Alasdair nodded. "As twins, my brother, Colle, and I have never been able to read each other. But now he can read me. Because I met you." He paused, and then added, "As can Tybo, who is younger than me and shouldn't be able to read me. New life mates and younger immortals can tend to project their thoughts without meaning to."

"Oh."

"Anyway," he said now, "the point is that constantly blocking incoming as well as outgoing thoughts can be exhausting. You can never really relax around anyone. It becomes easier to be alone, but the more time an immortal spends alone, the more chance there is that they could go rogue."

"Rogue?" she asked at once.

"Basically, they go mad. Suicidal really," he explained. "And then they go wild, usually harming mortals, which some think is the immortal version of suicide by cop, because Enforcers or rogue hunters will then hunt them down and—"

"Enforcers," Sophie interrupted quickly. "That's what you are. Vampire cops."

"Immortal cops," he corrected, and warned her, "The older immortals really dislike the name *vampire*."

Sophie waved that away. "But you are immortal police, then, right? You go after rogues?"

"Yes," Alasdair agreed.

"And then what?" she asked. "What do you do when you catch them?"

"We either take them in for judgment or just end them on the spot if they're bad enough and have a death order."

"But immortals can't die," Sophie protested with confusion.

"That's not completely true. We're very flammable and can burn to death, but it's pretty nasty. We can also die if we lose our head, but it has to be kept away from the neck or the nanos will just reattach and heal it."

"Oh," Sophie murmured. "But immortals who find their life mates don't go rogue?"

"It's never happened that I know of," he said simply.

"What about if an immortal went rogue, and then met their life mate? Would it save them?" she asked.

"That has happened, a rogue immortal finding their life mate. But it didn't save them. Although, there's some suggestion it did change them somewhat."

Sophie nodded, but her thoughts had already moved on to the issue of her and Alasdair. "You seem pretty sure that I'm this life mate for you."

"You are," he assured her.

"But what if the nanos are wrong? What if I agreed to be your life mate and we didn't get along in the end?"

"The nanos are never wrong, Sophie. I've never heard of life mates who didn't work out. In fact, Nicodemus Notte, my great-great . . ." Alasdair paused briefly as if working it out in his head, and then finished, "great-great-grandfather, and my great-great-great-great-grandmother Marzzia were among the originals from Atlantis, and they are still together and still madly, passionately in love now all these millennia later."

"And the sex is still good for them?" she asked, eyes narrowing.

Alasdair blinked in surprise, and then a laugh burst out of him that he appeared to quickly try to stifle.

No doubt to avoid waking everyone in the apartment, Sophie thought, and simply waited for his answer. Much to her relief she didn't have long to wait before he mostly sobered, although he was still smiling when he said, "I love your boldness."

"Boldness?" she asked with surprise.

"You're asking about the sex life of my great-great-great-great-grandparents who are thousands of years old. You don't think that's bold?" he asked with interest.

Sophie blew out a breath. "I suppose. But it's kind of important."

Alasdair stilled and tilted his head. "You're considering agreeing to be my life mate?"

"Well, duh," she said with disgust, hardly believing he'd think she wouldn't. "I mean, come on, the sex is killer, and we do seem to get along really well. And if you won't die, cheat, or leave me and the sex continues to be good for at least a couple hundred years or so . . ." Sophie shrugged. "I don't really see a downside."

Alasdair's eyebrows flew up, and then he announced, "My parents were mated barely nine months before Colle and I were born and are apparently still scandalizing the servants more than three hundred years later by getting caught in a state of dishabille in the dining hall, the library, the conservatory, my father's office, and the gardens."

Sophie felt her eyebrows climb as he listed off rooms. "Where do they live? A castle?"

"Yes," he said as if it was no big deal.

"Damn," she breathed, and then glanced at him sharply. "This is in Scotland, right?"

"Yes."

Sophie's eyes narrowed. "You don't have a title, do you?"

Alasdair shook his head. "My father's a baron, but that's hardly any title at all."

She snorted at the comment. It certainly seemed like a title to her.

"Sophie?" he asked, solemnly. "Will you agree to be my life mate?"

She peered at him for a moment, tempted to say yes, but then asked, "This turning business? Does it hurt?"

Alasdair stiffened, but it was his expression that answered her question.

"It does, doesn't it?" she demanded, her voice accusing, and before he could respond, asked, "A lot?"

"I'm afraid so," he admitted.

"Of course it does," she muttered with disappointment, and turned to crawl up the bed to drop with her head on the pillow, but her body on top of the covers.

"Is that a no?" Alasdair asked after a moment of silence had passed.

"It's an *I-need-to-sleep-on-this*," she growled into her pillow, and then lifted her head and glanced back at him to add, "And a *you-need-to-do-a-heck-of-a-lot-more-romancing-me-if-you-expect-me-to-suffer-agony-to-be-with-you*."

Alasdair's eyes widened, and in the next moment

he was crawling quickly up the bed. Sophie dropped her head back onto the pillow and smiled when he began nuzzling her neck and running his hands over her body through her clothes.

Sophie tiptoed up the hall, creeping past the guest bedroom as quietly as she could. Connor might have claimed they slept soundly, but she suspected it wasn't true. These men were Enforcers. She doubted any of them slept soundly. They probably woke at the slightest bit of noise, which probably meant it didn't matter how quiet she was, they'd wake up, but Sophie was still going to try.

It was only ten o'clock in the morning. She hadn't slept for more than three hours or so. She should still be sleeping like Alasdair was, but thirst had woken her up. That and hunger, but the thirst was worse. Or maybe the gnawing at her stomach was. Sophie couldn't be sure, they were both bad, and she supposed that was to be expected. They hadn't managed to finish either their food or drink last night before the men had shown up, and she honestly wasn't sure when they'd eaten or had something to drink before that. Which was the problem with amazing sex, Sophie decided now. They got so busy and distracted they forgot to eat and drink.

Of course, a lot of the time last night had been spent talking with Alasdair's uncles, brother, and Tybo. She and Alasdair had only actually managed one round of orgasm-inducing messing about after that. Then they'd passed out and slept straight through the last three hours. That messing about hadn't been sex. Alasdair hadn't had to remove even a stitch of her clothing or his to bring her to orgasm and she'd woken up still fully dressed.

Honestly, it was a bit embarrassing how responsive she was to him. Or maybe it was his skill, Sophie thought, and supposed she couldn't complain about the thirty to fifty thousand women Ludan had guessed Alasdair had been with if it had resulted in the skill that man had.

Thirty to fifty thousand women, Sophie thought with dismay. Alasdair had assured her it hadn't been that many while he'd sucked on her neck and caressed her through her jeans last night. He'd said it had probably been less than half that. As if fifteen to twenty-five thousand was better. But she was reaping the benefits, so . . .

Glancing around the living room as she crept through, Sophie noted with relief that all the uncles were sleeping. That or they were faking it, she supposed as she slipped into the kitchen.

Stifling a yawn, Sophie retrieved a glass from the cupboard and got herself some water. She gulped that down and had reached to turn the tap on to get another glassful when the sound of knocking reached her ears. Turning off the tap, she twisted her head to listen, unsure if it had been at her door, or across the hall. But a second tap sounded, and this time she was sure it was for her. It was probably Mrs. Abbott from next door, Sophie thought, setting her glass on the counter. That lovely older lady baked every Sunday and often brought her treats as a thank-you for collecting her mail for her when she got her own.

Sophie hurried out into the entry, desperate to answer the door before Mrs. Abbott could knock again and wake up the whole apartment. She did manage it, but then stilled in surprise when she saw who was at her door.

"Papa?" Her gaze slid over George Tomlinson, taking in his unusually disheveled appearance, along with the flowers he had in one hand and the bag in the other.

"I brought you flowers and a small gift to cheer you up," he announced, holding up both items. He then rushed past her, headed for the kitchen, saying, "We should put these in water."

Eyes wide, Sophie closed the door and hurried after him, glancing up the hall to the living room as she went. But with the curtains closed, it was dark enough that she couldn't see the men sleeping in there.

"I got your favorite: carnations and daisies," Mr. Tomlinson announced as he retrieved a vase from under the sink and began to fill it with water. "Hopefully they do the trick and make you feel at least a little better."

"A little better?" Sophie asked with confusion, not only at his words, but because he knew where she kept her vases, and had somehow got inside her building without her having to buzz him in. Megan had a spare key to her apartment, but Mr. and Mrs. Tomlinson didn't.

"I know you must be upset about your friend and not being able to go to Niagara Falls," he explained, quickly removing the wrapping around the flowers. "That must have been disappointing. And, of course, the accident must have been distressing too," he added, his voice a little stiff.

Sophie stared at his back for a minute as he worked, and then asked, "How did you know about my friend having an accident?"

Mr. Tomlinson turned off the tap with the vase only half-full, dumped the flowers into it, and turned to face her. "I love you."

"I love you too, Papa," she responded slowly, and then asked, "What's this all about?"

When he just peered at her kind of helplessly, Sophie swallowed the sudden lump in her throat and asked sadly, "Oh, Papa, what have you done?"

"I love you, Jasmine," George Tomlinson said desperately, and Sophie felt her blood run cold at his calling her by her mother's name.

Twenty-Seven

"I do love you, Jasmine. You must know I do," George said desperately, moving toward her. "I love you so much, I—"

He stopped abruptly when Sophie took a step back. Blinking in confusion, he breathed, "Sophie," with a small frown, as if just recognizing her.

She stared at him silently, not recognizing this man herself. This wasn't the friend of her parents, and the father of her best friend, who had taken her in and raised her along with his own children through high school. That man had always been calm and self-assured, a take-charge kind of guy. This man was disheveled, confused, and he'd called her by her mother's name. There was obviously something wrong with this man, and where she'd been certain her papa could not be behind the deaths, Sophie could believe this man was.

Mouth tightening, she asked point-blank, "Did you

run down Alasdair in front of my apartment Friday night?"

When her foster father stiffened, his eyes going wide, but his mouth unmoving, she asked, "Did you T-bone the tow truck yesterday?"

"I brought you flowers," George blurted, ignoring her questions. He picked up the vase and held it out to her.

Sophie's gaze didn't even flicker to the offering. "Did you kill Derek? And John?"

George shifted his own gaze down to the flowers and stared at the bloodred carnations among the white daisies.

"Beverly and Andrew?" she tried next.

He raised sad eyes to peer at her and the silence continued until she finally said, "My mom and dad?" the words little more than a whisper.

That brought a reaction. Whirling away, George smashed the vase into the sink, sending glass and water everywhere. Then he gripped the edge of the sink and stared into the red-and-white mess, his shoulders hunched.

Movement out of the corner of her eye caught Sophie's attention, and she glanced to the side to see Alasdair starting into the kitchen from the dining room entrance. She quickly held up her hand to make him stop. She wanted her answers, and she wanted to hear them herself, not from one of the men reading his mind. But if George knew Alasdair or anyone else was here, she was sure she wouldn't get those answers.

Alasdair hesitated, and for a minute she feared he'd continue forward, but then Ludan appeared behind him, caught his arm, and urged him back into the shadows of the dining room. A shuffling sound behind her drew her gaze over her shoulder in time to see Colle ducking around the entrance to the entry and out of sight too.

Letting her breath out on a slow hiss, Sophie turned back to stare at her foster father's back. George hadn't moved. He was still staring at the flowers, back hunched, head hanging slightly.

"I loved her so much, your mother," Mr. Tomlinson said, sounding more like himself, until he breathed, "Jasmine."

Sophie felt her hands clench at her sides, but stayed silent.

"She was the most beautiful woman I'd ever met. Inside and out. Sweet and brilliant and—oh my God, she was so good with the kids . . . and I wanted to tell her about my feelings. I tried to tell her a thousand times, but I could never get her alone to do it. Either your father or Deb were always there. Always getting in the way, interrupting me, driving me crazy," he finished, his voice becoming a frustrated growl.

Sucking in a long breath, George straightened and raised his head, and then let it tilt back on his neck so that he was looking up at the ceiling.

"That night—" He paused and swallowed thickly before continuing. "You were over playing with Megan and she asked if you could stay for dinner, and when Deb said yes, she then asked if you could stay the night." He gave an affectionate laugh. "Megan was always pushing it just a little, get permission for this, and then tack on that."

He sighed. "Deb hesitated before answering, and I

was sure she was going to say no, so I said, 'Sure, sweetheart,' before she could."

He lowered his head again to stare at the red and white flowers. "I knew your father would be working late again. He was doing that a lot, trying to get everything tied up at the office here before the move to BC."

Picking up a piece of glass, he held it in his palm and closed his fingers around it, squeezing until blood began to ooze out between his fingers. "He was a good friend, but I hated him for that. Taking her away from me to BC, I mean. I thought I'd never get to tell her how I felt."

He opened his fingers and let the crushed glass fall into the sink, then turned on the tap and stuck his hand under it to let it rinse the blood away. "Then Deb mentioned she should have you girls go ask your mother for permission to stay and to get some pajamas for you. But I told her to let you girls play, I'd take care of it. I'd just pop over, see if it was okay, and Jasmine could pack a bag for you that I'd bring back. It wouldn't take a moment, I assured her."

George turned off the tap and blood immediately began to bubble to the surface of the cuts on his hand. "But I knew that wasn't true. I really wanted to go tell Jasmine how I felt. And in the end, I had to pack your pajamas in a bag for you."

Turning, he peered at her miserably and said, "I loved her, but when I told her that . . . At first, she tried to laugh it off, as if she thought I was joking. But when I insisted it wasn't a joke, I really loved her . . . she got angry," he said with bewilderment. "Offended even."

"'I'm a married woman,' she said. 'You're married too and I love Deb like a sister. What were you expecting here? I'm not going to break my marriage vows, George. I love my husband. I don't love you.'"

Staring at her solemnly, he said, "She shouldn't have said that. It made me so angry. I don't even really remember hitting her. I was just so hurt and angry." His mouth twitched. "She fell, hitting her head on the table on the way down, and there was so much blood." His mouth tightened. "I just stood there staring, and the blood just kept coming, circling her head on the kitchen tile." Meeting her gaze again, George said, "I swear I thought she was dead."

He closed his eyes miserably. "I panicked. I didn't know what to do. First, I ran up and packed some pajamas in your little panda backpack, then I rushed back downstairs. At first, I was just going to go back home and pretend nothing had happened. Hoping that when your dad got home, he'd think a burglar had caught her by surprise or something. But then I realized my fingerprints would be everywhere. They'd know it was me."

His gaze met her cold eyes again and skated away guiltily. "As I was trying to figure out what to do, your dad came home. I didn't have any choice then. You can see that, can't you?"

"You killed him," she said, her voice flat.

George turned away and stared into the sink again as if he couldn't face her as he admitted, "I made a quick search through the drawers and found a rolling pin. Then I pressed my back to the wall next to the door to the garage, and when your father came into the kitchen, I bashed him over the head. Then I knelt on his back and choked him until he stopped breathing."

Sophie closed her eyes, her shoulders sagging.

"I almost started the fire then, but it seemed smarter to do it later when everyone would be sleeping and unlikely to notice too quickly. So, I left them there and went back home. I was a nervous wreck all night until we got you girls settled in bed and could go to bed ourselves. But then I had to wait for Deb to fall asleep too. It was so awful. I was in a cold sweat. Felt nauseous. Awful," he repeated with self-pity.

A strangled sound slipped from Sophie at that. Her parents were dead, by his hands, but it was so awful for him to have to wait to set them on fire?

Mr. Tomlinson didn't appear to have heard the strangled sound she'd made and continued, "Once Deb finally fell asleep, I slipped out of bed, retrieved the gas can from the garage—it was still full from the summer," he stopped to explain. "I'd thought I'd get in one more mow back in November, but then we got that unexpected snowstorm. The gas had just been sitting there waiting. Like it was meant to be."

Sophie turned her head away with disgust.

"I took it and made my way next door, splashed the gas everywhere, but a lot on your mom and dad. Their bodies might have evidence on them, you see." He frowned, and then continued. "Then I started the fire and hurried back home and got back in bed."

George fell silent briefly, and then Sophie heard him whisper, "I really thought she was dead." His voice growing in strength, he complained, "I nearly had a heart attack when she came stumbling out of the house on fire. I really thought she was dead. She should've been dead. It really would have been better if she had been," he added irritably as if she'd stayed alive to spite him.

"Your mother ended up with third-degree burns over sixty percent of her body. She would've been scarred for life, probably disabled if she'd survived, and I was afraid she was going to. Jasmine was a fighter. So strong. That's part of the reason I loved her, but it wasn't good in this instance. She was suffering, and of course, if she'd lived, she might have told them what I'd done." His mouth puckered with displeasure at that thought.

"I was beginning to think I'd have to kill her again. She held on for three days, and I was considering smothering her to death, or getting my hands on a syringe and maybe trying an air bubble in her vein. That's supposed to kill people." He shrugged. "Fortunately, she died before I had to do anything like that."

George was silent for a minute, and then said, "I miss her every day."

Sophie gaped at his back in disbelief, and then stiffened when he turned to face her again.

"I'm sorry, Sophie. I felt terrible when I heard that you ended up in a psychiatric hospital. I know it was all my fault and I am so, so sorry," he said solemnly. "I didn't really expect that. I didn't realize you were that weak."

She blinked at the insult.

"But you were a child," he added, excusing her, and then he smiled crookedly. "I was happy when Megan came home from her first day at high school and told us that she'd found you. From what she said you were obviously fine again, and I was glad you'd recovered from your breakdown and were good once more. Everything was fine. I could stop feeling bad."

Sophie just stared at him with disbelief. So, he

thought being parentless and living in a group home with no family was fine and he no longer had anything to feel bad about? What about her parents?

"But then she brought you home," George commented. "And you'd grown up. Three short years and you had blossomed into womanhood."

Sophie looked at him sharply as he lifted his head and let his gaze travel over her face and body in a way she'd never seen before. A way that made her feel gross, and want to vomit.

"You looked just like your mother. It was like she was walking in the door and smiling at me, and I knew I had a second chance."

"A second chance?" she asked with disbelief.

"Yes. Don't you see?" he asked, taking a step away from the counter. "I could take care of you, and love you, and you would love me back."

"Was killing Andrew and Beverly your idea of taking care of me?" she ground out, fury pouring through her like acid.

"Yes, of course," George said as if that should be obvious. "He was no good, Sophie. Just a punk. The kid of a drug addicted mother. He was going to get you in trouble. The boy was luring you into that shut down mall. Don't deny it, I saw. I followed you guys there several times. He'd do some skateboarding and then lure you into a dark corner and get you to make out with him like some little whore."

Sophie stiffened. He'd made it sound so dirty, but it hadn't been. Just kissing and mild petting. They'd loved each other. But it was somewhat tainted now in her memory by the knowledge that he'd stalked and watched them like some pervert.

"Then he gave you that damned ring," George growled with disgust. "I knew he'd be pushing you to have sex next. Maybe force you. You'd be pregnant before you got out of grade nine. I had to prevent that. So, I waited and watched for my opportunity, and when you girls left him to skateboard at the mall alone and headed away, I knew you were going to the library to do that group project and wouldn't return. Megan had asked permission to go after school to work on it with you."

He paused, his eyes growing distant and a smile curving his lips as he recalled. "So, I slipped into the mall, and stuck to the shadows to await my chance. There were other kids there at first. I thought they'd never leave, but then one of them said they'd better get back to the home, it was nearly dinnertime. But Andrew said he just wanted to do a couple more tricks and he'd follow."

George's smile widened. "After they were gone, he started doing this really rather impressive trick with his skateboard on the rim of the fountain. He never saw me coming. I pushed him off his skateboard, he hit his head when he fell. Then he sat up with confusion and stared at me asking, "What the hell, man?""

"I told him I was sorry. That I'd just been coming over to ask him something and had tripped and unintentionally bumped into him. Then I stepped into the dry fountain with him as if to help him up, but instead, I bent down and just slammed his head into the stone floor of the fountain a couple of times."

His smile turned into a frown now, and George admitted, "I thought I killed him too. I should have made sure. I guess I didn't learn from your mother, because—like her—he wasn't dead." He scowled, and then his expression cleared and he shrugged. "He might as well be. He's little more than a vegetable. But at least I saved you from his impregnating you and ruining your life."

Sophie was silent for a minute, at first bombarded with feelings, so many she couldn't clock them, and then she was suddenly just cold and empty inside. But she still needed to know.

"Beverly couldn't get me pregnant. Why kill her?" she asked flatly.

"Beverly," George said with a frown. "That was a shame. She seemed like a nice enough girl, but she was a group home kid too, and her mother—again—was a drug addict. I didn't mind that so much with her. I mean, I thought you were a good influence on her. But after Andrew's accident, you started talking about maybe you shouldn't move out of the group home and in with us. That you couldn't leave Beverly all by herself after what had happened."

He shook his head. "Sweetheart, you were going to throw your life away for this kid, and I knew you would do it too. Deb kept saying, 'No. It's okay, she just needs time. We'll convince her to move in as planned.' But I knew she was wrong. Bighearted as you are, you'd have stayed in the group home for Beverly's sake, and that bleeding-heart caseworker of yours would have understood and recommended allowing it, and the courts wouldn't force you, because you were old enough that they would have taken your choice into consideration." He held his hands out to the sides. "Don't you see? I had to take care of her. For your sake."

All Sophie could see was that Andrew and Beverly were dead because of her. Somehow this was her fault.

"How did you do it?" she asked, the not knowing gnawing at her. "Beverly didn't eat anything."

"She didn't have to," he told her with a smile. "Remember that morning? You and Beverly came over early to help Megan get your history project to school. It was a big two-foot-by-two-foot board with miniature buildings and people on it."

Sophie remembered. Their project had been on the War of 1812. They'd written a speech, dividing it in three parts so each would give a portion of it, and had built a model of Fort York and the surrounding area, including Lake Ontario, and models of the ships on it and such. They'd worked hard on that project.

"You and Beverly left your backpacks by your boots near the front door while you ran upstairs with Megan to put a couple of little last-minute touches on your project and make sure it was all ready. You were all so proud of it." He smiled faintly.

"Well, while you were upstairs, I went through Beverly's bag, pulled out her EpiPen and jabbed it into an orange to empty it." He clucked his tongue with remembered irritation, and told her, "It was only after I'd done it that I saw that the clear window on the pen was now shaded. I was afraid that would give away that it had already been used, but all I could do was hope that in the panic of the moment it wouldn't be noticed. So, I threw it back in her bag and then went out to the kitchen, pulled out the peanut oil Deb kept for cooking, smeared some all over Megan's insulated lunch bag, and then kind of half-ass wiped it off so it didn't look wet, but there were still traces on it. Then

I took that and Megan's school bag and put both in the trunk of the car, and called out for you girls to get moving or we'd be late. I was supposed to be driving you all to school with the model," he reminded her, as if she could have forgotten.

"Then at the school, I opened the trunk, got the model out and handed it to Megan to carry, gave you Megan's book bag, and Beverly Megan's lunch bag. Had Beverly not been wearing gloves, she would have reacted right away. But then that had been part of my plan. It was winter, damned cold that morning. Her gloves protected her. At least, until she took them off and touched the outside of them with her bare fingers to put them away. Then all it would take was rubbing her eyes, or putting her fingers near her mouth and—" George shrugged as if Beverly's life was of no consequence.

"It was for the best," he assured her. "She would have dragged you down."

Sophie didn't respond to that, she merely stared at him for a minute and then asked, "John?"

"He was no good for you," George said at once, looking irritated now. "No good at all. The kid was a partier. He was luring you to neglect your university classes. How many times did he convince you to by-pass studying to go to some stupid frat party? Time you could have spent studying."

"So, you ran him down," she said solemnly.

"It was easy," he said with a shrug. "I watched your dorm, waited for my opportunity, for a time when he was alone, and there was no around to see, then boom crash. He wasn't a problem anymore."

"Derek?" she growled.

"Derek." He laughed slightly. "Sweetheart, you guys thought you were so clever sneaking around dating like you did. Did you really think I wouldn't notice? What kind of father would I be if I didn't notice you whispering in the break room? Or disappearing into the bathroom when you thought no one was looking, and coming out a little disheveled. You forgot about the cameras, sweetheart." He paused, and then frowned and said, "Or maybe I hadn't mentioned them to anyone yet." He shrugged. "Anyway, I knew you two were dating."

"We dated for a year," she pointed out angrily. "Why did you wait so long to kill him?"

"Because it was fine. I thought you should get some dating experience. But then the idiot had the balls to ask you to marry him." George scowled. "He was an insurance salesman, Sophie. They're the scum of the earth. The only thing worse is a car salesman."

Sophie blinked in amazement. George owned the damned insurance agency. It seemed hypocritical to consider his employees, the ones who kept him in money, the scum of the earth.

"I knew he'd proposed," he bragged. "I saw the ring down your top when I stopped in your office one day to ask you about the monthly reports. You were seated at your desk, showing me the reports on your computer, and I was standing next to you. I glanced down and there it was, a diamond ring, hanging on a chain and nestling between your beautiful breasts."

Sophie nearly gagged at the idea of his ogling her "beautiful" breasts, but remained silent.

"I was actually relieved. It meant you two would have to come clean soon. You could hardly marry him without letting your family know. I thought once you came clean, I could point out to you that he had made you lie and sneak around. Make you see that a good man wouldn't have made you do that. Convince you to break it off with him." His mouth twisted. "But the little bastard handed in his notice, and I realized he was cleverer than I'd expected. I knew the plan must be to just pretend to start dating once he was employed elsewhere, and then eventually pretend he'd just given you the ring. I could hardly tell you then that I'd known all along. That I'd been watching the two of you on the cameras," he pointed out, and shook his head. "No. He had to be taken care of. But Derek wasn't some broke ass university kid who had to hoof it everywhere. He had a car."

He paused, his gaze glazing over slightly as if he was drifting somewhere else as he said, "That night on my way home there was an accident holding up traffic. When I finally got to it, it was between a car and a pickup with one of those snowplow blades on the front." He shook his head with admiration. "The truck was mostly fine. The blade took the worst of the impact, while the car was shredded." He smiled at the memory.

"That gave me an idea, and I stopped at a couple of used car places until I found one with a good, heavy-duty pickup that actually already had a snowplow blade attached. I thought I'd have to buy that separately and wait to have it attached, but no, it was there waiting for me. I knew then it was meant to be, and I bought it on the spot. Well, the company did," he said with a wink. "It was for clearing the parking lot after unexpected snows."

When Sophie didn't respond, he went on, "Fortunately, Derek had that little foreign car. From Korea, I think. It wasn't really a sturdy car. It folded up like an accordion between the telephone pole and my truck. The snow blade wasn't even bent from the impact. Too bad I wasn't driving it the night I hit Alasdair."

Twenty-Eight

"You're the one who ran him down in front of my apartment the other night," Sophie accused.

"Well, the poison hadn't worked, so I had to use a more direct method," he said, and then muttered, "Not that running him down did much good either."

"Poison?" Sophie asked with disbelief. No one had mentioned Alasdair being poisoned.

"It was me looking through the break room window Friday night. I saw where he was sitting and which drink was his and when the two of you rushed to the front of the building so that he could go search the parking lot for the person you'd seen, I slipped into my office through my private door, hurried to the break room, grabbed the rat poison from under the sink, and poured some in his glass," he said with a shrug, and then scowled. "But he must not have drank it."

Alasdair *had* drank it. Sophie had seen him down it quickly as they'd cleaned up before heading to her place. But where it probably would have had anyone who wasn't an immortal writhing in agony and dying on the break room floor, it hadn't seemed to affect him at all. Those nanos were really pretty amazing, she thought, but then focused on George again as he shifted impatiently across from her.

Mouth tightening, she asked, "Why kill Alasdair? He wasn't an insurance salesmen, or distracting me from classes, or whatever. We haven't even dated long. A lunch and a dinner, and—"

"And crawling all over him, first in your office and then in the break room," George interrupted with disgust. Crossing the distance between them, he caught her by the arms to give her a shake. "You would have fucked him right there in your office if Megan hadn't interrupted when she did. Don't deny it, I saw you on the cameras."

Sophie blinked. She'd known for the last six months that there were cameras in the reception area and on the entrances and exits, but she hadn't known there were any in the offices or the break room.

"Thank God I jumped in the car and headed down there then. Because while Megan's interruption stopped the two of you and you moved to the break room, you weren't there long before you were ripping your top open and wrapping your gorgeous legs around his hips like a stripper on the pole. By the time I got there and looked in the window, he had his mouth and hands all over you."

Sophie leaned away from him as much as his hold on her would allow, and stared up at him warily. He was breathing heavily, almost panting, but it wasn't purely from anger. She could see excitement on his face, as if the memory turned him on, and wasn't surprised when he said, "You're mine. You should be doing that with me, Jasmine, not some overgrown ape you only met days ago."

His calling her by her mother's name again made her jerk in surprise, but he didn't even notice and continued, growling, "So, yes, I tried to poison him, and when that didn't work, I gave him the same treatment as young John. Mowed him down like ninepins. I thought I'd surely killed the bastard then, and I came around yesterday with flowers to comfort you, but I'd barely found a parking spot when what do I see? The great ape coming out of your apartment to talk to a tow truck driver," he said with disbelief. "It didn't even look like he'd got a scratch from the night before. If I'd had a gun I would have shot the bastard on the spot. But I didn't have a gun."

Thank God for that, Sophie thought.

"However, I knew it would take a few minutes to get his SUV up on the tow truck's bed," he told her. "So I drove quickly home to switch my car for the pickup, and when I got back, they were just pulling away. I followed for a while to see where they were heading, then I passed them, sped up to get a bit ahead, and pulled down one street, drove up the next, and waited. Then I T-boned the bastard just like Derek."

The satisfaction in both his voice and his expression told her he'd enjoyed that, but then it faded to be replaced with irritation as he added, "I took care of Alasdair, but the tow truck was a sturdier build than Derek's car. My truck took a lot of damage. I was barely able to drive away from the accident. It's still parked on a side street a couple of blocks from the accident site," he added, obviously pissed. "It's probably done. But it was worth it. For you, Jasmine. I did it all for you, my love."

"I'm not Jasmine," she snapped, yanking her arms out of his hold. Stepping back toward the entry to the dining room, she added, "I'm not my mother, and I'm not your love."

Continuing to back toward the door, she took a page out of her mother's book and, using as much of her words all those years ago as she could, added, "I'm in a relationship. You're married to Deb, and I love her like a second mother. What were you expecting here? I'm not going to break my promise to Alasdair, George. I love him. I don't love you."

Sophie wasn't terribly surprised when he charged her. But she was surprised when she was suddenly snatched from behind and dragged into the dark dining room. It happened so fast, it nearly made her head spin, and then she stood completely still, her back to Alasdair's chest, his arms around her waist. She knew it was him. Her body was responding, despite the situation, but she tried to tamp down that reaction as George charged out into the dark room and stumbled to a halt.

"Where are you? Why the hell is it so dark in here?"

She heard him move cautiously toward the windows, and then the blinds began to open, allowing light to pour in and stretch partway across her living room area. In his blind groping he'd found the controls to the living room blinds rather than the dining room window.

Sophie bit her lip and glanced around for the rest of the men and thought she saw movement in the shadows on the far side of the living room, then her gaze slid back to George when he said, "Sophie? Is that you?"

Realizing he was squinting in her direction, she urged Alasdair to release her and took several steps forward until the light just reached her.

George started forward at once, but stopped abruptly after just a step when Alasdair moved forward behind her. She felt his chest brush her back, and then his hands slid around to clasp her waist, ready to move her if necessary.

"I killed you," George said with confusion, staring at Alasdair's face over her head. "You're dead. You have to be."

Movement drew Sophie's gaze to the side in time to see Colle stepping from the shadows in the entry up the hall.

George looked too and immediately began shaking his head with confusion. Stumbling back a step as he looked from one to the other, he said, "No. You're dead. How can there be two of you? What's happening? You're dead. What's happening?"

The uncles moved forward a step then, remaining in the shadows, but just visible enough that with their familial features similar to Colle and Alasdair, they could be mistaken for them.

Sophie watched as George freaked out and began mumbling to himself in horror about clones and robots, and nonsense. Part of her was enjoying it and thinking he deserved it after everything he'd done, everything he'd taken away from her, and all of her loved ones he'd killed. Not just for her loss of them, but for their loss too. Andrew, Beverly, John, Derek, and even her parents had all had their lives cut short, bright futures abruptly ended. Her parents would never enjoy their life in BC or see her children, their grandchildren. Beverly would never experience romantic love, marriage, birth, or any of the joys she could have had. The same was true of Andrew, John, and Derek. They'd all missed out on so much because of the man nearly blubbering in front of her.

She hated him for that.

Sophie had never loathed anyone in her life as much. She loathed him even more because she had loved him like a second father. Because she had been grateful for his part in fostering her. She had been so grateful she'd felt guilted into working for him for years despite it not being what she'd wanted. But it had all been a manipulation on his part, so he could stalk her, watch her, control her, and kill anyone she was foolish enough to care about.

However, while part of her was enjoying his confusion and fear, another part just wanted him away from her.

"What happens now?" she asked finally.

"What do you want to happen?" Alasdair asked solemnly.

"What are the options?" Sophie asked after a moment.

"There are a few. We can call the mortal police and let them handle him," he offered.

Sophie was shaking her head before he finished speaking. "I can't imagine how that would affect the family. Megan, Bobby, Mrs. Tomlinson . . . they're good people, Alasdair. They don't deserve learning the man they love is a sick, twisted, crazy asshole who killed so many people. They don't deserve the fallout from the press either, everyone looking at them, digging into their lives. The company would probably end up going under because it's owned by the family of a killer." She shook her head. "I can't do that to them."

"We could handle him, then," Alasdair offered quietly.

"How?" Sophie asked at once, noting that George had stopped mumbling to himself about Alasdair being dead, and yet there were now multiples of him. Instead, he was watching them and listening.

"A three-on-one mind wipe," Alasdair offered. "It might leave him a blank slate and rewritable, or might just leave him an empty vessel and in a bed in the psych wing of a local hospital for the rest of his life."

Sophie didn't get to ask what exactly a three-on-one mind wipe was. George was shouting "No!" now.

He stumbled back another step, coming up against the sliding glass door to her balcony, then quickly turned, unlocked it, and rushed out onto the balcony.

Sophie frowned and glanced around at the men. She could see they had those concentrated expressions on their faces that she suspected meant they were reading or controlling him. But they also all had small frowns on their faces. She didn't recall Alasdair telling her that immortals often couldn't read or control the insane, until the men suddenly all charged for the balcony door, including Alasdair, who took the time to shift her gently aside first.

Sophie hurried after them, but it was all over by the time she got out on her balcony. There was no sign of George and the men were all at the railing, Alasdair with his hand still out as if he'd tried to grab something. She heard the squeal of a vehicle's brakes, a thud, and a scream then, and hurried to the railing to push her way between Ludan and Alasdair.

"I'm sorry, love," Alasdair muttered, straightening beside her and slipping an arm around her waist as she leaned over the railing to peer at the circular driveway below. "I couldn't grab him in time."

Sophie stared at the scene below. There wasn't much to see, the top of a delivery van with dress-pant-clad legs sticking out from beneath it, and a woman running out from the building and into view.

"He fell right in front of the van," Connor commented. "It hit him before he hit the ground. It would look like an accident rather than a suicide if not for the witness."

"I'll take care of the witness," Tybo said, retreating from the sunny balcony. "I'll bring back another cooler of blood too when I return."

"I better go help him in case the police need handling," Colle commented. "We don't want the driver taking any fault for this."

The uncles grunted, but after a hesitation, Alasdair eased away from Sophie and said, "I'll give him your keys so they can both get back in."

"My keys are on the hall table," Sophie said, and then turned back to the railing to again peer down at the body of the man who had been something like a monster under her bed since she was eleven years old. She told herself, he was gone. He couldn't hurt anyone again.

Sophie was glad, but felt guilty for it, because she knew his death would cause a great deal of pain for Megan, Bobby, and Deb. While she felt nothing.

"It would ha'e been more painful fer them to learn what he'd done," Ludan said quietly. "At least this way, they're spared that."

Sophie turned to peer at the centuries-old man, surprised to see that his normally hard, grim face was almost soft with sympathy now.

"None of you could read or control him," she said.

"Nay." He glanced down at the scene below. "We should ha'e been quicker to give up and go after him."

Sophie stared at him silently, and then said, "I would have thought Alasdair could have reached him. He moved so quickly I could barely see him when he chased after George."

Ludan turned back and eyed her briefly, then nodded. "Mayhap we older, slower men got in his way."

Sophie snorted at that suggestion. She suspected that none of these men were slow. She also suspected that the uncles had let George jump and had hampered Alasdair to ensure George succeeded.

"It works out best this way fer everyone, lass," Ludan said solemnly. "He made his choice, and his family'll ne'er ken what kind o' man he really was."

"But the families of all the people he killed will never know what really happened either," she pointed out.

"Are ye happier kenning yer parents were slaughtered? Or was it easier thinking the fire was jest an accident?" he asked.

Sophie released a slow breath and nodded in understanding. Andrew's death was considered an unfortunate accident, as was Beverly's, and while John's family knew it was a hit and run, they believed it was an accident, a drunk who unintentionally killed their son. The same was true of Derek. Just an unfortunate accident that had taken his life. They would not feel better knowing it had been deliberate murder. That the men had been stalked and taken down by a madman. She didn't think so anyway. She didn't feel better knowing it.

Giving Ludan a nod, Sophie headed back into her apartment. She wasn't surprised when the men all followed. She wasn't sure, since nothing had been said about it, but suspected the sun wasn't good for them.

Kind of like vampires, she thought dryly.

"Yer a sassy wench," Connor said suddenly with amusement.

"And yer a rude old bastard fer listenin' to me thoughts," Sophie shot back, mimicking his accent.

Her words made the uncles all laugh, which brought a hint of a smile to her own lips.

Shaking her head at herself, Sophie stopped between the dining room and living room, debating what to do. She wasn't hungry anymore. Actually, she was mostly just tired, but doubted she'd get any sleep. As soon as Megan, Bobby, and their mother got the news that George had died in front of her apartment, they'd have questions for her.

A shower, she thought. That should wake her up enough to face what was coming.

The hiss of the blinds being closed drew her head around and she saw that Inan was closing them while the other men took up their spots on the floor again, huddling into their plaids.

"We're jest catchin' a nap ere the trouble comes knockin'," Inan explained. "You go on and take yer shower. We'll tell Alasdair where ye are when he comes back from chasin' his brother to give him the keys. Colle was already out of the apartment when Alasdair got inside," he added when she stared at him blankly.

"Oh." Nodding, Sophie headed for her room.

She took a long shower, half hoping Alasdair would join her and help her forget her life for a bit. But he hadn't shown up before her skin started to prune, so Sophie gave up and turned off the water. Stepping out, she pulled a towel off the rack and quickly dried her hair and body, then wrapped the towel around herself, toga style, and went out into her bedroom.

Much to her disappointment, Alasdair wasn't there either, so she fetched panties and a bra from her dresser. Closing the drawer, she turned, then stood still for a minute before simply walking over to sit on the end of the bed.

She just didn't have the energy to dress. Her mind and energy were taken up with fretting over Megan, Bobby, and Mrs. Tomlinson. Sophie knew they would be terribly upset. They'd want to talk about George, about how wonderful they thought he'd been, and how their life would be less without him in it. She just didn't know how she would handle it. Or if she'd even be able to pretend she was grieving his passing.

The sound of the door opening drew her from her thoughts, and Sophie glanced up to see Alasdair entering.

"I talked to my uncles and they're going to handle your family," he said quietly.

Sophie blinked at this news. "How?"

"They're going to come up with an explanation for his presence here, and put it into their minds that they talked to you to hear this story," he explained wearily, crossing the room to sit down next to her. "They'll give them a memory of you being as grief-stricken as they are, and then they'll ease their grief for them and send them home to handle the arrangements."

"They can do all that?" Sophie asked with surprise.

"They can," he assured her.

"Oh," she breathed, nearly giddy with relief. She'd been so worried about how to handle them. Now she didn't have to. Thank God.

"Sophie?" he asked suddenly.

"Hmm?" She peered at him in question.

Alasdair hesitated, and then growled, "You said you needed to sleep on it. We slept. Are you willing to be my life mate?"

A short laugh slid from her, and Sophie said dryly, "Well, don't sweep me off my feet with romance there, buddy."

Sophie was teasing him. Mostly. So she was startled when Alasdair immediately slid off the bed to kneel on one knee before her and took her hands in his.

"Sophie Ferguson, I vow to gi'e ye me heart, me wealth, me verra life, and amazing sex till the day we die, do ye do me the great honor o' being me life mate and spending however many decades, centuries, or millennia we're blessed with at me side. Will ye pledge me yer troth?"

A slow smile had spread across her lips as he spoke, and when he finally fell silent, Sophie admitted, "I do love your accent. When it shows itself, I just want to strip you naked and crawl all over you."

"Is that an aye?" Alasdair asked hopefully.

"You're damned right it is," she said, sliding off the

bed onto his knee and letting the towel drop to the floor as she planted her lips on his.

Alasdair had barely started to kiss her back when cheering broke out just on the other side of the bedroom door.

They broke their kiss and turned to peer at it briefly, then Alasdair barked, "Go to sleep!"

They listened as the men shuffled away, and then Alasdair turned back to her and smiled. "They like you."

"I love you," Sophie responded.

Alasdair froze briefly, and then asked, "Really?"

She nodded solemnly.

"You don't think it's too soon to call it love?" he asked.

Sophie narrowed her eyes. "Are you serious right now?"

A smile broke out on his face then, and Alasdair shook his head. "I love you too."

"How much?" she demanded as he scooped her into his arms and straightened to stand.

"More than my own life," Alasdair assured her as he carried her around to the side of the bed.

Sophie grunted at that and shook her head. "That's too much. I like you alive."

"I'll stay alive for you."

"Will ye sweet-talk me with yer accent every time ye bed me?" she asked, mimicking his accent. Apparently, not very well, Sophie decided when he suddenly dropped her on the bed.

He watched her bounce on the surface, and then said dryly, "Only if ye promise no' to try to imitate me accent yerself."

"You're no fun," she accused, and then changed her mind when he began stripping. "Maybe you're fun."

Alasdair chuckled and quickly finished undressing. Pausing then, he propped his hands on his hips and looked her over slowly before meeting her gaze and saying, "I love you, Sophie Ferguson. Thank you for agreeing to be my life mate."

Sophie swallowed and managed a crooked smile. "I love you, Alasdair MacKenzie. Thank you for having such a big cock."

"Wench!" The word came out on a startled burst of laughter as he launched himself onto her.

Sophie closed her arms around him and smiled inwardly as he kissed her. She knew she was in for the greatest, if shortest, sex of her life. But she also knew this was a new beginning for her. She could pursue the career she'd trained for now. She would have a huge family of her own if she were to judge from the many guests she'd seen at Valerian's wedding. But most importantly, she had a man she loved who loved her and whom she needn't fear losing. For the first time in a long time, she was looking forward to her future, instead of back at the shadows of her past. She was a lucky woman.